AMIDST
THE AMERICAN DREAMS

Stephan James Gathings

PublishAmerica
Baltimore

Hardcover 978-1-4560-5773-2
Softcover 978-1-4560-5774-9
PUBLISHED BY PUBLISHAMERICA, LLLP
www.publishamerica.com
Baltimore

Printed in the United States of America

Dedication:

Let these pages be my Epitaph to the "WHY" of it all.

ACKNOWLEDGEMENTS

My Deepest Love to:

My life & wife Juls for her help with this story.
You, who always encourages me to keep writing, but then has to grin and bear the process.

"You are the needle-true in my life's compass."

To the best of sons, Alexander and Benjamin, for both their computer tech support and being a reason to share this story.

"You are my branches, may you touch the sky".

To my good friend & Bro, Dan L. Norton: For comradeship and help with this work.

"It's the U and I in lunatics that makes the world think it's got sUperIority, but we're big enough to let them believe it."

And to these other fellow Jerseyans who've been such a blessing in my life:

Don & Claudia Ruiz: You two are the essence of my 'Joe and Cindy', because you have defined True Friendship for me.

To Joanne & Peter Schneider, Anna & Dale Lovern: You all exemplify 'Family'.

To my brother John (Buck) Gathings: The road less travelled has always been our way of life. While the dead rested in safe boxes, we travelled light and discovered new worlds. Therefore brother, I leave you with this.

Buck quietly laughed to himself as he threw more wood onto the dying ambers of our roadside campfire. "Say Jess. Since all we seem to live for is adventure, what do ya think we'll find when this life is over?"

I watched as a phoenix of flames began rising from the near-dead coals.

"I think we'll find that we lived it well."

FOREWORD

TRUE LOVE, is a perfect love.
It is pure, innocent, and everlasting.
It is softer than an angel's breath yet, stronger than the world.
It makes no effort to exist, it is its own reason for being.
It cannot be controlled, but it can guide.
It overcomes turmoil with patience.
It outshines the stars and outlives the darkness.
It consumes its consumer yet, none seek a cure.
It sings its own song, lives its own life, has its own purpose.
Hell envies it, while Heaven blesses itand the world can't change it.
Many seek it but its way is to find,
 IT IS A GIFT.

Table of Contents

Part I:

INTERLUDE

Part II

Part I:

INTRODUCTION

EVENTS OF 1965:

* Riots in Watts.
* Violence in Selma.
* The Great Blackout.
 *War on Poverty.
* 15 year old boy falls in love and brings present to girl one snowy Christmas Eve.

Popular songs of 1965:

1."The Sound of Silence" (Simon and Garfunkel)
2."My Love" (Petula Clark)
3."Soul and Inspiration" (The Righteous Brothers)
4."When a Man Loves a Woman" (Percy Sledge)

Popular Movies of 1965:

*Thunderball *Doctor Zhivago *Who's Afraid of Virginia Woolf?

EVENTS OF 1966:

*Ground breaking on the World Trade Center takes place.
*New Jersey: Christmas Break ends and the new year of high school classes resume.

Top songs of 1966:

*She's just my style (Gary Lewis and the Playboys)
*Cherish (The Association)
*Good Vibrations (The beach Boys)

Popular Movies of 1966:

*A Fine Madness
*The Rare Breed
*An American Dream.

Chapter One
"1966"

"I don't get it, are you looking for a fight?" Joe asked scratching his redhead as they walked up towards the high school entrance. "Cause if you are, this'll sure start one."

"No but I won't run from one either, you know that, especially this one if it comes to that."

Steve stared up at the darkening sky above. A storm was coming and he could feel the wind growing stronger as he walked against it.

Both were silent for several moments then, "Tell me something Joe," he asked as the two paused by a stop sign.

"Is falling in love just a chemical reaction
or seeing Heaven's face?
Is it a simple attraction
 or a blessing of grace?
And why does it make my heart so race?
Is it the touching of two lips or two hearts?
And does it have an end once it starts?
Is it the taste and feel of each other,
 or a breath of life shared?
A passing moment of pleasure,
 or a 'Oneness' forever—if we dared?
Is it what they claim it is in the world's marketplace?
And if so, how can that ever make my heart so race?
Is it a choice that we make,
 or a Gift that is given?
Is it of this world,

or sent from Heaven?
How can I know, and what makes it so?
Did I see the truth in her face?
Is that why her glance makes me stumble my pace?
Tell me why, oh why does my heart so race?"

"This poetry stuff you do has gone to your head," Joe said upset. "Forget your heart, you mess with her and the only thing beating will be his fist into your face! Look, I understand fighting for a girl but these kind of guys fight in packs, you know that, which is why I hate them."

"The whole world could stand with him against me Joe and I'd still fight for the dream of her."

Joe shook his head.

"Blasted it man," he said, "there are plenty of girls here, some even taller. Is this one worth getting killed over? You don't even know if she likes you! "

Steve stared off a moment, and then smiled.

"When I looked into her eyes I saw myself in them and I knew I never wanted to be anywhere else, just as she'll forever be in mine now."

"Steve, he won't play by any rules if you start this and with the others behind him they're gonna kick your …"

Joe stopped in mid-thought, seeing that anymore talk was useless."Come on Romeo," he sighed out, "we'll be late," and they started running for the glass doors.

When the first bell rang all of the students flung open the homeroom doors. The halls filled with the sounds of fast moving feet and chatty voices on their way to their first class of the day.

For Steve, that was a block class of English and history taught by the football coach of Parsippany High. It wasn't an easy class for him because the teacher tended to give a lot of slack to its several freshman football players. He ran track, but with a different coach, so he wasn't in this class's click.

As he made his way towards his seat a leg suddenly shot out in the aisle but he easily jumped over it. When he sat down he heard a voice say, "Hey, I heard about your little Santa visit over Christmas vacation."

Several footballers snickered but he ignored them, staring only at Mike for his remark.

When class ended, he was the first one out the door. He ran whenever he saw no hall monitors, darting in-between the sea of bodies, and made it to his next class in record time.

He sat down, watching the other math students as they leisurely wandered in. He glanced up each time one entered, until finally, he saw Sue walking quietly towards her seat in the next row. She looked his way for a moment and smiled, then turned and sat. He saw Mike's initial ring swinging on a gold chain around her neck.

She had on a soft blue sweater over a matching blouse and a neatly pleated skirt. When she brushed her hair aside, he noticed a small, gold earring as it flashed back at him for an instant. It sparkled like her eyes whenever he saw her smile.

The teacher entered the room and immediately started the lesson but Steve could only stare over at Sue as she opened her book.

Her hands were so small and delicate as they gracefully turned the pages. Her brown eyes were soft, shimmering pools and her light-brown hair laid gently across her small, sensuous shoulders.

He wondered what it would feel like to comb his fingers through it, then suddenly he felt silly, yet still he wondered.

He looked at her cute little nose, then secretly dropped his gaze to fantasize over the roundness of those perfect lips. A shiver ran down his back as she suddenly moistened them with the tip of her tongue. They now glistened like honey. He could almost hear them say his name; distant at first, then closer, louder and clearer.

"Steve …Steve …," he heard calling and he slowly sighed.

"The voice of an angel," he whispered softly.

"Thank you," responded his teacher now standing next to him, "I try my best to be pleasant. Now, would you tell us how you'd go about solving this problem?"

Several girls giggled and some of the boys grinned. Mike tapped a pencil on his math book as he shook his head with a smirk.

"I'd solve it the only way possible," he answered while staring at Mike, then looking over at Sue glancing down into her book. "By knowing that the shortest distance between two points is a straight line."

A snap was heard as Mike broke the point of his pencil on the desk.

"Are you sure you're on the same page?" asked his teacher checking her notes.

He glared back over at Mike. "Pretty sure," he stated.

When the final bell rang he hurried to his locker, dumped his books and grabbed an envelope, then he hurried to the main entrance and waited. He watched as students pushed through the doors, joking and calling to one another as they made their way down the walk to the street.

"I couldn't have missed her," he thought to himself as he checked faces in the huge crowd.

"Looking for someone?" came a gruff voice from behind. He turned to face Mike's large frame and two other apes in football jackets. "I heard you're fast."

"Fast enough to get by you," he stated while watching the faces of Mike and his big bookends.

"Well, maybe you better start using those running legs now," Mike snarled.

"No, I thought I might try my hand at making a pass today instead," he replied smiling over Mike's shoulder as Sue came walking towards them.

"Excuse me," he said as he slipped around them.

"Like hell," Mike growled, clipping him with a sucker punch in the face. He lost his balance from the blow and fell his knees. A moment later, all three were on him.

Just when he was sure he had pushed his luck too far, a familiar voice asked, "Got a problem here Sweety?" and suddenly there were occupied football jackets flying and lying next to him on their backs. He looked up at a smiling redheaded, freckled face. It was Joe Reily and next to him was his other best friend Kenny Tomineski.

"I had it under control," he said as Ken helped him up. He could feel the throbbing of his left eye and tasted the blood dripping from his upper lip. He was still trying to get his breath from the shots to his ribs.

"You do look better than them," Joe said, as the big Irishman's stare kept Mike and his buddies from getting up.

"What's wrong with you!" Sue cried out as she came running over. "Mike, are you crazy?"

She turned to Steve as he held his chest. "Are you all right?"

"Oh God, yes," he answered as she took a hankie from her purse and held it to his lip.

"You could have killed him," she said to Mike without looking down at him.

"And gone to heaven," Steve added as he gazed into her angel face.

"Maybe you should take him to the school nurse," Ken said to her.

"No, I'm okay," he stuttered out.

"You look a bit pale to me," Joe said with a slight grin.

"I think they're right," she said softly. "Come on, let me help you inside."

She put his hand on her shoulder.

"Oh no," Mike yelled as he started to his feet, "get your arm off her!"

"Stop it Mike," she said in a tone louder than he had ever heard her use before.

"You're my girl and you're not going anywhere with him!"

"That's it!" she yelled, then pulled the ring and chain over her head and handed them to him. "We're through!" She held onto Steve's side and guided him to the door with his arm on her shoulder.

"Oh God," he moaned as he felt her touch.

"Are you having trouble breathing?" she asked.

"Oh God yes."

Joe and Ken followed them in as they watched Mike over their shoulders. "Touchdown!" Joe yelled back as he flung up both arms into the air.

Sue stayed in the hallway with the guys while the nurse cleaned Steve's lip and checked his eye.

"You must have seen stars," the nurse muttered as she looked at his face.

"Heaven itself," he answered faintly.

When he came out Ken was talking with her by some lockers, then they came over.

"How do you feel?" she asked.

"Like I could do it all over again," he answered as he saw her look into his half closed eye.

"I hate fighting. Do you want us to call someone to come and get you?"

"Oh, I'm sure he's well enough to walk," Joe stated with a grin.

"I'm so sorry this happened," she said as she touched his arm.

He looked into her face and murmured, "And both were young, and one was beautiful."

Sue smiled warmly. "Who wrote that? Ken told me that you liked poetry."

"Lord Byron," he answered staring at her face like a child on Christmas morning seeing the gift he'd prayed for.

"Are you sure you're all right?" she asked again with a caring stare.

"Sweety's tougher than he looks," Ken said with a light laugh as he slapped him on the back, then he put his arm around Sue's waist. "Hey look guys," he said, "we're gonna take in a movie so I'll catch you later."

Joe looked at Ken, then at Steve.

"A movie?" Steve asked, suddenly shocked back into the moment, as Ken nodded with Sue smiling up at him.

"Hey, you sure you're okay?" Ken asked looking closer at his face.

"Uh yea, fine."

"All right then, see ya later."

Steve watched as they walked down the hall together. Ken smiled and waved as he walked through the door, while Sue paused to glance back at him standing there. He said nothing to her, but his eyes seemed to, then she continued out as Ken led her by the arm.

"Are you nuts?" Joe asked.

Steve just stared through the glass until she vanished from sight.

"Why didn't you tell him?"

"Ken's my friend. Besides Joe, didn't you see her face when she looked at him?"

"No, but I saw yours!"

"She looked so happy."

"What the heck is wrong with you?" Joe asked in frustrated disbelief. "She's all you talked to me about for months. I had to push you up that snowy hill to her house. I watched forever until you finally got the nerve to ring the doorbell and give her that Christmas present. Then you finally stand up to Mike and his monkeys, get pounded into play dough, and now you let one of your best friends take her out the door. They must have given you brain damage!"

"Joe, she's the most beautiful girl in the school. Why wouldn't she fall for a guy like Ken? He's good looking, dresses well, has style, fun to be with—a great guy!"

Joe just shook his head.

"You're a good friend Joe, one of my best, but it's still the three musketeers, right? You guys always come first with me and now, so does her happiness." Steve held up the envelope and smiled waving it. "Wanna stop at the Village Spa for a coke, then take in a movie?"

"I love you man, but I think this is a mistake."

"Joe, leave it alone," he said staring back at the empty glass door.

Chapter Two
Pride

"Did he drop it off?" Joe asked as he saw Steve putting books into his locker and he hurried over.

"Yea, my dad came by during my lunch period. I used it in math class when I needed to review for a test."

"So how do I work it?"

Steve pulled out the small open reel-to-reel tape recorder and handed it to him. "It's all set, you just have to turn this switch on while your teacher is reviewing the chapter. It should work just as well for you as it has for me to study."

"Thanks man. I'll get it back to you by Tuesday."

As he turned Steve saw Ken kissing Sue as she hurried to catch her bus. He stood quietly as Ken then came over.

"Hey Man, I haven't seen much of you lately, where have you been?" Ken asked with a smile.

"Been busy, you know," he answered staring out at her bus.

"Listen," Ken said as he put his arm around his shoulder, "I'm taking Sue to that church dance tomorrow night and I was hoping you could help me out."

"Help, how?"

"Ya see, things have been going nice between us for the past couple of weeks, but I need something to help me move on to the next level, you know?"

Steve stepped back a bit. "What are you saying?"

"You know, something to get her more passionate. I mean kissing and hugging are fine but I just haven't been able to find that right button. Then the other day it hit me, I've got you."

He paused grinning and raised his eyebrows, but didn't notice that Steve wasn't smiling back.

"She's been asking me to recite poetry lines to her and she looks forward to a new one each day. I've quoted all I could find but none have been the right one. I need one that will melt her down, ya know?"

Steve stared, then asked, "You need something that will make her swoon, is that it?"

"Yea whatever, as long as it makes her hot for me after the dance tomorrow."He winked and added, "I got a bottle of wine, don't ask how, and I plan on taking her outback in the pine grove past the church lot later."

Ken smiled as he pictured the two of them together. Joe watched as Steve's eyes widened and then saw his fist clench at his side.

"You're asking me to play your Cyrano de Bergerac to this pearl of Roxanne just so you can…Can steal her heart for one night?"

"I love it when you talk that way," Ken said as he gave his arm a slight tap. "So what have ya got? Come on, dig down deep into that poet's treasure chest and scoop me up some gems."

Steve turned away gritting his teeth, then mumbled. "The truly brave are soft of heart and eyes, and feel for what their duty bids them do."

"Who's that, Shakespeare?"

"No, Byron," he answered in a disgusted tone.

"Oh. Well I don't think that'll do what I need. Got somethin' else?"

Steve was silent with his back still turned towards him.

"Look Sweety, what would you say to her to make her feel that you loved her?"

Steve closed his eyes seeing her precious face then, without willing it, his mouth opened and spoke softly.

"Thy beauty humbles me,
its brightness is too great to look upon
lest I be blinded to all else and become thy servant forever;

but I am not worthy of thy gaze,
certainly not thy love,
for thou art pure as the morning dew
and better that I be banished from thy sight
than to ever dare to taste thy sweetness,
for I am not worthy of even thy smile,
let alone the lips from whence it came."

"Now you're cookin'," Ken said with a tone of glee, "let me write that down."

"No, don't say that to her!" he begged grabbing his arm. "Here, just look through the section on courtship and love in this book of quotations I got from the library. They're suppose to be some of the best ever written."

Ken took the book from the top shelf of his locker, thanked him and then walked off.

As they watched him strut down the hallway thumbing through the pages Joe asked, "That was no quote, was it?"

He didn't answer, just raised his hand and covered his mouth.

The next day, Steve went over to the church to help out with the preparations for the dance social that evening. As he was carrying out tablecloths to the huge banquet hall he bumped into Sue. She had her hands full also bringing in assorted desserts she had made to donate.

"Oh I'm sorry, I didn't see you around this mountain of linens," he said.

"That's okay," she said back with a smile.

"Please Sue, let me help you with those," he said taking her trays and placing them on a table.

"Thanks, are you coming to the dance tonight?"

"Yea, I'll be there," he said.

"This is the first church function I've been able to get Ken to take me to, besides Mass."

He spread out the first cloth then she laid out her cakes and cookies on top. As he went for the next linen she grabbed it with him and together they started to cover the table.

"Steve, would you tell me something?"

"Sure, if I can."

"Is Ken really into poetry like he seems?"

He fumbled a moment trying to open up the next cloth, then finally handed her an end and they spread it out.

"I only ask because if he is as he seems then maybe this is more serious than I thought." She paused with the look of one needing an immediate answer and he knew why.

"I'm not sure how to answer," he stuttered out, "Ken can sometimes be a bit complicated."

"Yes he can," she said grinning. "One moment I'm sure he's just putting me on, but the next he seems so sincere. I want to trust him and believe what he says but I have mixed feelings about it all."

He noticed her lost in thought as he stared at her face, but tried hard not to let his own true feelings become known.

"Sue," he said softly, "trust your feelings, they seldom lie to us I've found." He thought a moment then added, "Many of the ancient Greek and Roman myths tell of how women often tested their suitors with trials to prove their love."

Sue's eyes widened asking, "Like what?"

"Oh, sometimes a quest to bring her back something unique or of great value, but the risk often was dangerous."

"Oh, well, I wouldn't want him to do something where he might get hurt just to prove he cares for me."

Steve grinned and she saw it.

"What is it?" she asked.

"Nothing, its silly."

"Please, tell me," she pleaded and reached out touching his hand. He felt the softness of her fingers melting into him and quickly cleared his throat.

"Well, how about if you ask him to …?" He leaned down into her ear and whispered. A look of awe came to her face as she turned to him.

"Do you think that would work? Do you think he could do that?" she asked. She pondered a moment, then muttered, "Is there such a thing?"

"I believe there is," he answered with a smile. "Ask and ye shall receive we've been told, remember?"

Sue smiled warmly up at him, touching his hand gently.

That night, after eating and dancing, Ken led her out across the parking lot and into the grove of pine trees. As they made their way through the dense wooded area she asked, "Where are you taking me?"

"Don't worry it's just ahead."

Within moments they entered into a small clearing of the trees. There, spread out on the ground already, was a blanket with two paper cups and a bottle of applejack wine. They sat down and she looked up through the branches to see a near-full moon and a few stars shining down on them. Ken held up the bottle and showed it to her.

"I don't drink you know that," she said with a tone of reminder to him.

"I know, but I just thought that maybe tonight could be special."

He leaned down and kissed her gently on the neck, then up near her ear as his arm moved around her waist. Sue sighed a bit, then asked, "Ken, do you love me?"

"You know I do Baby."

She smiled as he continued to kiss her. "Would you do something for me to prove it?"

"Anything," he answered softly as he came to nibble under her chin.

She pulled back from him to look into his eyes.

"I have always believed that God would send me my perfect love, but I need to be sure who he is before I can give my love to him."

Ken smiled. "You can be sure with me Sue. I know I'll never find a more beautiful girl in the world than you, you're perfect for me."

She smiled up at him. "But I need to be sure," she repeated.

"So what can I do to convince you?"

"I need you to give me something that will be a sign from God that you are my True Love."

"Sure, but what?"

"I'll know it when I see it," she said glowing. "It'll be something He's made that shows how our love will be forever."

"You mean like a cross or something?"

"No. It has to be something alive and eternal as our love should be."

Ken looked at her puzzled. "There isn't anything that is alive and lives forever, is there?"

"I know there is."

"What?"

"I'll know it when I see it. Only then can I give my heart away to the man I will love forever."

Ken was silent for a long while, then asked, "What if I can't find this...Eternal thing?"

"Well then," she sighed, "I guess I'll have to just wait for the one who can."

"Wait, how about a nice ankle bracelet with a diamond in it? Diamonds are forever you know."

"No, it's not alive."

"I know," he said with desperation in his voice, "Flowers...Heart-red roses."

She laughed. "Yes they'd be beautiful and are definitely alive but they don't live forever. They blossom for a short while then they die."

Ken paced in a circle thinking.

"Oh," he said, "a living poem of love. Wait and I'll create one just for you right now." He paused a moment thinking, then said,

"Your beauty humbles me,
A ...It's so bright it blinds me,
and I'm not worthy to gaze at you or have your love
cause you are the dew, it's true, it's true!
a, a ...Oh, and to taste the sweetness of your smile
I'd walk another mile cause a ...a ...
From hence it came and I'm not the same;
oh, bid me leave thy sight, tonight
if my love be not true, for you!"

29

He looked back and saw her covering her face. He smiled for a few seconds until he realized she was actually hiding her laughter. In a panic, he quickly reached for his wallet to get out the wrinkled up slip of verse quotes he had stashed to use on her later.

As he unfolded it he said, "I have some verses that I did over to make them my own just for you."

"Okay, here's one based on some guy with a girl's name, Marlowe something or other. 'Love me soft, but love me a lot.'

No? Well here's another by a dude named Dollop, or is that Doltop? 'Make a woman love herself and the overflow is all yours.'

Wait, here's a better one. 'To just say I love you is a mouthful, but to hear you say it, it's a handful' . No wait, maybe that's heartful or soulful.

Okay listen, here's one I didn't change. It's by a guy named Anonymous." He cleared his throat and said, "When poverty comes in the door, love flies out the window!"

Sue fell back, laughing so hard and for so long that she had to roll over holding her side.

"Please Ski," she finally cried out, "just forget the poetry!"

Ken fell down on his knees into a pile of pine cones begging, "Aw Sue, just let me have some of your overflow, please!"

She shook her head, laughing even harder.

"Come on," he pleaded, "ya got to help me here. Just what is it that you want?"

"I really don't know what it is," she said composing herself. "I just know that I will once I see it."

Ken just stayed on his knees now shaking his head as she got up with the blanket and handed him the wine.

"Come on Lover," she said, "let's go and you can think about it."

It was just a few days later at school that Steve saw her crying at a locker with a girlfriend. He stood watching for several minutes until they walked off and into the girl's room. He wanted to talk with her, but didn't know what he'd ever say.

That night he went to the corner, where everyone hung out, and figured he'd tell Ken what he had seen. As he neared the corner he could hear Ken telling some of the guys how easy she'd been to make out with.

"Just a couple of dates and I had her bra size tag in my collection," he said. "We were making out everywhere."

Several of the guys snickered, then one asked, "How far did you finally get before you dumped her?"

"Are you kidding? She's so little, I couldn't have gone all the way with her if she let me."

The bunch roared laughing.

"But let me tell ya," Ken added, "once I even ..."

"That's enough!" Joe yelled as he came walking up from the far end of the block.

"What's with you?" Ken asked.

"Some things should remain private man."

Then one of the other guys said, "Hey man, if she's that easy maybe I'll take a shot at her now."

Steve lost it and ran up to the young dude and spun him around.

"Take a shot at me first, you dirty, lousy, piece of - - -!"

"Hey man, I didn't mean anything!"

"Take it easy," Ken said as he put his hand on Steve's arm. He turned with his fist cocked back as Joe came between them. He looked at Joe, both said nothing, then his eyes lowered and so did his fist. He pushed them aside and wandered down into the dark street.

"What's with him?" Ken asked.

"Come with me, now," Joe replied and they walked off by themselves.

Steve walked until he found himself standing across the street from Sue's house. He squatted down silently by the stop sign, staring until all the lights in the house were out. A tear finally broke and rolled down his face.

"I'm so sorry," he murmured softly over and over.

It was one in the morning when they found him. Ken held Joe back and went to him alone.

"I know sorry isn't gonna cut it," he said, "so if you need to swing at me do it. God knows I deserve it."

"I don't want to hit you Ken, but God, why would you hurt her like that?" He turned his head away so Ken couldn't see his eyes.

"Listen," Ken said softly, "nothing happened. I went back to those guys and told them that Joe was gonna beat the hell out of me if I didn't tell them the truth. I confessed that I lied, was just trying to cover up the fact that I couldn't even get to first base with her and I couldn't! So I told them I gave up and she was the one that got away. They knew I had a rep I was trying to protect."

Steve wiped his eyes and looked up at him.

"I don't understand how you could hurt her like that?"

Ken looked off a moment.

"Why didn't you tell me what she meant to you? I never would have even tried to touch her man."

"You were what she wanted, not me," Steve answered as he stared at the darkened upper windows. "You're my best friend and I just wanted you both to be happy."

"For God's sake Sweety, if you want that girl you've got to go after her and tell her! You almost did it once, I now realize, and took a pounding for it. How hard can it be now to just face one little girl after three apes?"

Steve remained silent, staring up at the dark windows.

"Come on," Ken said, "your mom's worried sick and we told her we'd get you home."

As he helped him to his feet he added, "You know, I hope this picking you up doesn't get to become a regular thing."

"All for one and one for all, remember? " Steve reminded him.

"Yea forever," Joe replied grinning, then together they walked down the hill.

The next day was Saturday. Steve spent the whole morning searching stores to find the perfect initial ring to give to her to go steady, just in case she happened to say yes.

At last he found it. It had a band of white gold, with a mother of pearl cut in the shape of a shield. The letter 'S' in yellow gold sat at its center, encircled with diamond chips. It cost him almost all he had put aside for some new high roll shirts, but she was worth it.

On Sunday the three walked up to St. Peter's together, as they always did, for the eleven O'clock mass. He kept his hand in his pocket caressing the ring.

"She'd be there as always," he thought and he'd talk with her after church. Surely she'd be calm and easier to talk to then; besides, he felt God might be on his side more there since it was Holy Ground.

"I'm gonna talk with her after church," he told them.

"Well Hallelujah!" Ken cried out. "Hey Joe, being that your older brother is studying to become a priest, do you know any special prayer that might help?"

"A prayer?"

"Yea, to keep Sweety on his feet this time."

"You know he's got a point," Joe said. "For being one of the school's best runners, those legs sure aren't worth much when you get around that girl. I'll bet she could beat you in the quarter mile by just walking past you."

Ken told him that he had wanted to date other girls while seeing her. When she pleaded with him not to, he decided it was just best to end it. Steve knew she was hurt, he just wanted to see her happy again.

He waited outside on the steps of the church while the guys went on in. He watched the cars as they entered the parking lots until finally he saw her family car pull in. She stepped out and he noticed that she was wearing all white. Her jacket, blouse, skirt, high heels, purse and even her small hat matched as if for a Holy Communion or even a wedding he thought. She looked beautiful.

As they walked up the steps he greeted them and Sue stayed a moment to talk with him.

"How have you been?" she asked. "I haven't seen you much lately."

"Just fine, and you?"

"Things are okay," she answered in a softer tone. "We'd better get inside."

They walked up the steps and he hurried to get the door for her. Inside, Sue dipped her fingers into the Holy Water and blessed herself. Steve also put his fingers into the water but paused to soak them a

33

moment before bringing them up to his lips. It tasted salty at first, then seemed to have a sweet aftertaste. He quickly blessed himself and then followed her.

He walked her down the aisle to where her family was seated. She genuflected and sat near the end of the pew. He paused watching her, then spotted Joe in the back mouthing, "Sit down."

He suddenly realized that he was just standing out in the aisle with several faces looking at him. Sue smiled and moved over to make room for him. He genuflected and slowly sat next to her.

"Oh God," he mouthed silently as he stared straight ahead at the altar.

Whenever it was time to kneel, he would always let her kneel first so he could catch a glimpse of her before he knelt next to her. Her soft brown hair reflected the light from the overhead hanging chandeliers like beams from heaven. Her scent filled his very being and he had to force himself to concentrate on the service before him.

He had to battle so much with his thoughts that when it came time to receive communion, she had to whisper, "Excuse me," to get by him to go up to the altar.

"Of course," he muttered as he stepped out to let her to the aisle. Her mother and father also went past him. Her mom smiled, but her father just looked at him.

"He knows," Steve thought and then he sat alone in the very long pew. He felt everyone could see the guilty feelings on his face and so he lowered his head.

After Mass, many church members went over to the auditorium next door to make purchases from the ladies bake sale. Her parents went in while she waited over by the large shrine on the front lawn. He came out and saw her walking on the grass.

"Well?" Kenny asked as he and Joe pushed him to move, "Go talk to her." He slowly walked out onto the lawn and she turned to smile at him as he came beside her.

"You look really pretty today," he said as he pointed to her outfit.

"Thanks," she replied with another smile, "and I like your shirt, I think the solid colors are always nice."

She then noticed him looking at her neck.

"Oh," she said as she held up the tiny gold crucifix on its chain, "my dad gave me this when I made my confirmation. Can you see how delicate it is?" She stepped closer holding the short chain for him to look at and carefully touch it.

"It's beautiful and it suits you."

"I always thought so," she said as she kissed it, then seemed lost in her thoughts.

"Uh, Sue," he said to get her attention again, "I was wondering if maybe you'd like to…" He stopped, then lowered his head.

"To what?"

"Are you going to the indoor pool party at the country club? It's open to everyone, even non-members, and the local favorite band 'Rizin Starz' is playing."

"Yea, I thought I might."

"Well, I was wondering if maybe you'd like to let me take you or I could meet you there if you'd rather."

He kept his head down, praying for the right words.

"That is, unless you already figure on going with somebody and that's fine cause …"

"No, I wasn't planning on going there with anyone. I think it would be nice to …"

She suddenly stopped as she stared over his shoulder. He jerked his head up, then turned around to see Joe and Ken standing in the parking lot watching them.

"So you want to go out with me?" she asked as she stared back into his face. "Why? What did he tell you? That I was easy!"

"No!" he answered as he saw tears coming to her eyes. "I want to go out with you because I …"

"I know what you want," she cried out. "I thought you were different!" She covered her eyes and ran towards the auditorium doors.

"Sue no!" he called out. "Please believe me!"

She didn't look back, just continued to the building and ran through the door out of sight.

"I just want to see you happy," he said softly. "I just wanted a chance to treat you like you deserve," he continued to mutter as he started walking home.

Saturday Joe and Ken dragged him out of his house to go to the pool party.

"You're gonna see her and explain," Joe said.

"She may not even be there," Steve replied as he threw his towel at him.

"You're going," he yelled, "even if I have to pound on you first, you're going!"

"If you don't straighten this out you'll never forgive yourself," Ken added.

"You've got a better chance to talk with her than I do Ken."

"I'm not doing your talking, anymore than you'd want me to do your fighting for ya. Now you go tell that girl what she means to you or so help me I'll ..."

Ken paused then yelled, "I'll take my whole collection of bra tags to your mother and tell her I found them in your locker!"

"You wouldn't!"

"In a heartbeat Sweety."

"You would," Steve stated with a look of horror.

"Now let's go!" Ken yelled walking away.

The club grounds were packed when they came through the gate and paid their admission. The smell of hot dogs and burgers cooking filled the air. They made their way inside, zigzagging around the towels, blankets and bodies that covered the walkways along the pool's edge.

It was mostly teens. Many were running around as guys chased girls and threw them into the pool. Others either swam slowly together or laid on blankets exchanging smiles and touching playfully.

"See," Steve finally said, "she's not here."

They made their way over to the game room and Joe pointed to a group of teens lying on towels near the wall.

"Hey, there's Janice," he said, "she'll know if Sue's here." Joe waved as they walked over and they waved back.

36

"Have you seen Sue?" Ken asked.

"Yea, she's here with Mike at her heels somewhere," she answered as she looked around. "They went over to get something to eat I think."

"Thanks," Ken said and they headed to the snack bar.

As they rounded the diving boards they spotted them eating at a picnic table.

"Go," Joe said as he put his hand on his shoulder.

"And don't stop till she listens!" Ken added as he got out of sight.

Steve watched a moment as Mike put his arm around her waist, talking in her ear. She stood up and walked over near the snack bar. It was then that she noticed him by the boards and looked away.

"She's beautiful," he thought to himself as he watched her standing there in a black and white one piece swimsuit. Her light golden tan skin glistened with a thousand water droplets as she posed with her left leg bent slightly and her arms crossed. He walked over and called her name.

"Please, just leave me alone," she replied.

"You were wrong, I would never ask you out for those reasons."

"So, you think they're true then?" she stated with hurt in her voice.

"No," he answered as he twisted his head to see her face. "I know what kind of a girl you are, the kind who deserves respect. The kind any guy with eyes in his head would see what a privilege it is to just hold your hand or to get a smile from you. To feel blessed just to sit with you and talk. To feel honored to hold an umbrella for you, give you his jacket when it's cold or to even open a door.

You're the kind of girl a guy falls in love with, dreams each night you might someday feel the same, and then ..." He paused, then whispered, "Prays that he'd be worthy of you. You're the kind of girl to die for."

She turned and looked into his face, searching in his eyes in silence as if to try and see the words he had just spoken.

"You really mean that?" she asked softly.

"Oh yes, with all my heart."

He slowly moved in to kiss her, but before they could touch he felt a sudden blow to the side of his face and fell to the ground.

"You keep your hands off her you make-believe jock," Mike yelled, then he kicked him in the chest.

"Stop it!" Sue cried out.

"No, you stop it," he replied and then grabbed her, breaking her shoulder strap.

Joe started over but Ken said, "Hold it, this is his fight. Just make sure no other football freaks join in, all right?"

Mike held Sue by both arms as he yelled at her. "You and I should be together, I know you love me Sue."

"I don't love you!" she shouted back as she struggled with him.

Steve looked up in a stupor. His ear was ringing and he tried getting a full breath back. As his vision cleared, he saw her fighting to free herself from Mike's grip and he quickly got to his feet.

"Get your paws off her!" he yelled grabbing the footballer by his inch high crew-cut but ending up with an empty fist instead.

Mike swung a right into his face, then a hit to his stomach. He fell to one knee and Mike kicked it out from under him, then jumped on top of him and pounded his fist into Steve's side.

"He's gonna kill him!" Ken yelled.

"No, he won't quit," Joe said, "let it be."

They both stood there, with fists clenched, as they watched their friend getting wailed on. Sue tried to pull him off but got pushed back by Mike as he lifted Steve to his feet to hit him again.

She ran over to Ken and Joe.

"Help him," she cried, "he's your friend, please!"

"Yea, he's our friend," Joe said as he looked over at her, "but this fight is for you and I wouldn't want to be the one to try and stop it. Win or lose, he'd never forgive us."

As Mike drew his right fist back, Steve suddenly butted his head into Mike's nose and was free from his grip. He was stunned and Steve hit him square in the eye.

"Don't you ever touch her again, do you hear me?" Then hit his face again. "Do you hear?" And hit him again. "Do you!" Then planted an upper cut to his jaw that later Joe said lifted both his feet off the ground.

It sent him sailing backward over the top of the picnic table and onto his back, flat out.

"You even say her name and I'll finish this!" Steve yelled.

Mike moaned holding his bloody nose with one hand and his backside with the other as he looked up at Steve over him.

"Do you understand?" he asked as he kicked the bottom of his shoe. Mike shook his head yes.

Steve turned to Sue, took two steps, then fell to his knees.

"You have that affect on him," Joe said to her.

She walked over and looked down at both of them on the ground. "I told you all. I hate fighting and I won't have anyone doing it over me like I'm some prize up for grabs!"

She turned and started walking towards the bathhouse with Joe quickly following her. Steve called out to her, but then just lowered his head when she wouldn't look back.

"I didn't want this," he murmured to himself.

"Will you just wait a minute!" Joe yelled as he got in front of her to slow her down. "You're wrong," he said, "and if you walk away now you'll be making the biggest mistake of your life."

"What do you mean?" she asked in an angry tone.

"Here read this," he said handing her a folded up paper he pulled from his pocket.

"I copied that down from a tape recording I did while he and Ken were talking in the hall at school the day before the church social. This is from the heart of someone who really loves you more than himself."

She opened the paper, read it, then her eyes started to water.

"Oh Joe, did he really say this about me?"

He nodded then she leaned up and kissed him on the cheek.

"Thank you Joe."

She turned around and walked back just as she heard Ken say, "Okay, here I go again. Hang on Sweety I'm coming."

"No," Sue said to him, "let me."

She took a napkin off the table, knelt beside him and held it against his bleeding lip with one hand while caressing his face with the other.

"Look at you," she said softly shaking her head. "Why?"

He looked into her eyes answering, "It's just a guy-thing and because I love you."

She held up the paper and read from it.

"Thy beauty humbles me,
its brightness is too great to look upon
lest I be blinded to all else and become thy servant forever ..."

He stared in shock as she recited his poem, then touched her lips to stop her.

"Did you really mean this when you said it?" she asked choked up. "I've got to know ... I've got to be sure this time Steve."

He smiled at her and said,

"Does the sun when it rises
mean to kiss the dew from the rose's cheek,
or the moon and stars each night
shine through the darkness to declare heaven's love?
So also, I can say only what my heart will allow
and then seal it as a promise if it be for your ears.
For into Beauty's eye one dare not lie,
lest I lie to myself and be shamed and cursed
or worst,
die a thief if ever then I would dare to take your hand."

"Oh Steve," she said with a near-tear, "who wrote that?"

"You did, across my heart with your smile."

He reached into his pocket and brought out a pine cone which he held up to her.

"As the evergreen is seen unchanged throughout the seasons, so too is my love for you eternal yet still ever growing."

She took the cone and smiled, wiping the blood from his lip with her thumb.

"Oh Steve you really are a Sweety." Then she paused. "But why do they call you that?"

"Cause I'm the youngest of these three Musketeers."

"The youngest, the bravest and My Love," she added as she kissed him.

Suddenly, both felt all the love within them flooding into their hearts. It was so great that they had to share its flow or they'd burst. In that moment they became One Heart.

She took the ring he held out and put it on her finger. The love she felt filled her eyes and then ran down to her smile where he kissed each tear joyfully.

"Touchdown!" yelled Joe and Ken with their arms held high.

"Would you like to dance?" he asked as the band 'Rizin Starz' began to play a slow song.

"I love to dance," she sighed putting her arms around him.

They swayed gently together gazing into the other's eyes as they softly sang the lyrics.

A sudden clap of thunder echoed off in the distance from outside as a storm began approaching. Several couples started to quickly gather up their belongings to leave, but they just listened to the music playing in their heart and danced on.

"Sue!" Janice cried out holding her beach-bag and hat by the door. "Come on or you'll get caught up in the storm!"

Sue continued to dance, smiling to his smile.

"I already am," she said seeing herself in his eye.

Chapter Three
A Matched Set

From the day of the pool party they were inseparable. They were always seen together. During school hours he'd run to walk her to the next class, then just make it to his own before the doors closed.

In spring after school, she'd sit and watch whenever he had practice for track and she never missed any of his meets. Later they'd walk downtown to the Village Spa luncheonette, sit in a booth sharing a cherry coke, and hang out with friends.

To be alone together their favorite place was to go to The Island, as it was called by the locals, down by the lake. It literally was an island of a few miles around. It was two-thirds covered with tall lush woods. Its center had a ball field and an open, grassy beach area with wildflowers facing the lake's shoreline. A serene moving river ran around it and fed into the lake.

It was completely cutoff from the rest of the town and, like an angel with a flaming sword, its isolation kept the outside world at bay.

Here they'd walk along the gentle washing of the water's edge and through the many colored paths of its peaceful woods.

Often they'd stand at the center of its wooden bridge, which separated the island from the road, and toss a penny over their heads into the river below. They'd make a wish for the fun of believing that maybe it could come true.

The only day she went home alone on the bus was Tuesdays. This was when he had to attend the fencing club he belonged to. Ken and Joe also were members.

It was started by a young math teacher, Mr. Biel, and taught in the gym on some mats. He was often several minutes late getting free from his last class.

During these unsupervised times, many guys would be found swinging on the climbing ropes as they dueled it out in mid-air like pirates.

Many times Mr. Biel entered the gym from the rear and would witness these antics, but he would always find Joe, Ken and Steve taking the sport much more seriously. They would spend that time checking their gear carefully, and eying down the blades of their foils to be sure they were straight and true and that the safety tips weren't coming loose.

He often commented on how proud he was of their professional conduct and how hard they applied themselves to each lesson.

Prior to each session, Steve would walk Sue to her bus before he headed off to the class.

He'd often kiss her cheek and say, 'Sorry my lady, but I have a dragon to slay' or 'Duty calls, for King and Country!'

Today he kissed her hand and said, "For my Queen will my sword defend."

She nodded a 'Thank you' and, with her smile in his eye, he hurried off to walk with the guys to the gym.

"I love this club," Joe said. "It's a place where I can go one on one with someone on an even playing field and our size doesn't matter, just our technique."

Steve knew what he meant. Joe was always being pressured by others to join the football team because of his size, but that was not something that fit the gentleman side of his nature. He wasn't a grunt, he was a guy with class and one he was proud to have as a friend.

Arriving late as usual, Mr. Biel entered but not alone. Ken tapped Steve on the shoulder and pointed to the door. Standing there was Sue. He smiled and was surprised Mr. Biel was allowing her to sit-in on the private club's activities.

"May I have your attention!" he called out. "I'd like to introduce a new member, Miss Susan LaRosa."

Joe dropped his sword. Ken fell back onto the bleacher. Steve stared with open mouth and raised eyebrows.

"I hope you all will make her feel welcomed."

He led her past the line of other disbelieving faces.

"Miss LaRosa these are my best students, my three musketeers I like to call them." He turned to them.

"Would you help her find the proper protective gear and show her the basics while I start the class session with the others?"

"Uh, sure," Steve answered, then walked her over to the equipment room.

"Sue, what are you doing?"

"I want to fence," she replied with a smile. "Mr. Biel said that size and strength don't matter."

"That's true, but …"

He stopped because he didn't know what to say. He wasn't sure why this bothered him. It wasn't a problem for the instructor, so why was it for the student?

He remained silent as he searched through the boxes to find safety gear that would fit her properly.

"Here," he said, "try this one on."

She took it but had trouble getting the vest secure so he reached over to show her how to adjust it. She could sense by his silence and his touch that he was upset.

"Steve, if you don't want me to do this then I won't." He looked at her and could see that she meant it.

"It's not that I don't want you to, it's that I don't understand why you'd want to. Are you trying to prove that you don't need anyone to fight for you?"

She put her hands on his arm and said, "To fight for me? No. To fight beside me? Always."

She paused as he turned to her.

"I don't want to be a princess in an ivory tower watching you go to battle for me. I want to be able to share in those struggles, to stand with you, to give strength to each other as we face them together. But first I need to find out what I'm made of so I can know what I'm able to give."

She looked into his eyes and asked, "Does that make any sense?"

"Somehow it does," he answered with a smile, "but don't ask me to explain it to anyone."

She laughed. "I love you, you know that?"

"The princess is becoming a Queen," he said with a sigh.

She hugged his arm. "And this knight, a King."

He pulled her close to kiss her. "Careful," she cautioned looking around, "there are others who still rule in this kingdom."

He laughed, then helped her to find the proper weight foil.

As they walked over to Joe he asked, "Would you mind walking her through the basics of steps and stance?"

Joe watched as Sue pulled down her mask.

"I can't fight her."

"Why not, afraid she might be a fast learner?" he asked with a grin. He looked over at Ken who took a step backwards.

She lifted her mask and asked, "Have any of you ever read 'The Three Musketeers'?"

None answered.

"Well if you do, you'll find out there were four! Now, on guard Reily!"

Joe looked at Steve smiling back, then he shrugged his shoulders and lowered his mask.

"First stance," Joe said as he positioned himself and Sue copied his movements as they crossed swords. "Heel, toe, heel, toe," Joe called out as they advanced and retreated.

"She's got the balance," Ken said watching with his arms slightly crossed.

"She's got a lot more than that," Steve added, "but yes, she's always had balance."

As the weeks went by she advanced her technique well, taking the sport as seriously as the 'Three'. Still she had a playful nature which came out every now and then.

During a match set between her and Steve, they went tip to tip back and forth for several moments; then she advanced two extra steps and pushed his foil back close to his chest and held it there. They were nearly mask to mask and he could clearly see her face.

She looked at him then, suddenly blowing him a kiss, quickly stepped back two and hit him straight in the heart.

"Point!" yelled ref. Biel as he looked at Sue. She lifted her mask and winked at Steve. He raised his foil and saluted her.

"Touche'," he said as he lifted his mask and shook his head. "You're only suppose to use one weapon in this sport," he whispered.

"Know your opponent's weakness," she whispered back.

Over the next few weeks, they learned that a sister high school had also formed a fencing club. Mr. Biel had been able to set up one tournament for them and it was to take place in the other school on Saturday. The team was excited to finally get to test their skills against new opponents.

They met at the bus loading zone and boarded quickly so they could arrive early enough to warm up. The opposing team began murmuring when they saw Sue gearing up. The word came back that no one wanted to be a matched set with her.

The instructors met together off to the side. They returned and announced that unless the match was set, the opposing team would have to forfeit the set to Parsippany High. The team murmured again saying, "We weren't told this sport was co-ed."

"Choose or forfeit," their coach stated again.

Sue stood quietly at attention in the team's lineup, showing no reaction and none of her teammates did either. Finally, they agreed to a set. Mr. Biel made a circular motion with his right hand above his head and they formed a circle. They raised their foils until all the tips touched above and yelled, "Pride, honor, and respect!" They then turned and saluted their instructor.

The sets seemed evenly matched as one by one they took place, but in the end it was a tie. It was decided by the two refs that the tie-breaker would be a final match set where each team would choose its own champion. The teams formed separate circles to discuss it.

"It should be one of the musketeers," Parsippany decided. "You guys choose," they said.

The trio remained standing as the rest of the team sat on the bleachers. They spoke amongst themselves, then walked over to Sue and saluted her.

"Oh no guys," she responded, "you are the best."

"Pride, honor and respect," Joe said. She looked at their faces. Ken smiled and Steve winked.

"It should be one of the musketeers," she insisted.

"And it will be," Joe stated, "there were four, remember?" He smiled, then added, "I got the book."

"And you read it?" she asked with a doubtful look.

"No not yet, but I got it. Don't know how it turns out."

She stood up and raised her foil tip to theirs.

"Pride, honor and respect," she said and then the three added, "One for All!"

"And All for One," she said joining in with a scared tone, then she looked at Joe and said, "but let it be on your head Reily."

She walked out towards the mat murmuring, "Size doesn't matter, size doesn't matter," and then she saw her opponent step out. Her small five foot frame dwarfed before Madison's six foot-one inch stature.

She heard his teammates snickering as she blessed herself.

"Oh you're kidding," one said.

"Maybe she thinks she's Joan of Arc," said another.

"Yea, and we all know what happened to her," laughed out another voice.

Joe leaned in towards Steve and said, "I read that story, it wasn't pretty."

She stepped onto the mat and saluted the instructors, then turned and saluted her opponent.

"On guard!" the ref called, and they crossed swords.

Not a sound was heard except for the echoing of clashing foils, then, "Point, LaRosa!"

Madison paused as Ken's voice shouted out, "The bigger they are, the quicker they'll crawl!"

"On guard!" called the ref and again the swords were crossed. A few more clicks of steel, then, "Point, Madison!"

His team cheered. The two paused, then took an opening stance again.

The swords engaged a third time then, "Point, LaRosa!" Again, set and engaged. The blades flashed under the above gym lights.

Madison held back a bit, then lounging forward and using his weight, he pushed his foil against hers and shoved her off the mat.

"Point, Madison!"

His teammates cheered out, "That's where she belongs, on the sideline!"

"Tied points, last set," announced the ref.

Madison raised his mask and smiled at her. "This is it honey," he said with a degrading tone, then lowered his mask as he prepared to use his advantage again. They took stance and crossed tips.

"Set!" yelled the ref.

Madison advanced on her quickly and she retreated, almost losing her balance, then she immediately hop-stepped forward.

"Heel-toe, heel-toe, heel-toe!" she shouted as she drove him back to the edge of his mat. He circled her foil with his, pushing it up, then went for a lunge, but just missed her mid-section as she turned sideways.

Steve's eyes remained fixed on her movements as she floated effortlessly across the floor with such grace. As he watched her he realized, that for the first time, he was not admiring the beauty of her physique, but the style, technique and skill she was showing. He smiled to himself as he whispered, "Go Babe."

"To toe! To toe!" Madison shouted as he advanced again upon her, forcing her to the end of her mat. She cross swung and pushed his blade aside. He jumped back before she could take a lunge at him. He twirled his tip in the air as he watched her standing in a defensive stance, breathing deeply.

...

She leveled her blade, then advanced. He engaged and foils blazed in flashes again. Forward-back, forward-back, then suddenly she advanced with added steps, but he forced her foil back to her chest and held it there. She stared at his face through the mask and could feel his hot breath.

"Know your opponent's weakness!" Steve cried out.

She looked into Madison's mask and smiled, then blew him a sweet, warm kiss. Her breath blew across his face and it went blank. She immediately pushed off him and leaped backward, then lunged forward to his chest with her blade's tip.

"Point, LaRosa, and match!" shouted the ref. "Parsippany wins!"

"Yes! Yes!" Joe screamed and all ran out to her. Joe picked her up and spun her around. She threw off her mask and hugged him.

"A true Musketeer!" he yelled as he kissed her cheek.

"A great teacher," she laughed as she kissed him back. He lowered her to the floor and into Steve's waiting arms.

"The youngest and the bravest," he whispered in her ear. She felt proud as she saw the way he was looking at her.

"So," she asked, "where's my victory kiss?"

"I think you just got it from Reily," he laughed, "but you deserve more than one," and as he slowly leaned into her she boldly pulled him close and kissed him.

Madison walked over and saluted her. She paused, then returned the compliment.

"Respect," he said to her with a smile and then returned to his teammates.Both teams formed lines and saluted each other.

On the bus home Sue fell asleep against Steve's arm. Mr. Biel came down the aisle, but then just smiled as he saw her sleeping.

"When she wakes up tell her how proud I am of her," he said, "and give her this." He handed him the winner's sash. It was red, white and blue with stars along the top and 'Fencing Championship Tournament of 1966' written across the middle in gold lettering.

"The team voted her to keep it," he said, "and I couldn't wait to give it to her."

Steve laid it across her chest and she slowly opened her eyes.

"Thank you," Mr. Biel said as he held out his hand to her. She reached up and shook it, then she saw the sash. "A token reminder from your teammates for what you've accomplished here today. None of us will ever forget it Musketeer," he said with a smile.

She looked at the sash, then at him. "I can't take this, it was won by the team."

"No it's yours," he replied, "because it was the team that was won over by you. You've taught them more this year than I ever could have hoped to. I talked with the other coach and his team. Next year the fencing will be an official sport, eligible for a letter, and of course co-ed. Thank you Susan from all of us."

"Thank you coach for letting me try."

He went back to his seat as she turned to Steve saying, "Thanks for believing in me."

"Angel, that's becoming easier by the minute," he replied as the right side of his smile rose up at her.

Chapter Four
Honor

Sue sat up high in the track field bleachers with Joe, Ken and their dates. This was an important meet to determine who would compete in the finals of the season. It was a damp day and the ground was still wet from the rain the night before. The wind was blowing also and felt cold.

Joe put his green dress leather coat over Cindy's shoulders as she smiled up at him. She was not a short girl, but next to Joe she could have set up house in it. Only the top of her brunette beehive could be seen above the large collar. She smiled out the front of it as he put his arm around her.

Ken's date, a girl he had just met today during lunch, was a pretty blue-eyed blond who liked to be called Mitzy.

As she sat, she shivered a few times to get Ken's attention. When he finally noticed he said, "Oh, yea," and held open the left side of his black dress leather so she could sneak inside under his arm. Once she was settled in, he focused his attention again at the line up starting for the 100 yard dash.

Sue sat wearing Steve's track letter jacket over her shoulders feeling content and warm.

"There's Sweety," Ken yelled as he pointed to the line below.

"Who's Sweety?" Mitzy asked.

"He's the guy we want to win," Ken answered as she started rubbing her head under his chin.

Steve took his place on the line, then, "Ready, set, go!" the coach yelled.

The line of bodies lunged forward. Steve and Frank Johnson quickly took the lead, running neck and neck. Their arms and legs were a blur as they left the pack farther behind. Steve could hear both their breathing as the finish grew closer.

"Go Sweety!" Ken yelled and jumped to his feet causing Mitzy to fall back against the seat behind.

"Good golly!" she yelped out.

"Run Sweety," Joe and Cindy cried out.

Sue stood up holding his jacket tight around her. "Go Babe," she said softly, "go!"

The final yards to the finish line were vanishing faster than his opponent's breathing as he inched out front. Suddenly his right foot dug into a patch of mud, slipped, and Frank flew past him. In a breath, it was over.

Both runners slowed to a stop, then bent down with hands on knees to catch their breath for a moment.

"Oh man!" Ken yelled out.

"Did we win?" Mitzy asked looking around.

"No," he answered, "it was called off due to bad weather."

Sue watched as he went over to Frank and they shook hands.

"Nice run Frank," he said.

"Thanks man, but it was too close for me."

"Thanks," Steve replied as he slapped him on the back, and together they slowly walked over to sit on the bottom bleacher benches.

Sue made her way down to him. "You ran like the wind," she said.

"But not like the winner," he muttered, "second place."

She knelt down to his face.

"You're number one with me," she said, then closed her eyes and posed puckered up. He leaned in and kissed her gently.

"Thanks Babe," he whispered smiling into her eyes.

"So what now?" she asked.

"I don't know," he answered, "that was my best event. If I don't win this last one, I'm out of the finals."

"What's the event?"

"The three mile run," he replied.

"I've watched you run that, you're still going when most are down to walking."

"I know," he replied with some hesitation, "but that last quarter mile lap is always my make it or break it point."

"I know you can do it," she whispered, "just find it in your heart to be your best."

He went over and did some leg exercises to warm up before the event was called. After thirty minutes, he stood with the others for the line up. He looked over at her sitting near the water table and she winked at him causing him to smile back.

"Ready, set, go!" yelled the coach and the line was up and moving.

He paced himself as he ran some eight to ten spots back, then maintained his position. The track was a half mile oval, so he kept even strides to be able to make it around the six times needed.

By the fourth lap, he had inched up to fifth position, which he held as he watched others drop to a trot, then walking as he passed them. By lap five, he was one of only three runners as they entered the final lap. He moved up to second as Bob Turner's legs began to shake beneath him.

As he rounded the last quarter, he was heel by heel with John Marsh, but felt his breathing lagging and his energy starting to evaporate into nothingness. John inched forward until Steve was watching the backs of his shoes as they were pulling away. Less than an eighth of a mile to go, but he couldn't find anymore to give.

He looked ahead to the line.

"An eternity," he thought, then some thirty feet past the line was Sue. She stood there with open arms.

"Run Babe," she called, "come to me!"

At that moment she was all he could see. The line vanished; he stopped thinking about his breathing or the pain in his chest and legs.

"Go Sweety, go!" yelled voices from the bleachers, but they were faint in the distance to him. He watched her blow him a kiss, then grab at the empty air with her stretched out fingers.

"Yes!" he heard her cry out.

He felt his legs go into overdrive without any effort. It was just automatic to her voice. His stretched out arms crossed the line just inches before John's, but as John slowed he kept running. He ran beyond the line, past his coach's cheer, through the ankle high grass at the track's edge and into her arms.

He swooped her up and they tumbled to the wet ground wrapped in each other. Without even taking a breath he pressed his lips to hers, then looked lovingly at her in his arms with mud on his face.

"Did I win?"

She smiled as she wiped mud off his nose. "A long time ago," she whispered.

That same afternoon they went to be alone out on the island. They laid back on the grassy knoll by the lake, surrounded by hundreds of small wildflowers.

She turned to him as she laid cradled in his arms and asked, "Why is it that guys like to fight so much?"

"Well it's just that, uh …Well, take a girl for example. It's often easier for us to fight for one than to say how we feel. I guess it's a matter of show vs. tell, a guy-thing."

"Hum," she said thoughtfully. "Maybe you should just show and tell but in more subtle ways. Girls do it all the time."

"I know, and I'm beginning to believe that's why you girls may really be the stronger sex."

"Why do you say that?"

"Girls can make or break a guy with just a simple glance and I've got the legs to prove it."

She looked at him questioningly. "You won that race today because you were smart, strong and fast."

He laughed.

"No, you won that race today, because your smile went straight to my heart faster than my legs ever could have reached that line."

"So you're saying that I should get the letter for my sweater?"

"Babe, you should get the whole alphabet!"

She smiled back. "But aren't you proud of the fact that you beat out over a dozen other runners?"

He looked up at the sky and sighed.

"When a guy beats another guy it's a temporary shallow victory, but when he wins the love of a girl it's a heavenly treasure."

"Touche'," she replied, "and to the winner goes the gold. Now, get over here and live up to your name Sweety."

They started kissing and necking as they felt their passions growing with each touch.

All of a sudden, he found his hand under her top and caressing her bare stomach, then slowly moving up her ribs towards her bra. When his fingers touched the bottom of its cup her breathing quickened and she moaned. Suddenly realizing what was happening, she quickly pulled his hand away.

"Please don't Babe."

He paused above her and looked lovingly into her deep brown eyes.

"I love you," she said softly, "and I want you just as badly but I can't until I'm married. I'm sorry."

"No, I'm sorry. I had no right to do that."

"I know you love me," she whispered, "and I want so much to please you, but not yet. God willing, maybe someday."

"I've waited this long for you," he said softly. "What are a few more years for the time to be right."

Her eyes widened as she leaned up, wrapping her arms around his neck.

"Hold me, tight," she told him and he pulled her closer. "I love you so much," she sighed, "but sometimes I don't feel strong enough to stop either."

She became quiet a moment, then added, "My dad is afraid for me, he thinks we're getting too serious and I'm going to get hurt. Sometimes I wonder if he might be right. I don't know how much longer I can say no."

She pressed her face against his chest as he gently stroked her hair."Promise you'll help me to be strong?"

"I promise," he answered as he put his chin on top of her head and closed his eyes. "When the time comes I want to be able to look into your eyes and not see guilt or regret, only love shining back at me."

She closed her eyes as they teared up. "I've always felt safe in your arms but never as much as now."

He felt her breath through his black t-shirt burning his chest.

"Oh Steve my heart is bursting," she cried, "there's so much love to hold."

"Maybe love shouldn't be held inside, just given to another. Give me all the love you can't hold back until the time is right to give me all of you."

She turned her head up to meet his lips as the salt of her tears mingled with the passion of their kiss. He brought his hands up to wipe away her tears as they rolled over. Her hair flowed wildly, filled with the perfumed flowers from the bed on which they laid upon. Their breath quickened as they moaned to the other's touch.

There was a fire between their lips as they exchanged heated breath into one another's mouth.

"Every breath I take is for you," she sighed out in a whimper.

"Then breathe life into me Angel," he whispered back as he drew her sweet, moist lips to his again.

Their chests heaved to take deeper breaths, so as to make each kiss last longer before having to come up for another swallow of air. Their skin was like electrified velvet against each other as they stroked hands, arms, faces and necks.

She paused once, to put her ear to his chest and listen to his heart. It was beating wildly, pumping out love for her. She kissed it through his T-shirt, then laid a track of hot kisses up to his neck where she declared, "I love you. Oh Steve, I love you so."

Moments later, each began to rein in their passions as their kisses and touching became slower yet still gentle.

"I think our hearts can hold the rest," he said, gazing into her melting eyes. Her chest was still heaving as she felt him stroke her hair ever so gently.

"I guess," she whimpered, "but what about thirty minutes from now?"

"God she's so beautiful," he thought, "who could wait thirty minutes?"

He suddenly leaped to his feet and yelped out, "Well then!" Turning quickly, he ran towards the lake, where with clothes and all, he dove into the cold water.

"Oh God!" he screamed as he surfaced.

"Are you crazy? You'll freeze!"

"That's the idea," he said looking at her. "Come on!" he shouted as he started walking out towards her.

"Oh no," she replied getting to her feet, "not a chance!"

He kept coming and she backed up.

"Steve I'm warning you. Don't you touch me you nut!"

He fell dripping wet at her feet. "See," he said, "it works!"

"I'm in love with a crazy man," she said as she knelt down in front of him.

"Crazy about you," he stated shivering.

She kissed his cheek.

"Let me get you home to dry out," she said smiling as she grabbed his side to help him up.

"Oh God," he moaned as he felt her touch again. "Quick, let's hurry."

Chapter Five
"1967"

It was a beautiful morning as Steve made his way up her street. He could smell the rows of flowers in front of the other houses as he passed. The sun warmed his face as he looked up and felt the gentle warm breeze as it blew the treetops above. They swayed, as if to the songs of the sparrows that were busy flying about keeping an eye on the chicks trying to leave the nests.

When he came up the steps Sue was at the window and saw him then ran to open the door. Her father was in the foyer and asked that he might have a word with him. She smiled and said, "Of course Daddy," then opened the door and met him with a smile as she blew him a kiss.

"My dad wants to talk with you a minute. I'll be back down, I'm almost ready."

"Sure," he replied and looked over at her dad who called to him.

"Steve, I'd like to talk to you."

"Yes sir."

"Let's go into the living room." He went over and sat on the couch while Mr. LaRosa remained standing.

"Steve, you're a nice boy and my daughter is very fond of you," he said as he pointed up the stairway.

"I care for her very much too."

"Yes well, you two have been seeing quite a lot of each other and I've been getting concerned that maybe it's too much. Perhaps it would be better for her, and for you, if you dated a little less."

He paused, then added, "To give yourselves a chance to see other kids and to do different things."

He turned to see his reaction. "Do you understand what I'm trying to say?"

"Are you saying that you don't want me to see her anymore?"

"No, just not so much. I just feel that you might be getting too serious for your ages."

"Mr. LaRosa we're both going to be seventeen in the next few months, we're not kids."

"That's very young," he replied, "and it's very easy to make mistakes. I won't let my daughter get hurt over some puppy love, do you understand? She will be going on to college when she graduates and start making a real life for herself."

Sue quietly came down the stairs, but stopped halfway to listen more as Steve stood up to face him.

"What we have is not puppy love. It is real and our lives together now are real. She loves it and so do I. We both plan to go on to college, we talk about it all the time."

"Talking and dreaming are easy when you're so young but making sure it happens, that's up to me as a parent. I won't let a mistake ruin it."

Steve crossed his arms as he stood firm. "Our love is not a mistake. I stand by her decisions all the time."

"There are some things she is too young to decide about. And love? …Oh please!" he said waving his hands in the air. "You can't possibly know what love is at your ages."

"Can't we?"

"No, one moment of weakness could wreak her life."

"Don't you trust us, me, to act as adults?"

"When you become adults, then yes."

They were both quiet for a moment, then, "Look son you have to understand. She's my whole world and I can't take the chance of letting her get …"

"I do understand and I would never hurt her. She's my world too."

"I'm sorry, but I think its best. It would be better if you left and I'll explain it to her."

Steve walked towards the door as Sue watched from the darkened stairwell, out of sight. She covered her mouth with one hand and put the other over her chest to hold her heart steadfast as he opened it.

He suddenly stopped to stare at the outside steps where once he stood in the snow, holding a near-frozen present, feeling scared and insecure. He remembered that moment when he had forced himself to ring the doorbell, asked to see her and then handed his gift to her without knowing what would happen. She was someone else's girl then also, but he could only follow his heart. In those few moments came a courage that had never left him, the courage to believe.

"No sir I won't," he said looking back at her father. "When you were my age, did you ever fall in love?"

"Of course," he answered, "many times I thought so, and it will happen to you again and again until …"

"But was there ever one so special you couldn't forget her? One worth risking anything for? Someone you thought about all the time and who made you feel like you could do anything, as long as you were together? Was there ever someone you thanked God for putting into your life and knew you didn't deserve her? Did you ever love anyone like that?"

He looked down a moment, then over at his wife standing silently in the kitchen archway as she smiled at him.

"Yes I have," he answered with a distant look of reflection.

Steve walked over to him asking, "And you just walked away and let her go?"

"No, he didn't," answered Mrs. LaRosa as she came out to them. "He told my father and two brothers that he loved me and that they better just accept it, because he wasn't going away."

Steve smiled at her, then looked back at him. "I'm not going away either sir. I'm in love with your daughter and I always will be."

Her dad sighed. "All right," he replied as his wife looked at him lovingly, "we'll watch and we'll see. I am trusting you with the most precious thing I have, my daughter's happiness."

"Yes Sir, and thank you both."

Sue composed herself quietly, then came down to the landing.

"I'm all ready," she said smiling.

They turned as she entered wearing a light-blue blouse, to match the solid blue shirt she saw he had on when he arrived. She also now wore a darker knee-length skirt with stockings, instead of socks, and a pair of easy walking dress shoes.

Her father looked her over then nodded in approval saying, "You look very nice sweetheart, where are you going?"

"We're meeting Joe and Cindy to take the bus over to Caldwell to window shop and have lunch."

"We'll be back before dinner," Steve added.

"Can I drop you off downtown," her dad asked.

"Yes," she answered, then leaned up and kissed him. "I love you Daddy," she whispered as she gave him a tight hug.

"I love you too baby," he replied softly and then she hugged her mom.

"Thank you Mom, I love you." she whispered in her ear.

"And I love you," she said with a smile.

"Okay," said her dad, "let's go then," and he walked her out to the car with his arm around her shoulder. Steve smiled from behind, then ran to open the car door for her.

"It might be a bit cramped up front," he said looking at Steve, "maybe you'd be more comfortable taking the backseat?"

"Frank!" her mom called as she locked the front door, "Wait, I need to go downtown and get a few things."

She hurried to the car and told Sue to sit in the back as she winked at her. Sue smiled and winked back. Her father adjusted his rear view mirror, seeing her smiling up at Steve, then they drove off.

On the bus, the girls chatted away about some of the stores they wanted to explore. Joe leaned over to Steve and asked how much he thought lunch might cost.

"I didn't get to go caddying this week," he said, "I had to help my dad clean out the cellar, so I only have about six bucks left."

Steve reached into his pocket and quietly slipped a ten dollar bill into his hand."I don't need that much."

"Then use what you need. Cindy's worth it, isn't she?"

"Yea, she is," he answered with a tongue-in-cheek look as he twisted the ring on his finger and rubbed the circle of diamond chips around the big 'J' on its face.

"You gonna ask her today?" Steve asked.

"I sure want to," he replied in a nervous tone, "but what if she says no, that'll ruin everything. What if she doesn't want to go out anymore?"

"But what if she says yes," Steve asked, "isn't it worth the risk?"

Joe glanced over at Cindy as she was telling Sue about a sale she read about for one of the stores.

"I can't," he murmured. "Maybe you could ask her?" he said with a begging look.

"I've already got a girl, thank you."

"Yea," Joe replied, "but it was easier for you."

"Easier? Are you kidding!" Steve asked dumbfounded.

"Yea," he replied, "all you had to do was beat up one guy. I'd pound ten into the ground for her but there's never any around when ya need them."

"Joe, you know how hard it was for me to talk to Sue and to ask her out. You've already gotten that far on your own. Trust yourself, be honest with your feelings and the right words will come."

They both looked over at the girls. The girls noticed them staring and they smiled back, then continued talking.

"Believe me Joe they're worth it, even if you don't have to fight to get them."

When they first got off the bus, they walked together as couples. Sue and Steve walked with arms around each other's waists. Joe and Cindy also were together, but with arms each behind their own backs holding their own hands.

They stopped to look in windows as they strolled along the main street. Sometimes, they went inside to browse and the girls would hold something up for them to comment on like a dress or sweater.

Later, they were looking through baby clothes and pointing out how cute the tiny booties were; but when they hit the nightgown section, Joe went out for some air.

Sue came over to Steve. "What's wrong with Joe, doesn't he like Cindy much?"

"Like her? He's crazy about her."

"Well he doesn't show it. I know how much she likes him," she said as she held up some lacy red panties to look at.

Steve turned his eyes to the ceiling, blushing.

"Are you embarrassed?"

"Oh no, I just need some air too I guess."

"You are!" she said grinning. "Oh you really are a Sweety," then she kissed his cheek.

"Maybe I should just go out and tell Joe how much she likes him?"

"Don't you dare," she replied, "you can't do that!"

"Why not?"

"Cause it would kill her to know he knew."

He turned to her and asked, "Am I missing something here? We both know that he likes her and she likes him, so why don't we make it easy and tell them?"

"We can't do that," she said with a look of surprise. "He has to show her he cares by holding her hand and whispering in her ear. Maybe say how nice she'd look in that dress and that he'd love to see her in it at the dance next Friday night. He has to show her that he cares in subtle ways, in gentle ways... You know what I mean."

"All I know is that unless we do something to help, there are ten guys out on that street who are about to have a real bad day."

"What are you talking about?"

"Never mind," he answered, "you've got to help me help them now."

"Okay, follow my lead."

She found Cindy and they all went outside to find Joe. He was kicking at a parking meter with the toe of his now scuffed shoe.

Sue looked across the street at a fashion boutique called 'Anna Amora's' and said, "Cindy, let's go look in there." The girls started across the street as Steve grabbed Joe's arm.

"Come on," he said, "before some guys try and pickup our dates."

Joe perked up. "You think some might try?"

"I know I would if I were them."

"Yea," he responded with a grin. "How many do you think, four or five maybe?"

"Maybe."

"I hope they're football players," Joe muttered as he hurried to catch up.

They came up behind the girls as they were pointing at the dresses in the window.

"Look at that white laced one," she said to Cindy. "It even looks your size."

Steve leaned into Joe and said, "Go tell her how nice you think it would look on her."

"Okay," he replied as he walked slower.

"Then when she smiles, tell how nice it would be to see her in it at the dance on Friday."

"Right, the dance," he repeated.

"But that no matter what she wore, she'd always look beautiful to you. Then wait for her response and look her in the eye and tell her how you feel."

"How I feel, right."

"Then ask, 'Would you go with me as my steady date?' and then hold out your ring."

"The ring, got it."

Joe called out to her as he walked up onto the sidewalk from the curb. Cindy turned around to smile at him just as a short, slim guy was walking past and she bumped into him.

"Well pretty lady," he said, "if you wanted to meet me, all you had to say was hello," and then he put his hand against the window as he leaned into her.

Cindy looked at him in surprise. "Oh, no, I was just looking around to see …"

She stopped as suddenly the young dude was lifted up over her head. She looked down at the pair of green eyes that were looking back at her as he held the guy vertically overhead with both arms.

"Joe," she asked puzzled, "what are you doing?"

He put him down and the guy scrambled to get up, but Joe held him by the collar with one hand.

"Oh God," Steve said as he hurried over and tried to get the guy free from his grip.

"Cindy I think you'd look great in that dress if you wore it to the dance this Friday. Or if you wore nothing you'd still look beautiful, cause you're the greatest girl I've ever known."

Joe went down on his knees.

"Would you go steady with me?"

"Oh Joe," she sighed.

"Please say yes," the dude moaned as he pulled at the huge hand under his chin.

"I'd love to go steady with you," she answered smiling.

Joe let go of his grip so he could remove the ring from his finger. The young guy scrambled to his feet.

"Congratulations, you make a great couple," he said, then ran down the street.

He slipped his ring onto her thumb and she closed her fingers gently around it so it couldn't fall off. "I'll buy you a gold chain for it," he said and they kissed.

"Oh," Sue sighed as she hugged Steve's arm, "I love it when you guys are romantic."

"It must be the musketeer in us," he said as he rolled his eyes.

"See, I told you it would all work out," she added. "You just have to be subtle."

"Yes you did, and there are nine more guys out there who are very grateful."

Sue turned back towards the window display.

"Oh, look at this wedding dress," she said as she walked up against the store glass in front of it. "Such a soft white glow, and those tiny pearls on the headpiece and along the neckline, isn't it just beautiful?"

She turned around to see his response. Her outline blocked out the mannequin's figure. All he could see was the gown's fringes around her, with the white veil above and around her head, and falling behind her shoulders. He was speechless for a moment as he stared at her.

"What do you think?" she finally asked again, "Don't you think it's just beautiful?"

"I do," he answered as he reached out and took her hand, then leaned in and kissed her gently. "The most beautiful vision I've ever seen," he whispered as he looked into her shining eyes.

She smiled, then looked downward for a moment and began to blush.

"How about lunch you guys?" called Cindy as she pulled Joe by the hand.

"I thought it might be nice to have a sit down lunch of Chinese," Joe said as he let her lead off.

"Oh, that sounds nice and cozy," Cindy replied, then called back to Sue, "don't you think?"

"I do," she answered softly as she looked into his rich blue eyes, then led him down the walk as well.

During lunch they joked and laughed as Cindy tried feeding Joe noodles with her chop sticks one moment, then he'd try to get her to eat more of the hot mustard as she fanned her tongue in-between bites.

Sue did a tea ceremony with Steve she had learned from her grandmother. She filled the cup, took a sip, then turned the cup one full turn and he sipped. They continued until the tea cup was empty.

"Each turn completes a cycle in our lives," she explained, "and we share the taste of each together. Then, when the cup is empty, I look at the bottom later when it has dried and try to see our future in the design."

She moved the cup aside and shared more tea from his cup during the meal.

As the dishes were taken away by the waiter, Joe asked about their fortune cookies.

"I will get for you now," the elderly gentleman replied and carried away the tray. He returned with four cookies in a bowl.

"Let the guys go first," Cindy said, so Joe took one and opened it.

"The sun sets best on the day you made."

"Awe," Cindy said as she hugged his arm, then she pointed to Steve. He fished one out, opened it and read it aloud.

"Your greatest strength is found in your greatest weakness."

"They must be talking about your legs," Joe remarked with a laugh. "Sue?"

"No, you go next," she said.

Cindy took the one farthest from her and cracked it open.

"The happiness you give others will return in abundance."

"Starting right now," Joe said as he gave her a kiss.

Steve lifted the bowl and held it out to Sue. She carefully took the cookie, gently opened it and read silently.

"Well Babe?" asked Steve.

"Love is a flower that blooms through a winter's storm," she read slowly and thoughtfully.

"And lasts forever," he whispered in her ear.

Sue's expression went blank and she suddenly reached out for the cup. She quickly looked inside and her eyes widened.

"Can I look too?" Steve asked as he leaned over.

"Oh no," she answered, "only the girl can see!" and she quickly poured more tea into the cup.

Later on the bus home, Sue was quiet as she held her head against his arm and slowly stroked it.

"Did you have a good time?" he asked.

"A wonderful day, but I guess I'm just getting tired is all."

They sat quietly as the bus continued down the highway, pausing only for its scheduled stops. Sue watched the seats empty as passengers got off each time. The bus grew emptier with each side trip. When it turned off Route 46 and onto North Beverwyck Road towards its last stops in Lake Hiawatha, she squeezed his arm.

"Afraid you'll get hurt?" he asked as the bus made the turn.

"Yes," she answered as she stared at all the empty seats. He put his hand on hers as she continued to squeeze.

The bus pulled over at the corner of Vail Road and Joe said he was getting off here to walk Cindy home. They waved and Steve waved back as they got off.

"It was a great time!" Joe yelled back and his words echoed in the empty space.

The bus started rolling again with only the two of them left in the rear seats. The bus now echoed its own emptiness off the walls as it made its way along the bumpy road.

Sue felt her heart begin to race as she watched the scenery run past too fast for her to hold it in her mind for even a moment. Each second was new, then gone behind her.

Finally, the bus pulled over and stopped at the corner of Lake Shore Drive.

"Last stop!" the driver called out. Steve got up and started down the aisle, but stopped when he saw her not moving.

"Sue?" he questioned as he held out his hand.

"I don't want to get off, " she replied.

"What?"

"Please don't leave," she cried softly and he came back to sit with her.

"What's wrong?"

"I don't know," she answered as he put his arms around her and could feel her trembling. "I don't want it to end," she said tearfully.

"You mean the ride? The day? What?"

"This time we have, I don't want it to pass," she cried.

"Hey, hey," he said softly as he touched her face and wiped away the tears, "what we have will last forever, I promise."

"Promise me, really promise me!" she cried with fright.

"I promise to love and cherish you the rest of my life, no matter what."

"Miss!" yelled the driver. "I'm sorry, but this is as far as you can go."

Sue got up and walked to the front. "I know," she replied, then got off.

Later after dinner, she went up to her room and called her grandmother on her princess phone. She told her all about the wonderful day she'd had.

"But something is wrong?" her grandma asked.

"Yes," she answered in a choked up tone.

"You love this boy, yes?"

"With all my heart Grandma."

"And he loves you, this you are sure of?"

"Oh yes, in every way he has shown it."

"He is Catholic?"

Sue smiled. "Yes Grandma, we go to Mass every Sunday together."

"Then that is good. God will guide you both then." There was silence then she asked, "He is respectful, yes?"

"Always."

"And he honors you?"

"Honors?"

"Does he ask you to do things that you should not?"

"Grandma!"

"I know you would not do such things my angel, but does he know?"

"Yes Grandma, he knows without my telling and he's never asked. He said he wants to be able to look into my eyes and see only love, not guilt or regret."

"Oh, what a good Catholic boy. I will keep you both in my prayers."

Sue was silent.

"There is something else?"

"Yes, today when we did the tea ceremony I looked into the dried cup."

"Oh? And what did you see?"

"I saw two light circles next to each other but not touching, and the bottom of the cup was dark stained all around them. Each circle had a jagged line through it. I was frightened as I looked at them."

69

"Oh my," she responded, "you don't need to be frightened. You are both young and will face many hard times, but things will always get better. You will both come through the darkness."

"The jagged lines in each, what do they mean?"

"Broken hearts my angel, but God made our hearts that way. If they were hardened, then we could not love." She paused, then asked, "Susan, do you know what the shortest sentence is in the Bible?"

"No," she answered with a tear.

"Jesus wept."

"Why?"

"Because of His love and because of your love you both will cry and hurt. Then if God Wills, you will heal and if your love is true it will last forever."

"So I should pray and leave it in His hands?"

"Pray without ceasing Paul tells us and our Lord tells us not to worry about tomorrow. God has a plan for each of us, trust in Him."

"I love you Grandma."

"I love you too child. You sleep now and have wonderful dreams."

"I will and you too, bye."

She hung up and started to go downstairs to watch a little television. She could hear the family talking in the living room as she opened the bedroom door, but she paused and came back to the phone and dialed.

"Hello?"

"Hi, Steve?"

"Hi Babe, are you okay?"

"I'm fine. I just wanted to hear your voice and tell you I really did have a great day, thank you."

"Oh you're welcome. I'm glad you enjoyed it as much as I did."

"I also wanted to tell you how much I love you."

"And I love you too," he said softly, "but I still love to hear you say it."

She kissed into the phone and heard him kiss her back.

"Mom," she heard his little sister yell in the background, "Steve's kissing the phone and talking mushy to it!"

"Would you go watch the television!" she heard him say and she laughed."Sorry about that," he said.

"Are you getting embarrassed again?" she asked with another laugh.

He was silent.

"It's okay Sweety," she said, "you just listen while I do all the mushy talk. But first, I want you to know that I couldn't have asked for a better man to stand beside me than you were today. I love you with all my heart for what you said to my father. I was never so proud of anything as I was today to be your girl. God bless you My Love.

I'm sorry I got upset on the bus, but I know now that everything is going to turn out fine. God has a plan for our lives and we can trust in Him. The promise you made me on the bus, I now promise to you also. I will love, honor and cherish you forever. My father was wrong. We can know what love is at our age and it's so beautiful that it makes me cry that I could ever be this happy. Thank you for loving me the way you do."

There was silence, then, "Sue I know it's getting late, but could you find a way to be at the end of your driveway in about ten minutes?"

"I guess, but why?"

"Cause I need to kiss you right now and I can't wait till tomorrow."

"Oh Babe I have to get to bed soon, it's after nine, and you're over ten blocks away."

"Okay, give me eight minutes."

She laughed then said, "I'll be there. I can't wait till tomorrow either."

She heard him hang up, then lowered the phone to her chest and held it there for a moment before putting it down. She reached for a small bottle of perfume and lightly sprayed some on her neck, then smelt the bottle and the thought of him filled her completely. She savored the feeling for a few moments as she caressed the bottle. Then, seeing the clock on her nightstand, she hurried down the stairs and went quietly out the back door.

As she came to the end of the driveway, she could hear footsteps down the street. She looked at her watch. "Seven minutes, twenty seconds," she noted, then smiled as she closed her eyes.

There was no need to look. He was already there, in her heart.

Chapter Six
The Promises of Camelot

As their junior year ended and the warmth of summer approached, they dreamed sweet dreams of fun and freedom. They waited in agony for their seventeenth birthdays so they could be able to drive. To go when and wherever they pleased, but of course, this meant getting a car of their own.Steve had taken auto shop and landed a job after school at the Sunoco in town owned by his father's best friend, Chuck Wade, or Uncle Chuck, as Steve had grown to call him.

He would start work at four O'clock each day and work until six on weekdays, then on Saturdays he was eight to five but was off on Sundays.

He started out cleaning the restrooms, pumping gas and doing tires and oil changes. Later, he learned how to do battery work, tune ups and brakes. By the end of six months, between auto shop and working side by side with Uncle Chuck, he was able to do most of the work that came in the bay doors.

He enjoyed learning his way around cars and Chuck made it fun, more than just a business to him. He soon became very confident as an apprentice mechanic.

When school was done, he was allowed to work more hours so he could save for a car. He already had in a savings account over five hundred dollars from all his past part time jobs. His grandmother had told him always to save part of everything he earned since he was little.

Aside from buying a few new clothes as he needed them, and taking Sue out on modest dates, he had managed to save regularly.

He was proud that he was able to buy the extras he wanted on his own, without asking his parents; after all, he was the oldest of seven siblings and his father already worked hard to provide their necessities.

Sue admired this independence in him. She was quite content to enjoy their time together in the simplest of ways. She understood his need to get a car on his own and she loved him for it.

She'd often come down to the station and bring a lunch she had prepared to share with him. He missed not having the time together that they use to have, but promised that he'd make up for it. He just wanted to find the right car for them that he could afford and she understood.

"Only a few more weeks and we'll have our driver's licenses," she would hear him say, "and then, wheels of our own."

She asked what color he wanted the car to be and he laughed.

"I don't know, how about red?"

"That's a good one, passionate, full of energy …"

"And fast I hope," he added.

"You don't intend to race, do you?" she asked.

"No, but it would be nice to know the power's there if you need it?"

She glared at him, then said, "Maybe we ought to stick with affordable and reliable."

He smiled with a chuckle. "I'm just hoping to get something you would be proud to be seen in."

"I'm proud on the bus with you, you know that."

"I know Babe but I just want to give you what you deserve, the best."

It was mid-afternoon on a Saturday when a call came into the station for a tow. Uncle Chuck went out with his wrecker as Steve continued to watch the gas pumps while plugging a flat that had been dropped off earlier.

As he was checking the tire repair for any leaks, he heard the pipes of the Mack wrecker roaring back up the road. He looked up and saw the most beautiful car on its hook that he had ever seen. It was a

Pontiac convertible. Chuck backed it into the garage bay and dropped it down.

"Check the undercarriage for damage and see if it'll start," he yelled as he prepared to park the tow truck around back. "I had to winch it out of some woods off Edward's Road after the driver told me it had lost power."

Steve jacked up the front nose and put some safety stands under it. He grabbed a floor creeper and slid underneath looking over the front end as he pulled away grass and mud from the A-frames and steering linkage. He went to start it but the starter would only click, not turn over.

"How's it look?" asked Chuck as he came in the bay door.

"Well the oil pan is leaking; the inner and outer tie-rod ends on the driver's side are bent like pretzels. The stabilizer links have popped on both ends and the front exhaust pipe is ripped away from the manifold. Oh yea, it's got a dent in right front fender and a smashed headlight."

Steve paused, then asked, "What happened to it?"

Chuck just shook his head saying, "The price for street racing. How about the engine?"

"The starter didn't seem to have been hit, but it won't turn over."

"Better see if we can turn the motor by hand with a breaker bar, to check if it's seized up," Chuck told him.

Steve got the tools and was able to move the crankshaft just an inch. "Feels like it's hitting something."

"Pull out the spark plugs," Chuck said then went into his office to start on an estimate.

When he returned he took a long screwdriver and proceeded to lower its tip down into each plug hole and move it around.

"Just as I thought," he stated, "it's dropped a valve down into the piston and put a hole in the top, maybe even scored the wall too. Let it sit while I call the owner," and then he went back into his office.

Steve just stood looking at the car.

It was a 1966 Le Mans, red with a white rag top and black interior with full carpeting. There were bucket seats with an automatic shift on the console. Under its hood was a 326 cubic inch V-8 engine with air conditioning, power steering and brakes. It had rally wheels and dual pin-stripping along the side. A radio with an 8-track player and custom stereo speakers, front and rear, completed the package.

"Man, just look at you," he thought as he slowly walked around it, stroking its smooth paint job as if he could feel its pulse.

Chuck walked back towards him and saw him sitting in the driver's seat stroking the wheel.

"If you were mine," he heard him say, "I'd show you the respect you deserve."

Chuck smiled from behind him as he said, "I gave the owner an estimate and he's coming over to talk."

Steve didn't comment, just sat lost in his daydreaming.

"I'm getting hungry," Chuck said. "How about you call Sue and ask her to join us for some pizza, I'm buying."

Steve suddenly turned and looked his way. "Oh sure Uncle, that would be great, thanks."

Chuck ordered the pie and Sue gladly picked it up.

As they sat eating, Steve said, "Let me show you something," and took her by the hand into the last bay.

"Oh Steve, it's beautiful," she said as she reached out to touch it.

"It's a '66 and it's red," he said with excitement, "and it's loaded!"

"It's actually maroon," she corrected as she read the registration over the visor, "but the color feels so warm and inviting."

He slowly opened the passenger door for her and let her slip down into the seat. She ran her hand over the dash as he turned on the key and the radio.

"It even has an 8-track!" he said, as she tuned the radio to her favorite station. She closed her eyes with her head back and listened to the music.

"This is the kind of car I'd love to have for us, cause it's like you. It's got style, it's got class and it deserves respect," he whispered to her.

She smiled as she sank down into the seat saying, "It doesn't scream 'Race Me', it says come 'Ride with Me' on warm summer nights around the lake."

"And up to the mountains," he added.

"And down to the shore," she said softly.

"And to the senior prom," he whispered.

"Is it for sale?" she asked.

"Could be," came a voice from behind them and they jerked their heads up to look around. Standing there was Chuck and the owner, staring at them.

Steve got out of the car and apologized. "Oh God, I'm sorry, we didn't mean to take advantage, it's just that it is such as beautiful car."

They came over and the owner said, "That's all right, you both look good in it.

I've been talking to Chuck here and decided that between the cost of the repairs needed to get it back on the road, and the fact that my son has no respect for my car, I would like to sell it."

Steve and Sue's eyes widened.

"Really?" he asked, "How much would you ask?"

Mr. Wallace smiled over at Chuck, then asked, "How much did we say?" Chuck grinned with his hand half over his face.

"I believed we figured it was now worth around eight, maybe nine hundred. Of course, there still could be more damage yet to find for a complete estimate."

"Yes, you're right," agreed Mr. Wallace. "Well, maybe a more fair price would be say, six hundred-fifty. What do you think?" he asked Steve as he turned to him.

"Oh Mr. Wallace, this car is worth a whole lot more than that."

"Maybe so, but I want to see it driven by someone who can appreciate it and would care of it. Would you be interested?"

Steve looked down at Sue as she shook her head yes, then mouthed, "Please." He smiled at her, then at the others.

"I'd love to buy this car. Thank you sir, thank you!"

He slowly closed the door and stood next to it. "I'll be able to give you the full amount when I get paid on Friday, will that be all right?"

"That'll be fine son," he said, "just promise me you'll treat her special."

"I Promise," he replied putting his hand on Sue's. "Yes sir, I promise!"

Over the next couple of weeks, he worked on it every free moment. Uncle Chuck let him order the parts on credit and deducted a set amount out of each of his paychecks.

Sue came to help him everyday. She brought lunches, handed him tools and helped clean, vacuum it out, and give it a real toothbrush detail, as he worked on and under it. He pulled the heads off both sides of the engine and gave it all new valves. Uncle Chuck helped him with the new piston, and was glad the cylinder wall wasn't damaged, then let Steve put up the new oil pan and filled it with the station's best oil.

Several nights the three would sit in it with the top down as they ate sandwiches and drank coffee, while Uncle Chuck would tell them about his first cars.

"My very first one was a '42 Ford pickup. It had a six in it but man it could run. It had only two rear wheels when I got it."

Steve smiled. "Then how'd you drive it?" he asked with a laugh.

"Easy," he answered with a smirk, "I did wheelies all the way home!" and they all laughed out loud.

One early evening, as he was finishing tightening in the last spark plug and attaching the wire, Chuck came in with a funny looking suction cup tool.

"What's that?" he asked.

"This, my boy, just might save you from having to replace that front fender." Steve watched as he attached it over the dent.

"Okay," he asked, "now what?"

His uncle put his hand on the tool's handle grip and said, "Well, if we're real lucky, one good pull and that dent might just pop out without needing major surgery." He paused on the handle then said, "Here, you do the honors," and put his hand on Steve's shoulder.

Steve gripped the handle, but paused.

"No, I'd rather let it be done with a tender touch," he said, then stood up looking into the back seat where Sue had fallen asleep.

"Hey Babe," he called as he looked at her with a smudge of grease on her cheek. She opened her eyes and smiled up at him. "We got one more job left but it requires a delicate touch. " She got out of the car and walked around to the front.

"We've got a chance to fix this fender with one pull." he said.

"But it has to be done gently, yet firmly," Chuck added, "and we believe you could do it best."

"Oh no guys, it should be one of you," she replied with wide eyes."Neither of us has ever tried this before, so it's a first for all of us. We've chosen our champion, 'One for all'," Steve whispered. His uncle nodded with a smile.

"You can do it," Chuck said.

She put her hands onto the handle grip tightly and applied pressure slowly until she could feel the resistance.

"I'm not gonna hurt you, I promise," she said softly to the car. "You push and I'll pull, okay?"

She closed her eyes and said, "I love you," then gave it one smooth, steady pull. A loud metallic 'Pop' was heard echoing through the shop as the fender gave way. She opened her eyes and the crease was gone!

"We did it!" she cried out.

"No you did," he said with a hug, "and I never had a doubt."

"Oh," Chuck said as he removed the tool and checked the repair, "it's perfect! You got the mak'ins of a real body man, uh, woman."

She smiled as she caressed the spot. "There, no more hurt," she whispered, and then gently wiped it with a towel.

"Well then," Chuck said, "only one thing left to do now." He gathered them all at the front of the car as he closed the hood. They looked at him and at each other. "The christening of course," he said, "it's got to be given a name."

"You name it," Steve said to her.

Sue paused thinking, then took off her white scarf and holding it over the hood said, "I dub thee, EXCALIBUR!" and then knighted it gently on both fenders. "Defender of all that is good in our lives."

She turned to Steve and said, "Legend says that as long as Arthur had Excalibur he could not be defeated."

He took her face into his hands and said, "And for as long as My Lady loves me," then tenderly kissed her.

By July they had gotten their driver's licenses, a week apart. So to celebrate, they planned a trip to the shore at the boardwalk of Seaside Park. They decided to go on the Saturday following the Fourth of July weekend so it would be less crowded. Uncle Chuck said he could have most of the weekends off for the rest of the summer to enjoy themselves.

At nine in the morning, Steve pulled up to her house as planned and parked out front on the street. He waited, listening to his new eight track tape of the American Breed.

As she came flying out the front door in her yellow halter top and white shorts, struggling with a large beach bag, he cranked up the music singing the song 'Bend me, shape me'.

She reached the car and tossed the bag into the backseat as she caught up with the song to sing along with him. She jumped into the front and turned to sing the last verses with him, then they kissed.

As they drove down the street they already were imagining the fun. The salty breeze, the open beach and the cool waves. The great assorted eats and treats, and the rides and games of the boardwalk that beckoned to their free-spirits.

As they made their way down the Garden State Parkway south, they watched each other enjoying the openness of the top down and the wind blowing the other's hair wildly.

The sun warmed their faces and its brightness glared off of their sunglasses as well as Excalibur's highly waxed hood like pure rays of energy; each moment building with the excitement of a freedom they had never known.

As the three roared forward across the black pavement, Excalibur carried its precious cargo as if they were children in his charge. It glided across the hardtop like a sailboat over a calm, mirrored lake, not one bump was felt. It gripped the road, whenever it changed lanes, as if its tires had steel claws.

It smoothly passed by all the station wagons, work-vans and common commuter-type cars as each driver's head turned to admire its air of freedom and fun-in-the-sun.

Steve loved how he never had to fight the car as he drove it, the two had a natural flow together. It was as if Excalibur could read his mind and he learned to trust its feel as he lightly gripped the wheel.

Sue would gently stroke its vent window as she sang along with the radio. The motor seemed to purr along with her from its dual exhaust pipes.

As they made their way further south, she kept fine turning the radio to keep listening to her favorite station.

"Come on Baby," she would say to Excalibur as the station faded, "don't lose it now," and suddenly the music came back stronger.

"Thanks Love," she'd whisper, then got ready to start singing along again.

***

"Hey to all my listeners out there! This is Bad Boy Bob coming to ya live from the greatest station in Jersey and now I've got a song for all of ya that are heading out for a great weekend. Here's Steppenwolf telling you to take a Magic Carpet Ride."

***

She closed her eyes as she sang, but smiled and rested peacefully, knowing she was being taken away by the two loves of her life.

As she held the hand of her shining knight and slipped off her sandals to caress her feet against the rich magic carpet, they carried her through the wind to new worlds.

Suddenly, she realized she was breathing in salt air and she sat up looking through the windshield for a glimpse of the ocean. White seagulls flew overhead, swooping, diving and some hovering as they drove beneath them under the full blue sky hearing them sing.

Moments later, she could hear the excitement of the boardwalk as music was playing and voices calling out, "And we have another winner! Step up and try your luck, everybody wins here today!"

As they drove passed the rows of summer houses and motels, she ached with anticipation to see the water's edge. They finally passed a sign which read, 'Welcome to Seaside Park,' and she pointed to it as she put her hand on Steve's shoulder. He turned down the next road leading to the main drag.

When he reached the stop sign he paused to watch all the cool cars cruising the strip. As soon as there was an opening, they pulled out and joined into the parade of cars.

Excalibur blended right in with the classic 57 Chevy Belaire, the Firebirds and GTOs, the S.S. Chevys, Mustangs and a coupe Dodge Hemi, all cruising and looking good. A sense of pride filled them as they got thumbs-ups and 'High' signs from other drivers as they made their way to the beach front parking area.

As they pulled into a space, Sue stood up to look over the windshield at the turquoise waves. They roared onto the cream beach like huge cupped hands grabbing a chuck of sand to bring back with it as a prize, as each returned to the vast openness that sent it.

The air was alive with music, voices, birds, salt, the roaring water, the clicking of a hundred game wheels spinning towards a winning number. Of course, the smell of fresh fish, clams and other sea-foods begging to be sampled drifted down the boardwalk. The aromas of hot sausage and peppers, spicy meatball subs and sizzling pizza quickly followed.

"I'm starved," Steve said as he put up the top and locked the car.

"Oh me too, but please, let's first run along the shore okay?"

He laughed. "Last one to touch a wave has to sit down in the next one, deal?"

"Deal!" she yelled and then darted off ahead of him into the sand.

A flock of gulls squawked loudly as they took flight from her sudden invasion through their beach gathering. She waved her hands laughing as she made her way past the fluttering feathers about her. Then she looked over her shoulder to see him closing fast.

The surf was still some forty feet away as he finally came running by her side.

"Oh Steve!" she suddenly yelled out to him and pointing, "Grab me that shell, please!"

He immediately slowed down to pick it up before he realized she was still running at full speed.

"Oh, you're gonna pay for that!" he yelled, then dug his bare feet into the sand to try and catch her again.

She screamed out a laugh as she reached the edge and stood in the water with the waves splashing against the back of her legs.

"Your wave is waiting!" she yelled and pointed to his cutoff blue jeans.

He dropped to a slow walk.

"You're coming with me for that stunt," he said as he kept moving closer with a grin.

"Oh no!" she yelled laughing, "I won fair and square! Know your opponent's weakness, remember?"

"Touche' again," he answered laughing, then stooped down for the next incoming wave.

She stood by him as she watched it coming, then he grabbed her and pulled her down into it just as it splashed his backside.

"Don't get my top wet!" she yelled as the water hit her waistline and he immediately held her up so it didn't get her completely wet.

After the wave passed he lowered her down and kissed her.

"I love you," she whispered, then pushed him backwards and he went under as she ran for the beach.

When he came up for air and shook the water from his hair and face, he saw her sitting on the sand smiling. He got up and walked out slowly.

"You mad?" she asked.

"Of course not," he replied as he sat down beside her, taking his black T-shirt off and shaking it, then he held it over her head and wrung it out.

"Steve!"

"Nope," he said, "not a bit, now."

She grabbed it and put it over his face as she pushed him back onto the sand.

"For that, you buy lunch and I get to choose."

"Fair enough," he replied as he reached into his pants pocket and pulled out a wade of soggy dollar bills.

"I forgot to check before the race."

"I think they'll still take them," she said covering her smile, then helped him to his feet with a tug on his arm.

"So," he asked, "what do you feel like having?"

"Me? I'd love a shrimp basket and you get the fries."

He looked at her blankly.

"Well, maybe we can share," she added in a forgiving tone, "if I dry out before they serve them." They walked lovingly, arm in arm, back to the car for a towel and their sandals.

On a boardwalk bench, overlooking the sand and surf, they sat and fed each other from the basket lunch. When they finished, they made their way past the game-stands and souvenir shops.

They stepped into Lucky Leo's and played a little skeet-ball. When they cashed in their tickets at the redemption center, Sue choose a small, silver-plated clip with a wave on it for her hair.

As they came back out onto the sunny boardwalk a voice called out, "Here dude, how's about winning the pretty lady a nice prize?"

They both stopped and looked at the young barker wearing a straw hat, with a long blue feather in it. His colorful vest of stars, over a red and white striped shirt, flashed in the sunlight as he waved a carnival cane.

"Come on," he motioned, "try your luck and you might get lucky! Every girl loves a winner and our prizes are the best on the midway and that ain't no hay!"

"Why not," Steve said as he walked up to lay down a quarter on a number. He hit the button and wheel started spinning but slowly came to a stop on another number.

"Oh, so close," the dude said, as he scooped up the quarters from across the board.

"Try again," he yelled as another couple turned to walk away. "I've given so much away today I may be out of business in the morning, but that's how the luck runs here, to my customers!"

Sue tugged on Steve's arm.

84

"That was fun, but let's go on some of the rides."

He started to walk away until he saw her staring at the huge colorful animals hanging above the stand.

"Just one more time," he said, "here you choose," and he handed her a quarter. She looked at the wheel full of numbers, names and symbols, there were over thirty of them.

Finally, she reached over and let the coin drop in the center of a red heart. She pushed the green button and the wheel started spinning. Several other people rushed up and laid down quarters on other spaces.

She watched as the wheel slowly came to a stop and landed on her space.

"You won!" Steve yelled and hugged her.

Her eyes widened as she held a hand to her mouth. "Oh wow, I really did!"

"Another winner here!" cried out the barker. "A choice of stand big winner! Everybody wins!"

She looked up at the animals, then saw two beautiful white owls. Each had red feathers on its head and was wearing a graduation cap. One was over four feet tall and the other about two feet in height, each with large blue eyes looking at her.

"Could I have him?" she asked. "Yes, the smaller one."

The barker handed it down to her, still crying out, "Here goes another big winner out the door, come play while I still have prizes left!"

"Oh, thank you so much!" she told the young man as he handed it to her.

"You're welcome, enjoy it."

Sue took the owl into her arms.

"You want me to carry that for you?"

"Oh no, I got it," she answered with excitement and they walked off towards the ride pier as she petted it.

"Oh, I just love him," she said. "Steve he's so soft, feel him."

He reached out and felt its furry feathers.

She gave it a hug, then they headed for the Ferris wheel.

When they got into a seat he told her he was glad they didn't charge extra for the bird.

"Shamus," she said, "that's his name, Little Joe Shamus," as she sat him between the two of them.

Steve peered over the owl's head to see her.

"Is this guy gonna sit between us on every ride?" he asked.

She let out a short laugh.

"Feeling neglected over there?"

"Well yea, a bit," he answered shaking his head. "I just never thought I'd see the day that an Irishman named Joe would come between us."

She let out another laugh, gave Shamus a kiss, then reached under its wing and held his hand.

"I can't resist him he's got your eyes," she said while batting hers.

"Okay, I'll tell ya what," she added while squeezing his fingers. "After Little Joe gets to see everything from the top he can go and guard Excalibur for us, I promise."

"That's fine," he said with a raised brow, "but he rides home in the backseat, and alone."

They rode several more rides throughout the rest of the day, in-between browsing the shops and walking back out on the beach. They got separated once when Sue wanted to checkout a clothing shop, while he headed down the boardwalk to catch a look at a roadster that kept cruising the drag.

When she finally came out onto the walk he wasn't anywhere in sight. She started walking down where she thought he had headed, then paused to wait on a bench. A moment later, an older guy in his late twenties sat next to her.

"Hi," he said, "I'm Andy."

Sue smiled back.

"Hello."

He moved closer and asked, "Would you know a good restaurant here that serves Italian and maybe a little wine for dinner?"

"No I don't, I'm not from around here."

"Oh, then maybe you'd let me show you around and together we might be able to find that dinner spot along the way?"

She became nervous as he kept moving closer to her as he spoke.

"No, I can't," she replied, then went to get up. He reached out and took her hand as he stood up also.

"Hey nothing serious, just for some fun. What do you say?"

"Thank you, but no. I'm waiting for someone."

Steve made his way back up past the shops and games, looking from side to side, but he couldn't spot her. He had passed her in the crowd and didn't realize it.

"Come on doll," Andy said as he squeezed her hand, "my car's right over there. We could cruise down the shoreline, have a couple of drinks, a few laughs…you know?"

"No," she said, "now please let go of me!"

Steve heard her voice as he exited the shop. He ran over and stood up on a bench to look over the crowd.

Andy let her hand go, but then put his arm around her waist as she tried to pull away.

"Hey, calm down," he said, "I'm not a bad guy. I just want to show you a good time since you're visiting here all alone. Come on, it'll be fun."

"Would you stop!" she finally yelled out as she pried at his grip around her. "I'm not alone."

Steve spotted her, jumped down, and ran zigzagged through the crowd to reach her.

Sue struggled as he pinned her tight against him, then finally stopped resisting and just smiled.

"See there," he said in a relaxing tone, "isn't that nicer?"

She looked him in the eyes.

"Much better," she answered softly as she felt him lighten his grip. She then suddenly butted her forehead into his nose, pushed off his chest and stepped back free.

He looked at her stunned, holding his nose.

"When I said no, I meant no! "

Steve finally got within ten feet of them and he saw her snap out a punch, hitting him straight in the chest.

"Now do you get it!" she yelled.

Steve paused, somewhat startled also, as this six foot guy cautiously backed away from her fiery stare.

She turned around as a group of younger teen girls started clapping.

"We don't have to take that stuff!" she told them and they smiled, then she noticed Steve behind them clapping also.

"You tell'um Babe," he said with a grin of wonder and a shake of his head. She looked at him, then began to blush.

"Well I'm sorry, but he just got me mad!" she said as she moved along side him. "Besides, I couldn't let someone like that ruin one of the best days of my life, could I?"

"Absolutely not," he answered still grinning, "and I'm sure there are nine more guys out there who got the message also. You sure Little Joe didn't rub some Irish off on ya?"

She looked up at him, then let out a laugh.

As the sun set they made their way back to the car. The boardwalk lights started coming on like a carnival as they came into the parking lot. They saw several other teens sitting on their cars with all the radios playing the same station as they talked, while others danced. She grabbed his arm and said, "Lets dance," and they joined in.

More teens starting showing up until it became a full party. Cans of sodas and chips started coming out of backseats and trunks for anyone to share. The parking lights came on overhead as the boardwalk lights flashed around them.

The two lost themselves in the lights, the music and in each other's arms as they danced wildly to each new song the radios played out at full volume.

Girls and guys were laughing, kissing, and sharing sips of water and sodas as they danced themselves into a frenzy, then the D.J. called out another song from the radio.

***

"Get ready to move in the groove now with Wilson Pickett's 'In the Midnight hour,' now that's a song I can howl to with all you wild ones out there!"

***

Steve pulled her closer as they danced slower, looking into each other's eyes and singing along. Other voices around them sang with theirs as the sea of lovers swayed beside the ocean's roaring surf.

Sue flung her head back as he held her. She gazed up into a ballroom of swirling stars above, sparkling around the white spotlight of a full moon as it shined down on them.

He kissed her exposed neck and heard her sigh. She closed her eyes as they caressed each other, then again became lost in the music.

"Oh no, look how late it is," said a girl's voice next to them. "I have to get home!"

Steve looked down at his watch.

"It's nearly nine o'clock," he said with a look of fear. "I promised your folks I'd have you home by ten and it'll take two hours!"

Sue smiled saying, "It's all right. I'll just call them and let them know what happened and that we're on our way."

"But your dad!" he replied.

"Shh," she whispered as she touched his lips, "I have a secret weapon."

He looked down at her as she kept dancing in his arms calmly.

"My mom, she trusts us," she said, "she'll understand. Everything will be fine, just trust me."

When the song ended they left the lot and found a phone. She called and, as she thought, her mom said that her dad was working overtime.

"I don't expect him home until midnight," she said, "but you better be here by then."

"We'll be home by elevenish Mom. Sorry, we just lost all track of time."

"Sounds like you had a nice day together."

"Oh Mom," she sighed, "it was the best. It's like a dream that could go on forever. We'll see you shortly, I love you, bye!"

She hung up the phone and turned to him as she heard the end of a song playing in the distance.

"Give me one more dance?" she asked with the midway lights blazing in her eyes. He put his arm around her waist and a hand to her cheek as they leaned their heads against one another singing and dancing in circles as Sergio Mendes sang, 'The Look of Love'.

As the song ended, their lips melted together while their one heart sang on.

Chapter Seven
The Seniors Rule

Music blared out from Excalibur's speakers like a concert, as they turned onto Ken's street and then up his driveway. The garage door flew open and he ducked under it carrying his notebook and a small, brown bag.

His tall, lean build molded perfectly inside his new outfit. He had on dark dress pants, a double knit shirt of black with a gray vertical stripe down the front and polished new feather-weight shoes. With his dark hair hot-combed back, he took his time coming to the car, then slid into the backseat with Joe and Cindy.

"You brought a lunch?" Sue asked looking back at him. "I thought you were always too cool for that?"

"Oh this?" he answered holding up the bag with a grin. "This here is love bait!"

"It's what?" she asked.

"Polish love bait," he repeated. "The contents of this little bag are guaranteed to win over the heart of the hottest cheerleader in our school."

"Pam Wiseman?" Steve asked.

Sue turned and punched his arm.

"I just heard she was," he remarked looking back at her stare.

"But didn't you date her last year?" Joe questioned.

"Yea, but it's not for her," he replied, "it's for her sister Paula."

Sue looked back at him.

"You're going after both of the twins now?" she asked with a dead stare.

"Well, I think it's only fair after the good time Pam and I had, don't ya think?"

Sue sighed.

"Joe, smack him real hard," she said, "and then toss out his little bag of lust into the dust."

"Don't you dare!" he yelled. "This fudge is a secret recipe that's been handed down to each male member of my family as soon as he reached manhood."

"Toss it Joe, " she repeated as she waved back with her hand in the air.

"So how did you get it early?" Steve asked with a laugh.

"Go ahead and make your jokes," he replied holding the bag safe from reach, "but this treat is an irresistible special blend of chocolates, nuts, raisins and fiery passion that goes straight to a woman's greatest weakness."

"And what's that?" Steve asked as he slowed for a stop light.

"Well," he answered, "me!"

"Joe please," Sue called back, "either the bag or him. I don't much care now."

"Could I try one?" Cindy asked.

"Oh no," Ken answered, hanging onto the bag tightly, "it's just too strong of an advantage for you ladies. Even with the guys here, I might not be able to stop you."

"Please Joe! " Sue cried out, then she suddenly turned around and said, "Ski give me that bag, now!"

"Better do it," Steve said, as he watched in the rear view mirror. "Trust me, it's for your own good."

Ken slowly handed her the bag.

"I'll give it to you at lunch, I promise," she told him, "if, you promise not to open it or talk about it until I'm out of sight, deal?"

"Okay deal," he replied. "If you want to try some later together, I'm sure it would be fine."

"Thanks anyway," Steve said, "but I'm getting the feeling that it won't work very well on her."

They turned into the parking lot and drove up to the 'seniors only' spaces. As they got out of the car, Ken spotted some new freshman.

"Hey there, newbies!" he yelled. "How about helping me with these to my homeroom?" then he held out his notebook to one and a pencil to the other. The two freshmen hurried over and he handed them their first hazes.

"Yep," he said to the group, "gonna be a great year."

Sue waited as Steve came around to open her door and help her out, then he helped Cindy out of the back as Joe followed. The two couples slowly walked up to the main entrance, quietly holding hands.

"Ken's right," Steve said, "it is going to be a great last year here."

"Have you two made any plans yet for after graduation?" Joe asked.

"We'll be checking out the colleges," Sue replied. "I'll be starting next fall."

"I guess I should be able to start behind her in the next year, after I can work and save more for it," Steve added.

"You guys want more school?" Cindy questioned.

"I just want to find something I'm good at and stick with it," Joe stated, "then get a home of my own."

Cindy smiled up at him and squeezed his arm.

"I've always planned on college with my parents since I was little," Sue said, "and I'd love to see him go and learn to use the gifts God has given him to their fullest."

"Which ones do you mean?" asked Joe.

"Well for one," she answered, "his leadership qualities. I've seen him use them many times when instructing the fencing classes and on the track field."

She looked up at him adding, "You're patient, compassionate and I think you have a lot to give others."

"So," Steve responded, "you think I would make a good teacher then?"

"I do," she said firmly, "and Lord knows, we could always use a few more who care about teaching then just a paycheck."

The first warning bell rang out and they hurried to make it to their homerooms on time.

The first weeks passed without much incident. Most of the hazings were mild and expected. Steve and Sue also enjoyed having some fun with the newbies they encountered, but always in a playful way, never hurtful.

It was early one morning when they witnessed something neither would soon forget. As they were walking together to their next classes, Sue stopped when she heard sobbing coming from behind a closed door. She opened it and there, crunched down on the floor of the janitor's closet, was a young boy in his underpants only.

She quickly covered her eyes as she called Steve over. He looked inside as the boy turned away.

"Hey man," he asked, "are you all right?"

The boy only waved him to leave.

"You wait here, I'll be right back."

Steve closed the door and told her to stand in front of it until he got back, then he ran towards his locker.

He grabbed a clean pair of long sweat pants, a track T-shirt, socks and his sneakers, then hurried back. Sue stood at the door, holding her books against her chest nervously, until she saw him.

"Stand watch," he told her as he partly opened the door and handed the items to the boy.

"Here, put these on," he whispered, then closed the door. A moment later, the young man emerged wearing the clothes and Sue went over and rolled up the pant legs so he won't be walking on them.

"Sorry about the fit," Steve said, "but I guess they'll do until you can get home later today, don't you think?"

The boy nodded, without looking either of them in the eye.

"Listen," he said, "don't tell anyone about this, please!"

"Not a word," Sue replied, "we promise," as she noticed bruises on his arm and face.

He looked up at Steve and said, "Thanks."

"Your welcome, and listen, if anyone bothers you again, you tell them the Musketeers said to back off or else."

"The Musketeers?"

"You just tell that to any senior and they'll know what that means," Sue answered, "now, get to your next class."

They watched as he hurried down the hall and out of sight. She turned and put her head into his chest.

"Why would anyone do such a thing?"

"It's called bullying," he replied, "I remember it well, but it's not gonna happen this year I promise you."

"Are you lost?" called a voice from behind them. It was a new teacher walking towards them. "May I see your hall passes please?" he asked.

"Sorry, we …," Steve started to answer until Sue interrupted.

"I wasn't feeling well," she said, "so we had to stop to rest a bit, sorry."

"Do you need to see the nurse?" She shook her head.

"No thank you, I'm feeling better now."

He handed them each a slip saying, "Here are two temporary passes, now hurry and get to your classes.

"Thank You," they said and walked down the hallway, picking up the pace as they moved on.

The next day, while waiting with Sue at the car for the others, Steve noticed the same freshman walking towards them.

"Well hi," he said to him, "nice to see you again."

The young dude handed him a paper bag.

"I had them washed," he said as Steve looked inside.

"So you did, thanks."

"No thank you, both of you."

Sue smiled and touched his arm.

"Are you feeling better today?"

"A lot better now that I know some of the Musketeers," he answered smiling back. "You guys sure have a reputation around here."

"So that means no more getting picked on?" she asked.

"No more for sure. In fact, a lot of people want me to introduce you to them."

"Maybe you'd like to introduce them to all of the Musketeers?" and she pointed as Joe, Ken and Cindy walked towards them.

"Wow," the boy said. "Are you really Big Joe Reily?"

"What do you think gave him away," Steve whispered to her.

Joe paused and looked down at the wide eyed face.

"Just Joe," he replied, then noticed the little guy turning pale as some jocks passed by. Joe glanced over as Mike's brother and some other teammates looked their way. The group quickly moved on when they saw Reily staring.

"Footballers," Joe grunted under his breath as he looked back down at the freshman. "They been giving you any trouble?" he asked, then added, "You aren't one are you?"

"Oh no."

"Good. Well then, ever give any thought to learning to fence? We could use some new Musketeers to take over when we graduate."

"I don't know if I'd be any good at it."

"Never know till you try. The club meets every Tuesday after school, so think about it."

"I will, thanks."

"Listen to me," Joe said as he leaned down. "The best way to get over being afraid is to stand up for yourself no matter what. You may take a pounding, like Sweety there did, but it's the only way you can live with yourself, understand?"

"I think so," he answered, then turned to Steve and asked, "Sweety?"

"That's my nickname for him," Sue said taking Steve's hand.

"Oh…yea," he replied as he walked off with a wave.

"And it's a great way to get girls!" Ken added with a yell. "They'll love ya for it!"

"Ken! Don't tell him that!" Sue yelled as she smacked his arm.

"It did with you," he snickered back.

"Come on," Cindy said, "who's for a coke at the Spa?" as she climbed into the backseat with the guys following.

"Sounds good," Steve said back, "then we're gonna head out to the Island for awhile."

"Hey Ken," Joe asked, "how did go with Paula?"

"Not so good. It seems she's allergic to nuts and has to avoid them at all costs."

Steve leaned over to Sue as he started the engine. "Don't you have gym with Paula before lunch?" he asked with a grin. She just smiled.

Later on the island, as they stood on the wooden bridge, she noticed that he was being usually quiet.

"What are you thinking about?"

He stared down into the dark swirling ripples of the river and said, "Being afraid to walk the halls."

She turned to him. "What do you mean afraid? You aren't afraid of anything I know of."

He lowered his head and sighed.

"I was once, for nearly a year back in eighth grade. I use to wait until the last possible moment, then run like a deer to my next class so I wouldn't be late."

"Why?"

"Because I didn't wanna to run into three guys who enjoyed pounding the hell out of me on sight."

He turned to her adding, "I'd walk home, instead of taking the bus, to avoid getting hit during the ride and beat up again when I got off at my stop."

"I'm so sorry, I didn't know," she said softly as she held his arm.

"How could you? You didn't go to Central Junior High."

She thought a second, then asked, "Didn't they come here to Parsippany High with you?"

"Oh yea, they did."

"Who are they?"

"One moved away at the beginning of freshman year. The other was Mike."

Sue closed her eyes. "You must have hated me for dating him."

He put his arm around her. "I never hated you, don't even think that."

Her eyes teared a bit as she asked, "and the third guy?"

"It was Joe."

She jerked her head up in disbelief. "Reily?"

"Yea, Big Joe," he murmured.

"So what happened?"

"I liked to go bowling back then, but only went after school when I knew none of them would be there. There was a girl I liked then and she came to ask me if I'd bowl with her that Friday night. I was thrilled, until I found myself outside the alley with Joe and Johnny Millane waiting for me."

She slowly moved her hand onto his back, gently rubbing it.

"Yea, and?"

"Well Johnny didn't hesitate at all. He walked right up and pushed me back flat onto my backside asking, 'Did I say you could hang around here?'. I noticed the girl from my class standing in the doorway watching and I knew I had been set up."

Sue turned sideways to look into his face. "What did you do?"

"I got mad as hell as they laughed, but when I saw her laughing too something snapped. I got up and said, 'If I ever want your permission to do something, I'll write it on toilet paper and send it down to ya.'. "

"Oh Steve, you didn't?"

He smiled. "I guess Johnny couldn't believe I'd said it either, because he paused a second too long and I kicked him square in the…"

Sue put her hand to her mouth. "Oh you didn't!" she said with a covered laugh.

"Just as hard as I could."

"What did he do?"

"Not too much as I recall, but it was the first time I ever saw him cry and without making a sound."

Sue turned away, choking on another laugh she was trying so hard to hold in. Finally, as she wiped back a mixed emotion of tears, she asked, "What was Joe doing all this time?"

"He just stood there watching, he never made a move. Even when Johnny finally got to his feet and took a swing at me. He missed, due to blurry vision I guess, and he fell to the ground. I lost my balance ducking and ended up sitting on him."

She turned away again, hiding her face.

"Look," he said to her, "things happened pretty fast."

"But you still found time to rest," she said not turning around.

"Anyway," he continued, "Johnny got up and hit me in the ear. I grabbed his tie, then started pulling his face into my fist, over and over…"

Sue spun around and started laughing so hard, she had to hold her stomach."Sue!"

"I'm sorry," she cried out still trying to compose herself.

"You have to understand," he said as he walked to the middle of the bridge, "I was only trying to stay alive. I didn't have a clue how to fight!"

"Okay," she said catching her breath, "then what?"

"Well, I finally let him go when I got tired and saw Joe walking towards me."

"Did he hit you?"

"Not right away. I let out a screaming yelp and he stopped. Then I reached out and grabbed his tie and pulled."

"What did he do when you started hitting him?"

"Well I never did hit him. He was wearing a clip-on and it just came off in my hand."

Sue leaned over the railing.

"Oh Steve!" she laughed out hard, "Stop please!"

"Sue! It wasn't funny, he whipped the hell out of me!"

"With his own tie?" she asked bent over again holding her side.

He stopped talking and looked upwards in silence.

Finally she was able to compose herself enough to walk over and wrap her arms about him.

"Oh Babe, I'm sooo sorrrry," she said softly, then laughed again into his chest. He paused listening to her, then started laughing himself.

"I guess it was pretty funny, but you could give me a little break here."

"You're right, I'm sorry," she said still grinning. "Here, let me lie down so you can sit on me and take one."

"That's it!" and he started chasing her down onto the dirt path and up into the grassy beach of the island. As he caught up with her he pulled her down onto the bed of flowers.

She was panting, trying to catch her breath, as he looked over at her.

"If you weren't so darn cute, you'd get yours." he said.

"You mean you'd clip me?"

"That's it!" and he started tickling her until she begged for mercy. She took in one last deep breath as he leaned in for a kiss.

"Wait a minute," she suddenly said staring. "If he just hit you some more, that doesn't explain how you became friends. What happened?"

"Well I only remember throwing my arms and fists at him like some windmill. I think I hit him a couple of times, but I sure remember each time he hit me."

"Yea, and …?"

"Well what it came down to was the fact that, no matter how many times he knocked me down, I kept getting back up. Finally, he grabbed my fist in mid-air and said, ' Enough all ready! You made your point, you win.' I told him in a half daze that I'd stop when they stopped.

'You can't beat a man who won't quit. You're all right Clayton. I'd rather have you with me, than trying to sit on me. Come on, lets go to the diner and have some coffee and a buttered hard roll.' and he brushed me off."

"Aw that's Joe all right," she said, "and did he buy?"

"He had to because I'd lost my wallet fighting. I didn't know it until we had finished eating and well I guess, sealing a friendship. He hardly ever said but a few words to the other two after that."

He turned and looked into her eyes.

"I guess my point is that when I saw that guy in the closet, I knew what he was feeling and I hated it."

"I've seen girls do things to others also and it seems to be getting worst each year. What can we do to stop it?"

"Maybe nothing will change in the long run," he sighed out, "but if we can help just a few to be safe, it'll be worth it."

She leaned up and kissed him gently.

100

"I love you honey and I know together we'll make a difference just for the trying."

"Together, together …," he kept repeating. "Yea, not one doing the fighting but side by side! That's how we'll do it Babe!"

His face lit up as he turned to her.

"Remember what you told me? To stand and fight with you, not for you. That's how it'll work. Come on," he said helping her up, "we got lots to do."

The next day all four Musketeers went to see Mr. Biel and discussed their ideas with him.

"I take it you're all committed to this project?" he asked.

"Yes we are."

"All right. I'll have to run it by the principal, but I think he'll see the light of it like I do."

At the next Tuesday club meeting there were some twenty-six freshman who showed up. Young Adam Goldberg, whom they had befriended, had brought most of them to meet with the Musketeers.

As they waited in the gym they watched the present club members practicing their warm-ups. They noticed two girl duelists working out by themselves in a far corner and seemed impressed.

"See how neat it is," Adam told the others, "and we can learn from the best if we join."

Steve came in and waved. Most of the group waved back as he rolled out a large blackboard with him. Within minutes, Joe, Ken and Mr. Biel entered and the session started.

"I want to thank all of you for coming, "the instructor said to them. "This meeting is really two-fold. First it is for anyone who wishes to register for the club. Second, we're going to discuss the subject of bullying and how to help end it in this school."

Steve noticed Adam slump down a bit so he stepped forward.

"I also want you to know that we are not here to embarrass anyone. No names or incidents will be ever be talked about here. All we want to show you is how you can feel safe during this year."

"These are my three Musketeers," Mr. Biel said pointing. "This is Steve Clayton, Joe Riely and Ken Tomineski. They are three of the senior instructors here."

Joe stepped forward.

"For those of you who haven't read 'The Three Musketeers' as I have, you might be surprised that there were actually four of them."

He turned and pointed saying, "And here is ours, Miss Susan LaRosa."

All turned their heads to the far corner as Sue removed her mask and stepped forward with her freshman sparring partner.

"There are 56 ribbons, trophies and award plaques won by this club sitting in our trophy case since it was founded. Eleven of those were won by Susan, including 'First Champion' Tournament winner'. She's earned the respect of this club's members forever."

"Thank you Joe," she said, "and this is Lori Manning. Lori has just earned her first stripe for the basics in fencing and did it in less than three weeks!" Sue led the applause in her honor.

"We pride ourselves in giving recognition when it is earned, " she continued. "Here you excel both as a team player and as an individual. I look forward to working with all of you."

"Pride, Honor and Respect are the foundation for this club," Mr. biel stated. "No member is more important than another and we all help each other to excel."

He pointed to Steve and the words on the blackboard.

"Pride, Honor and Respect," Steve repeated. Believe me when I tell you, everyone in front of you today has learned what those words mean.

Everyone you meet…Your teachers, friends, classmates and yes, even your opponents. Whether they are those here on the mat, on the bus, in the halls or the street. No one is without worth and everyone deserves to receive these three things from you. You will always get them from us and now, from many of the other seniors in this school."

The main gym doors opened and a procession of students entered.

"In this school, there are one hundred and thirteen seniors and these are seventy four of them. They've all signed a pledge today to instill pride, honor and respect in all of the underclassmen of this school.

Look hard at their faces and remember the pins that they're wearing. It has two foils crossed with this club's motto, 'One for all, and All for one'. Any senior wearing this pin will treat you with the respect you deserve."

"In this club everybody works in pairs," Ken added. "They spar together, practice together and support one another as a team. If you join this club you'll wear one of these pins, but that means you'll be expected to help anyone who needs it. You will stand side by side with them to defend what is right, what is good and what is true. You do this and you will never be alone. You do this, and you will be on your way to becoming true Musketeers for the rest of your lives."

"Okay so," asked Mr. Biel, "who'd like to join today?"

Every freshman leaped up and ran to the registration table where Sue was standing with Lori.

"Just fill out this form with your parents then drop it off here tomorrow," they told each. "Your pins will be waiting."

Steve winked over at Sue and she smiled back, while Joe, Ken and Mr. Biel shook the hands of each senior who came to support the project.

In the weeks that followed, more seniors and underclass men and women signed up for the pins and many for club membership.

Any time a student was feeling threatened all they had to do was call out 'One for all and All for one' and they'd find other students standing next to them for support.

Within two months, there were no more reports of bullying and the school's morale was soon considered the highest in the county.

It was in December, as they were preparing for the Christmas season, that the call came to the house. Mrs. LaRosa answered it as the family sat on the floor untangling the lights for the tree.

Sue opened up another box of ornaments as she overheard her mom on the phone.

"Merry Christmas Martha, how are you?...What?...Oh God, I'm so sorry. How is George taking it?"

She stopped unpacking as she watched and listened to her mom.

"Maybe they just made a mistake and the letter was for someone else...Oh I see, you checked all ready. "

Suddenly the whole family sat quietly listening as she continued.

"Listen, I'll talk with Frank and call you back...Yes of course we will and please go see Father Paul together, I know it will help...Okay Martha, you both will be in our prayers...Yes, goodbye."

Mr. LaRosa got up and went over to her.

"What's happened?"

She started crying and he held her.

"It was my sister. They just got a letter from the war department." He held her tighter and patted her shoulder.

"It was about Billy. Oh Frank, their son is dead and they don't even have his body to send home for them."

"Cousin Billy's dead?" cried Sarah and Sue put her arms around her little sister. "It'll be okay," she whispered, "come here," and together they cried in each other's arms on the floor.

"They're all alone now Frank," she said, "they can't spend Christmas in that house without family."

"We'll get mom and drive out there on Wednesday," he said. "The kids will be out of school on vacation. It'll be fine."

Sue looked up at them and saw a tear roll down her dad's cheek. She had only seen him cry once before when his brother died. She knew how much he loved Billy. She remembered how he would take him downstairs into his workshop to teach him woodworking. When he got older, Billy had made him a wooden-model plane as a birthday gift. Her dad always kept it on his dresser.

"You go get ready for bed," she told her sister, "and I'll be up to read to you." Sarah slowly made her way up the stairs and Sue went over to her parents and hugged them.

"I'm so sorry," she said. "I'll miss him badly."

"We all will Angel," her dad whispered.

She started crying, then asked, "Why Daddy?"

"He was called to do his duty and he answered it like a man. We can be proud of him and thankful for such men. Everything is in God's hands and whatever happens is, in the end, to fulfill His purpose."

"I'll make us some coffee while you two finish up in the living room for the night," her mom said walking slowly into the kitchen.

Later, she called Steve from her room and he tried to comfort her as she cried on the phone.

"It's hard enough to realize that he's gone," she said, "but not even to be able to have him home to bury, that hurts forever."

" I know it does," he replied softly, "but know in your heart that he's here in God's earth. Whenever you touch the soil anywhere, you'll feel him resting in it and sense his love for you."

She stopped and thought about that.

"Oh Steve you're right. He doesn't need to be under that headstone for us to feel or talk with him. He's in the very earth itself."

She suddenly felt a feeling of relief, as if an added burden had been lifted from her heart and replaced with one of peace.

"Thanks, that helps to make it easier. I'll try and share that with the rest of the family."

"I love you Babe," he whispered. "Now, why don't you get some sleep and I'll pick you up early so we can stop for breakfast before heading off for school. Deal?"

She wiped her eyes with a tissue and said, "I love you so much."

"And I love you. Please sleep well and have a good night Babe."

She sensed him waiting quietly for her to hang up first. She kissed the phone, then gently put it down.

"It's always good because of you," she thought.

She reached for his picture on her nightstand, kissed it and then fell asleep with it in her arms.

***

INTERLUDE:

Introduction of
1969

Major News Event:

*500,000 march on Washington, D.C., for peace.
*Woodstock festival. 500,000 people gathered for 3 days of music and peace to change the world.
*Death and injury toll of U.S. Troops in Vietnam reaches over 100,000.

Top songs of 1969:

*Bad moon rising.
*This girl's in love with you.
*This Magic Moment.
* Love theme from Romeo and Juliet
*This girl is a woman now
* Suspicious Minds

Top Movies:

*True Grit
*Easy Rider
*Alice's Restaurant

***

It was a new year when Sue and her family returned after spending Christmas vacation with her aunt and uncle. She was glad they had gone, knowing how much it helped the family and preserve a sense of joy in the season for all.

Still, she had missed him so much during these weeks and couldn't wait to see him again. She had gotten a call from him on Christmas morning and the sound of his voice was the only gift she had wanted.

When she had tried to call him on New Year's Eve his brother told her that he had gone to help their dad. He had some car trouble and needed him.

When she finally got home, she flew upstairs to call him.

"Hello?" answered a little girl's voice.

"Hi Anna this is Sue, is Steve there?"

"No. He went roller skating, I think."

"Oh, well could you tell him to call me when he gets home?"

"Okay."

"Thank you and Happy New Year."

She hung up and went downstairs to help bring in the last of the luggage from the car.

"Did you talk to Steve?" asked her mom.

"No, he's out skating at the Denville Rink."

"Well we're done, so you can take the car and go there if you'd like to skate with him."

"Oh thanks mom," she said with excitement, "I'd love to surprise him like that!"

She helped with the last suitcase and then headed to the rink.

As she pulled into the parking lot she spotted Excalibur and parked. She walked up to car and stroked its highly polished trunk lid.

"Hello Baby, did you miss me?" she said softly, then suddenly she heard a noise inside. A girl's blond head was against the rear side window and she slowly walked over to look in.

The windows were fogged up, but she could see the girl's face looking her way. The boy's jacket read 'Parsippany Track Team' across its back.

She covered her mouth to hold back a scream as the girl sighed out, "Oh Steve." Seconds later with tears, she threw her hands onto the window and let it out.

"You lousy, cheating, no good!——How could you!" she cried out. She turned yelling, "Happy New Year to you too!" as she ran towards her car.

"Sue?" came a voice from inside, but she continued to run off. "No, wait!" she could hear from its backseat.

She started the car, then screeched the tires out into the street and up to Route 46. She finally slowed down a bit to reach into the glove box for some tissues so she could see past the tears.

"Oh God!" she cried out again and again. "Why?——You said you loved me, so why!—- How could you! "

The tears just kept coming so she pulled over to the shoulder and stopped. She held her face in her hands and felt like she was going to be sick. She rolled down the window and took several deep breaths until she was calmer.

"How could you do this?" she muttered in disbelief. "You promised to love and cherish——You promised me forever!"

She cried harder, almost choking on the tears. She took another tissue and a deep breath, then pulled back out onto the highway and headed for home.

Snow flakes began to fall like dancing stars from above onto the dirty black road ahead of her. She felt them under her tires as they slipped and skidded away from what was behind her. Her heart ached in her chest, as if it had been cut open and all the good ripped out. She felt empty, used and cheap inside.

As she neared home she realized she needed gas, so she pulled into the Sunoco to fill it. Uncle Chuck came out and waved.

"Hey Sue, Happy New Year! Glad to see you're home."

She just smiled as she sat behind the wheel.

"How much you want?" he asked as he unscrewed the gas cap.

"Fill it please," she said back to him.

When he was finished he came up to her window. He noticed several tissues on the seat and in her lap as she fumbled through her purse for her wallet.

"Steve know you're back yet?" he asked as he watched her reaction.

"Yea, kind of," she answered as she kept digging in her purse.

"How's about coming inside for some coffee?"

"No, I need to get home, maybe another time."

"Oh, just for a couple of minutes to keep an old man company. It's been pretty slow here tonight and it would sure help, please?"

"Well okay," she replied, "but just for a few minutes."

She pulled the car away from the pumps and parked it out in front of the bay door.

Once inside out of the cold, he poured two cups and handed her one. "Thanks," she said, "it's getting so cold out tonight."

"Been out anywhere special in this weather?"

"Not really, just out and about, you know?"

Chuck nodded, looking at her in the light and could now see how red her eyes were.

"Been walking out in this cold I guess," he said with a feel of prying in his words.

"No, why do you ask?"

"Your eyes, they're all red from the wind?"

She looked over at him and couldn't hold back the tears.

"Oh Chuck," she sobbed out, "he's with someone else."

"What? No, that can't be."

"It's true!" she said louder. "I saw them tonight at the skating rink in the backseat of Excalibur. They were …," then she cried.

He leaned over to her and said, "Honey that can't be, you have to be mistaken."

"I saw them together, on top of her as I stood looking in! They were kissing and, and …" She stopped as she choked up again.

"Susie, listen to me. He loves you more than any person could ever love somebody. Why all he's done is mope around here for weeks while you were gone. Ken and Joe had to come several times to get him to go out anywhere. He would never do that to you."

"I know what I saw!"

Chuck sat quietly for a moment, then said, "Oh, I'd better ring up your gas before I forget."

She searched her purse for her wallet, took out a ten and handed it to him. He rang it up and counted back her change, then went over to his desk. He picked up an old bolt and removed the washer from it then sat back down.

"Let me show you something," he said as he held up the washer in his right hand.

Sue watched as he took it with his left hand and then put it into her palm and closed her fingers over it. He waved his hand over hers and said, "Take a look." She opened her hand and in it was a shiny quarter.

She looked up and smiled.

"How'd you do that?" she asked.

"Do what?"

"Change that old washer into this quarter?"

"Did I?" he asked.

She smiled as she held up the coin and shook it at him.

"Oh you had that all the time," he said and immediately reached up behind her ear with his right hand and pulled out the washer.

"Did you really think a steel washer could change into a silver quarter?"

"No," she laughed, "but it sure looked that way."

"Listen Susie, there never was a old washer in your hand. You had the quarter all the time, no matter what you thought you saw. It didn't change and neither did he. Whatever you think you saw, we both know, was not what happened. Then he took her hand and closed it back over the quarter. "You hang onto what is real."

She stared at her hand and squeezed the coin. "Thanks Uncle Chuck," she said giving him a kiss on the cheek.

"Oh my, that's got more kick than the coffee."

She smiled then a car pulled in. It was Excalibur. She got up and moved from the window. " I don't want to see him! Please, tell him to go away. The magic's a lie."

"Susie, real magic is in your heart. If you want it then you've got to believe it."

She stared at the door, then went to slowly open it. Steve came out of the car and ran to her. "Sue please, I can explain!" he said with pain in his voice.

She touched her fingers to his lips. "I believe you," she whispered then smiled into his eyes and kissed him.

"Oh God," he whispered back in her ear as he held her tight, "I thought I'd lost you when Ken said you ran off crying."

She looked up at him. "Ken said?"

A hand came out of the rear of the Le Mans and waved. "Hey Sue," followed a voice, "Happy New Year to you too!"

She walked over and peered in. There was Ken sitting with the blond under his arm.

"Ken, why do you have Steve's jacket on?"

"Ken? What does she mean, KEN! This isn't your Varsity Letter?" questioned the blond now staring at the name on the coat.

Ken smiled uneasily.

"Uh …no, but did I mention that I'm on the fencing team and one of the Musketeers?"

"Why you sneaky! - - - Lying! - - - Good for nothing!"

Sue turned back to Steve. "I love you and I'm so sorry."

"I love you too and I'm sorry I let you get hurt. I should have known better than to give him the keys, after all, he's Ken."

"Yes," she laughed, "yes he is."

Steve reached out to her and she threw her arms around him again.

"Oh Sweety, I'm the one who should have known better," she said softly. "So Happy New Year My Love."

"It is now Angel," he whispered back with a smile.

They slowly touched lips and savored a long, loving kiss, then, "Wait a minute," she said suddenly and turned towards the car.

"You thought that you were going to do what? - - -And in THIS CAR!"

Ken started rolling up the windows as he heard her. "But we didn't really do anything, did we, a,a,a …?"

"Brenda," the blond stated with a stare towards him.

"Right," Ken said as he reached to lock the doors.

Sue grabbed at the door handle just as he hit the lock button. "Open up Ski!" she yelled.

Ken looked to Steve who just waved his hands saying, "No way man, you should have known better."

"Ski! Open this door now or so help me!" She turned to Steve and said, "Give me the keys!"

"No!" Ken yelled, "Call Reily! He's the only one who can handle her when she gets this way! Tell him it's a CODE RED!"

"I left the keys in the ignition," Steve said and she turned back to the door.

"Tomineski, I'm warning you!"

Ken slouched down next to Brenda.

"It'll be all right," he told her, "she'll calm down. We just have to wait her out is all."

"I swear, if you make me hurt this car trying to get it open, you'll wish you were born a monk!"

"See," Ken whispered, "she's starting to talk religious, it won't be much longer."

"I better call and try to find Joe," Chuck said as he quickly went inside.

"SKI!!!"

Chapter Eight
"New Decisions for a Clear Dream."

Winters pass quickly when summer lives in your heart and excitement filled the afternoon spring air as they drove onto the island.

It was always thrilling to drive over the old iron bridge from the back of River Road. Many locals seldom chanced it, believing it was not safe, but Steve knew it was as strong as when it was built.

Excalibur glided effortlessly across its wooden planks as they creaked, but held firmly as he knew they would. He had watched county work trucks cross it many times as they came to do work on the ball field.

With the top down they felt invigorated by the crisp air. They drove up the dirt road, under overhanging branches of oak and maples beginning to bud, until they reached the ball field. He pulled close to home plate where the sun was shining warmest and parked.

Sue reached to the backseat and brought out packages of college catalogs for them to explore. It was fun showing each other the different courses available and looking at the pictures of the campuses. Of course, tuition costs were discussed as well.

"Oh, look at the art studio they have!" she said with wide eyes to him as she pointed at the photo. He looked over smiling.

"Very nice, I think you should take some art classes, you draw really well and enjoy it so much."

"I've thought about that too," she replied with her head down turning the catalog pages.

"You know," she added, "I think going first for the two years at Morris County College, and then entering with a AA or an AS into a four year college is the best way for us to save money on all of these costs."

"That's for sure," he said shaking his head as he read some of the fees.

"Maybe we could finish our last two years at this new college they're building up in Mahwah?" she said. "It's called Ramapo and says it will be ready to take in students in two years."

She showed him the write up and the pictures of the grounds where it was to be.

"They say here that it has plans for dorms in 1971, set back near this wooded area. Yea, it looks nice," he replied with a nod.

"I was thinking," she said feeling him out. "I thought maybe I'd take some art classes and some business courses, then do a concentration in advertising to combine the two. What do you think?"

"Sounds like something you could really make use of when you get out, besides, you do have great taste and creativity."

She smiled at him.

"Well thank you, and what courses interest you?"

He turned back to some pages he had dog-eared.

"Oh lets see. Sociology, Creative Writing and Philosophy seem interesting, but I've often thought I might like some business courses also.

I like the independence and the idea of one day owning my own company. The challenges of building it up and creating jobs for people with good incomes. Knowing that I helped make their lives a little better."

"You're something, you know that?" she said as she put her chin on his shoulder and glanced into his face. "You just keep on giving me more reasons to love you."

He kissed her on the forehead.

"That's because it's you who brings out the best in me and I love you for doing that."

She nuzzled into his neck and kissed it gently, then again, and again. His eyes closed as he brought his hand up to caress her cheek, then ran it up into her hair as he gently cradled her head. Passion grew inside him steadily as her hot lips touched his neck, throat and then onto his chest.

"I love you so much," he heard her say between kisses.

"Oh Sue," he moaned, as he felt a volcano beginning to erupt within him.

The warmth of her mouth, the touch of her fingertips as they ran over his burning skin was more than he could contain as he sighed and moaned over and over.

Sue had lost herself in wanting him so badly.

"Four more years, more years ..." The thought kept running through her mind and her gentle touching soon became one of beckoning, of coaxing him to taste more of her also.

"Oh yes," she sighed softly as she felt his hand finally move onto her waist, then under her shirt to her bare stomach and stroked it. She lay back against the door and pulled him to her.

He watched her chest rising and falling. He stared at the 'V' of her neckline and dove down to kiss it.

"Oh Steve," she cried softly, "I love you ... Yes Babe, I need you," as she struggled to pull off his shirt. He looked into her wanting eyes and he knew.

He reached and opened the door, climbed out and lifted her into his arms. She said nothing, but tightly wrapped her arms around his neck. She continued pouring hot kisses onto his chest, as he carried her up to the grassy knoll, above the bed of blooming red, white and blue flowers.

"You are so beautiful," he whispered as she looked up to him with those melting, chocolate-brown eyes and those perfect lips now quivering. Her breasts heaved as they strained against the small buttons of her shirt.

"Tell me to stop," he pleaded to her softly.

He searched for some sign of resistance; but she only whimpered. "Shh, please Babe, just love me," she said with a beckoning surrender in her voice. She pressed tighter against him, her eyes drawing him into the world wind of her love.

"Please Sue, I need you to say it."

"I can't," she moaned out. "I can't think it anymore. I love you, but four more years …I'm just not that strong anymore."

He watched a tear form in her eye, then the other. He burned for the want of her as he knelt to gently lay her down in the perfumed bed. He pulled her hands from about his neck and kissed them, they were now cool and trembling. His dream laid before him and he ached for her sweetness.

She gripped his waist and pulled him down to her. He lowered himself above her and took her honey-drenched lips to his starving mouth as heated breath poured from each.

"You are my love and my life," he heard her sigh. "I need all of your love."

Her arms swung again about his neck as his left still held her around the back while his other hand slipped under her thighs.

"Forgive me," he whispered and he rose up, carrying her slowly towards the lake.

"Oh God!" she cried out as she felt the icy cold water begin to cover her as he wadded in. She kissed him hard and passionately as he held her waist deep and shivering.

"All my love is here, in these arms," he cried to her with a tear.

She couldn't answer, only continue to kiss him, but now softer and with open teared eyes as she put her hand onto his face.

"You're my world Angel," he said softly, "and I live in the palm of your hand."

She smiled remembering a shiny quarter.

"Our love is real and true and forever," she said softly to herself.

He turned his head and looked at her hand.

"The day you give yourself to me, you will have a gold ring on that finger, I promise."

"You just keep giving me more reasons," she said crying. "Don't ever stop."

"We're meant to have forever together, not just a few moments," he cried softly into her ear with a kiss, "that's what you deserve."

He carried her back to the car and got a blanket from the trunk to put around her.

"We better go get changed," he said as he put up the top and turned on the heater.

"My heart was just too full," she said, then laughed. "I guess you have that effect on me."

"We all have our weaknesses," he told her with a glow of love in his eyes, "and you will always be mine, and my strength."

She sat up on the console and put in a tape of Jay and the Americans into the eight-track. It started playing 'This Magic Moment.'

He put his arm around her as she whispered, "The magic really is forever."

"Angel, Romeo and Juliet got nothing on us."

For the following Saturday, they had decided to ride up to Denville for the carnival which had been going on all week.

Sue had taken Excalibur in the morning after dropping Steve off at Joe's so he could help him work on his Chevelle. She planned to do some shopping at the Willowbrook Mall. She picked up Cindy so they could make a girl's day of it while the guys hung out together.

"I can't believe Steve lets you drive his car," Cindy said.

"It's because we have an understanding."

"What is it? I'd like to have the same one with Joe."

"Oh," Sue said stroking the dash, "I don't have one with Steve about the car, I have one with Excalibur about Steve."

"Huh?"

"I agreed to share Steve's love with Baby here, in exchange for an equal amount of driving time. It's worked out quite well, Steve has so much to share."

Cindy shook her head.

"You two, eh three, sure have a strange relationship that's for dang sure."

Sue just smiled as they turned off Route 46 and into the huge mall lot. She parked some distance from the entrance.

"Why are you parking so far away, there are some spots closer over there?" Cindy asked questioningly.

"I don't want to take a chance that someone would slam their door into this beauty. Besides, Excalibur enjoys the sun," she answered, trying to have some fun with her.

Back at Joe's, the guys had the Chevy jacked up with stands and Steve was underneath trying to get the old mufflers off.

"Is it coming loose?" Joe asked from above.

"Yea, slow but sure. Hand me the five pounder from the box."

Joe went and got the hammer and handed it under to him. He listened as Steve gave the muffler a few good whacks. Seconds later he heard 'Clang!' and it dropped to the ground.

"Got it!" he heard as Steve slid out the side holding it up to him."Man, you sure got you money's worth from that one."

Joe looked at the rusted out holes and shook his head.

"Yea, I sure did, but now it's time for this babe to have a new voice." He reached back and opened the box.

"A pair of Cherry Bombs?" Steve questioned as he noticed the picture on the side. "Man, that'll sure make the duals of this 327 sing, but are you sure Cindy won't mind the louder tone?"

"Naw," he replied, "we have an understanding."

"Oh yea, what kind?" Steve asked as he slipped the first custom muffler onto the pipe.

"Well," Joe answered with an air of 'as-a-matter-of-factness', "she knows that this car's my domain. My personal chariot pulled by a lot of horse power and she is the princess I get to carry off in it. How it runs is up to me; after all, what does she understand about cars? That's a guy-thing."

Steve stopped working and looked out from underneath.

"That's the understanding you both share?"

"Okay," he replied, "maybe we don't share it, but we have it."

Joe paused, and then asked, "All right. I watched Sue just take off with your car and I didn't hear you say she could, so what kind of an understanding do you two have there SWEETY, hum-mm?"

"Sue and I don't have one about the car," he answered as he tightened up the exhaust clamps with the ratchet.

"I didn't think so," Joe said with a smirk.

"She just has one with Excalibur," he added as he pointed for Joe to hand him the next muffler.

Joe paused again. "She has one with the car?"

"Yea, it's a kind of love triangle but she'd have to explain it to ya," he answered. He tapped the second cherry bomb lightly to be sure it was seated into the pipe.

"A love triangle? I wouldn't have even thought you could do something like that in a car, let alone with one," Joe said in a pondering tone.

"Yea," he heard him add from below, "it's a very complex and personal relationship, but it works for us."

"Dang," Joe mumbled to himself. "Are you sure this is allowed if you're Catholic?"

Steve stopped working and said, "Hey, this is Sue we're talking about, would she do anything against the church?"

"No," he answered, "no she wouldn't."

"Well," Steve said from under the car with a grin, "there you are."

"Yea," he remarked, "there I am."

He thought a moment then asked, "Where am I?"

Steve slid out from under and said, "You're about to road test this baby."

"All right!"

The girls arrived back shortly after they had taken the Big Red, as Steve quietly referred to it because of its color, for a nice long test drive. They had driven along River Road, up into town and back down to Joe's driveway.

"Aw man," Joe said with a thrill in his tone, "she's awesome! Just listen to the power screaming out of those pipes! I can feel the added horse now that there's less restriction. Thanks man."

"My pleasure, glad you like it."

"It sounds different," Cindy commented as she stood back a bit, "and so much louder!"

"It's the cherry bombs," Joe replied, "like um?"

"Cherry Bombs? Well good, they'll match the rest of the car, wherever they are," she said as she looked the Chevy over.

"Come on, hop in," Joe said to her, "I'll take you for a spin."

She walked over to the driver's door, opened it and asked, "Could I take it around?"

Joe turned off the engine.

"You mean, drive it?"

"Yea."

"But you don't even know how to drive a stick shift," he stated in shock.

"Well, I thought we could go out on the island and you could teach me."

She was quiet as she smiled up at him. He stared over at Steve and frowned as she finally added, "I just thought it would be nice if I could understand the car better and share your love for it together."

Joe looked back at her with his head tilted slightly.

"Kind of a triangle sharing thing, huh?"

"Exactly, we could share the driving equally and you could enjoy relaxing as a passenger too. What do you think?"

Joe turned to look at Steve smiling.

"I think …" he muttered under his breath, "I think I'm gonna have a long talk with my brother when he gets home about the church's definition of triangles."

"Good," Cindy replied. "Now, which one is the clutch?"

"Hey guys," Steve said waving, "we'll meet you later up at the carny," and he slipped into the passenger bucket seat as Sue started to pull out. Cindy waved as Joe just pointed his finger at them.

It was a little after one O'clock when he had taken a shower and got changed into some nicer clothes. Sue waited, talking with his mom and three of his five sisters around the table over some coffee. She showed them some of the things she had bought at the mall.

"Oh," his third youngest sister Anna said, "This scarf is beautiful!" as she saw her open it up fully. "Can I touch it?" she asked cautiously.

"Of course," Sue smiled, "I got one for you and your sisters."

She turned to his mom and whispered, "They were on sale and I couldn't resist. It's all right I hope."

"Yes of course, and thank you for thinking of them."

Steve came out of his bedroom combing his hair.

"Hey," he said, "it's still a bit early, wanna go up to the Spa and have some lunch?"

"Sure, she answered and handed him the keys.

"Bye mom," they said as they headed out the door. Anna ran over to Sue and hugged her arm.

"Thank you for present," she said smiling as she petted it.

Sue stooped down.

"I'm so glad you like it, and you know something. Now that I look closer, it matches your eyes."

Anna gave her a kiss.

"Well thank you, now you go make sure all your sisters pick one to match their eyes too."

"Okay."

Sue waved as she closed the door and ran to the car.

As they backed out of the driveway, she looked at the small bungalow house. It was only a one bedroom, but his father had converted the front porch into two tiny bedrooms. Each side had a set of bunk beds and a divider wall between the two. Steve shared one side with his younger brother James, while the two older sisters shared the other.

There were two more little ones that shared a corner in the living room with partitions and the baby girl was in a crib in his parent's room.

She was amazed how so many people could live in such a small place, and yet get along so well. She had never been to his bedroom, nor had he ever seen hers, but she could size up the space he shared from the outside.

She knew she never could have reason to complain about the room she had to share with her little sister. Both were houses of love and that was what was most important.

As they walked into the Village Spa luncheonette, they found it nearly empty.

"Hi Mrs. G.," they said when they saw her looking out from the kitchen.

"Oh hello," she waved smiling, "if it isn't one of my favorite couples. Want the usual cherry cokes?"

"No, we thought that we might have hot chocolates today," Steve replied, "it's a little cool out there today."

"Not cold enough for the carnival," she said. "Business hasn't been too good lately, everybody's gone to it all week."

Sue noticed she seemed a bit down.

"I'm sorry to hear that."

"Yea," Steve said, "we were thinking of …" He stopped talking as Sue squeezed his arm.

"Yea," she finished for him, "we were thinking that too when we pulled up."

"It will be hard," Mrs. G. continued, "we were hoping for a good week so papa could go get checked by that specialist for his back. He's been getting worst and I worry about him."

"I'm sorry," Steve said, "but maybe things will pick up tonight."

"I don't think so," she replied. "The carnival is supposed to stay on for several more days and with what we've taken in, we will be hard pressed to just make expenses. Oh well, nothing to do but pray. I will get your drinks lovies."

"I wish we could help," Sue sighed as she noticed him staring off into space.

"Babe, what is it?"

"I got an idea," he answered, and then called to Mrs. G., "two of your best burgers, we'll be right back."

He grabbed Sue and left the shop. They went over to the pay phone and he began dialing.

"Hello Joe?…Yea it's me, listen. Don't meet us at the carny, come to the Spa and call Ken to grab a date and get here too. Then call up anybody else you know that planned on going up to Denville and tell them to come here instead. Tell them to bring anyone they can and tell them it's a 'All For One' alert, got me? I'll explain later. Right, see ya."

"What are you up to?" she asked with a questioning grin.

"How'd you like to skip the carnival and go dancing with me tonight, with the stars?"

"Of course!" she cried out with bright eyes and she grabbed the phone book. He handed her the phone and she started dialing.

"Hello Janice?... Yea its Sue. Look, how'd you like to pick up Walt and come to a dance? ...Yea, now listen ..."

They continued calling until finally she turned to him and said, "Well, that's everybody we know, but I'm not sure it'll be enough to help."

He thought a moment, then said, "Not everybody," and asked for the phone book again.

"Hello Andy? ... Yea, this is Steve Clayton. Look, I need a favor. I need you to come down to the Village Spa by 4 O'clock and to call up every freshman you know...Tell them to be here as well. Tell them it's a ' All for One' alert and to bring money with them, got it?...Yes, by four O'clock. Tell them that if they care about the Spa they'll be here, I'll explain more later ...Right ...Thanks a million man, bye."

Sue threw her arms around him.

"That's it, I know they'll come through!"

"They have to," he grinned, "there all Musketeers."

They went back inside and sat at the counter.

"You were gone so long I kept your food warm in back. Is everything all right?" asked Mrs. G.

"We hope it will be soon," Sue answered.

They tried to relax and enjoy their burgers slowly to give everyone enough time to start arriving. As they watched the old black cat clock on the wall, with its eyes looking left and right and its pendulum tail swaying to and fro, its hands slowly approached four O'clock. Steve smiled and decided to try adding frosting to the cake.

"Mrs. G.," he asked, "how about trying a special tonight to help business?"

"Well sure, but what?"

"What do you have the most of?"

"Uh, crackers," she answered.

He glanced over at Sue with a lost look.

"Crackers?" Sue asked.

"Oh yes, we got a whole delivery for the soups," Mrs. G. said, "but not much call for it this week. I hope they'll stay fresh long enough to use them."

"What soups do you have ready now?" Steve asked.

"Oh, Papa was hoping for a good crowd today cause of the cold, so he has made both chicken noodle and vegetable."

"Great!" he said. "How about a soup and sandwich special, and maybe a free refill on hot chocolates, coffee, teas, and sodas, or is that too much?"

"No, we can do that," she replied, "but who am I making these specials for?" He turned around as Joe and Ken pulled up with their girls in the cars.

"Steve," she said, "Joe has a great appetite, but I don't think he could do more than three specials, six, counting the others."

"You wait, I'm hoping the count will get higher."

He and Sue went outside and explained what was happening to the group.

"But the carny is not the only problem," Steve told them. "With the coming of the new mall, business here has been dropping steadily and it might mean the end of the Spa soon."

As he spoke, a couple of more cars arrived with more seniors. Then several freshmen started walking in from the street and through the wooded paths behind the buildings.

"This place has been home to us for over four years," he continued, "but what about the next four? We have to show this new generation of Musketeers why it is so important to help keep this little social haven. We have to help save it for those coming behind us or they may never have what we had here together."

He looked at all the seniors. "Besides, I think we owe it to the Goldbergs for making it such a welcomed place for us teens to hang out, don't you agree?" Every head nodded and smiled.

"So, what do we do?" Ken asked.

"You and Joe, pull your cars next to mine and wait in them."

As he finished, he saw Andy coming into the lot with over twenty freshmen. He waved them over, while Sue gathered the others coming from the back.

"Well Steve, we're all here and more coming," Andy said. "What's the alert for?"

He explained to the group the situation, then asked, "Is having a place like this worth it to all of you?" Most nodded, but some wondered what the big deal was.

"We can go over to the mall by bus everyday and have fun, hang out together and do stuff," several freshmen said, "there's nothing to do much around here."

"What if I could show you how to have a good time right where you're standing and you could spend your bus fair on drinks and food instead?"

He turned to Andy. "Did you find one?"

"Yea," he answered, and he called out to a friend. The girl walked up carrying a medium sized portable radio.

Steve took it and held it up. "Here is your answer," he said and then tuned it to Jersey's best rock station and pumped up the volume.

"Hey gang, here's one for those of you who had a long week. It's their hottest one yet and climbing the chart to becoming the new number one hit. Here's the Fifth Dimension singing 'Aquarius'."

Steve turned to the guys.

"All right, how about some more volume over there!" and both cars turned on their radios and cranked them up. Sue went and turned on Excalibur and all six of them started dancing in the lot.

Several other seniors joined in, and finally, the freshman smiled as they grabbed a partner.

Steve and Sue went into the shop and said, "There are your specials Mrs. G.!"

"They certainly are, aren't they? Well, I'd better get out the sandwich makings and lots of crackers too." She quickly headed for the kitchen yelling for papa to put on more soups.

Sue got some sheets of paper, markers and tape from their back office. She quickly made up ' special of the day ' signs and taped them on the windows and walls.

Steve made up a starting round of hot chocolates and put them onto trays with a sign hanging off it, 'Special: Buy One, and the refill is FREE!'. He and Sue handed the trays to Joe and Cindy who went outside and started selling.

Ken went into the kitchen and started helping with the sandwich orders as they came in. Mr. G. filled the carry out cups with soups and handed them to mama who brought them on a tray with plastic spoons and napkins out to the front door where Joe was collecting the money.

As they were handed out to the very cold crowd Mama G. yelled to each, "And take plenty of crackers!"

Sue filled the soda orders as teens came inside to get warm or just to talk in-between the dancing outside. Papa got sore and tired after awhile, so Steve took over the soup making, under his careful supervision.

"Just a pinch of salt at a time in the chicken soup," he said, "we don't want it too salty now."

"Yes sir," he replied.

"Every bowl must taste as the last." Steve smiled and nodded.

It was around nine O'clock that Officer Meads arrived in his squad car with lights flashing. He stepped out and yelled over the music.

"Okay, turn down that music."

Sue went up to him and asked, "Hello Officer, can I help you?"

"Everybody has to leave, now."

The front door opened and Mr. And Mrs. Goldberg stepped out.

"Oh Bobby," she called as she saw the uniform, "come have some soup and crackers to warm you up!"

"Mrs. Goldberg," he said, "you can't have a block party with all these teenagers hanging out unsupervised and loud music playing."

"This is not a block party," Joe said, "just some customers trying to stay warm is all."

"And I have been meaning to put out front some speakers to play music for my customers to enjoy as they eat out here on my sidewalk tables," Papa declared.

"And Bobby," Mama said, "these young people aren't unsupervised. I am watching over all of them. So you see, everything is fine."

"Here," Papa said, "have a cup of soup while I get your coffee."

The officer readjusted his hat as he shrugged his shoulders and asked, "Is it chicken noodle?"

"Yes Bobby," Mama said, "and lots of fresh crackers."

"Yes!" Andy yelled out as he cranked up the portable radio again and the eight cars now in the lot joined in.

Steve smiled as he watched the freshman singing and dancing. Sue came beside him and he put his arm around her as they watched together.

"You two saved us," Mrs. G. said from the front door.

"No Mama," Sue replied as she pointed to the next generation dancing, "they did, because they've learned what's important." Then she grabbed his arm and said, "Hey, you promised to take me dancing!" and she led him out to dance among the stars.

Chapter Nine
"THE PROMise"

The senior prom was barely two weeks away and Sue was in a panic because she hadn't yet found the right gown. She was becoming irritable and short tempered and she found herself often snapping at others.

"What if we made the gown?" her mom asked.

"Mom, we have just two weeks!" she cried. "Rome wasn't built in a day!"

Her grandma got up from her chair and came over to her.

"Angel, now you stop this and you no talk to your mama this way, you hear me?"

Sue lowered her head.

"I'm so sorry. I don't know why I'm acting this way. Please forgive me, both of you."

Grandma hugged her and said, "That's my Angel, you're a good girl," as she patted her on the back. "Now, you tell us what it is that you want, eh? "

Sue thought hard, then said, "I guess what I want is a gown that will make me feel more like a woman, instead of a high school teen. Does that make any sense?"

"Perfect sense," her mom said.

"Not to me," Grandma replied and she looked Sue in the face.

"You turn round," she told her. Sue slowly turned as her grandma watched her carefully.

"You look like a woman, but you don't feel like one?" she said shaking her head. "Angel, you are not a woman cause of what you wear, you are one or you are not! So tell me, are you one?"

Sue turned to her and said, "Yes Grandma, I am a woman," and she smiled.

"Good," Grandma stated, "now we make you a dress, because it is the woman that makes the gown beautiful, eh?"

"In just two weeks?" she asked softly.

"Only if you can pick a color by today. Come, we begin."

The three drove down to the fabric store and Sue went looking through assorted textures and colors. She finally narrowed it down to three different ones.

"Which one do you think Mom?"

Her mother held each one up against her saying that any would be beautiful for a gown. She turned to her grandma with a perplexed look.

"A woman knows what is in the heart," Grandma said in answer to her unspoken question.

Sue looked again and then said, "Yes, this one."

"Good, now we can begin. I will need more thread."

That afternoon, and nearly every night, the three worked on the dress in Grandma's small, back sewing room. She came after school for fittings and to help.

Sue marveled at how Grandma's feeble fingers could do such meticulous work. She noticed that with each piece, her grandmother labored on it as if that were the only important one to do until the next item was needed.

Slowly, piece by piece, a gown began to materialize before her eyes. Her grandma had sewn rows of tiny white pearls along the neckline and sleeves. It was so well done, you couldn't even see the threads.

"Come stand here," she said to her, "we need another fitting for the waist and length."

Sue put the gown on and admired herself in front of the tall, lean mirror as Grandma pulled at the dress and placed in pins.

"Ouch!" Sue cried as a pin stuck her.

"You move too much," Grandma replied, "now, pay attention. You hold here and I pin."

"Grandma, how old were you when you married Grandpa Dom?"

"I was eighteen but age is not important, it is the heart," she answered as she gazed over at a picture of her wedding on the dresser.

Sue saw her face in the mirror.

"I know you miss him, so do I," Sue said sadly.

"He will be there when I come home."

"I think I'd die if Steve were gone."

"There is always the pain and everything will make you think of him, but you don't think about dying. God gives you love to live and He expects you to make it grow."

She stopped working and smiled.

"My love for my Dom. It grew greater than I could hold in my heart or he could take, so I had to put the rest into everything else the Lord sent me."

Sue smiled. "Like making a prom gown?"

"Yes well, you help here or you be dancing with half a dress."

"I love you Grandma."

"Put your finger on this spot, good. I think I need to shorten this some."

Sue smiled down on her as she started working again.

Steve joined the guys at Tony Rudy's men shop in town to be fitted for a tux. They looked over the styles as they browsed about the store, then Mr. Rudy approached from the back room.

"Ah," he said with big smile, "the Musketeers getting ready for the big night?"

"Sure are," Ken said with a grin, "and you should see my date."

"Oh? Do I know her?" he asked.

"Sure do, "Ken replied still grinning, "we met here in the store once."

Mr. Rudy paused, then asked "You met a girl here in my men's shop?"

"Yea, right over there," he answered pointing to the register. "She was going out with someone at the time, but as of last week, she's free and available."

Mr. Rudy glanced at the counter, thinking. "I've only had two women work here, one was Mrs. Hoggins and the other was my niece Renee. I'm guessing it's not Mrs. Hoggins?"

Ken smiled as he felt the sleeve of one of the tuxes.

"Renee, that's the one. Sweet girl. I thought after the prom I'd drive her up to Lake Hopatcong."

"Oh? To the amusement park up there?"

Ken slipped on a jacket and checked it out in the full length mirror. "The park?" he replied, "Oh yea, there too."

Steve interrupted asking, "Could I try this one on?"

"Of course," he said as he eyed Ken. He pulled it off the rack and held it for Steve to slip on.

"That's a popular style," he said as he straightened the shoulders for Steve to look at in the mirror.

"Yes, it is nice, but maybe I should be sure and just try on some others."

"Anything you want to see, just call," he replied and he left them to explore on their own.

"Hey," Ken said as he pointed to a hot red tux, "pretty nifty! That'll make me stand out from the crowd."

"Like a safety flare for your date," Joe remarked.

Steve cracked up laughing and said, "You know what's really sad Joe? He might just end up with something like that."

"God help that poor girl," Joe muttered to himself.

As they wadded through the aisles of jackets, one caught Steve's eye. It was black and simple in design, yet with a slight boldness still coming through with the softer lapels. He found his size and tried it on. His shoulders filled it nicely without any extra bulk. It closed perfectly about his waist with the one button and best of all, it fit his long arms which were always a problem.

"What do you think?" he asked as he saw Joe working his way around the rack next to him.

"Yea, looks good," he said checking him out front and back.

"Yea, and it does feel good too." Steve said with a smile. "I really want to be comfortable that night so I can dance without fighting with a jacket."

He stared at the coat again in the mirror.

"But do you think Sue'll like it? I really don't want to disappoint her."

"I think you look great in it," Joe remarked, "but it's you she'll be seeing."

"Yea I know, but when it comes to things like proms I'm not sure that girls always think that way. This night is gonna be just too important for us and I don't want to disappoint her."

"Hey guys," Ken called from across the room, "what do ya think?"

They looked up to see him posing in the mirror as he admired a lavender tux jacket with blazing red lapels he had on.

"Does this say, 'Be prepared for an unforgettable night baby', or what?"

They gawked for several moments.

"I got a feeling that no matter what you pick out," Steve stated, "she's never going to forget this night."

Ken smiled at himself as he kept turning.

"Yea well, that goes without saying," he said back, " but you don't think it's too much?"

"No," Joe answered, "if anything you're too much. The jacket just tones it all down a bit."

"I guess, but maybe something with orange?" Ken mumbled.

Later Sue heard a car pull into her grandma's drive, it was Steve. As he walked up the walkway she came out the door and met him.

"Hi Babe, your dad said you were over here. How come you're spending so much time with your grandma, she isn't sick is she?"

"Oh no she's fine. It's just that, well, we decided to make my gown than buy one and I have to be here to keep getting fitted for it."

"Wow, you really are going all out, that's great. Can I see it?" he asked in fun.

133

"Of course you can, when you pick me up on prom night. Oh," she said nervously, "I pray it's ready."

He put his arm around her shoulder and smiled down asking, "Who's helping you with it?"

"Mom and Grandma."

"Well there you are. Three LaRosas on one gown, how can you miss?"

"But we haven't much time left and…"

"And it will be perfect I'm sure."

"Oh God, I am so nervous," she muttered as she walked him back to the car.

"Hey," he said as she opened the car door for him, "I came to see you and maybe go to the Spa for a quiet lunch together."

"Eat? I can't eat! I have a gown to finish creating. We still have hemming to do and a waist which needs, oh something, and then there's the lace to do yet…"

"Whoa," he said as he touched her hand, "I understand. Man, I thought I worked hard finding a tux? Listen Angel, calm down and believe in yourself and your folks, okay? They won't ever let you down, trust them."

"Oh I know," she replied with her head on his chest, "I guess I just need to know that it'll be perfect."

"Tell ya what," he said. "You go back to work while I run down to the Spa and have Mrs. G. put together a few of her specials. I'll bring them back here for us to all share out on the steps, sound okay? "

"Okay," she answered with a smile, "I'll tell them!"

"I'll be back in about forty minutes." He closed the door and backed out onto the street waving. She blew him a kiss, then ran back inside.

As he pulled into the parking lot, he recognized a car parked with several underclassmen. All were wearing football jackets and sitting on its hood. They started horsing around as he got out and headed towards the door.

"Well if it isn't Captain Clayton, Parsippany's own buccaneer," said one as he passed and he ignored the comment.

"Hey," came another voice, "how's that little hottie you stole from my brother doing?"

He stopped as they laughed, then turned to Mike's little brother and said boldly, "I think you'd better apologize for that."

Brad hopped off the trunk then asked laughing, "And if I don't?"

Steve hit him with a right and he slide down the trunk to the pavement in a daze.

"When he wakes up," he said to the rest, "tell him that wasn't an option." Then he turned and went inside. The group ran over to Brad and shook him back to his senses.

"When he comes out," he told them, "he's dead, get me?"

Steve placed his order and sat down with a cup of coffee to wait. A moment later, he saw Mike come out of the restroom. He smiled and waved him over.

"Hey Mike, how've you been?"

"Good," he answered, "you ready for the prom?"

"Oh yea, just picked out my tux the other day, and you?"

"Yea, I got mine. It should be a great time. Sally is really looking forward to it."

"So is Sue, I just left her working on making her own gown. She's a bit nervous that it won't be done on time, but I'm sure it will."

He pointed to the stool asking, "Why don't you sit a moment and have a coffee, I'll buy?"

Mike smiled. "Yea why not. I got a few minutes to kill before I have to drive my brother and his friends over to the field to throw the ball around a bit."

"Good," Steve said, "we haven't had much time to just talk lately and I'd like to discuss something with you."

When his order was ready, the two walked out together. They paused as they spotted the line up outside waiting for Steve.

"Brad," Mike said, "I understand you owe Mr. Clayton an apology."

"He punched me Mike, I owe him good."

"You owe him what he asked for, so tell him, unless you want both of us to teach you about respect."

Mike took a step forward and added, "and I want your jacket."

135

"What for?" Brad asked.

"I'll give it back when you won't disgrace it, and don't any of you ever say anything like that again about a lady like Miss LaRosa, do you understand me!" All nodded but Brad.

"He hit me and I'm not gonna take that."

Mike laughed. "He only hit you once? Hell, you got off easy."

Brad stood his ground, ready to fight.

"Let me talk with him, all right?" Steve asked.

"Sure," Mike replied as he took the package from him.

Steve walked slowly towards him saying, "You know Brad, I've found that there are a few things you should never do in life. One is to never belittle another person. The next is to never insult the one they love. The last is to never pick a fight with a man who's sure he's in the right because you can't beat him. He won't quit and he'll never stay down."

"He's telling ya the truth," Mike said. "I learned and so did Big Joe Reily."

Brad lowered his fists slightly to ask, "You fought against Joe Reily?"

"He sure did, and he won," Mike added.

Steve looked at Brad and said, "Joe and I both won that day, because we ended a fight neither could win. He had the power to keep knocking me down and I had the willpower to keep getting up. So we did the only thing that made sense, we became the best of friends."

Steve held out his hand. "You look like a guy who just won't stay down, so are you ready to win that kind of a fight also?"

Brad looked away to the others for a moment, then towards his brother. Finally, he smiled and shook his hand saying, "I guess maybe I am."

"Good," Steve said, "I'd much rather see you use that kind of tenacity where it counts, out on the field in a game."

"Yes sir," he responded, " and I'm sorry for what I said about Miss LaRosa. "

"Apology accepted," Steve said with a smile, "and now my friend, you're a Musketeer."

136

Brad laughed as he turned to open the car door. Mike came over and handed Steve back his dinners.

"Now that's worthy of a Varsity jacket," he said with a grin. "Come on, let's get to practice."

"Thanks for your help here Mike. I'm glad we could settle it peaceably, as always."

Mike laughed shaking his hand. "Say hi to Sue for me will ya?"

"Sure will, and we'll see ya at the dance."

They waved and then drove off.

When he got back up to the house he saw them sitting on the porch and Sue came down to help with the dinners.

"Any problems?" she asked as she glanced into the bags.

"Not at all. Oh, I saw Mike and he said to say hi."

"How is he?"

"Fine. I also met Brad his brother, nice kid."

"I'm so glad you two have been able to get past your differences," she said smiling.

"Well, it helps to be sensible about things like that." He took her arm gently and whispered, "I love you."

She looked up at him and studied his face a moment.

"I love you too, " she replied, "is everything all right?"

"Yea, of course. I just like hearing us say it."

Sue handed out the dinners and they all began to eat as they talked in the warm evening. When they had finished, she ran him off so they could get back to work.

He got back into the car and she said, "Now, get going so missing me will be worth it."

"I love you," he said again.

"I know," she replied anxiously, "but absence makes the heart grow fonder, remember that from English class?"

He thought a moment, and then remembered the rest of the poem.

"Isle of Beauty, Fare thee well!"

She smiled kissing him saying, "I love you too, now get out of here!"

Each day they would drive into school together, see each other in-between classes, then go to the Spa for a quick soda. He would then drop her off at Grandma's and her mom took her home later.

When the day of the prom finally came it was full of both excitement and tension. Sue spent most of the day with her mom and Grandma; first spending the morning in the beauty salon having her hair done, then the afternoon running up and down stairs looking for something or someone.

Her mom and Grandma took shifts helping her find or do whatever she needed, including trying to keep her calm. Her dad stayed out of their way for the most part, watching television, or reading the paper over and over. Sue sensed they were as nervous as she was.

Steve laid out his tux outfit on the bed and searched for the shoe kit to polish up his feather weight shoes. He had taken two showers that day. The first was his normal shower, the second because he was nervous and started sweating, so he grabbed his dad's special deodorant soap and wanted to be sure he was safe.

He got frustrated when he got to the bathroom mirror. All of that water had washed out the hot-combing the barber had done to his hair. It just flopped around on his head as he mumbled about it.

"Use a little hair spray," his mom told him as she handed him the can, "but just a little to hold it until they take your pictures, then you can comb it out so it's soft again."

As he finished his hair, he felt a slight stubble on his chin so he got out the razor again.

"Ouch!" he cried out.

"What's wrong?" his mother called out asking from the kitchen.

"Oh, I just cut myself shaving."

"Didn't you already shave before?"

"Yea, but I wasn't able to ruin my look so I thought I'd give it another try. Oh man, it won't stop bleeding. I can't go to the prom wearing a Donald Duck band aid on my face!"

"Use some tissue paper on it," she called out.

He tore off a piece and held it asking, "Should I wet it first?"

His mom turned to look at his father sitting with the paper shaking his head with a grin.

"Your father says no, just press it on until it sticks!"

A few moments later, he came out putting more deodorant stick under his arms and then walking around the house flapping them to dry it. As he passed the bathroom each time, he'd go check that his hair hadn't moved.

Meanwhile, Sue was watching the clock every fifteen minutes as she checked her gown over and over. She laid it out across the bed with her purse next to it and her now matching, French-heeled sling backs on the floor in front.

She checked her purse again to be sure that she had the mirror compact from Grandma inside, together with a comb and a handkerchief scented from the bottle on her nightstand. Still, she felt something was missing. She walked the room pondering the scene on the bed.

"What's the matter?" her mom asked as she entered the room.

"I feel like I'm overlooking something, but I can't figure out what."

"Is it the something of mine that I promised you?"

Sue's eyes lit up. "Yes Mom, that's it."

"Wait here," she replied and went over into her bedroom.

A moment later, she returned with a small, black box that read, 'Tiffany's' and she opened it. Sue smiled as she watched her take the fine banded piece out.

"Turn around," her mom said and she proceeded to place it around her neck.

Sue walked to her vanity and sat down looking in the mirror.

"Oh Mom," she sighed, "it's beautiful."

She admired the way the half inch wide blue band laid against her white throat, with the black and white cameo of an angel at its center.

"I was given that on my prom night when my mom said I needed something grown up to wear. Now, it's yours."

Sue turned and hugged her. "I love you Mama."

"Now," she said, wiping away a tear, "you better start getting ready soon, your date will be here to pick you up at five O'clock, remember?"

"I will, and thank you for all you've done," she answered with a loving smile.

Sue opened her top dresser drawer and took out her diary. She wrote the date, then added 'tonight I am a woman'. She stopped when she heard a knock at the door.

"Can I come in Baby?"

"Yes Daddy."

He walked into the room and sat on a chair.

"Well," he said, "tonight's the big night huh?"

"Yes, it's finally here."

"That's a beautiful gown you designed there. I hope he appreciates all the work you three did on it?"

"I know he will Dad, he's a lot like you when it comes to my feelings."

"Well good, then he knows what I expect from him on this special date."

He got up and reached into his pocket to bring out a twenty dollar bill.

"Here baby, I want you to put this in your purse, just in case you find you need a cab or something, you know."

She smiled, got up and hugged him tight.

"Yes Dad I know and I love you too."

She could feel him hold her tight also. When he finally did back away she saw a look of distance on his face. He turned and stared at her bed.

"Do you remember when you'd make me to check under the bed and in the closet before you let me close the door?"

"I remember," she said softly. "You'd always do it night after night saying, 'all clear here' as you went from place to place until you knew I felt safe."

She walked over to him.

"I was always safe with you Daddy, and he knows you expect no less from him. I love you both more than I can say."

"He is a fine boy," he replied as he looked into her eyes. He kissed her on the forehead and walked to the doorway where he looked back.

"No, a fine young man," he said, then slowly closed the door.

She picked up her diary and added, "A woman, because my parents love me enough to let me become one."

At the Clayton house, Steve was almost finished getting dressed when he realized that his ruffled shirt had French cuffs.

"Ma!" he called out, "I can't find my cuff links!"

"Check the box on your dresser, I think your brother was using them as shields for his Roman soldiers."

Steve scurried through the box of plastic soldiers and found two sets of links attached to guys with spears.

"You're a pip James," he murmured as he undid them.

At last, he felt he was ready. He did a final check in his wallet to be sure he had brought enough cash, and then he walked out into the living room.

"You look so nice," his mother said. "All grown up, soon to college then … Soon you'll be having a family of your own."

She stopped and he noticed her eyes tearing up. She reached up and gently pulled off the tissue still stuck to his face.

"She's a wonderful girl," she said.

"I know Mom, she's the best."

"You want something to eat before you go, they might not serve dinner right away and you'll be hungry."

"I'm fine," he said as she turned and went into the kitchen.

He followed her in and watched as she put a couple of apples into a bag and handed it to him.

"You both can eat these and not worry about having already brushed your teeth." He took the bag and thanked her.

"You'd better get going. You don't want to keep the young lady waiting on the most important night of your lives."

He started for the door, then turned back and gave her a hug.

"I'll always love you, you know that."

She hugged him back. "I know," she answered as she patted his breast pocket, "but you always put her first now, you hear?"

"I will Mom."

"Go," she said, and he went out the door and ran to the car.

As he started down the street, he smiled as he looked over the car. He was glad he had spent so much time waxing it and taking the extra time to give it a toothbrush detail inside. Excalibur shined like the full moon above.

He drove up and parked out front. Grabbed a colorful bag he had on the seat and went up and rang the doorbell. He checked his watch, it was five to five, and then he took a deep breath and slowly let it out.

When the door opened, it was her mom.

"Well there you are," she said, "and don't you look so nice, come in."

He entered slowly as she closed the door behind him.

"Frank!" she called, "Come see if Steve needs something to drink."

"Oh, no," he said as he glanced in the hall mirror at himself, "I'm fine."

Her dad came out of the kitchen and paused to look at him. He could feel himself being checked out and when her dad finally moved towards him smiling, he began to breathe easier.

"Well," he said, "you look very nice."

"Thank you. Is Sue ready?"

"Almost," answered Grandma, "I will go and let her know you are here."

He watched as she went up the stairs.

"You might want to wait in here," her dad said, pointing to the living room.

Steve followed him in and sat carefully on the couch, still holding the bag in his hands tightly. When Mrs. LaRosa came back with a camera he got up and handed her a long stem rose from the bag.

"This is for you, for all that you did to help make this night perfect for us."

Her mom took it and smelt it slowly.

"Thank you Steve it's lovely, but I loved every moment of helping."

142

He turned to her dad and reached into the bag.

"I got this for you, because I know how much you enjoy them," and he handed him a El Producto cigar.

"What's this for?"

"For giving me a chance to prove myself. Thank you."

He rolled the cigar between his fingers, then put it in his top pocket and smiled.

"Are you sure I can't get you some coffee?" Mr. LaRosa asked as he leaned into him. "It might be awhile yet," he added.

"Yes, maybe a small cup then, thanks."

He sat back down carefully again on the corner of the couch and held onto the bag.

Her grandma came down and told her mother that she was needed upstairs.

"She'll be just a lit'l while more," she told him.

"That's fine," he answered as he checked his watch to see its hands moving towards fifteen after the hour.

"Oh," he said as he rose again, "I have this for you Grandma," and he pulled out a small corsage he had made. They were the red, white and blue flowers from the island, and he pinned it on her.

"Oh my," she said as she gazed at them, "wild flowers."

He looked at her and said, "I thought of when you told us about his picking some for you on his way home from work on special occasions." She smiled at him.

"Always he came with the wildflowers," she said softly as she smelt them.

"I wanted this night to be special for you too," he said as he kissed her cheek.

"Oh," she cried, "you are so like my Dom. My Angel could not have found better," and she patted his face.

"I think we're ready," they heard her mom say as she came down the staircase. "Oh, where's my camera?" she asked and Mr. LaRosa handed it to her.

143

All stood at the landing as slowly she came into view at the top. Steve stood at the very last step looking up and holding the colored bag in his hands.

Sue paused looking down at their faces, then quickly fixed her eyes on his. He watched as she slowly descended from above. The walk lights along the wall shined upon her like a heavenly path to him.

He watched as her pearl shoes carefully took each step. The pale blue gown flowed over the stairs like a clear summer sky, with sparks of brilliance flashing from the tiny milk-white, seed pearls. Its flared skirt swayed with each step as if in a waltz by itself.

As she got closer, he could make out the beauty of her arms beneath the near-see-through chiffon sleeves. He followed them down to where they flared out at the pearled wrists like a flower about to bloom. He saw the cameo angel beneath her chin, looking upward with raised hands as if to cradle her glowing face. He could not take a full breath for she was a vision.

His legs weakened more as she got closer until at last, as if for mercy's sake, she stopped on the bottom step and smiled into his eyes.

"She walks in beauty, like the night," he whispered, quoting from their literature book. She smiled, blushing slightly.

"You look so lovely," he said. "I wouldn't have believed you could ever outshine the last time I saw you."

"It's you that makes me feel beautiful," she said lovingly into his eyes.

He reached into the bag and brought out a box. He opened it and showed her the corsage.

"Oh Steve, it's beautiful!" she exclaimed as he pinned it carefully on her.

"Let me take a picture," her mom said, as she positioned them in front of the stairs. She took several shots, and then Sue noticed that he was only looking at her.

"Look at the camera, they need one shot of your whole face, not just the side."

"I'll do my best," he whispered.

"We better get going," she told them.

"All right, but wave from the car," her mom said.

They walked out and stood by the front of Excalibur and waved back. A flash bulb went off, then another. He opened the door and helped her into the seat, then quickly ran around to the other door. and jumped in. They waved again as they started pulling away, with flashes in their mirrors.

As they drove, both were unusually quiet. He drove very carefully and slower than normal. Sue looked out the window as they left town and made their way to the highway.

"Your gown is really beautiful," he said.

"Thanks. I really like the tux you chose, it fits you so well."

"Thanks."

They sat quietly again as he crossed Route 46 and headed towards Morristown.

"I hear they're going to serve us our choice of steak or chicken." he mumbled.

"Yea, I heard that too. Which one do you want?"

"Oh the steak I guess, we don't often have that at home. And you?"

"I think I'd like to try the steak also," she answered, as she sat with her hands folded in her lap.

He wondered why he suddenly felt so awkward. He watched as she too kept fidgeting, checking and adjusting her gown every couple of moments.

Sue felt the tension also in both of them.

"What's wrong here?" she kept asking herself. "We should be laughing and as happy as can be."

Still, they made only polite conversation all the way to Whippany Road.

As they were about to turn into the main entrance of the Governor Morris, he stopped and parked out on the road.

"Something wrong?" she asked.

He sat thinking for a quick moment, then asked, "Are you as nervous as I am?"

She smiled shyly and nodded. "And I don't know why."

They looked at each other, as they listened to the faint music playing from the banquet room up the drive.

"I've been scared all day," she confided. "I was so worried about making this night perfect."

"Me too," he said, as he turned in his seat towards her. "I shaved twice, doubled showered, and must have spent over an hour trying to make my hair perfect."

He looked into the rear view mirror and saw that it was flopping around, in spite of the hair spray.

Sue smiled again saying, "I drove the hairdresser so crazy today, I don't think I can go back until it has new owners. Oh, and my poor mom and grandma. I must have taken years off their lives as they kept running at my beckoned call for the smallest of concerns."

She suddenly laughed under her breath saying, "At one point, I got so upset when the zipper of my gown got stuck in back. I kept insisting it was because I had just gained weight from having eaten a pastry an hour earlier."

They both laughed.

"And I was almost ready to kill my brother for hiding and using all my cuff links as shields for his Roman soldiers."

"He didn't!" she cried out as she laughed with him.

"Then," he added, still laughing, "I realized at the last minute that I was out of shoe polish, so my mom gave me butter to use on them. I've been in a panic since. I was sure a cat would come along at some point tonight to try and lick them clean."

Both laughed for several moments, then looked at each other smiling.

"It's all been kind of crazy, hasn't it?" he asked.

"Yea, it has," she answered back, still laughing a bit, "and I still don't know why really. I just know that I love you."

"And I love you too, and I still love to hear us say it."

She grabbed her dress and slipped up onto the console for a moment to kiss and hug him.

"Now," she said, "let's go dancing and have some fun!"

He laughed and said, "Tell ya what. How about we leave worrying for tomorrow? Tonight, let's just be ourselves and have a special time to remember that'll always be ours."

"You promise to kick off your shoes on that dance floor, no matter what songs they play?"

"Babe, my buttered shoes will be the cat's meow tonight!"

"That's probably the worst metaphor I ever heard, but if you do try and sit one out I'll come down on you like a ton of pastries. Now, kiss me you fool and let's get to dancing!"

He drove up the drive to the main entrance and the valet came over.

"Do me a favor," Steve asked as he slipped him a couple of bucks, "please be sure to park Him next to a classy set of wheels, okay? I want Him to have a good time too. He's particularly fond of other convertibles, especially the dark topped ones."

"Uh, yes sir," he replied as Steve gave him a wink, then the young man smiled as Sue patted Excalibur on the hood.

"Have fun Baby!" she said.

He continued to watch the two of them as they danced in circles up to the doorway, making a grand entrance.

The valet got into the Le Mans and said, "Say, how about a black top Mustang whose doors, I happened to know, are unlocked?"

He started the engine and raced it a bit. "I thought you'd like that," he said with a grin, then drove up into the lot.

They laughed together as he swung her around in the huge main entrance hall, then walked together up to the podium for check-in.

As they entered the grand banquet room, they heard their names being called out from a front table by Joe and Cindy. They made their way across the ocean of faces and joined them.

"We were beginning to wonder what happened to you two," Cindy said lightheartedly.

"Oh," Sue replied with a grin, "we had to fix Excalibur up with a date last minute, and you know how fussy he can be."

"You really do have a strange relationship, don't you?" she stated, not sure if she was serious. Sue laughed and then she did also.

"So," Steve asked, "do you guys know when they'll be serving dinner?"

"In about an hour the waiter told us," Joe answered.

"Well good," he said as the live band started playing, "gives us time to build up a good appetite first."

He grabbed Sue and they were out on the dance floor in seconds.

"Let's not let them have all the fun, come on Joe," Cindy said pulling on his arm.

"Couldn't we wait for a slower one?"

"No, I like this song and now it's time to put all of that practice time we did to good use."

Joe looked over at Steve and Sue dancing. It was as natural to them, it seemed to him, as breathing.

"All right," he said, "but no laughing if I look like a drunken gorilla out there, promise?"

"Of course I promise, now loosen up and let's have some fun."

They joined the others out on the floor and started dancing. Sue noticed them and made her way over.

"Joe," she said with a look of surprise, "you're looking good! I never realized how well you could dance."

He suddenly had a smile on his face.

"We've been practicing these past weeks."

"Well it sure has paid off, have fun!" and she turned back to Steve just in time for him to spin her around.

When the song ended, all four sat down to order something to drink.

"I wonder where Ken is," Joe said as he looked around.

"If he rented the last tux we saw him trying on, they might not have let him in," Steve said grinning.

"He always has such good taste," Joe replied, "I don't know what got into him with those tuxes."

"Yea I know, it was like he had gotten a sudden case of color blindness. Well, we'll know when he finally gets here."

Joe leaned over to him and said, "I wish they'd play a slow song. I like it better when we get to dance close, ya know?"

Steve nodded with, "Well let me see what I can do."

He went over and spoke with the lead guitarist. A moment later, the band started playing 'Wedding Bell Blues' from the Fifth Dimension. Joe winked at him as they held out their hands to the ladies and led them to the floor.

As he danced holding Sue gently, she sang softly into his ear. He closed his eyes and kissed her hand, feeling the love in their heart.

"I do love you," she whispered, "and always will."

They gazed into each other's eyes as the band started playing something with a faster beat. Joe smiled when he saw them continue to dance slowly on the floor and it gave him the courage to stay also.

When dinner was served Joe and Cindy shared their chicken and steaks with each other as usual.

"I'm gonna eat up Ken's dinners too if he doesn't get here soon," Joe said as he soaked up the last trace of gravy from his plate.

"Maybe I should call and make sure he's all right," Steve replied, but then he spotted Ken at the entrance way.

There was no missing him standing there. He was wearing a red tux with fire engine flames on its lapels. Smiling next to him was his date. She had on a gown of orange and yellow that could have glowed in the dark. He waved to them and the couple made there way over.

"Oh my God!" Cindy yelped as they sat down. "You two look like you could start a fire together." Then she quickly covered her mouth, realizing what she had said out loud.

"We do look great, don't we?" Ken asked, and he hugged his date as she smiled. "We had a hard time finding just the right clothes for this special night."

"You both got together on this I gather?" Steve asked.

"For awhile now," he answered. "We wanted to be sure that when we danced, we had everyone's attention."

"Well, I think you can count on that," Joe stated as a fact.

"Good," Ken said smiling, "but let's eat first, then it's on with the entertainment."

They all ate and talked, then when the band took a break Ken went over to talk with the Disc Jockey as she prepared to play dinner music. They noticed him hand something to her, then return to the table.

"We've had a special request and all of you are welcomed to come up and join in at any time," the D.J. nervously announced.

Ken took his date and they quickly stepped to the center of the dance floor.

"What in the world?" Sue thought out loud, as she watched them standing there waiting for the tape to begin playing.

The music began as Ken pulled a rose out of his jacket and put it between his partner's teeth.

"Oh my Lord," Steve laughed, "they're doing a tango!"

Sue and Cindy both brought their hands to their faces in disbelief as the two proceeded to dance in perfect sink together. Not a voice was heard anywhere as they moved across the floor. At one point Ken paused to smile, then quickly pulled his partner back into his arms and carried her off.

Howls and cheers came as he dragged her across the floor. He pulled her up into his arms again and, with a quick side look, paused for more applause.

It was about half over when Sue grabbed Steve's arm.

"Come on, let's try it!"

He sat with a blank look on his face.

"A ton of pastries are coming," she said with a smile and he got up.

They tried to follow the other matched set, but within minutes, they were doing it their own way and loving it. A few more couples joined in as they realized they too could just come up and wing it for fun.

As it ended, Ken suddenly swung his date outward, and then snapped her back to his side. She put her head onto his shoulder and stroked his chest, then he flung his free arm into the air and yelled, "O lay!"

They both got a standing ovation as they took a bow, and then made their way back to the table.

150

"Where in the world did you learn to do that?" Sue asked with a look of awe on her face.

"I learned it from her," he said looking at his date. "This is Renee, she studied dancing in France."

"Allo everyone," she said with a slight accent.

"Well hello," Sue replied. "You sure are a great dancer and teacher."

"Thank you, but Kenski made it very easy to want to teach. He was highly motivated."

"I'm sure," Sue remarked with a nod.

They danced more, sometimes changing partners for the fun of it. Joe felt extremely awkward when he started dancing a slow one with Renee.

"You seem tense," she said. "Here, let me massage your neck a little."

"Uh, no I'm fine thanks," he quickly said with cheeks now blushing as red as his hair. "I can fix it," he added, then snapped his neck to the side with a audible crack. "There see, fine now."

Ken had Cindy all over the floor.

"You sure got some moves there," she told him just before he dipped her. Joe gave him a stern look and he quickly pulled her back up.

"Sorry," he said with a tilt of his head, then made some space between himself and her.

Steve finally danced with Renee while Sue took to the floor with Ken.

"So," Sue asked, "where did you meet Renee?"

"Oh, she worked one summer at Tony Rudy's but she was seeing someone at the time. When she came back I ran into her and, well, here we are."

"Do you think she might be the one?"

He looked at her blankly.

"Sue, how long have you known me?"

"Right," she answered nodding her head.

"But if I ever was to look, I'd want what you two have found," he said smiling.

151

She smiled back at him.

"I love you, you know that?"

"Yea I know, everybody does," he replied and then felt a light slap to the back of his head.

"Kenski tells me you handle your foil very well," Renee said to Steve.

"My what? Oh fencing. Well, I had a good teacher."

"Maybe you could show me sometime?"

Sue was dancing behind them and overheard their talk.

"Could I handle it?" Renee asked with wide eyes.

"Oh sure, Sue took to it without any trouble. It's just a matter of balance and focus."

Sue laughed quietly to herself.

Renee put her head on his chest. "You have such a strong heart," she said, "you must have great endurance."

"I ran track. It helps the circulation, as well as muscles like the heart."

She moved her hands up his arms as they danced. "Oh yes, you have strong firm ones."

"I work out with weights a bit too," he said while enjoying the song that was playing. "It's good for the arms, but my legs are in great shape from the running."

"Are they?" she asked as she pressed closer against him.

"Well I think it's time we switch back again," Sue said to Ken, "and before your date forgets your name."

"Huh?"

"Never mind. Here you go lover," she said putting his hand on Renee's shoulder. Renee turned around and Sue quickly slipped into Steve's arms.

"Sooo," she asked as they started dancing, "how did you enjoy being Frenched?"

"What?" he asked with the sudden look of a deer in headlights. "I never kissed or touched her!—-We were just dancing Babe!"

"I know, but boy did she ever handle you."

She let out a laugh as she saw his lost look.

"Oh, could you show me zometime?" she said with a sultry look. "Oh, you have zuch strong, firm muzzles. Oh, I heard you have a Le Mans. Oh, that's so French, oh yes, oh yes, oh, oh …"

He looked at her blank-faced a moment. "Are you saying that she was coming on to me just now?" he finally stammered out.

She let out another short laugh and pinched his cheek.

"Oh, zometimes you guys are just so naive."

"Oh man," he replied rolling his eyes jokingly, "I feel so cheap."

She laughed again adding, "But I can't really blame her, you do have that effect on women."

"You really think so?" he asked as he pulled her closer with a smile.

She put her head on his chest and sighed.

"Oh yes. Especially when I can hear your heart like this as it goes LE THUMP, LE THUMP, LE THUMP!"

"You're just not going to let it go, are you?" he asked as she laughed louder, then gave her a squeeze.

"Could I have your attention please?" asked the student class president, Robert Barr, over the mike.

"First, I want to thank all of you for coming and making this such a memorable prom night."

He waited for the applause to stop, then added, "and a special thanks to Ken Tomineski and Renee for leading us in that wonderful tango!" Again, more applause as the two stood up for a bow with Ken waving and Renee blowing kisses.

Cindy leaned over to Sue.

"Did she seem a bit over friendly with the guys to you, or was it just me?"

"No you're right, she was getting way too friendly," Sue answered with a bold defensive tone. "And French or not, if she ever tries scoring on my matched set again I'll show her Le Foil. Mine!"

Cindy half-grinned as they both politely clapped for the duo dancers.

"Thank you," Robert said, "it truly has been a fantastic four years here at Parsippany High for all of us. Now, it's time to announce our choices for King and Queen!"

He motioned for Carla Anderson, the head of the committee, to bring the envelope and she stepped up waving it. The band did a drum roll while she opened it and they looked inside.

"And our Homecoming Queen is," she read aloud, "Paula Wiseman!"

Paula let out a scream as she ran up for her crown. Everyone clapped and many whistled.

"And for King, it's Ken Tomineski!"

"Oh my Lord," Sue said as he ran up, "he still got her after everything I did to try and stop it."

Ken held up the crown.

"I want to thank all of you who voted for me. I know how much this means to you."

The band started playing as the Royal couple lead off the dancing. Ken put his arm around Paula and whispered, "So, your dream has finally come true at last." Paula took both his hands in hers as they swayed about the floor.

"Oh come on," he said softly, as he lowered his right hand down around her back. "Let me lead you into dancing bliss and then seal this memory with a kiss."

She motioned for him to glance over at her table. Ken turned and looked into the stare of a huge guy in an undersized tux watching them.

"Who's he?"

"That's Brock, 'the steamroller', Brown from Dover's Varsity team. He's my date and maybe just a little more," she answered with a smirk.

"Oh my," Ken commented with a slight grin, "he's a big one isn't he?" then he spun her around gently.

"So," he continued as he held her close again, "how about we waltz our way into the wings and go make some memories out in my Charger?"

As other couples joined on the floor, he slowly started dancing her towards the side curtain. There he paused, stroking her face with his finger and looking deep into her eyes.

154

"Paula, you truly are the most beautiful woman I could ever hope to find. You're perfect for me." He then pulled her to him and tried to kiss her.

"Someone warned me about you," she said pulling back.

"Oh yea, what did they say?"

"She said I should avoid you, because you can't make a commitment to any one girl."

"Like you and Steamroller out there?"

She smiled with a tilt of her head.

"Well, he and I just have a kind of understanding is all."

"I like understandings," he said kissing her cheek. "They can be so …" and he kissed her again on the lips.

"So understanding?" she asked with her eyes closed.

"Oh, so very understanding," he sighed out, then kissed her hard and long.

"Wait here a moment," he whispered and then he hurried over to his table."Renee, there's someone I'd like you to meet." He grabbed her hand and led her over by Brock.

"Hi Brock, I'm Ken."

"Yea I know," he said as he looked around. "Say, have you seen Paula?"

"I think she had to go to the powder room, but she did want you to meet Renee."

"Allo," Renee said with wide eyes.

"Hello."

Ken pulled up a seat for Renee and sat down with her.

"Brock, Paula was telling me how much she'd like for you to learn a few new dance steps. I told her that I was sure Renee here would be more than glad to walk you through a couple."

Ken turned to her. "Would you like to show him some now?"

"Oh yes, I would love to," she answered taking Brock's hand. "My you have such a strong grip, do you like fencing also?"

"No, I play football," he replied somewhat confused.

"Oh, I can see why," she said as her hand hugged his upper arm, "you are so rugged."

155

Ken smiled as they hit the dance floor and faster than you could say 'hike!', she was wrapped tighter on him than a lace on a pigskin. Ken quickly ran back for Paula, took her by the hand and headed out the back door towards the parking lot.

In the meantime, Steve and Sue were talking with Mike and Sally as they were all getting drinks.

"So what are your plans after graduation?" Mike asked.

"I'll be starting at the County College in the fall," Sue said, "and he'll be joining me the next."

"Yea, I'll probably be looking for a better paying job to earn what I'll need," Steve said shaking his head.

"Have you ever considered doing special duty for a security service?" Mike asked. "My cousin does it and said that they pay well for short term assignments.

"I might look into that, thanks. Wanna dance some more?" he asked looking back at Sue. She glanced over and saw Renee with her head on Brock's chest as they rocked back and forth in one spot.

"Yea, I think its safe now," she said grinning and he laughed.

Outside, Ken led Paula by the arm to his car.

"Oh what a beautiful convertible," she said as they passed Excalibur. "Isn't that Steve Clayton's car?"

"Don't even breathe on it," he said nervously, "just look ahead at the pretty Dodge Charger."

The band played 'Light My Fire' by the Doors as Steve and Sue swung around each other, singing along face to face.

As the song played, more voices around them screamed out the lines also, as they all swayed, swung, flung and spun together in the intoxication of the amplified music.

For Steve and Sue, music was a natural high and one that they had always loved to share. In the outside world of events, it carried them to a private place. It offered shelter from the storms of an often chaotic world and let them live in One Heart as they dreamed.

They always played music when she worked on her drawings and he wrote his poems or short stories. They had secret artistic souls and each inspired the other but here, on the dance floor, the music was just for the pure delight of it.

As the evening grew late many couples began leaving. Some to head home, while others just went to be alone. For them, it was to be a night visit to the lake, to talk, hold each other and to dream.

Joe and Cindy left for a drive as Steve went to the cloakroom for Sue's sweater. As he was putting it over her shoulders, Ken and Paula reappeared in the entrance way.

"Oh, is it over?" she asked, hanging on Ken's arm.

"No, there are still a lot of couples dancing," Sue answered, then watched as Paula began fixing her hair and checking herself over in the cloakroom mirror.

"Oh great," she said turning to Ken. "Kennie-Bear, I'll go and get us something to drink, then I'll be right back." She smiled at them, and then headed inside.

"Where in the world have you two been?" Steve asked, prying a bit as he noticed that Ken's tux was a little out of sorts.

"We were out in the car," he said. "In MY Charger!" he added quickly glancing over at Sue.

"Well, you just had to take out the other twin, didn't you?" she asked with a shake of her head.

"Well you know," he mumbled out. "But let me tell ya, she's nothing like her sister. She's wild and a little bit scary."

He paused a second. "You know what?" he whispered, "I think I like it."

"You are too much," Steve said with a half laugh.

"Well, let me go get her," he said. "I promised to take her up to Lake Hopatcong and teach her about the submarine races."

"Kenski please," Sue said, "don't ever change. You are the constant we can always measure our lives by."

"Okay," Steve said as he put his hand on Ken's shoulder, "but I have a feeling that by tomorrow, you may need me to help you get to your feet."

"Yea," he said staring over a Paula, "maybe so."

As they waited for the valet to get the car, Sue leaned on his arm.

"Tired?"

"Oh no, not a bit," she answered smiling. "Let's go and make a wish on the bridge."

"My very thought," he said smiling back into her eyes.

They drove to the wooden bridge and parked. He came around and helped her out so she wouldn't catch her gown on anything. A full moon brightly lit their way and its beams danced in glistening starbursts across the silent lake as they walked the bridge.

It was a warm mid-May evening. Several crickets were calling to each other, but then stopped as they heard the footsteps. The treetops were still, as was the very air itself. It was as if the island was holding its breath.

He stood behind with his arms around hers, as they stared silently together at the peace about them.

"It's been a magical night," she said, "thank you."

"We're the magic Love," he whispered as he kissed the back of her neck lovingly.

"I love who we are together," she sighed caressing his hand.

He smiled saying, "Two clouds, but one sky. Two stars, but one heaven. Two souls, but One Heart." He turned her face gently. "And two lips, but only one breath shared." Then he kissed her.

"I want to share everything with you Angel, forever."

"You do," she sighed with melting eyes.

"Do you remember the first song we danced to?"

She smiled with a glow and then began to hum it. He listened, then sang the words into her ear softly.

"I wanna make all your dreams come true," he said, "because your dreams are my dreams."

He got down on one knee, opening a small box from his breast pocket and he held up the ring to her saying,

"Of all the riches to be found in life,
none dare compare to the one called wife."

He looked up at her as she stood with the full moon behind her, causing it to glow all around her like an aura.

"I love you Sue, as a flower loves the warmth of the sun
and the moon, the brightest star beside it.
I offer my life as a promise you can hold true,
and this ring a token, of that love and life for you."

He took the ring out of the box and said, "Will you honor me with a yes and marry me?"

"Oh Steve," she said as she slowly moved to touch the perfectly round diamond. Its purity brought the moon's rays up into her tearing eyes as she spread her fingers for him to slip it on.

"Yes," she answered softly. Then, as she fully realized the moment she cried out, "Yes! Oh Yes! Of course I'll marry you!"

As he rose up to her, she saw the light from above shining in his eyes and they kissed as if for the first time.

"Oh Sweety," she cried out through the tears, "you just keep giving me more reasons. I love you so much. I will love you forever!"

"Forever, I promise Angel," he whispered as he picked her up in his arms securely.

"You are a gift from God that no man deserves," he said as he held her beneath the starry heavens. Then spun around and carried her across the bridge and through the gate to their Excalibur.

"We need to tell someone," she said to him as he started the car. She looked at her watch and saw how late it was getting.

"I don't think I can wait until tomorrow, please," she said with urgency in her voice.

They thought for a few moments, then, "Uncle Chuck!" they cried out together.

"He'll just be closing up now," he told her.

Her face lit up. "Go Babe!"

They pulled out to Lake Shore Drive and roared up the hill towards town. As they came to the light, they could see him locking the front door and they blew the horn several times. He turned around staring, and then waved as he recognized the car. They drove over and into the drive entrance calling to him.

"Hey!" he said, then asked, "How was your night? Did you have a good time?"

"The best! Look!" she cried out, holding up her hand as she ran.

"Easy there," he said, "don't get hurt."

When she reached him he saw the ring. "Oh honey, I'm so happy for you," he said hugging her tight. "God bless you both."

"I can hardly believe it," she said.

He took her left hand and closed it tightly saying, "Remember, hang on to what is real."

"I once almost threw it away but for you," she said softly. "You helped me to keep believing. Thank you."

He walked over and shook Steve's hand.

"Congratulations," he said, "and you take real good care of that lady, you hear me?"

"Yes sir, I will."

"Have you told your folks yet? "

"No, it just happened," she replied, "but I'm so glad that you were the first to know. We love you."

"And I love both of you, but wait a second," and he went over to the coke machine. He got out his key and opened it, then took out three bottles.

"A toast, to the most precious couple I know. May your lives be full of love for one another forever."

They held the three bottles up high touching. "One for always!" Uncle Chuck said as they drank.

"Let me break it to my folks gently," she said to him as they pulled into her driveway.

"Of course," he replied with a smile.

The lights were still on in the living room as they got out of the car. Her mom came to open the door when she heard the doors close. As soon as Sue saw her, she ran up the steps.

"Is everything all right?" she asked concerned.

"No," Sue cried out, "everything is perfect!" and she showed her the ring.

"Oh Baby, I'm so happy for you," she said, then reached out to hug Steve as he came up from behind.

"Your dad's watching television," she said excited.

"May I speak with him alone?" he asked.

"Sure," she replied, letting him go in while she and Sue continued to hug out on the porch steps.

He went into the living room and saw her father sitting in his chair.

"May I talk with you for a moment?"

Her dad turned off the television, and then motioned for him to sit.

"I've asked your daughter to marry me tonight and she said yes, but I would like to ask for your permission and blessing."

Steve paused, studying his face, as Mr. LaRosa stared into his eyes in silence.

"I know how important it is that she finishes college first and have a career doing something she loves. She will, I promise. We'll both be in careers we love, using the gifts God has given us, then we plan on getting married."

"I see, and what'll happen when a child comes?" he asked in a 'must-need-to-know' tone.

"We do plan on having a family. When and if we're blessed with a child, there isn't any reason why she shouldn't be able to continue working her career. She has so much to give. We're both looking forward to sharing in the raising of our children together. We know that the family must always come first, and for me, that means her happiness as well as that of the children. Our home will be built on love."

He got up and went over to get his lighter and the cigar Steve had given him earlier. He was silent a moment as he lit it up.

"You're a fine man Steve and I can't think of anyone I could trust her happiness with more. I'd like to believe that you will always be there for her and make the kind of life together that she deserves."

He held out his right hand and took Steve's. "You promise me, as you will later before God," he said with a firm grip, "to always love her with all of your heart."

"Oh that I promise," he said smiling. "Your daughter is now my life, as she has been yours. Thank you for such a wonderful gift and trusting me with her care. It means everything to both of us that you believe in us."

Frank smiled. "I'm glad to be able to give my blessing for my daughter's marriage to someone like you," he said and then they shook.

He then turned and went to the door. "Come inside," he told the ladies, "and welcome my new son to the family."

"Oh Dad, I love you," Sue cried with relief as she ran to hug him. "Thank you Daddy, oh thank you!"

"Well, it's getting late," her father said. "Why don't we all say goodnight and we'll talk more in the morning." He led her mom up the stairs, leaving the two of them alone at the door.

"Goodnight," he said as he kissed her.

"I was so worried waiting out there," she confessed. "What did you say to him?"

"It's a guy-thing," he answered smiling, "but mostly that I loved you."

She smiled and let out a short laugh.

"Oh, this has been the most magical night I could have wished for. I love you Steve and I'll see you tomorrow at church."

"I love you too, and I'll see you later in my dreams Angel."

He kissed her once again and then went to the car as she waited by the door until he flashed his lights. She blew him a kiss then went back inside and stood silently caressing her ring.

"I know I don't deserve it Lord but thank you for this love. I promise to make it shine forever." She went up to bed, falling asleep with the ring over her heart.

Chapter Ten
"Graduation: A time to reflect, a time to envision."

As the senior class of 1969 sat in rows, girls on the left, boys on the right, they smiled towards each other.

A major milestone was about to be acknowledged and they would soon be looked upon as men and women from that day forward. Family sat proudly behind them as they waited to hear their children's names about to be called.

First came the faculty speeches, then the awards, followed by the valedictorians speaking of their class's accomplishments, hopes and dreams.

As it came near an end, a last minute guest speaker arrived and was invited up to the podium. It was the deputy mayor.

"I am so glad to be here today. There are some things that deserve the respect of our attention and I am proud to be here for this one."

He pointed out into the body of students.

"This High School has set the standard for the entire county of Morris on how its students are to conduct themselves both in and out of school. It has inspired a community to aspire to becoming a family.

"It is you as role models," he said focusing on the parents, "and your influence that has helped to bring about these dynamic changes we find here today in these halls. It is a legacy I hope will be carried on for years to come. A place where students respect each other and their teachers. Where every student from freshman to senior can come and feel safe and welcomed.

This class of 1969 here today has forged that legacy. Together with the board of education and this faculty I will do all I can to see that it continues and grows."

He opened his briefcase and placed a box from it onto the podium.

"I wish I could give each and every one of you a personal acknowledgment, but I believe that is already inside you all. What I do have here is a plaque I want to present to this school and is dedicated to the students of your class who started the momentum of this team effort. I would like the following students to please come up here, Joseph Reily, Kenneth Tomineski, Susan LaRosa and Stephen Clayton."

They all stood and looked at each other as they came forward and assembled in line on stage.

"Here are the spearheads of your legacy. Here ladies and gentleman, are The Four American Musketeers!"

There was a standing ovation for them as they smiled out into the audience. The Mayor then presented them with the plaque for their school. They, in turn, handed it to Sue as the applause subsided for them to give a few words.

Sue nervously urged Steve to step forward with her to talk.

"On behalf of ourselves," he said, "the graduating class here and the school, we all thank you for this honor. In all honesty though, the inspiration first came from this young woman who taught us to stand beside one another, long before it was popular to do so."

He smiled at Sue and joined in the applause as he urged her up to the mike.

"Most of you who know me also know I am one who, like my foil, comes to the point."

There was laughter and applause for a moment.

"So, if there has been only one thing that this foursome has learned together, it is that 'What you leave behind is just as important as what you strive towards'. We hope it is what you have learned from us also.

I see here on this plaque we have a new school motto. It makes us proud to have helped leave this behind as an echo for all time."

She held up the plaque which read, 'ALL FOR ONE, AND ONE FOR ALL!'.

"God bless you class of 1969!"

The applause continued until they were able to return to their seats. Steve held her hand as they walked and winked to her smile. The closing was the handing out of their diplomas and when each musketeer received theirs, the house went into an uproar and each waved.

Finally, they moved the tassels of the caps to the opposite side and then all let out a cheer as threw their caps into the air.

Outside, all the families were busy hugging and taking pictures. Several wanted a group shot of the four musketeers, so they kept getting calls to regroup for another picture.

Steve and Sue were at last ready to go over to her house. Her parents had prepared a backyard cookout for a combination graduation and engagement party for the two of them. Of course, both families and friends were invited as well.

They said goodbye to everyone, then got into the Le Mans. He put the top down, as Sue took both of their graduating tassels and hung them from the rear view mirror. Joe, Ken and Cindy said they had parties at home also, but would stop by later for the engagement end of their get together at Sue's. All waved as they pulled out onto the street and they drove down Vail Road.

"It feels funny leaving for the last time, doesn't it?" she asked.

"It sure does. Summer coming or not, it's hard to believe we won't be here next year."

"I can hardly believe that next year both of us will be in college together. I guess in some ways it'll still be the same," she said thinking about it.

"As long as we're together it will," he said, "no matter how hard some of the classes are."

"Don't worry," she said, "when you come in the spring, I'll be there to help you with the math."

They stopped off at the Spa for a few minutes to see the Goldbergs. As they started to get out of the car, Mama came out the front door waving.

"We were hoping to see you today," she cried out, "Papa has made something special, come see!"

Steve held the door for Sue as they entered peering around.

"Now just wait right there," Mama G. said and she went to the kitchen.

As they stood, they could hear the couple talking in back, then Papa came out carrying a huge sheet cake with 'CLASS OF 69' on top and four foils crossed in the center.

"We actually made it for the whole senior class when they come in," Mama said, "but you two are the first so here, you must have a slice!"

"Oh Papa," Sue said smiling, as she slapped Steve's hand for trying to taste the icing, "it's beautiful! You two shouldn't have gone to so much trouble. "

"What trouble? I love to bake, besides, we love all of you and we owe you all so much."

"You owe us?" Steve asked. "It's the both of you that have given so much. You have always made this place a second home, so we thank you."

Mama smiled as she cut out two pieces.

"Here, you have some and I will get your special order cokes."

They ate, talked and then thanked them again as other students came in and had cake with their orders. When they left and went up to the LaRosa Ranch, as Steve often referred to it, they were just in time to help her parents with the food.

Steve helped cooking burgers and hot dogs with her dad on two grills. Sue worked with her mom in the kitchen on the salads and with Grandma on the desserts. There was so much food that more tables had go come out of the garage to hold it.

As they continued to work guests kept on arriving. Steve's family, friends and several relatives also came for the celebration. A special table had been set up in the yard to place any gifts on, so the two could sit together later and open them.

Steve's mom went right to the kitchen to help out, as his siblings ran around the yard playing horseshoes and bad mitten. Some of the adults enjoyed a game of boccie ball in the far corner of the yard, while others just sat talking.

When Janice arrived alone and sat under a tree by herself in the yard. Sue spotted her and went over to take a break and talk.

"I'm so glad you could make it," she said, "it is a perfect day for a barbecue, isn't it?"

"Yes, it's really nice out today," Janice replied in a low tone.

"Isn't Walter coming?"

"No, he said that he had to go straight home from graduation."

"Oh, too bad," Sue said, noticing that she just didn't seem herself. "Are you all right?" she finally asked.

"I'm fine," Janice answered, "but I was hoping that we could talk later?"

"We could talk now. They can do without me for awhile," Sue answered concerned.

"No, later would be better, after everything has quieted down."

"Okay, sure."

The two watched the activities about them for a few minutes, then "Come on Janice, help me with the drinks," and she coaxed her to go inside.

Sue showed her where the pitchers and glasses were as she brought out the punch mixes.

"I have cans of assorted sodas in the fridge for the ice chest. We can put the flavored ice pops in with them for the kids," she said as she opened the mix and put it into the first pitcher.

"The finger sandwiches over there on the counter are for the kitchen help only, us," she told her. "Grandma made them and they are sooo good. It's a secret recipe, try one!"

Sue knew something was troubling her and did her best to keep her busy until they could talk alone later. Within a short while it seemed to be working as the two kept rushing to keep the drinks coming out for the guests.

"Burgers and dogs are ready," Steve called out, "bring a plate and who wants theirs with cheese?" The kids all ran up first as he panned out one after another to the lineup.

"The chicken and steaks will be done shortly," Mr. LaRosa said, as he checked under the second grill cover. "Who wants theirs well-done?" and he counted the raised hands.

Sue had sent the moms and her grandmother out of the kitchen to relax for awhile at a table in the shade. She and Janice stayed to finish bringing out the last of the salads, then cleaned up the kitchen messes before joining them.

After everyone seemed full, they resumed with the yard games again. She got Steve and Janice to organize some games for the kids to play. Each child got to win some small bags of penny candies and little prizes.

They did sack and relay races, tried hula hoop spinning and played guessing games. All three even joined in a try at 'Twister'.

The little ones laughed at how they tried to stay up with kids hanging onto them for balance. In the end, all just fell in a pile of giggles.

At last the coffee and cakes came out.

The one her mom made for graduation was coconut. It stood three layers high, with two black grad caps that were actually candles. 'Congratulations' was written in blue icing and the year at the bottom.

The second, by his mom, was a chocolate iced sheet cake for the engagement. Their names were in two white hearts next to each other but not touching. There was an squiggly arrow through each heart with Love Everlasting across the bottom. It had one red and white striped candle on it that sat over the two hearts.

The moms each lit the candles of their cakes and called them both to blow them out. On the count of three, they blew out the two grad ones, but when they tried the one for the engagement cake, it kept on reigniting.

Steve's little brother laughed.

"I bought the candle, it is one of those that won't ever go out!"

"We'll see," Steve said as they tried again and again.

"I can do it!" cried out some of the younger ones and they all blew over and over, but it would not go out. Sue laughed as they all tried in vain.

Finally his mom took it off the cake, dipped it in some water and laid it on a saucer. It sizzled but continued to glow.

Afterwards, they all gathered around the gift table as the two opened the boxes and cards. They showed everyone each gift as it was unwrapped, most of which were serving sets ranging from a cream and sugar bowl, to flatware and even a punch set. They thanked each person for their gift. They also received cards with cash, a check or a savings bond, all of which went for her hope chest.

They had saved an unusually colorful box for last. It was from Joe and Cindy. As Sue finally got the wrappings off and lifted the lid, she paused to take a breath. She carefully lifted out the most gorgeous candy dish she had ever seen. It was crystal, with woven patterns of colorful hand painted wild flowers all around. It had the scene of a lake in the background with wild ducks flying beneath some clouds, even the wooden bridge where they became engaged.

"Oh guys," she gasped, "it's our Island!" She paused to hold it up for all to see.

"It really is," Steve agreed as he studied its detail.

"How in the world did you ever find this?" she asked them.

"My uncle," Cindy answered, "he has a shop out in Washington and this is what he makes. Joe and I took pictures of the Island and sent them to him, he did the rest."

"It certainly is a one of a kind gift to treasure," her mother remarked.

"A gift forever," Sue said in awe as she turned it round and round.

"One last thing," Joe said, "look at the bottom."

Sue turned it over carefully to reveal a sword with the letters EXCALIBUR stamped across its blade.

"We'll never forget this," Steve finally told them as he watched Sue getting emotional.

"I love you guys," she at last could say and quickly hugged them both.

It was about five O'clock when the last of the guests were leaving. The couple said their goodbyes, and then went to help with the last of the cleaning up. Janice was rinsing dishes for the dishwasher as Sue came in the kitchen, while Steve carried tables back into the garage.

"Do you want to talk now?" she asked her.

Janice lowered her head, and then turned to her with watery eyes. "I'm late," she said, "I haven't had my period."

Sue went to her and held her. "Does Walt know?"

"Yes, I told him and he won't talk about it. I call and he won't come to the phone. I go over to his house and he won't see me. Even today, he wouldn't even look at me the whole time, then he just left and went straight home. He hates me, I know it!"

Sue held her close whispering, "Shh, he doesn't hate you. When did it happen?"

Janice was silent, then answered, "On Prom night. I had said no for so long, but that night was so magical, you know?"

"Yes it was."

They heard Sue's parents coming so they dried her tears and went back to cleaning.

"Mom, would it be all right if Janice slept over tonight?"

"Of course."

Sue turned and said, "Come on, I'll drive you home to pick up what you need to stay." Janice nodded and Sue went to find Steve for the keys to the car.

"We'll be back soon," she told him.

"You want me to come?"

"Oh no, I'd love to have you stay and keep helping my dad finish up, would you mind?"

"Sure, but don't be too long all right?"

"I won't. Love ya, bye."

The two got into the car and drove off down the street.

"We've been going together for almost two years," Janice told her choked up. "He always wanted to do it, but I just kept saying no. I wanted to so many times, I loved him so much, but I kept telling him we had to wait.

It was so hard to say stop. It got harder each time to know where to draw the line. I was afraid I'd lose him if I didn't give in a little more each time, you know?"

She pulled over and parked in a dead-end street.

"Yes," Sue answered holding her hand, "Oh yes, I know. Sometimes you just want to scream it hurts so bad."

Janice looked at her crying. "I got to the point where I wasn't strong enough to say no anymore, I wanted him just as badly." Sue pulled her head down onto her shoulder and they cried together.

"I know, I know," she kept telling her, "I got to that point too. It ripped at my heart until finally I pleaded with him that I needed all of his love."

Janice raised her head and asked, "So you both have …?"

"No, we didn't," she answered with a sigh, "but we came real close to it. So very close," she repeated softly.

"I know you love Walt like I love my Steve, so I know that he will come to you. You just have to keep your faith in that love."

"What about this baby?" she asked.

"Hey," Sue whispered, "you don't even know if there is a baby yet, right? So, let's pray right now together and leave it in God's hands."

They both lowered their heads and blessed themselves. Then Sue said, "Father, we ask that you forgive us for our weaknesses and our trespasses against Thee. Help us now. Send us the strength to do Your Will, whatever it is, for you know better than us what is best. We ask this in Jesus' name, Amen."

Janice looked up at her with tears and said, "I love you Sue."

"And I love you," she said with a smile, "and so does He."

After a few moments, she started the car and drove her home to get her things.

As they pulled into the driveway, they saw Walt standing by his car. Janice got out slowly, and then he walked over near her.

"Oh honey," he said with a pleading look, "please forgive me. I am so sorry for the way I've acted. I was scared. My scholarship for college, the plans I had …The plans we had."

He stopped and lowered his head a moment.

"I was just riding around and suddenly I felt so selfish as I realized how scared you must be alone. I love you and whatever happens I need to be there with you, please."

Janice started to cry, then ran to him.

"I love you so much," she said, as they held each other tightly. "I don't even know for sure if I am," she whimpered.

"Then we'll wait and see it through together, I promise," he told her with a kiss.

She looked over his shoulder at Sue in the car, seeing her eyes closed and head bowed.

"Thank you Father for Your love of us," Sue said humbly, "and for hearing our prayer and sending us the strength we needed."

The two came over to her as they heard her say softly, "Amen."

"We're going off to talk," Janice said. "Thank you for being my friend."

"Always," she replied smiling, then she backed out onto the street and headed for home.

When she came through her front door, she called out for Steve.

"He's out in the garage," her mom said. "Your father asked him to rearrange some things to make room for the car."

She went and found him lifting boxes and chairs up out of the way of the garage entrance. His face was sweaty with smudges of dirt on it from the work. He turned and smiled when he finally noticed her standing there.

"Oh man," he said, as he got out his handkerchief to wipe his face and opened the garage door for some air, "I must look a sight."

She went over to him without a word and kissed him long and hard.

"Wow, what was that for?"

She laid her head on his shoulder, hugging him tightly.

"It was a thank you."

Chapter Eleven
"A Tear in the Tapestry."

Steve came into the plaza headquarters and signed in on the duty rooster, then he headed for the locker room to get changed into his security uniform.

"Hey Clayton go to the Inspector's office," the Sergeant called from the desk. "Matthews wants to see you before you report for post duty."

He headed up the stairs and down the hall to the last office door and knocked.

"Come in," came a voice and he entered. "Close the door please," the Inspector said, "and have a seat." Steve went and sat in front of his desk quietly.

"I've been reading your daily officer reports and those of the site Captain. It seems he holds you in some high regard in conduct, attendance, punctuality and says you are well liked by the client there."

He walked over to a table and poured himself a cup of coffee and motioned if he also wanted a cup.

"No thank you," Steve replied politely.

"I see here in one of your reports that there was an incident at the plant while you were on duty on September 25th at 2230 hours. A breaking and entry attempt?"

"Yes sir."

"According to your report, and your Lieutenant's, it says that you encountered two intruders during rounds. They were stealing large platinum and copper wire spools and you witnessed the loading of these onto a non-company truck. The reports go on to say that you confronted them, were attacked, yet overcame both. You then, it says, made a citizens arrest. You cuffed them together and brought them to the gate house to be held for the police."

"Yes, that's correct."

He paused to sip from his cup.

"Why did you confront them? You know it's our policy to observe and report."

"Yes sir, but they saw me as I came around a corner and stood only a few feet away. I recognized one of them as an off-duty worker and started questioning why he was on the site and about the unauthorized vehicle. They both then jumped at me without answering, so I had to defend myself."

The Inspector sat down looking at the reports again.

"According to this they both had crowbars, but it doesn't say here how you overcame both?"

Steve adjusted himself in the chair.

"There were several three-foot lengths of thin rod iron on a table next to me, so I grabbed one to use."

"You fended off an attack of two men with crowbars using a thin three foot rod?"

Steve smiled. "Yes, it made a fine foil."

"A what?"

"A light-weight sword," he answered. "I was on the fencing team in high school. Besides, their attack was so disorganized and clumsy that I was easily able to disarm them within a couple of moments."

Inspector Matthews lay back in his chair eying him silently.

"A regular Errol Flynn hey?"

"A Musketeer actually," he answered, "it was on my employment application."

"Well," he said sitting upright, "I see that your Captain was correct when he told me you were a rare breed in this business. Tell you what. I am putting together a new unique team of security officers for very special duties."

He showed him a sheet listing some of the duty expectations, from a folder on his desk.

"The training is advanced and takes about three weeks at the regular pay rate until you graduate the courses. It then would increase substantially and give you a new rank of Captain. Of course it involves some overnight traveling and a little nerve at times for this type of duty. Do you think you might be interested?"

Steve read the list over as he thought about the offer.

"I have to tell you that I plan on entering college classes in the spring over at the County College of Morris for two years, before transferring to a four year one."

"Okay," he replied, "not a problem. If you decide to do this and after you get some field experience, then perhaps I can arrange to make you an assistant instructor for these classes here at the plaza. How's that sound?"

"That would be great," he answered with a smile. "When can I start?"

He passed his training and then was assigned with a team of other officers to be taken down to defend a manufacturing plant in Camden County, New Jersey.

It was a wildcat strike and their job was to secure the grounds from the strikers picketing, as well as protect all office workers on the site. It seemed like the perfect opportunity for the team to test its new skills.

Sue was a bit concerned as he told her about it.

"Where exactly is this place?" she asked.

"We're not told for security reasons," he answered, "just that it is in south Jersey for sure."

"Will you be gone long?"

"As long as the strike lasts I guess."

He saw her face and said, "I'll call you everyday, I promise."

"It sounds dangerous," she remarked, "is it, really?"

"No, it's just people striking for better benefits and such, our job is just to protect the office workers and the grounds. There will be over twenty of us there, plus supervisors, and besides, I need the money for college."

"I know," she said softly, "but still, please be careful."

"I will," he said with a kiss on her forehead.

The team was brought down by an unmarked bus the next day. When they arrived, they could see that each gate had over thirty picketers or more. They got off and split into five teams of four each. His team had to enter through gate three.

As they approached the entrance the picketers turned on them. They shouted in their faces, intimidating them verbally any way they could to turn them back. They moved focused through the angry bodies without saying a word. When they reached the fire barrel some fifteen feet within the grounds they relieved the guards from their post.

"The company hasn't gotten a court injunction yet to limit the number of picketers per gate but it's in the works," one of the guards said as he was relieved from his shift.

"So far," said another, "there have only been a few minor incidents. We logged them in our reports for you to read over."

They thanked them and then took their positions for the next shift of twelve hours.

The first day went by with only more minor incidents. Picketers banged on the car doors of office personnel as they were escorted through the gates. Attempts to harass the officers continued, but all stayed composed.

He called Sue after he got off duty at eight O'clock in the morning from his motel room.

"Everything went fine," he told her, "just nonsense type things that were to be expected." She was just relieved to hear his voice and let him ease her anxieties about the whole thing.

"Sleep well," he said, "I love you, and I'll be home before you know it."

"Will you call tomorrow again as soon as you get off?" she asked.

"Just as soon as I hit the bed," he promised and they kissed goodnight into the phone.

The next day, an office person was working late until almost midnight. She called the guard gate and said she was ready to leave by gate three. The supervisor radioed the men stationed there to watch for the car. As the green Buick appeared from the lower parking area Steve stepped up to meet it.

"Just follow us as we walk along side you and go nice and slow until you are out in the street," he said to the young lady. He led her up to within five feet of the gate, then stepped to the side of the car as it continued to move forward.

About halfway through the ocean of bodies, one picketer threw himself against her driver's window yelling obscenities at her. She panicked and her foot slipped hard onto the gas pedal, causing her to suddenly bump several bodies with her front bumper. Within seconds, the car was covered with screaming picketers trying to open her doors and banging on her windows.

Steve and the other officer ran to go between them and the car door, but suddenly a side window was broken and the door was opened. The woman screamed as she was being pulled out of the car and shaken by several workers yelling at her.

The other officer came to her first and tried to pull the hands off her, but they turned on him and knocked him to the ground. Steve climbed over the hood and grabbed her, then shielded her from the wild blows flying in the darkness. He pulled her coat up over her head as the other officer got to his feet and together, they worked their way back inside the gate.

As they made it to safe ground a bottle came hurling from behind, striking Steve in the back of the head as he was continuing to protect her. He fell to the pavement unconscious as the other officers came to help.

Sue was jarred from her deep sleep and sat up in bed.

"Steve!" she cried out. Her heart was pounding in the darkness and she ached as his face came to her mind.

She grabbed her phone and called his room number. It rang and rang, but no answer.

"Of course," she remembered hanging up, "he's working. It was just a dream," she said to herself. She laid back down to try and sleep again, but the feeling grew to numbness inside her.

The next morning she sat anxiously but no call came. Finally, at ten O'clock, she called his house and his mom answered.

"I just got off the phone with the company," she said, "they told me there had been an accident and he was at the hospital."

"What kind of accident?" she asked franticly, "Is he all right!——What did they say!"

"They didn't, they said they would call me back in about twenty minutes."

Sue asked her to stay there until she arrived. She grabbed the keys and ran out to Excalibur parked in front where he had left it for her.

"He's hurt Baby," she said as they drove over to his house. She trembled as she held the wheel but the car carried her safely to the drive.

As she came towards the door his mom opened it. "Did they call back?"

She shook her head. "Not yet, come have some coffee while we wait." It was over an hour before they got the call.

"Hello, Mrs. Clayton? This is Inspector Matthews, I am at the hospital now and he is resting."

"What happened to him?"

Sue leaned near her as she spoke.

"He was protecting a client and got hit with an object. He is still unconscious but stable and has a few stitches. They feel he will be fine, but want to keep him overnight in case he has a concussion."

"Thank you Inspector. I will be coming down this afternoon to see him…Yes, goodbye."

She hung up the phone as Sue asked, "Couldn't we talk to him?"

"He's unconscious," she replied, "but they said he should be fine."

"Let me drive you down, please."

"Of course, we'll go as soon as my mother-in-law gets here to watch the kids."

178

It took about three hours for the drive to the hospital. Along the way they talked to calm each other.

"I know he'll be fine," his mom kept saying.

"I want him back home," Sue said. "I didn't plan on him becoming some kind of a police officer or getting hurt like this. No, he can come back and do his old job in the garage where it's safe."

When they arrived the front desk gave them directions to his room.

They quietly opened the door and found him asleep, so they sat on each side of his bed. His mom held his hand and Sue kissed his forehead.

"We're here Babe," she whispered but he didn't move.

His mom went out to find his doctor as she stayed by his side talking to him. She saw his blue uniform lying on the dresser, his blue hat with a shiny badge on front and the red stain at the back. She cried holding his hand to her face.

"I love you," she said over and over. "Please be all right."

His mom returned with the doctor and Inspector Matthews.

"He was hit with a bottle in the back of his head," the doctor told them," and I had to give him six stitches. He's stable, doing fine, and he should come around anytime now."

"He's a good man," the Inspector said, "he kept a young lady from serious injury."

Sue was silent, not turning from the bed as she held his hand.

"You can both be proud of him."

"Proud?" Sue asked. "I was already proud of him before this. He has nothing to prove to me. Why didn't you tell him this was dangerous work?"

"Miss, this was an accident. This kind of thing doesn't happened all the time, it was brought on by a mishap."

She turned to him coldly adding, "And it could have gotten him killed. No, he's coming back with us, as soon as he's able."

"I'm very sorry," he said. "I'll stop back later."

It was around dinner, when she noticed him first showing signs of coming out of it. He moved his head and hands and moaned slightly at times. Sue called his name each time, but he didn't answer.

A nurse came in with some sandwiches and coffee for the two of them.

"I know it ain't much," she said, "but I could tell you two weren't about to leave."

"Thank you for your kindness," Sue said smiling.

"He'll be just fine baby," the nurse told her with a wink. "I can spot the tough ones when I see one, and honey, you got a bear there."

Sue smiled up again and then poured some coffee for the two of them.

Inspector Matthews came by the room again at nine pm, opening the door quietly. He saw Sue sleeping in the chair by the bed. His mom waved to him and they stepped out into the hall. As they talked, two uniformed guards approached and greeted them.

"This is Captain Kevin Hurley and Captain David Conners," Matthews said to her, "they work with your son."

"We were hoping to see him for a moment, if it's all right?"

"Of course," she said and led them in.

Sue awoke and saw the uniforms at the foot of his bed.

"You must be Sue?" one asked. "I'm Kevin and this is Dave. We work with your fiancée."

She sat up saying hello as they took her hand.

"He wasn't kidding when he said you were pretty," Dave commented lightheartedly to help break the tension.

A sudden intenseness filled her eyes. "Were you there when this happened?"

"I was," Kevin replied in a more serious tone. "If it weren't for him that poor girl might have really been hurt, me too probably."

She noticed he had a small bandage on the other side of his face.

"It just got a little crazy when the car accidentally bumped some of the strikers. I'm just glad we were both able to keep our heads and act fast enough."

"I'd want him by my side anytime," Dave said, "how's he doing?"

"He hasn't been awake yet," she said, "but when he does and is able, he's coming back home."

"Before the job is done?" they heard him say. Sue turned to see him smiling.

"Hi Angel," he said as she came to him, "sorry I scared you, but I'm fine."

"I'm fine too now," she said, "and as soon as we get you home, you can work with Chuck again on cars and forget all this."

"I've got to finish what I started," he said to her. "You know I've never walked away from anything left undone. Besides, I think I may be good at this."

She stared at him.

"I want you to come back, please."

"I will, as soon as the job is finished."

"Why are you being so pigheaded," she suddenly said in a louder tone, "you could have been killed!"

"And that young woman also," he replied with a firm tone, "if it weren't for us. I'm glad we were there."

He held out his hand to her saying softer, "It's my job and I'm not alone." He pointed to the others. "I work with the best. We can do what has to be done here, it's what we've been trained for, so don't worry."

She stopped talking, but he knew it wasn't settled between them yet.

Later, when everyone had left, she asked him again to quit.

"Sue, come here," he said softly and she got up and sat on the edge of the bed.

"I know this has been upsetting to you, but believe me, I'm not about to do anything I can't handle. They have trained us well. I love you and in the spring we'll be in classes together and I'll just be teaching this. That is what you wanted isn't it, for me to teach?"

She sat quietly a moment.

"I just want to know that you're safe," she finally said putting her head on his chest.

"I am. We watch each other's backs all the time. It's a trust we have with one another, like ours. I'm helping people and it makes me feel good, understand?"

"Yes, I do, but I want you to do something less dangerous for me. Please quit."

"I can't, besides, I need the kind of money I'm making here to be able to afford college by spring."

"Then do something else and start in the fall or the year after, I don't care when just not this!"

She turned to his mother. "Mom please, you talk to him."

"Steve, maybe we could refinance the house for your tuition and you could pay us back later as you went along. What do you think?"

"I think you and Dad are already overburdened. No, I'll pay my own way."

Sue got real upset. "Fine, have it your way!"

He got out of bed and began getting dressed into his uniform.

"What are you doing?" Sue asked.

"I'm reporting back for duty. I can still work the second half of my shift instead of leaving the others shorthanded."

"You're not up to it," his mom said. "Let them send someone else."

"I'm fine, besides, they don't have anyone else trained to do it and these guys need me."

"And we don't!" Sue cried out.

"I'll be fine, don't worry."

"I won't!" she yelled. "Go ahead and get your head knocked off again but I won't be here, I'm going home!"

She went out into the hall and cried as she headed for the stairs. She sat down in the main lobby trying to dry the tears that kept coming. When his mother found her, she asked if he had left and his mom nodded.

"Oh Mom," she cried, "what's happening?"

"He's become a man and a man has responsibilities he can't shirk, even when it hurts those he loves."

"I just want to go home," she said quietly.

The strike went on for over three more weeks and everyday he would call her, but she wouldn't answer her bedroom phone. He tried calling the main house number, but her mom said she was out or was not feeling well enough to talk.

Sue couldn't let go of her anger, or her fears, over the fact that he made this job more important than her feelings.

"I'll let him come to me," she kept saying to herself, as she was sure he'd miss her so much that he would quit and come home on his own.

As the weeks went by and he still stayed away, she grew more upset.

"How can he be so stubborn!" she asked out loud to his mom over coffee. "How can he not miss me as much as I miss him?"

"He calls you everyday, doesn't he?"

"Yes, but he knows that won't cut it. He knows I want him here and safe."

She crossed her arms and said, "Well I'm not giving in, he's wrong and I'll make sure he understands it."

It was two days later that he came home. The strike was over. He hugged his mom and sisters as he handed out some small gifts he had gotten for them.

"I tried calling Sue when the bus came into the Headquarters, but no answer. Have you seen her Mom?"

"Not for a couple of days now. Why don't you go over, she left your car here since we got back."

"Yea, I saw it."

He got showered and changed into some nice clothes, then drove up to her house. Her dad answered the door and let him in.

"She's up in her room," he said, "but she has been mad as a wet hornet over this job of yours."

"I know and I'm sorry, but I had to see it through."

Mr. LaRosa smiled saying he understood.

"Could you tell her I'm here?"

"Why don't you go up and knock yourself."

He went up to the second floor and paused in front of her door. He took a breath, then knocked.

"Who is it?"

"It's me."

"Go away."

183

"Sue open the door please, I want to see you."

"If you wanted to see me, you'd of been back long before this, now go away."

"Come Babe, we need to talk."

"Have you quit that job?"

"No, I have another assignment to go on this Thursday, so please, come talk with me." He listened, but no answer.

"Okay," he said grinning, "I'll just stay here until you come out." He pulled up a hallway chair and sat at the door. "You'll need the bathroom sooner or later."

"I just went," she said back.

"Look Babe, I'm sorry about all this. Can't we just talk it over?"

"Talk is cheap, I want action," she fired back through the door.

He thought a moment, then said, "The woman we helped, remember?"

There was silence.

"Well, her husband came to see us at the motel after one of our shifts."

"Did he thank you for being such a hero?" she asked with sarcasm in her voice.

"Well, he did come to thank us, right before he told us that she was two months pregnant and that both mother and baby were doing fine."

There was sudden silence, and then a moment later he heard the lock click. It opened slowly and he saw her crying. He stood up and she slowly came into his arms and put her head to his chest.

"Oh my God," she sighed. "Oh, my dear God."

They held each other without saying anything more for a long while.

"God bless you," she finally whispered from beneath the tears.

"Then am I forgiven?" he asked softly.

She looked up at him and said, "Please forgive me. I didn't understand how important your work can be and I'm so sorry."

"You're forgiven," he said with a smile but she kept looking into his eyes.

"Please help me feel it with a kiss."

He scooped her up in his arms and tenderly put his lips to hers.

"I love you Captain Clayton," she said with half-closed eyes, then tilted her chin upwards for another kiss.

"It's been weeks you know," she added.

It was in late November, after he had returned home from an assignment near West New York in Jersey, that he got the letter. He opened it slowly, read it and went for a drive alone.

Sue called for him after her last class, but his mother said he went out and hadn't returned. She drove her parent's car around then spotted Excalibur parked near the entrance to the wooden bridge. She parked and walked over it to see him standing alone out by the grassy knoll.

"A penny for your thoughts for the bridge," she said as she came up behind him.

He turned to her and held out his arm silently as she came to stand with him looking out over the lake.

"A rough assignment?" she finally asked.

"I love you," he said still gazing across the water.

"I love you too, what's wrong?"

He took the letter from inside his coat pocket and showed it to her.

"I have to report to the draft on Tuesday," he said.

She felt her heart sink, as she immediately thought of her cousin Billy. She grabbed his waist and pulled him close.

"Hold me," she said, "as tight as you can." He opened his coat and took her inside it as he wrapped it around her.

"It'll be all right," he whispered, "so I won't be going to college for two more years. I can still meet you at Ramapo and start there as a freshman and Uncle Sam with flip the whole bill, right?"

"Right," she answered holding back the tears, "and you can be the envy of the entire freshman class by dating a junior."

"There you go, that'll be hot."

She laughed softly.

"I guess all of this traveling you've been doing was just preparing me to handle you being gone for much longer." She smiled up at him and said, "I can wait. What's a couple of years more for things to be right, remember?"

They both fell to their knees as he gazed into her face.

"I love you," he said. "You are my life and I will be back, I promise you. No matter what the world throws at us, I will always get back up and come to you. We will be happy, together forever, I swear this before God."

They kissed and fell on their sides to the cold ground, still breathing life into one another.

"I will pray for you day and night," she said in between the hot kisses, "and light a candle every Sunday … and keep your picture next to my heart, and, and …"

She suddenly burst out with in loud cry. "Oh God why! Please Steve, promise to come back to me!"

"The gates of hell won't hold me Angel," he declared pulling her closer to his heart. She continued to dig her nails into his back, unable to stop crying, except to pause to kiss him.

He went to Fort Dix in Jersey for a total of eighteen weeks of basic training. This included advanced training for search and rescue. He was to be assigned to a combat support-re con platoon for MAAG (Military Adviser Assistance Group). It was with combined forces of Naval/Air Force Rescue.

He would come in by chopper and set up a fire line. Extract troops, retrieve dog tags from the dead, destroy weapons and any crept-o or radios.

He had spent Christmas with the family before leaving two days later to start his training. He and Sue went to both homes to celebrate. Hers on the Eve and his for Christmas morning. She wouldn't stay far from his side as he went visiting friends and family.

On their last night together, they went to the Village Spa early and Mama G. got them a quiet booth by themselves near the back. A fine lunch was prepared by Papa and it was at no cost. He also slipped them each a glass of red wine, even though they were underage.

"Here's to us," she said as they toasted the glasses.

"And to our time together again," he added. They took a sip and found it bitter tasting, but drank it all as they sat pressed against each other.

It was in mid-May that he was to leave and be flown out to Nam. On the day before, they spent it together alone. They drove around, playing their favorite tapes, then stopped for a brunch at Steward's drive-in before noon. They tried not to think about tomorrow, only today.

In late afternoon they went to the Island with a picnic basket she had prepared. They sat sharing tuna sandwiches, chips, moon pies and their dreams out on the knoll of flowers. Tomorrow was a million miles away on the other side of the bridge.

When they came back to her house in early evening, they went to the couch together talking. As he sat Sue lay against him, with her shoes off and legs curled beneath her and rested her head on his arm.

"I'm scared," she said at last quietly, as if by saying it made it more real, "aren't you?"

"Yes," he answered without hesitation, "I haven't been this scared since I had to fight Reily and Johnny.

"You mean the 'face to fist, clip-on tie match'?" she laughed under her breath as he reached immediately to tickle her side.

"Promise me something?" she asked.

"Anything you want," he answered with a kiss on top of her head.

"Promise that when you write me that you will tell me everything that's happening to you, the whole truth in detail. What you're going through and how you feel, everything. Please don't try and shield them from me. I need to know and share what you're dealing with, so promise?"

"I'll never hold back anything from you, I promise, and you do the same."

"I will," she sighed softly, trying not to think about what might happen.

Her parents overheard them from the kitchen as it became quiet when the dishwasher stopped running. Her mom opened it up and started to remove the dishes, then choked up and began crying. Frank got up from his newspaper and put his arm around her.

"It's just not right," she cried softly. "Why Frank? First Billy and now him. Why the good ones? Why the ones we love and need so much?"

He pulled her head to his shoulder as he held back his own tears. "It'll be all right, we have to have faith June."

As she raised her head to look up at him, he could see the loss already in her eyes.

"If he dies, she will too," she whispered. "I know it Frank, it will kill her."

He held her face, still fighting back his own feelings, and said, "She's a strong young, Catholic woman, she gets it from us. No matter what happens she'll accept God's Will in her life."

"I know," she replied and then turned to continue with the dishes. He kissed her cheek, then put on his reading glasses and went back to his paper.

She stared towards the living room as she wiped the spots off of the glasses before putting them away into the knotty pine cabinet. She listened as their voices came through the archway. They were voices of joy, of hopes and dreams, of love and tenderness. They were the sounds of life, the sounds of the heart.

"I know," she repeated to herself, as she went to place the last two glasses into the dark cabinet, then slowly closed it. "I know," she muttered a final time.

Later, when her parents came to check on them, they were both fast asleep on the couch. Sue was lying with her head resting on his chest and under his arm, while Steve's head leaned against hers.

Her father moved to wake them.

"No Frank," her mom said, "they'll be fine there. Let them have this time together."

He nodded and went upstairs as she went over and put a comforter across them both. Sue stirred slightly but did not wake up, only readjusted her head on his chest with a sweet sigh of contentment. June smiled as she knelt and lightly touched each on the arm.

"I pray that He will bless and watch over you both," she whispered. She reached and turned off the lamp as she walked quietly to the staircase and paused.

"I love you," she said softly, as the moonlight through the window held them amidst the surrounding darkness.

Sue wanted to drive him down to be flown out but he asked her to stay. "I want to remember you here at home," he said. "And I want you to keep Excalibur."

"Don't say that," she replied in a tone of fright. "The car will stay in storage in your family garage, waiting until you come home."

He agreed and she took the keys to give to his father who, with the rest of the family, had driven up to her house to see him off.

He kissed his mom and sisters, then hugged his little brother and his dad. When it was time for him to get into Joe's car and leave, Sue walked out to the Chevy with him and they kissed.

"Please, just stay alive," she begged, "that's all you have to do and come back to me as you promised."

"I will," he answered gazing into those beautiful brown eyes, "cause you're what I live for." Then she handed him something wrapped in tissue paper and told him to open it later.

"I love you more than the words can say," she whispered.

"But I still love to hear you say it," he replied and then softly sang some of their song in her ear. He reached down and kissed the open palm of her right hand, then rolled up her fingers to make a fist.

"Save this," he said, "in case of emergencies."

She raised the fist up over her heart, then hugged and gave him one last sweet kiss before closing the door. They smiled as she watched them drive off and saw him look back before the Red Chevelle vanished from sight.

As they drove, he opened the tissue paper and found the Pontiac key fob from his set of keys that he had given her. On the tissue was written, "As long as he has Excalibur, he cannot be defeated."

The families went inside to talk as she stood looking down the road, then she went up to her room. She grabbed the blue-eyed stuffed owl to hold on her bed. She moaned into her pillow for a few minutes, then went to her window and sat for the longest time staring up at the sky.

She watched the clouds as they drifted by, most as small as a wisp of smoke and noticed how each would fade quickly and be gone.

Then two touched and became one, solid and brilliant like a perfect pearl. It allowed the winds to carry it along, yet they were unable to change it as it continued its journey past the end of the world.

Her mother called her down for supper and she came to help her set the meal out. They said grace and then began eating.

Her folks were unusually quiet and her little sister asked, "Are you mad or something?"

"No Baby," her mom said, "we just will miss Steve is all."

"Oh, me too," she said, "but he promised to bring me back something neat." She looked over at Sue and asked, "Did he promise you something too?"

She smiled. "Yes he did, and he always keeps his promises."

Chapter Twelve

"The Green Weenies of D. L. Norton."

Shorty after his arrival, Steve was taken with other recruits by bus to their assigned posts and report to their superiors. He and three others were dropped off at a small airbase and told to report to a Sgt. Norton.

They walked around the barbed wired compound bewildered as to how to find him, since most of those they asked either ignored them or cussed them away. Finally, they just sat on their bags and watched the activity about them.

"Maybe if we sit here long enough," one said to Steve, "the war might pass us by."

"If only it could be that easy," he replied.

"I'm Tucker," he said, "Ladermier Tucker, from Georgia."

"I'm Steve Clayton, out of New Jersey."

The other two were called Patrick Huff, Maine and James Yeats, from central Texas.

"I wonder when it's time to eat around here?" Tucker asked.

"When you can do it while sleeping, working and killing," came a voice from behind. "Have you earned that piece of dirt you're sitting on? Then get the hell off it and follow me you bunch of weenies."

The Sergeant walked ahead of them saying, "I'm your team leader, Sgt. D. L. Norton. If you do what you're told, when you're told and exactly how you are told, then D. L. may mean Damn Lucky to some of you. Lucky enough that you might just survive out another day, get me?

The life expectancy in a chopper for a door gunner is about six minutes. If you get past that then your odds may get better. The same goes for the gun in a scout jeep and the newest weenies always get to man those M60 machine guns.

I am not your friend, so don't ever wave to me. I am not your nursemaid, so don't expect me to carry you unless you are shot. If you are dumb enough to get shot and make me carry you, then I may shoot you later myself. You left your nose-wipers back in boot camp, so tough it out."

He stepped up the pace.

"I am the one who, if you so much as breathe too loud when in the brush with me, will shoot your sorry behind. If you sneeze around me in the open, I'll cut off your nose and feed it to the weenie next to you, and do you know why? Because I will not let your green weenie ways bury me in this 'Not a Jersey beach' sorry excuse for dirt.

Now, maintain a safe fifteen feet behind me. It's time to check in with your platoon leader Lieutenant Hall but be prepared, he's not as nice and easy going as I am."

Four months later, it was Steve or Tucker meeting the new weenies with him. Yeats was blown to hell and Huff, dead from a snake bite.

Back home, Sue was writing her next letter to him as she sat in the student lounge. Cheryl, a classmate, came to her and said that she heard there was going to be a big anti-war demonstration in Morristown.

"You can ride with us if you want," she said excited as she tried to coax her to join the group going over.

"No thank you," Sue replied.

"It's our civic duty to protest against these things," she stated.

"I am not interested in going," she repeated.

Another girl overheard her and started putting her down for not wanting to participate.

"If you're not against the war, then you're for it," she said wearing a large button with a peace symbol on it, as well as others with anti-war slogans and the like.

Sue stopped writing and looked up at them.

"The man I love is over there, this very moment, fighting just to stay alive. I don't care about your politics, your anti-war marches or your make love-not war rantings. I won't disgrace what he is doing."

"He's only over there because of people like you not caring enough to put an end to this war," the girl said with an air of arrogance.

"How," Sue asked, "by wearing buttons? By making a 'Fun-To-Do' party out of it? I pray for him, that's my duty."

The girl said nothing more and turned away as Cheryl came to sit with her.

"I didn't know," she said, now looking at the ring on her finger. "How long has he been gone?"

Sue thought and answered, "Three months, three weeks and now, five days."

"What does he do?"

"Mostly he does search and rescue by helicopter and scouting out areas."

A couple of guys sitting behind them overheard her.

"My brother was over there," one whispered, "and he said that the guys in those choppers have a life expectancy of less than ten minutes! Can you believe that? You'd have to be nuts to do that."

Sue closed her eyes and said a silent prayer.

Cheryl turned around and said, "You're a jerk, you know that!" and the two hurried away. "I'm sorry about that," she said touching Sue's shoulder.

"It's all right, I hear things like that a lot. It doesn't change the fact that it's all in God's hands."

Sue went back to writing her letter to him as Cheryl got them coffee. When she finished, she kiss the page and sealed the envelope.

***

Steve and the others were in stand down, watching the fire base. After three weeks of continuous patrols he was looking forward to this one week of R&R. D.L. came up from behind and called to him and Tucker.

"Here you go Farm Boy," he said to Tucker as he handed him some mail.

"Oh man," he said as he grabbed the letters, "the whole family must have sent me one!" and he went off to start through them.

"Hey Clayton, I got one here for you too," and as he held out the envelope, he noticed the return address.

"So, you're from New Jersey too? How come you never said anything?"

"Didn't think you'd of much cared about a weenie's hometown," Steve replied.

"That's true, but where the heck is Lake Hiawatha?"

"A small town in the Northern part of Morris County," he answered, "and yours?"

"I come from further south, Flemington," he said with pride.

"Oh," Steve replied, "from fur coat country hey?"

He handed him the letter and asked, "What's the best thing about Jersey?"

Steve smiled and answered, "That it's separated by the Hudson from New York City."

D. L. let out a laughing roar.

"You're a Jersey boy all right!" Then he watched as he opened the envelope and smelled the letter. "From your girl, huh?" he asked.

"Yea, the most beautiful woman you'll ever see."

"She has to be, if she's Jersey born and bred," the Sarge added.

"Right down to the beach sand in her shoes."

"You both hit the beach a lot?" he asked.

"Every weekend that we can, even in the off season, just to smell the salt air and walk the boardwalk together."

"Which one?"

"We're partial to Seaside," Steve answered with a smile.

"That's a good one," he replied pointing his finger, "but me and Audrey Ann mostly go to Wildwood. We use to go to Asbury Park but it's not the same anymore, besides," he added grinning, "we like the great seafood down there."

Steve smiled and said, "As long as it's the Jersey shore, it's perfect."

D. L. looked at him and together they recited the New Jersey motto, "New Jersey and you, perfect together," and then they laughed.

194

He left him to his letter as he delivered the rest of the mail. Steve opened the folded pages and read.

My dearest Love,

I just started my third semester and the classes are wonderful. I am taking an Art class and for my first assignment I drew the view of the knoll from the wishing bridge, like in my earlier sketches, but this time with us there. I could only think of you with each stroke.

I miss you so My Love. I light a candle for you each Sunday and pray each day that you are safe. I often hear bad things about the war here with all of the protests, but I know you are only doing what you have to and I am proud of you as always.

Tell the others I pray for them also and give your Sergeant a chance, after all, he's from Jersey too.

Your family sends their love also and yesterday, your brother cleaned and waxed Excalibur while your dad checked the engine and ran it awhile. I think your brother loves it as much as we do.

Last Saturday, I went and just sat in the car and was thinking of you. I played a tape, the one of Jay and the Americans that you like so much. It made me dream of our last trip to the shore. I will always cherish when you…

Suddenly he stopped reading as there was a yell from the line. He put the letter into his pocket, grabbed his M14 rifle and ran up.

It was sniper fire coming from several tree lines and one man was hit. He laid down next to Tucker and both opened up on the smoke from the trees.

"Hey Seaside," D. L. cried out to him, "I need you to help me with getting this weenie back, he's got to weigh close to my ex-wife!"

Steve ran over with head low and grabbed the other arm and together they carried him away from the line.

"Is it bad Sarge?" the kid asked.

"I told you to keep your head down at all times, didn't I? No it's not that bad, so when we get out of range, I'm gonna shoot you in the other butt cheek for making us carry your sorry tail across this compound."

Later, when the shooting was over and they found several of the dead snipers, Steve went to find a quiet, safe place to rest and finish reading her letter.

As he came up to an empty ammo box, he adjusted it to sit on and her letter fell out of his pocket. A couple of new weenies were walking by and one picked it up. Steve turned and saw him with it as he was searching his pockets.

"Looking for this?" he asked with a Brooklyn accent.

Steve nodded and reached for it but he snapped it back.

"Hey man, not so fast," he said as he saw Sue's name on the return and then smelled the inside of the envelope.

"Great smell'in broad," he said holding it to the other's nose. "I think I'll keep this and dream about her tonight as I read, 'My dearest Love'."

That was as far as he read. He was suddenly kicked between the legs and dropped like a mercury reading in an ice bucket.

"What the hell?" he moaned as Steve took the letter from his hand and sat down to read it. He slowly got to his feet to hit him back as D. L. watched from behind.

"Hey you, weenie! What do you think you're doing?" a voice yelled from over his shoulder.

"I'm gonna kick his...," the recruit growled back but stopped when he felt the tip of a knife under his chin.

"If you ever touch anything of mine again," Steve said, "I'll carve you into briskets and mail you back as a roach coach special one piece at a time. Do you understand me Brooklyn?"

"I'd listen to him weenie, if you have any hope of seeing tomorrow," D. L. told him. "We Jersey boys don't have a great fondness for you New Yorkers to start with."

The recruit nodded as Steve put his knife away slowly, then sat again to read.

"I don't have to take this crap from you," he said through a dry throat. "I can report this to the Lieutenant, and even higher. My family knows a lot of important people. When I'm done, you won't even think about threatening anybody again."

Steve folded his letter, stood up and looked him in the eye.

"Jersey's surrounded by water on three sides and we're use to making a lot of waves, so don't mess with us.

As for you running your mouth," he added, "it will only get you killed here. If we don't show you what to do, when to do it and how to do it, you are dead. Guaranteed to be either shot by a sniper, eaten alive by animals, bitten by snakes and insects, or blown up where you stand."

He paused a moment, looking him coldly in eye. "Or maybe you'd prefer to be eating maggot rice with Charlie for breakfast tomorrow?"

He stepped even closer into his face and sniffed him.

"You're a green weenie and you reek of it! You are nothing and you know even less. You're a danger to yourself and everyone around you. If you don't respect us then you die, fast. Is that clear enough city dweller?"

Both only nodded, looking back at D.L., then quietly walked off.

Steve sat back down and finished reading his letter. He smiled, then took out his pad and pen to immediately start to write back to her.

Hello my Angel,

I got your letter, thank you. I miss you so much Babe, but I'm glad to hear that you are enjoying your classes.

As for me, I just had to scare the hell out of a pair of new recruits. If no one does, then they will remain a death trap to themselves and others around them and die within a week.

The few of us who do this to them only do so to save their lives and give them a chance to get back home. I don't enjoy it, but it is the only thing that works quick enough here to help them. By the way, Huff and Yeats are dead, they didn't learn quick enough. There's only me and Tucker left from the original bunch.

As for your drawing, it sounds like home to my heart and I look forward to seeing it as well as some of your advanced work to come when I get back. It's good to hear that…"

He looked at his watch and realized that he had to give relief on the line in two hours, so he decided to finish his letter to her later.

He, like everyone else, was on 'Super Alert' all the time. A fully awake awareness and readiness even while resting.

He laid back onto his poncho in the dirt and let himself lightly drift off, yet, maintain awareness of his surroundings. The dirt against his back, softened by the poncho, reminded him of the grassy knoll and he drifted back to a moment on the Island.

In his mind's eye he felt the cool breeze off of the lake, smelt the fragrance of the wildflowers, and could hear the wild ducks quacking from beneath the tall cattails covering the inlets along the shoreline.

He could see Sue, standing at the water's edge, wearing tight blue jeans with a white halter top. She was barefoot, holding her sandals, as she let the gentle waves lap against her feet. She was throwing the crust from their sandwiches out to the ducks and fish swimming quickly to her.

He laughed as a group of six little ducklings came up behind her from the brush and walked between her legs for a chance at some of the pieces. She jumped as she felt the fuzzy feathers against her ankles and let out a yell, then saw them and laughed.

"Oh, she said, "aren't they adorable?"

She started to break up the bread into tinier pieces for their little beaks to be able to eat.

"They are so hungry," she said, giving more and more crumbs to the peeping lot encircling her.

As she reached down to pet them, a full grown white duck came charging from the bushes quacking at her. She ran knee deep into the lake, yelling for him to help her.

"That won't do any good," he laughed, "mama can swim you know?"

"Steve!" she yelled, trying to dodge the quacking beak snapping at her heels. "Stop her!—-Get her away!"

He got up and shook the blanket at the charging bull-like duck. It quickly turned aside and swam off back to the little ones eating on the shore.

"My hero!" she declared with a smile and threw herself into his arms. "I am yours! Come take your reward, a kiss for the knight of the lake."

He could see the brightness in her laughing eyes. He smelt her scent of light perfume and felt the softness of her brown hair against his hands as they laid upon her milky-white shoulders.

As he leaned in to claim his prize he could feel her gentle breath on his lips. Then suddenly, she faded from his grasp into a distant image and was pulled away into the darkness.

His eyes opened slowly and he saw the fading light behind the trees before him. He checked his watch and saw it was nearly time to relieve T. C. Parker on the line. He gathered up his gear and rifle, then started walking across the compound, lowering his head.

***

Sue went with Joe and Cindy to the Par-troy drive-in to see the opening of 'Beneath the Planet of the Apes'. She was glad to spend time with them whenever she could between her heavy load of classes and the stress of mid-terms coming up.

As she sat in the back seat alone, watching the movie through the windshield, she found herself glancing as Joe and Cindy held each other. They would give each other an occasional kiss as he held her under his arm.

She smiled and was so happy they had found each other.

She pulled her jacket over her shoulders and rubbed her cheek against the collar. She closed her eyes, remembering how his arms felt around her. She could smell his aftershave; feel his moist lips against hers, his warm breath on her face and neck.

She saw the moonlight reflected in his sky blue eyes. His soft brown hair flowing between her fingers as she ran through it to cradle his head. His voice whispering in her ear; each word dripping with his love for her.

The excitement of his touch as he caressed her arms, then slid his fingers down her back and onto her waist, then tenderly across her bare stomach. She felt an ache inside as she sensed him with her.

She could hear his love of poetry speaking to her softly again as her emptiness watered in her eyes. She smiled, remembering his favorite line from Byron he'd say to her when she cried.

"So bright the tear of Beauty's eye,
Love half regrets to kiss it dry."

She opened her eyes fully as the scene before her suddenly flared into a violent explosion of fire, and a bomb brought the world to an end.

Joe looked back and saw her tears.

"Did it frighten you?" he asked.

"Yes," she answered, taking a deep breath.

***

"I got green smoke ahead!" Tucker yelled out.

Steve looked out the side door of the Apache airship, over the machine gun. "I got more a bit south," he yelled back.

"We'll set down in that midway clearing. Stand-by," the pilot said. Steve opened up with the gun into the wooded area where he saw rifle smoke as the men of the first platoon began to appear for extraction. Three other airships landed and they began to load the men.

He gave the door gun to a weenie as he left the copter with Tucker. They fired their M14s on automatic as they ran into the jungle's edge line.

"Farm boy," he called to Tucker, "I got two down here!" as he lifted one and Tucker came over to carry the other back.

They fired their rifles at smoke on the run, while under machine gun cover from their Apache weenie. At the door, both loaded the men on board, then ran back.

D. L. made his way to the south smoke with a recruit. They pulled tags off the dead and searched for survivors from a crossfire.

"Keep your nose down kid, " he said quietly. "I can smell their sweaty eyes on us." They continued slowly, staying low, as they worked towards the tree line.

Steve made his way deeper into the jungle as men ran past him to the choppers. As he came under fire, he nosed down behind a tree next to another soldier face down and hanging onto his helmet.

Steve took a look around the tree and was fired upon. He returned some, then went back down again as he heard the guy next to him mumbling.

"One day your eating in the Village Spa with a hot chick, the next day some guy's trying to part your hot comb with a bullet."

Steve turned quickly. "Ski?"

Ken jerked his up head. "What the heck…Sweety?" He grabbed him around the neck and shook him. "I knew they'd never get a Musketeer!" he laughed out.

"How did you end up here?"

"Same as you, I won the wrong lottery."

"Why didn't you marry Paula like you talked about to stay out of this?"

He laughed again, almost bellowing for all to hear, as he shook his head.

"Marriage! No thanks. I figured a year or so of this would be enough fighting for me. I didn't need to sign up for a lifetime of it."

They laughed together under the surrounding gun fire as if back home at a July 4th picnic. Suddenly a wild-eyed figure leap out of the tall grass, wielding a knife towards Steve's back. Ken grabbed the hand and as they wrestled, the knife plunged into his mid-section.

Steve turned over with a scream. He drew his 45 and emptied a partial clip into the soldier's face and chest. He felt his heart pounding as he watched the life drain from the now startled eyes as the soldier fell back limp. He sat Ken up and checked the wound. It was deep and he was losing a lot of blood.

"It's nothing like fencing class," Ken said, then, "oh damn, it burns man!"

"Hang on!"

"Hell, its set and match," he said spitting blood.

"You stay with me," Steve yelled, "or I'll send that bra tag collection to your mom!"

He laughed as Steve helped him up to his feet. "Now here's a switch," Ken said laughing and choking, "you picking me up." He

201

leaned on Steve, then glanced over into his eyes coldly and said, "It's bad, isn't it?"

"Naw, nothing to worry about," he said pulling Ken's arm over his neck. "He didn't get any of the vitals. He only got you above the waist."

Ken choked out a low laugh as they made their way out to the clearing for the choppers.

Halfway Ken collapsed, so he lifted him onto his shoulder and ran with him under fire for the last 30 yards or more. The Apache gunner saw them coming and opened up on the trees behind them.

When they reached the door, the gunner said, "There's no more room, we've got them packed and over the limit."

Steve pointed his rifle at the weenie."You take him or I'll shoot you and he can have your place."

"'Okay!" he yelled back, "but where?"

Steve looked then said, "Toss out their packs."

The crew threw out all they could find, then pulled Ken up and over the top of others.

"I'll wait for the next ride," he told them, "now get going!"

The copter tried to lift but was stuck, having sunk deep into the muddy ground from the weight. Steve got under it and let out a scream as he pushed up hard with his shoulders. A second later, D. L. appeared next to him with the young crewman and together they lifted it.

It finally gave way and rose up slowly as D. L. tossed the bag of dog tags to the door gunner. Ken came to just in time to see him and the others being left behind.

"No!" he screamed, reaching out for him.

"All for one, forever!" Steve yelled to him, holding up his rifle.

Ken struggled and crawled towards the door as the crew hung onto him.

"Tell her I promise!" he cried up to him.

"Go! Go!" D. L. ordered them.

Steve watched as the copter lifted and flew far into the south. He turned back and ran towards another soldier down and calling out in pain.

"You'll be fine," he told him as he checked his wound, "now, on your feet!"

He held the young man up as they scurried to make the last copter now filling up.

As he put the man on board, he reached up to the crewman for a hand. The door gunner grabbed him by the collar and pulled, just as another round of machine gun fire came and Steve was hit. He fell back and laid unmoving on the ground. The gunner froze looking down at him, holding Steve's torn off dog tags in his hand.

"He's dead!" yelled another crewman as he took the tags and tossed them in with the rest. "Let's go, now!" and the copter lifted up quickly and made for the river.

When it had finally appeared to be safe D. L. came crawling over with the recruit. He knelt down by Steve and lifted his head up.

"He's still breathing," he said. "Here, help me get him out of the open."

Together, they carried him to the jungle line and deep into the brush for cover. He checked the head wound, he had been hit on the left side of his head. The wound was long, but wasn't deep and no bullet could be felt.

"You are one lucky beach bum," he said to him as he laid there unconscious.

Steve finally awoke after nightfall.

"God," he said holding the bandage around his head, "I feel like the top of my head is missing."

He turned suddenly to D. L. as he continued to feel the wound.

"No, you still got what little brains God put up there. You'll be fine."

The sergeant looked at him a moment, then said, "We gotta move in deeper and hide until we can raise a pick call. You well enough to walk now?"

Steve nodded as he patted his boot lace and murmured something to himself.

Chapter Thirteen
"The shortest distance between two hearts is ..."

"If you could just tell him that I'm here and I need to see him," Sue asked a third time.

"I told you," the orderly replied, "I have just as I did yesterday and he doesn't want any visitors."

"Come on," Joe said softly to her, "we'll try again tomorrow."

He took her under his arm and walked her down the hallway. Sue looked around at the patients, some in wheelchairs, some missing limbs and many with blank faces.

They walked out the doors of the V. A. hospital and towards the parking lot.

"You wait here," he said, sitting her on a bench and pulling her coat closed, "I'll get the car."

She watched as cars and people passed by on the snowy streets, all smiling under the brightness of a welcomed sun after several days of winter bleakness.

The streets and buildings were decorated for the season with red-ribbons and green wreaths. Large red and white striped wooden candy canes hung on the lampposts, and bright strands of silver and gold tinsel sparkled from the store windows and houses.

A live nativity scene was being enacted across the street on a church lawn. She watched as the wise men each brought a gift. It was Christmas, but even under the sunlight, she felt numb in the midst of it all.

Joe parked at the curb and called to her when he noticed she wasn't getting up.

"Sue, come on little one."

She got up slowly and went to the door, but paused as she looked back at the third floor of the building.

"I've got to see him," she said firmly to him.

She started back towards the entrance as Joe called to her, then she began to run.

"Sue wait, they're not going to let you see him!"

Joe got out and left the car as he chased after her.

She ran to the elevator and pushed for the third floor. As the door opened he caught up with her and got in also.

"This is crazy," he said as they went up to the wing again.

"I'm not leaving again without seeing him," she said in a determined tone.

As they exited onto the floor, there was a commotion and people were running to the far end of the hall. The two of them stood still, out of the way of the panicked workers, until they heard his voice coming from the room.

"Stay here," Joe told her and he went down to the room and entered.

He watched as Ken was throwing things at the attendants and nursing staff, yelling at them.

"Get out or I'll kill you!" he heard him scream, as a tray came through the doorway.

"Why won't you just leave me alone!" he screamed again.

"Because we love you man," he heard a familiar voice answer, and he paused holding a clock in his hand over his head staring at him.

His eyes widened, then he threw the clock against the wall.

"Go away Joe, leave me alone."

"What's wrong with you?" he asked, as he moved closer.

"Joe please just go, I can't talk with you now," he said in a quieter tone as he slowly went and stared out the window.

Joe looked at the room, it was a war zone. Clothes thrown about, chairs over, food and juices dripping down the walls.

"If not now, then when?" he asked.

"Maybe never," Ken mumbled putting his hand against the window pane.

"Sue is here and she needs to see you badly."

Ken spun around with his hands held out in front of him and cried out, "No! I don't want to see her, ever!"

He paused, panting in a cold sweat.

"I can't," he said waving his hands. "I can't look at her. Take her home now, please, and don't bring her back."

"Ski?" came a soft voice from the doorway.

He turned and saw her looking at him. His wildness instantly turned to a look of despair.

"Oh no," he whimpered, falling to his knees sobbing.

She ran to hold him but he fought her off with waving hands as he hid his face from her.

"Oh please go away," he begged with tearing eyes. "Oh God please go! Don't look at me or touch me. Don't ask me anything. Don't care, just leave."

He dropped his head onto his knees and cried harder and louder. She fell on top of him and held on tight as he violently tried to shake her off.

"We love you," she cried out, "so hurt me if you have to but we're not leaving!" She tightened her hug around him and repeated, "We're not leaving you ever."

Joe closed the door on the gawking faces and went over to kneel by them.

"It's all right," she whispered in his ear, "you're home now with us." She caressed his head, then pulled it against her chest. "Shh, you're safe, it's over. We love you and everything is gonna be all right now."

He squeezed her and cried hard again, as she cradled his head and kissed it. Her tears fell on his face and mixed with his as Joe put his huge arms around them both and all cried together.

"I'm so sorry, he moaned to her, still with his head down.

"Shh, it's fine…I'm fine," she whispered back, "you don't have to say anything."

"I shouldn't be here," she heard him say.

"It's God's Will that you are," she softly replied.

"He should be here with you, not me," he added as he finally brought his face up to meet hers. "He put me on that copter and stayed behind. He gave me his place, me!"

He choked and coughed.

"He said he'd wait for the next pick up but there was none, not for any of them!"

He looked off into space as he added, "I can see their faces looking up. I can see his face, waving his rifle, calling out 'All for one!' and smiling. Yelling for me to tell you, to tell you …," then he cried again.

"To tell me what Ken?" she asked trembling as she put his face into her hands.

His eyes opened into hers and answered slowly and carefully. "He said, 'Tell her, I promise!'"

She closed her eyes and sighed, then took a deep breath and smiled upwards. Looking back down to him again she said softly, "Thank you Ski, oh thank you." She leaned against him tightly, kissing him several times.

Ken looked back at her perplexed. "That helps?"

"Oh Ski," she replied shaking his head in her hands with joy, "that's everything!"

"Come on," Joe said as they lifted him to his feet, "you're spending Christmas with us," and they helped him get dressed.

Sue straightened up the room and found a box with a purple heart in it. She put it in his bag with his other belongings and handed it to Joe.

"I have to stop for gifts," Ken said as they headed for the elevator. Sue held his arm and said, "I have mine. You're home and he will be."

***

"King's pawn two, this is Queen's Knight, over." Steve paused for a reply."King's pawn two, this is Queen's Knight, over!"

Norton came up from behind.

"No answer yet?"

Steve just shook his head.

"Okay," he said, "you can try again later, we've got to move."

Steve closed up the radio and swung it over his shoulder as together they looked at the other faces.

"One vet and a bunch of weenies," he heard D. L. say in a low frustrated tone. "I can't believe we've lasted out here this long."

He looked at Steve. "You've got to help me keep these guys moving until we get a chance for a pick up."

He nodded but asked, "What's up?"

"The vet there told me we are sitting in the middle of Arvins, so we've got to keep low and on the move carefully."

"What's Arvins?" asked one weenie as he came walking over with a can of rations.

"A bed of roses with a lot of thorns," D. L. answered in a gruff tone.

"It's a huge elite group of Charlies," Steve said to him softly, "well trained and well equipped."

"What'll we do?" the recruit asked nervously.

"We stay low and keep moving, that's what," Norton answered with a growl. "Now get your sorry butt up and stop talking so loud."

The group made its way through the thick jungle with Norton at point and the vet, Sgt. Axle, with Clayton at the rear. They watched every step they took and stopped for anything out of the ordinary.

Norton heard a rustling sound ahead and waved silently for the group to drop and be still. He waited, then heard it again. He raised his rifle and took aim, then made out the stripes as something moved just ahead.

It was a tiger and the weenie next to him suddenly jerked his rifle up to shoot. Norton grabbed the barrel and lowered it gently.

"No, just sit still," he whispered as they watched it pass by without noticing them.

When it was safe, he turned to the shaking recruit.

"I can't take it anymore," the young man said in a whimper.

"Look you sorry sack of cow pies," Norton said to him, "you will pull it together."

"I can't," he said sobbing and shaking. "We're gonna die, all of us. We're never gonna get out of here."

Norton looked into the frightened black face and said firmly, "You will do what you were trained to do, understand me?" He placed his hand on the man's shoulder and added, "It'll be fine kid. When it's time you'll do well. Now let's go."

He waved the all-clear and the group continued onward through the thick brush quietly.

They came to an open field of rice patties and stayed out of them, as they made their way under cover along the jungles edge line.

As night came again, they set up a tight cold base camp, no fire, huddled together in a small opening of jungle. Sentries were posted at all sides, with the others resting and eating in the center. Shifts changed every two hours.

Steve brought out the radio.

"King's pawn two, this is Queen's Knight, over."

Again, no reply.

He continued to try as Norton checked with Sgt. Axle on his feelings of their situation.

"I think that if we don't get picked up soon, our luck won't hold up much longer," Axle said quietly so as not to be overheard.

Norton nodded.

"Maybe we would be better to split up into two groups. Less chance of being spotted, and better our chances of us getting out of here. What do you think?"

Axle agreed.

"Most are your men," he said to D. L., "so you pick out four and I'll take the others."

He looked around. " Okay, I'll take Clayton, Barnes, Darnel and the new black boy there."

"Preston," Axle said, "but watch him he's still real green."

"King's pawn two, this is Queen's Knight, do you read me? Over." Steve waited, but nothing, so he turned it off to save the battery. D. L. looked over to him, but he just shook his head again, then both laid back with rifles and closed their eyes.

Before the sun had yet risen above the tree line, they had left in two groups.

209

Norton led, Clayton covered the rear.

By mid-day, they came to a river. They checked the maps they'd found from the pack of one of the dead they had left behind.

"I can't tell if this is the one shown here or not," D. L. said, looking out before him for some landmark.

Steve checked the compass and pointed to the right for south. "Let's stay with the river and just keep heading south."

Norton agreed.

As they made their way along the bank, they heard the sound of a motor coming from upriver and dropped.

It was an American gunboat and they stood up waving as it saw them and turned into the bank.

Suddenly they were opened up upon from the brush. They watched as two were hit and fell overboard. They ran closer and fired at the brush smoke. Within minutes, both groups had bullets flying about them like anger hornets.

Preston worked his way around to the right and Barnes on the left. Norton gave them cover by keeping the enemy's focus on him and Steve. There was a loud noise, then they saw the boat blown out of the water. Its pieces drifted back down in the air onto the water's surface. It was too late now, all they could do was continue to fight on.

Steve opened up the radio and began calling.

"King's pawn two, this is Queen's Knight, over! King's pawn two, this is Queen's Knight, do you read?"

He stopped when he felt a cold rifle barrel being held against his head. He looked up and three more were on Norton as he dropped his gun. They were motioned to move and both did as directed as they heard from behind, "Queen's Knight, this is King's pawn two, go ahead."

Together with Darnel, Barnes and Preston, they were marched for what seemed like forever. Finally they came to a set of huts and were thrown into bamboo cages, which were suspended five feet off the ground.

They were so small that they could only sit inside with their legs pulled up tight against their chests. Once secured inside, they were left to just sit and spin in the wind until night fell. No water, no food, just silence in the darkness.

"What's the D. L. stand for?" a voice asked in the darkness to see if he was awake.

Norton smiled to himself.

"Daniel Le Roy," he replied with an accent on the Le Roy.

Steve laughed.

"It almost sounds like my car," he commented. "I've got the most beautiful Pontiac Le Mans you'll ever hope to find."

"You got a middle name there Seaside?"

"It's James."

They were silent for awhile, then, "You plan on marrying that Jersey girl when you get back?"

"Not till we both graduate college. It was part of a promise. What about Audrey Ann? Married, engaged, or what?"

"Uh," he answered with a hint of hesitancy, "or what, I guess you could say."

"That's probably for the better. I'm sure she's too good for the likes of you."

Norton laughed back.

"They all were," he said as they laughed together in the pitch blackness.

"Ya know what Seaside?"

"What?"

"From the moment I got over here, I've been terrified more of being captured than of dying. Now that it's happened I actually feel relieved," he said as he swatted another mosquito biting on his neck.

Steve didn't answer; he just raised his head up and watched as a dark cloud passed over the moon.

"Happy New Year Sue," he whispered.

D. L. heard him and then, for the first time in a long while, bowed his head and said a prayer.

***

As the clock stuck midnight, they held up their glasses and cried out, "Happy New Year!" Then they drank a sip and hugged and kissed all around the room.

Joe picked Cindy up and kissed her in mid-air as her parents hugged and kissed.

Ken took Sue's hand."This is from him," he said, then kissed her softly on the lips. She thanked him, then hugged him tight.

"Welcome home Ski," she said rubbing his back, then they went around the room exchanging hugs and kisses with the others.

On New Year's Day she went out for a drive to be alone with her thoughts and noticed that the Village Spa was open. She pulled into the lot and went inside. Mama was serving lunches at the counter and smiled.

"Oh my Sue, so good to see you," she said, "and Happy New Year!"

"To you too," she replied. "I'm surprised to see you open today."

"We figured that there may be some people out and about who needed a place to feel welcomed with a good cup of coffee, you know?"

"I know, and I do need one."

"Coming up!"

She sat down on a stool as a girl in the booth near her got up and came over.

"Aren't you Susan LaRosa?"

She nodded.

"I thought I recognized you," she continued as she sat next to her. "I heard that your boyfriend was fighting over in Nam. What's his name?"

"Steve, and he's my fiancé," she said holding up her ring.

"Oh, and is he home now?"

"No, not yet."

"Don't you just hate how this war goes on and on? He didn't volunteer?"

"No he was called, and like a man he did what he was asked to do."

"Oh good," she commented, "at least he didn't support it."

Sue didn't reply, just looked away.

212

"When's he due back?"

"Soon I hope," she said, then excused herself and got up to join Mama in the kitchen.

One of the other girls called out from the booth. "I'd never date a soldier."

"That's a cruel thing to say," Mama cried out as she overheard them. "Her fiancé is one of the finest men I know and you should be ashamed to say such a thing!"

"It's all right Mama," she said softly, "they don't know any better. Could I have that coffee to go please?"

She left and drove down to the Island, then walked out in the snow to the knoll sipping from her cup. At the frozen lake's edge she dug down deep for the sandy dirt. Taking a handful she closed her eyes as ran her fingers through it.

"Hi Billy I miss you," she said smiling, "Happy New Year. I miss him too, so please watch over him for me."

She cried as she let the dirt fall to the ground and raised her cup.

"Happy New Year My Love," she said softly through her tears and she suddenly could feel him close as her heart sang to him.

Chapter Fourteen
"Uncharted Waters."

It was the first day of her last semester and she was running late. Sue parked the car in the lower lot because it had the only available spaces, then ran with an arm full of books up the steps.

As she got to building B, she reached for the door and lost her grip on the books and they fell all over.

"Oh no," she said as she knelt to pick them up.

At that moment, a well dressed, strikingly handsome, young man came from behind her and stopped to help.

"Thank you so much," she said to him, noticing the latest fashion of suit he was wearing.

He smiled at her as he held open the door.

"Nice suit," she said, "and thanks again," then she ran for her class.

She entered the classroom and found a seat empty near the back. Her professor opened his notes and told them the chapters they would have to cover for the next class.

She jotted them down as he commented on paying particular attention to the advertising and accounting principles.

The door opened and a young man entered as the professor waved him in. It was the same man who had helped her with her mishap with the books moments before. He came to the front and was introduced as Mr. Lance Graham of Bartley and Company Accountants in New York City.

"Mr. Graham is a recent graduate of ours and has acquired a fine position with this firm. He has been gracious enough to come here today and discuss what he and the firm do so well for their clientele. You'll soon learn why they have such an excellent reputation."

"Thank you Professor," he said, "and thank all of you for inviting me." He looked at their faces, then noticed Sue and smiled.

The lecture lasted nearly the entire time period, then he wished them well and left.

"I hope you all took good notes from Mr. Graham's lecture and read the chapters so we can discuss them in Wednesday's class."

Sue gathered up her books to leave and dropped some again.

A young man with dirty-blond hair sitting across from her reached down to pick them up. He glanced at her legs as he rose to hand them to her.

"You got quite a load there," he said smiling.

She nodded trying to sort them large to small for better balance.

"Hi, I'm Wil Walker," he said as his gray eyes stared at her. He placed the last book on top of her pile as she squared them up.

"Hi, Sue LaRosa."

"You sure you can handle those all right?" he asked as she was making her way to the door. "I'd be glad to carry some for you."

"I'm fine thanks," she said, then stepped out through the doorway.

Wil waved to her, then secretly opened a folded letter which he had palmed from her fallen books. It was the beginning of a letter to Steve. As he read it, he could feel her loneliness crying out between the lines. He smiled as he stared back at the doorway.

"Hello again," Mr. Graham said as he stood in the hall.

"Oh, hello."

"Did you find the lecture interesting?"

"Oh very," she said, still struggling with the books.

"Here, let me help you with those," he said taking most of them.

"Do you plan on being an accountant when you graduate?"

"No, I want to understand business principles," she answered," that's why I majored in Business but my real love is art. I hope to be able to enter into Advertising with a bachelor's degree. I plan on transferring up to Ramapo College next fall."

"Oh, but you could enter with the two-year degree you get from here as I did. I think a four year one is overrated myself."

She just smiled, then said she had to go.

"Another class?" he asked as he walked along with her.

"No, I have a break period before my art class begins. I usually like to sit in the student lounge and read and catch up on my writing."

"What do you write about?"

"I try to use that time to write letters to my fiancé. He's stationed over in Nam."

He walked with her into the student lounge and they sat in the quieter area of the room. She went to get some coffee and asked if he also wanted some.

"Just black thank you," he said as he sat on the couch and watched her get in the service line.

He eyed her shapely figure and followed the curves of her legs as they vanished beneath her plaid knee-high skirt. He scanned her chest and shoulders as she turned sideways in line. He found it hard to take his eyes off her.

"Here you go," she said handing him a cup.

"Thank you. How much do I owe you?"

"Oh, my treat," she replied with a smile.

"Well, thank you again. Say," he said as she began to take out her letter writing materials, "if you are free this week, I would be glad to take you to see my company and let you get a feel for the business world first hand. We could even have dinner on the way back. What do you say?"

"I wouldn't feel comfortable doing that."

"Oh of course, how stupid of me. I shouldn't have even asked."

They were quiet for a moment, then he said, "Okay, but what if you could bring along a friend? I just would like you to see for yourself what business is all about. I even have a friend who works over at Davies and Blanche in the advertising department and I'm sure she wouldn't mind showing you around. She could answer any questions you may have in that field also. What about that?"

She paused looking at him. "No dinner then, just the tour?"

"Strictly a business show and tell, I promise. How about it? After all, I came here today to help students prepare for the real world, this would just be like a field trip."

She felt excited about the chance to see a real advertising department. To be able to talk with another woman who was actually working at it was appealing, but she still felt uneasy.

As they sat, Cheryl came over and asked if she had notes on the lecture she missed today.

"Sure here, and this was our guest lecturer, Mr. Graham."

"Oh hi," she said surprised.

"Well hello, and you both can call me Lance."

"Nice to have met you," she said. "Sorry but I gotta go, classes wait for no one." She smiled back as she ran for the door.

"Maybe she would like to come with you since she's taking the same course?" he asked in a coaxing tone.

"May I think about it and call you?"

"Of course," he replied handing her his card.

She looked at her watch and told him she had to go for her next class.

"I'll talk with you later in the week then," he said as he waved to her heading to the door.

He watched as she walked away, noting the movement of her hips and legs.

"Very nice," he said to himself, then he eyed a blond student as she sat cross-legged reading in a lounge chair and he went over to talk.

Sue turned back outside the glass doors and saw him now with her.

***

They were brought inside one of the larger hut-like buildings one at a time. Steve and D. L. stood tied to staked poles, with their arms suspended up over their heads. They could hear some of the words being said from inside, as the interrogator spoke in English.

"Where is your unit?" the voice asked.

They waited, then heard a scream of pain.

Steve lowered his head, trying to block out the sound. It had been several weeks since they were captured on New Year's Day. They had been moved from one encampment to another and always treated poorly; but this was the first time they had to face possible torture.

They watched as the prisoner was dragged from the building by two guards. They couldn't tell if he was dead or had just blacked out.

Steve was untied and brought in next. He was placed in a chair and his hands tied. He remained quiet as the officer just kept his head lowered reading papers on his desk.

Finally, he looked up at Steve.

"It says you were found near the river, some twenty miles into our borders. This is true is it not?"

"I don't know for sure. We were lost and trying to just follow a compass."

"You lie!" he shouted and struck him in the face. "You were found radioing in information. What information did you send?"

"I was calling for a pick up, a rescue copter for us, that's all."

"Lies!" he said again and motioned for the guard to strip away his shirt and hold his head.

"You will tell me what you were there for, you understand?"

"We were lost!" he cried out. "Just freak'in lost!—-We were left behind that's all!"

"How many of you were there?"

Steve thought of Axle and the rest, then said, "Stephen Clayton, private, serial number 138661829."

His head was pushed forward down near his knees, then held there as the officer opened up a straight edged razor and ran it across his back. He let out a scream, then went quiet as his head was jerked up again.

"I will not play games with you soldier. Now tell me, how large was the force you came with?"

"Steve Clayton, private, serial number 138661829."

Norton could hear what was said and then the screams as he struggled against his ropes.

"Pass out," he whispered to himself, "just pass out."

Again he heard Steve repeat his name, rank and then another scream and another, then silence for a moment.

"You will tell me. We've only just begun," said the voice in a tone of finality.

Steve slowly raised his head in a daze.

"Wait, wait," he said laughing, "I know that one. 'We've only just begun'. It's sung by the Carpenters."

He began to sing the lyrics in a tone of semi-consciousness. Seconds later another long, chilling scream rang out, then nothing but dead silence.

After many agonizing minutes the door opened. D.L. watched them drag him, with a bloody backside, across the compound and throw him into a dirt floored lockup.

Norton was taken in and tied.

"Now Sergeant, perhaps you will be more reasonable and tell me what I need to know. Yes?"

D.L. looked at the bloody razor, then glared up at him.

"Sure," he answered with a hint of sarcasm. "The way I see it, if you plan on shaving guys for a living ya might wanna do barber college first." He grinned coldly then added, "Cause from what I've seen, you really stink."

***

Sue called Lance to have him drive her and Cheryl out to the city on Friday afternoon from the college. She had on her best business suit and waited, talking with Wil Walker, out front of the student lounge. When Lance pulled up in a new Cadillac he asked Sue about Cheryl.

"Oh, she couldn't make it so I invited another classmate. This is William Walker. He asked me if he could come along instead, okay?"

He opened the front door for her and answered, "Uh sure, that's fine I guess," as Wil got in the back.

"This should be fun," she said smiling as he drove out of the lot and onto Route 10 headed east.

When they came out from the Lincoln Tunnel into New York, they turned left. He made his way through the crowded streets like it was his hometown. Within a few blocks, they pulled into an underground garage and parked.

"We walk from here. It's just down the block, a nice walk," he remarked with a grin. They went to the stairs and Lance followed from behind as he enjoyed watching her climbing the steps.

"We go this way," he said as they hit the street level and he led the way with Sue at his side. When they went through the revolving door together he pressed up against her in the confined space.

"Here we are, New York, the place where it's all happening."

She looked up at the sky high buildings for a moment, feeling both excited and uneasy.

They walked a block or so, then went into the main company entrance. As they approached the reception desk, Lance winked at the man sitting there.

"Just a couple of guests here for the day," he said, then turned to them. "You'll have to sign the guest register. Here Sue, use my pen." He pulled out a gold fountain pen from his breast pocket and handed it to her. "It was an award for the ranking of top service in my department last month," he told her with an air of self-importance.

She smiled and signed in, then handed the pen to Wil as Lance guided her over to the elevator holding her arm firmly. Wil signed and then paused to admire the expensive pen's engraving. "Success is always within your grasp," it read. He looked over at them, then put the pen into his inside coat pocket as he hurried to catch up.

They were met by a male co-worker moments later who seemed puzzled by seeing Wil with him. Lance shrugged his shoulders as the four entered the elevator and went up.

"Max," he asked, "would you mind taking Mr. Walker here over to the accounts payable?"

His friend nodded and led Wil out when the doors opened.

Sue started to follow but he took her arm.

"Wait, I have something I want to show you first." The doors closed and he hit the top floor button.

When they opened again, they found themselves stepping into an unfinished part of the building.

"Oops too far," he said. "I must have hit the wrong button, but since we're here let me show you a view you'll never forget."

He took her by the arm and they walked over to the huge glass windows.

"Didn't I tell you it was a great city? You can see clear back over the Hudson to Jersey from here."

Sue took in the view, then walked along the wall to look from another direction. The city was in full swing as she watched the people, buses and cars all moving below. It was like being on top of the world, but was a bit scary looking down for long.

"It's very nice," she said, " but shouldn't we be getting back with the others?"

He took her arm again and walked her back to the window.

"Can't you feel the excitement of the city?" he asked as he slid his other arm around her waist.

She pulled away.

"Maybe we should go down to the offices now Mr. Graham."

"Sure, if you like," he replied and patted her hand. She was starting to panic all alone until the elevator doors opened and Wil stood there smiling at them with Max.

"So there you are," Wil said taking Max's arm. "We were beginning to worry about you both, weren't we Maxie?" Wil added, acting gay as he smiled up at him in a suggestive way.

Max removed his hand from his arm and said, "Let's get going, shall we?"

They all entered the elevator and went down, as Wil winked at Sue and she covered her mouth to hide a laugh.

After showing them many of the departments within his company, he suggested that he take Sue to meet with his lady friend at the advertising company a few blocks away.

"Oh," Wil said, "I just adore advertising. What with the way they use such colors like lava red and passion purple in those boxer shorts commercial ... Oh, it's just to die for. Yes, let's go!"

The three went out to the street and he hailed a cab. He gave the driver an address and they headed uptown.

Sue watched out the window at the many stores and restaurants they passed.

221

"So many people," she thought as she watched them all moving in such a hurry.

The cab pulled up to the curb and he paid as they stepped out.

"This is it," he said to her.

She read the name on the face of the building and felt excited. Once inside, they went to the desk and he asked to use the in-house phone so he could call his friend and let her know they had arrived.

When he got off, he turned to them.

"Sorry, but it seems Karen is out today, but a co-worker of hers said he'd be more than glad to let us take a look at the department."

They waited in the lobby until the elevator opened and another young man stepped out and greeted them.

"Well hello, I'm Jessy Powers," and he shook their hands.

"Oh my," he said as he shook hands with Wil, "aren't you a strong one. Such a grip!"

Wil looked at Sue and she shrugged her shoulders with a smirk.

"Just follow me and we'll show you what we do here," Jessy said taking Wil's arm.

After seeing most of the departments and talking with staff members, Sue asked if she could see where the artwork itself was done. Jessy led and they went up to one of the top floors.

"This is Janet Sims deary," he said to Sue. "She oversees and approves all of the work done here before it reaches layout and is prepare for photo."

"Hello and welcome," she said. "Let's start over here and I can show you some of the ideas we're working on now."

Sue was bubbling with excitement as she was shown the pen and ink work sketches on the drawing boards. The near finished colored ones for fashion dresses, full evening wear, perfumes and other types of Fifth Avenue specialties delighted her as well.

When the tour was completed, Jessy insisted they all go round the corner for an early supper and a drink.

"We're underage," Sue said quickly.

"Oh, not in New York," Lance said. "The drinking age here is eighteen."

Wil and Sue both became nervous, but followed them around the block to the club entrance of 'Le Brie's Way' on a side street.

It was extremely dark inside as they entered. Sue was led by Lance to a far corner booth as the others followed. He let her slide in first, then sat next to her as she was pressed against the wall.

The waiter came and winked at Lance as he ordered a round of martinis.

"No," Sue said, "I'll have a coke thanks."

There was a small live band playing and Jessy grabbed Wil's arm, pulling him to the dance floor.

"Looks like fun," Lance said and he reached for her hand.

"I'd rather not," she said putting her hand under the table nervously.

Several more drinks were ordered and consumed before the meals arrived. Wil was busy trying to keep his distance from Jessy's wandering hands, while Lance kept moving tighter against Sue in the near pitch darkness. Only a red candle on the table offered any light.

"Here try just a little sip," he said to her holding his martini glass. "It's really good."

"No thank you, I would just like some water with my meal."

"Come on just a taste. It'll relax you to have some fun."

She shook her head and reached for her fork, then she felt his hand touch her knee and move up her thigh quickly.

"No don't!" she cried out. "Please, stop it!" She struggled but had no where to move away to avoid him.

She finally was able to grab his hand and pull it off her leg.

"I want to go home, now!" she said boldly.

Lance looked at Jessy, who then turned to Wil and said, "Sure. Let's go find us a cab cutie," and they got up to leave.

Sue stared at Wil with fear in her eyes as he stepped away.

"So the whole evening isn't a loss," Lance said, "how about a goodnight kiss?"

He put his arm around her shoulder and moved close, pinning her against the wall and began kissing her neck. She turned away struggling and felt his hand on her leg again. She started to cry, then grabbed her fork and jabbed it into his hand below the table. He pulled back and cursed at her, then slapped her face.

"You lousy tease," he growled while she held the side of her face in a daze.

Wil jumped back from the table as she suddenly pulled the table cloth, with drinks and full dinners, up and over the top of Lance's head.

As he struggled and cursed beneath it, she pushed him out of the booth and onto to the floor. Sue slid out quickly, then both she and Wil ran for the door as Jessy stood by stunned.

Once outside in the light she paused, then turned and calmly walked back in alone. She went over to him as he sat on the floor dazed, covered in tomato sauce, and punched him hard in the nose.

"As it says in Don Quixote, 'between a woman's yes and no, there is not room for a pin to go!' So Buster, there aren't any grey areas. When I say no, I mean it!"

She quickly swung a hit into his eye and he fell back and out. The waiter then asked her to leave.

"Glad to," she said with satisfaction, "now that I've put out the trash."

Back outside, Wil had been able to hail a cab to take them to the bus terminal. As they waited for their bus to be called, he tried to console her as she continued to tremble.

"I was a fool," she kept saying. "I just knew this didn't feel right from the beginning."

"We all make mistakes," he said, "but at least we did get to see the workings of some powerful companies."

"Oh, I've gotten an eyeful and handful of the workings of big city business," she said tearfully. "I feel so dirty and I don't want anything more to do with it. I'm never crossing that river again."

Wil looked up as the numbers were called.

"That's our bus," he said to her as she continued sobbing. "Come on, let's get you home."

***

Steve stared dazed from heat and exhaustion. One by one, the guards dragged him, Norton and Darnel up out of the stinking pit of swamp water and human filth. They had been forced to stand in it since the day before. Endless hours up to their necks with hands tied behind them as they slowly sank in the muddy bottom. Lifting their legs every few minutes to keep from sinking over their heads. More than once, each had almost drowned in it as they felt their legs weaken. Whenever one started to fall, the other two would press against him to hold him up so he could rest a moment.

"Stand together or we die!" Steve cried out again and again.

The guards had found this amusing and placed wagers on who would finally survive to face the commander's return to question them again.

Dark leeches could be seen on their backs and legs now as they were dropped in front of the officer. He had water poured on them to wash away the stench.

"Perhaps you feel more like talking now?"

Steve looked up coughing. "Stephen Clayton, Private, Serial ... " The officer kicked him in the chest and he fought hard for a breath.

"Another nameless face no one will know or care about."

D. L. squinted up into the sun at him and remarked in a raspy voice, "It was kind of like being buried in the sands of Coney Island after a Labor Day weekend. It just made us a bit homesick for Jersey."

***

Sue noticed that after nearly every class, Wil would be right there at the doorway when she came out. He seemed to be rearranging his day to be sure to run into her. By the time their semester was half over, she had started to become accustomed to having him nearby as a companion.

"I was wondering," he finally asked as they were studying together in the lounge one afternoon. "Since we seem to like each other's company, would you like to go to a movie with me this weekend?"

She looked up from her book slowly, trying to think how to say no to him.

"It wouldn't be like a date or anything," he said, "I just thought we could share some time off campus as friends."

"Wil I like you, you're fun to be with," she said cautiously choosing her words, "but it wouldn't be right for me or fair to you to date. I have someone that I love and I'm already gladly spoken for."

"I understand that," he responded quickly, "but that shouldn't stop you from going out and having some fun with friends. You're alone so much it seems, we could go out with others at the same time."

She sighed. "I do go out with friends, good caring friends. They know what I'm going through and love me enough to help me deal with it."

He got quiet and looked away a moment.

"I just enjoy your company is all, I don't have a lot of friends."

Sue thought to herself.

"Tell ya what," she said trying to lift his spirits. "I plan on going out Saturday with the gang up to the amusement park in Lake Hopatcong for its season opening. You are more than welcomed to join us."

He spun his head around to her and smiled."That would be great! I love Bertrand Island! I've won a lot of prizes there and I can show you the best ones to play and win!"

"All right then, you can meet us up there in the main lot."

"Would you mind if I drove up with some of you instead?"

She hesitated, then said, " Okay, I guess the guys will have some extra room in the car."

He gave her his address and they agreed on a time.

That Friday when she pulled up into her driveway, Ken was parked outside.

"Hi Ski," she said waving, "what's up?"

"I've been worried about you lately. You don't seem as happy as I'd like to see you and I do understand why, believe me."

She came over to him as he leaned against his front fender and hugged him. "Thanks for being here," she whispered.

He looked down at her and asked, "Have you got a little time to spare? I'd like to show you something that might help both of us."

She smiled. "I'd like that." Then they got into his Charger.

He drove out to Hanover Airport and showed her the 'Take a Ride' copter as it was preparing to give another passenger flight. He stood behind with his arms around her as they watched it take off.

"He did this nearly everyday," he said softly in her ear, "and safely brought a lot of guys home. He brought me home."

Sue squeezed his hand as she watched it rise into the air.

"I know there's one that will find him and bring him home soon too Angel."

She was silent as the whirlybird flew up and off over the treetops, then went out of sight.

"Oh find him," she whispered. "Please bring him back."

Ken held her tight and kissed her cheek.

"They will," he said in a firm tone, "he'll make sure of it. He promised, didn't he?"

She looked up at him with a tear. "I love you Ski, you know that?" He smiled.

"As sure as I'm breathing," he sighed out.

On Saturday, when they came to pick up Wil, they found it to be a tight squeeze. Joe and Cindy were in front with Ken's date at the passenger door, and in the back were Ken and Wil, with Sue in-between.

"Good thing this is a short ride up Route 10," Joe commented looking in the rear view mirror and headed up the highway.

At the park, they stayed pretty much together as a group. They made the rounds down along the midway near the lake's edge, trying their luck at some game stands.

Cindy won a small stuffed mouse on a wheel while Wil won choice of stand, but had cheated. When no one was watching, he lifted the game coke bottle upright into the target circle with his hand instead of using the plastic ring on his fishing pole.

"I won!" he shouted out and called Sue over to come and pick out a prize. "You can choose whatever you'd like," he told her as they looked over the prizes.

She smiled as she tried to decide, then suddenly froze and felt a chill as she spotted a plush owl sitting on the top shelf.

"We'll take that one!" Wil yelled, seeing her staring at it and the attendant handed the stuffed bird to her.

"No, I can't," she said backing up and Wil took it for her.

"It's a really nice one," he said smiling. "Want to name it?"

She closed her eyes, shaking her head no.

"All right, you can decide later. Come on, let's go on some rides."

She walked on the opposite side as he carried the bird on the other. He went and bought tickets and took her to the line for the Ferris wheel.

"We'll be able to see the whole lake and park from up there," he said excited.

When they got into one of the swings and the safety bar came down in their laps, she asked, "Please just hold the prize, okay?"

"Sure," he said with a smile and moved next to her holding the owl at his left side.

As the wheel started turning, she could only think of Steve again at the shore and didn't even feel Wil's hand on hers as they rode.

Later, they caught up with Ken and his date Sally and they went to the villa for a soda and to buy some sandwiches. Wil slipped the server a large tip to get a beer as he placed his order. The four sat down at one of the tables and watched as people got onto rides.

"Let's go on the Lost River ride next," he said to her. She half-smiled, then asked if the others wanted to also.

"Sure, sounds like fun," Sally said and they finished eating, then got in line for the next boat to go through the tunnel. Ken got in back with Sally, with Wil and Sue in the middle seats and another couple sitting in front.

As the boat was released, it slowly drifted into the semi-darkness and lights flicked on to show strange jungle animals on each side as they passed through.

Ken started kissing Sally as Sue knew he would and she smiled trying not to look back much. About halfway through, the couple in front also got romantic and then appeared to start making out.

Sue got uncomfortable and glanced downward to the left, away from seeing them or looking at Wil.

Her thoughts returned to Steve's smile, his touch, his warm tender kiss and she sighed out loud without realizing it. A moment later she felt an arm around her shoulder and Wil trying to steal a kiss from her.

"Stop it Wil!" she cried out in the near darkness and moved away.

He was taken back. "I thought you wanted me to kiss you."

"No! I was just … Well, no I didn't."

He moved closer again. "It's all right, just forget it okay? Then as he leaned to try and see her face more clearly he suddenly felt a hand on his shoulder.

He smiled until it pulled him back and a voice asked, "Got a match there friend?"

"No," he answered Ken over his shoulder.

"Didn't think so," came a reply and then he felt the hand pushing him back over to the other side of the boat's seat.

When the ride ended Ken helped the girls out. He asked Sally to take her over to get some cotton candy, seeing Joe and Cindy at the stand.

Sue touched Ken's arm lightly and he smiled. "Go ahead," he said to her, "we'll be along."

As they left he turned to Wil.

"Didn't you see that ring on her finger?"

Wil nodded.

"Then that says it all. Respect it, understand?" Ken stated firmly. "The man she's engaged to is one of my closest friends. I would die for him and for her."

Wil backed up a bit seeing his facial expression and feeling threatened.

"I didn't mean to upset her, really. When she sighed I just thought she was giving me, you know, a signal that she wanted me to do something. She's just so pretty."

"What she is, is pretty-well spoken for," he replied. "A friend doesn't try to do something with an engaged woman. A friend respects her enough to back off when she's emotional and vulnerable, not take advantage. A friend is just a friend, you understand me friend?"

Wil nodded again.

"What she wants is miles away. What she has are good friends to be here for her. There's only one man worthy of that special lady. You respect her and him. Am I being clear?"

"I'm sorry," he answered.

They returned to the group and Ken took a bite out of Sue's Cotton candy stick, then out of Sally's.

"You girls don't need that much sweetness," he said, then offered his stick to Wil. He smiled, then accepted it as a peace offering.

When they stopped off for a small cone at Dairy Queen on the way home, Joe's treat, they ran into Janice and her friend Tina. Sue introduced them to Wil and told Tina how much he liked brunettes.

Wil blushed and Tina came by him saying, "Mine is natural, here feel. " He slowly touched it as he looked over at Sue winking. She left them talking awhile as she went over to sit with Ken.

"What are you up to?" he asked her.

"Me? Nothing. I just thought they might have some things in common."

"Like what?" he asked with a smirk.

"Oh, I happen to know how much he enjoys walking, eating good food, talking on the phone, driving in his car, you know, fun stuff," she answered grinning.

"Really? He sounds very deep," Ken remarked, "and this all makes him a perfect match for her how?"

"Oh that's easy," she said smiling, "Tina likes guys."

Ken laughed lightly.

"You are so deviously subtle sometimes, it scares me."

Sue turned to him and smiled again.

"Uh Ken," she said taking his arm, "have I told you about this great classmate of mine Linda? She's studying to become an drafting board engineer. She just loves fast cars, like your Charger, so she can study them up close and get some hands on. I'll bet I could get her to come over sometime and make a beautiful sketch of it for you, as a keepsake. I know she's free on Saturdays."

When Sue got dropped off and came into the house, she was surprised to see Steve's parents there.

"Hi," she said smiling and giving them a hug. "It's so late, did you guys have dinner together tonight?"

"No," her mom said, "they had some news about Steve."

"Oh," she replied sitting down.

Mr. Clayton spoke up saying, "We got a letter here from the army."

She smiled. "Is he coming home? He's due stateside soon he wrote me in one of his last letters."

"No," his mom said with tears. "It says he was killed in the same battle Kenny fought in."

Sue looked at her for a second.

"Oh no, that can't be. Ken told me he saw him alive and well as he was flown out. They just made a mistake is all, it happens a lot I heard. He's fine, you'll see."

"Sue, they called the army and it's been confirmed," her mom said coming to sit next to her. "They have his dog tags Baby."

"What about him? Did they find him?"

"No," cried his mom, "they only have his tags."

"Well see," she said smiling, "they don't know anything for sure. Don't worry, I know he's alive. I know it, I can feel it."

She stood up and walked to the stairs.

"I'm sorry but I'm very tired. I think I'll just go up to bed, goodnight." They watched her slowly vanish up into the darkness, but said nothing more.

She told Ken the next day and he agreed that it had to be a mistake. He said he'd try and look into it for her.

Wil kept up their friendship. Upon hearing the news, he started to try and convince her that she should accept it and move on with her life.

"You are going to be starting your junior classes in less than two weeks. You have to focus on the future now and what you're going to do with your life," he said. "Isn't that the kind of thing he would have wanted for you?"

She knew he meant well but couldn't explain what she was feeling. Only Ken seemed to understand it.

On a late afternoon in September, the day before she was to move into the dorms at Ramapo College, she went with Ken to the island. They sipped the coffee he had brought as they gazed out over the glass surface of the lake talking.

"I know in my heart, that if I say the words then he will be gone forever," she told him. "I can't say them Ski, I just can't."

"Then don't."

They held each other tight as she cried. Ken thought of his face looking up at him from that clearing, as she trembled in his arms."I promise," Ken heard his words as if there again, and repeated them softly to himself.

Sue was lost in her despair as they lay together on the knoll. She heard him, closed her eyes and reached up to stroke his face. She kissed his neck, then pressed her lips hard against his.

"Oh Sweety," he heard her say and suddenly he pulled away and held her face in his hands.

"Sue no, he's gone!"

She gasped, putting her hand to her mouth. "What? Oh my God!" she moaned out loud.

Ken knelt up and pulled her back into his chest.

"He's gone," he repeated, "oh my God I'm sorry, but he is really gone! I checked and read the report from the soldier who saw him die."

She let out a long, loud, agonizing cry and pushed him away.

"Oh Ski no! - - -Oh please he can't be. I love - - - I need him too much!"

"I know, I know, and so did I," he said touching her face.

They fell together again and cried until they just couldn't any more. Finally, he looked at her and wiped away her tears gently as Steve would for her.

"Stay here," he said, "I'll go get the car and take you home."

He got up and walked slowly over towards the Charger parked in the ball field, then he heard splashing behind him. He saw her running into the chilling fall water. He ran back, throwing off his jacket and shoes, then dove in following her as she screamed and swam out farther.

He made his way through the murky water, sweeping aside the red and brown decaying leaves that were floating on and just under its face. As he touched them, they oozed through his fingers like slippery worms and floated behind him in black swirls in the wake of his passing.

"You promised me Steve!" she cried out, choking on the water as it came into her mouth. "No, you can't have him! We are forever! It was a promise!"

She was already out in deep water when he could have just touched her feet as they were kicking wildly, but then she turned to him.

"No!" he heard her scream repeatedly. "Ken no, I need him! Please don't!- - - Just let me go to him, please!"

He reached out for her and she disappeared below the surface as if being taken by the lake itself.

"Sue!" he screamed, then dove beneath the now choppy surface. He couldn't see her through the dark green water and he reached out franticly grabbing at the darkness about him.

Many moments later, they surfaced and he wrapped her in his arms. She was no longer struggling. She was just limp as he pulled her towards shore.

"Please dear God," he prayed, fighting to keep her chin out of the water as he swam, "don't take her, please."

The shore was so far away and the cold crept into him like the numbness of death. He felt his strength and focus draining with each stroke. His clothes bonded to him like a heavy, frozen straight jacket, getting tighter with each movement. He felt himself starting to sink but he refused to let her go.

"Just one more stroke," he told himself each time, until his arms seemed to move without his having to will them.

The moment finally came when he was able to stand up on the muddy bottom and hold her in his arms above the water. He stopped a moment to breathe deeply against the tightness in his chest.

As he paused, she suddenly started choking up water and gasping for breath. She opened her eyes and he smiled down at her.

"It's God's Will that we're still alive," he said. "I ran out of strength long ago."

"Oh God …Oh Ski," she cried choking. "I'm so sorry. I didn't want to do that. I just died inside and, then suddenly, I just couldn't feel him anymore. Oh God please forgive me."

"He does, it's all right Angel, and I understand too. Listen, what we really need is to go on living. Promise me that you'll honor that love you shared and do something special with your life."

"I'll try," she cried, "I promise Ski."

He carried her back and put his coat around her. Then they went to the car to warm up and drive home.

"Thank you and please forgive me for what I did and how I acted," she said shivering, "I feel so ashamed."

"There's nothing to forgive Little Sister. Just know that Joe and I will always be here for you."

She took his hand and kissed it.

"I love you," she said as he kissed her forehead.

"I was ready to go," she confessed, "until I felt your hand grab me and pull me up."

He turned to her.

"I never touched you, I couldn't find you. I didn't even see you until I came up for air and there you were with me."

She looked down at her wrist and saw the bruises of fingerprints around it. Ken reached over and put his hand on them. They appeared larger than his.

Over the next few weeks Wil was glad to have her alone at the college. She still wore the engagement ring on a chain around her neck, but seldom talked about Steve to him. He was feeling sure that she was getting over him and now he'd have a shot at her.

It was mostly at night, alone, that her grieve took hold of her. Her emptiness gnawed at her heart like a starving dog on a dry bone. Sucking out the last of its marrow as she'd stare up into the darkness.

"Oh God how I miss you," she'd cry out quietly, then often fall to her knees sobbing, moaning and begging for his touch again. She'd take out his picture and hold it to her face asking, "Oh Stephen, why does it have to be like this?"

Each night she felt herself weakening, yearning to join him. The hole that his passing had left behind inside her was becoming a grave to her soul. The brightness and warmth of his smile soon could no longer be felt with just a picture to hold.

The light of each of life's joys they once had shared were being extinguished, one by one, as she neared drowning in the tears of a bleeding heart. She wasn't sure just how much longer she could keep pretending that she was fine.

She saw Wil everyday to his joy and they were seldom visited by the others, except maybe two or three times a month or on holidays when she'd go home. He spent all his free time trying to let her know, in subtle ways, that he had fallen for her and that he needed to be with her.

By the New Year, it began to frustrate him that she continued to look upon him as just a friend. He had invited her to a New Year's Eve dance, being held at his father's Elk's club and she thought it might help her, so she accepted.

When they arrived he introduced her to many of his acquaintances as his girlfriend. At first she was put off by this. Not wanting to hurt his feelings, she decided it wouldn't do any harm for him to pass them off as a couple for the one night.

When midnight struck and the horns blew and the cheers for the new 1972 began, he leaned over and kissed her on the lips firmly. She backed up, surprised at his boldness. It was then that he pointed at the mistletoe hanging above them and she laughed it off shaking her head.

Over the next few months, she began to appreciate his little acts of consideration and attentiveness. He was sweet and it felt nice to have someone near who tried to make her feel special again. Still, her loss continued to grow like a cancer inside her. It kept eating away at her will to go on with life.

Her appreciation of Wil's friendship grew slowly, but as graduation neared he started to invade her personal space more. A lot more than she wanted.

One time, her roommate said that she heard he was booking the two of them for a weekend at the shore for her upcoming birthday. When she confronted him, he said it was for two separate rooms and because he knew how much she loved it down there.

"I only wanted to give you something really nice as a gift," he told her.

"It was a sweet thought and thank you," she replied, "but I could never do that."

He dropped his head and said that he understood. Later, he canceled the reservations for the joining suites he had booked.

On graduation day he found out that she was considering an advertising position with a company she had sent a resume to in Short Hills, New Jersey. He had been offered a great job out in Oakland, California and didn't want to pass it up. The thought of losing her wasn't acceptable, so he decided to try and persuade her to look for something out there also.

"I don't ever want to leave New Jersey," she said. "I love it and I need to be here."

As the time came closer for him to inform the western company on his decision, he was left with only one option. He went and spoke with her roommate and asked her if she knew what Sue might really like for a graduation present.

"I'm not sure," she told him, "she doesn't seem to like much but art and music. She often sat in her room playing her phonograph while she worked on her art sketches, but it nearly always was the same song every night."

"Really," he asked, "which one?"

"It's that 45 over there on her desk. Go see for yourself."

She left the room for a soda as he picked up the record. He noticed that it was worn. In its dust jacket he found a picture of her and Steve kissing on a bridge. Written on the back were the words 'I Promise'. He played the song, then suddenly he smiled to himself.

He made reservations for the two of them to have dinner in a very exclusive restaurant in West Orange. She considered it to be a farewell date since he had said he was taking the job offer, so she thought little more of it. She knew she'd miss him and it would hurt to say goodbye.

During the evening he ordered wine and their better cuisine. They toasted to the years they had together and they danced to the live band music. She seemed to be having a wonderful time as he had planned.

After dinner he invited her up for one more slow dance. As it ended the band leader paused for an announcement.

"We have a very special moment to share with all of you," he said as he motioned for a spotlight to fall onto them.

Wil stooped slightly down in front of her as he signaled for the band to begin playing, 'God Only Knows,' by the Beach Boys.

She gasped hearing it playing and her hand went over her heart quickly.

"Sue I won't go west. We can stay here in Jersey together forever, if you'll marry me?"

She was speechless as the music played on and looked down at him. She stared around at the faces watching as they stood on the dance floor alone in that blinding spotlight. She started to tremble, then closed her eyes and cried mournfully, "Oh God."

"Say yes, please," he begged. "I've wanted you since we met. We'll have a perfect life together and be happy forever."

He paused, then added, "Sue, I promise," suddenly smiling as he took her hand.

"I promise, I promise," she heard echoing in her head and her heart. Suddenly, like someone near drowning and now being thrown a lifeline, she felt herself screaming inside to be saved.

She looked into his eyes for hope and in a moment of desperation heard herself say, "Oh yes, promise me." Quickly she covered her mouth just as the song ended.

He got up and held her firmly as she cried harder, gasping for each breath. As he kissed her neck the band started again, but now played a different and unfamiliar melody. She stared up into the dark ceiling and sighed quietly, "Forgive me."

While they danced he pushed an undersized ring onto her finger. He tried but couldn't get it to go all the way so she had to make a fist to keep it.

They set the wedding for the first Sunday in September, as she convinced herself she was doing the right thing moving on with her life. Wil took a job in New York City and commuted from an apartment he had rented in Fort Lee, New Jersey.

This was where they would live after they were married. She had refused to move any closer to the city and he said that he understood. He had told her that she could later look for a position in advertising there in Bergen County and she agreed.

The plans were moving along smoothly as the date approached. Wil was overjoyed to finally realize she would soon be his. When the day arrived he seemed anxious but she appeared nervous.

The wedding seemed to be going as planned even though Wil had gotten to the church on time while Sue arrived late. As the wedding march tried to begin playing for a third time, she stood out in the vestibule with her father and began to tremble.

"Baby, what's wrong?"

"I'll be fine," she said taking a breath. "I had dreamed of this day for so long, but you can't live a life while dreaming, can you?"

He kissed her hand.

"If I could change it, I would Baby." He paused, then asked, "Are you sure this is what you want?"

"I need to … I have to move on Daddy," she said with hurting emotions echoing in her tone. "What we had is forever in my heart, I loved him so. What I have now is a chance to live again. Wil's a good man and I do care for him, but it's still so hard to wake up and let go, you know?"

The doors opened and they slowly started down the aisle. She saw Wil smiling up front as she came forward. She felt her gown flowing. In her mind's eye, Steve appeared waiting for her at the bottom of the staircase. He was smiling in his tux, holding her corsage as her gown waltzed about her with each step towards him.

She heard his voice again saying, "She walks in beauty, like the night."

She glanced up for a second at the crucifix of her Lord bleeding for the world's trespasses. She lowered her eyes, bowed her head and stood silent before His altar. The ceremony began as her father gave her away.

She posed, half listening to the words spoken, staring at Wil's flowered lapel. She thought of the wildflowers, that bed of American dreams, now fading with the coming of the fall. Wil stood staring at her as her eyes rose to meet his.

"Do you William Walker, take thee, Susan LaRosa, to have and to hold, for better or for worst, in sickness and in health, for richer or for poorer, to love, honor and to cherish, till death do you part?"

"I do," she heard, as she remembered his face looking at her against that storefront window of the bridal shop in Caldwell. His eyes reflected his love then like the beacons of a lighthouse guiding her to his soul.

"Say I do," she suddenly heard the priest whisper to her and she snapped back.

"I do," she heard herself say.

"What God has joined together, let no man put asunder. You may kiss the bride."

Wil leaned into her, as she stood unmoving, and kissed her. She pulled her veil back down to hide a tear as they walked the empty aisle and out into the day's chilling air.

At the reception Sue remained seated most of the time, except to visit the tables and dance with her dad and with Wil. She lit up when Joe and Ken asked for a dance and she held them close each time.

"Are you happy?" Ken asked as he carried her across the ballroom floor.

"You, most of all, know where my heart is," she said, "but yes, I will try as I promised."

"If you ever need me," he whispered.

"I know Ski, and thank you," she said with her head against his arm.

Wil continued to drink, laugh and dance with all the women at the reception, including Sue when she was feeling up to it. They left at last around eleven and she drove because he had drunk too much.

Over at his apartment in Fort Lee she packed up the last of their luggage for the honeymoon flight in the morning. She put him onto the bed to rest and removed his jacket and shoes. Taking off her gown, she boxed it away quickly and then showered.

When she came back out in her nightgown he was asleep. She got into bed and laid there with the light still on thinking, then dreaming again.

She reached for her purse and took out Steve's engagement ring hanging on the gold chain. She held it in her palm, caressed it gently, then closed it tight in the fist of her right hand.

Wil's hand laid on her side and he awoke, pulling her over to him.

"Hey honey," he said softly.

She smiled putting her hand to his face.

"Hi," she said. "Why don't you get some rest now and I'll see you when you wake up, all right?"

He started kissing her neck then she felt his hand grab her leg.

"Don't please," she said, smelling the liquor on his breath, "not yet."

She turned over to him and said softly, "I just want this night to be special that's all. Let's just wait a bit."

"But I want you now."

"Please," she replied nervously, "just hold me for awhile and let's just be together."

He put his arm around her as they lay still, but within moments his hands were on her again and removing her nightgown. She didn't resist, just closed her eyes. Once it was off he just stared, then began to move his hand over her.

"Please turn off the lights first Wil," she asked softly and he did.

She remained still in the darkness, feeling him hold her, groping her and kissing down her neck and shoulders. His lips kissed across her chest as his hand moved to her thigh. She closed her eyes tighter as he moaned above her and her lips trembled.

"Wil wait, you're hurting me." She tried to move from beneath him but couldn't.

"Stop please!" she cried out, but he wouldn't. She gripped the pillow as she felt him and tried to prepare herself.

As he took her she cried out softly, "Oh Sweety."

She turned her head aside as a tear fell, mixed with eye shadow, and it stained the pillow.

***

Steve was suddenly jarred from his sleep as he cried out to her in the darkness of the cage.

"Sue! I'm here Love!"

He paused, as if for a reply from out of the black emptiness about him, then felt an ache in his chest. Slowly, he laid back down and turned on the dirt floor, trying to fall back into his dream of her again.

***

Later in the early hours of the morning, when Wil had long since fallen sleep, she went out onto the balcony. She had a blanket wrapped around her as she fell to her knees. She felt ashamed and sobbed quietly beneath a starless sky. There was a burning in her chest as she held her hand over her heart with the ring and chain cutting into her clenched palm.

"Thy Will be done," she finally sighed out, then cried until dawn.

On May 15, 1974, nine months later in Paterson General Hospital, Sue gave birth to a beautiful nine pound baby girl with a touch of brown hair. She had been in labor for nine hours and was drained. She laid quietly holding this gift from God in her arms. She had delivered alone. Wil had to be out of town on business in California.

When she was first shown her by the doctor, after he had gotten her to cry and take a breath, Sue reached out to wipe the tears away. Now, as she held the infant close to her heart, she began to cry.

"You have my eyes, my nose and the sweetest smile My Love."

She lowered her head and then ever so gently blew her breath towards the tiny mouth. "That's life from one who loves you and me." The baby gave her a half upturned smile as Sue wiped her tears on the child's tiny hands.

The nurse came into the room and asked for the child's name to be recorded.

"Her name is Dawn," she said. "Dawn Evelyn Walker."

Sue looked down into those precious eyes. "You are my Alpha and my Omega," she whispered.

Chapter Fifteen
"All roads don't lead home."

Norton sat up on the dirt floor and checked his leg wounds for infection. Preston moaned in the corner from a fever, as Steve went around retesting the strength of the bamboo bars.

"Still thinking about escaping?" Norton asked with a chuckle under his breath.

"Always," he replied pulling on the bars again.

"We've been in this how long now?"

"It'll be the Christmas of '74 in three weeks or so," Steve answered in a frustrated tone.

"You still thinking about that lady of yours, ain't ya?"

"Every moment that I breathe. Don't you think about Audrey?"Norton sighed. "Yea everyday. Course, I doubt she's still waiting for the likes of me."

He propped himself up as he watched Steve continue to check out their cage.

"Won't do either of them ladies any good if we die trying to break out of here," he said feeling him out on how intent he was to try.

"My Sue," he said, pausing his search to turn and look him straight in the eye, "is a woman worth dying for."

Steve stared up at a couple of clouds as they floated by, then continued with his work.

He glanced out through the bars and watched as a guard across the yard acted suspiciously, looking around, and then ducking into a small hut used as a tool shed. A moment later, he saw a girl's head move inside between the partly pulled cloth curtains.

"Looks like they got themselves a little gal barn going over there," he said to D. L. who got up to see.

"Yep it does. Just another way to torture and get to us," he mumbled.

"Maybe so," Steve muttered softly, thinking and watching.

"I wondered how these guys lasted without any women here, seeing how that old Ho Chi Minh wanna-be wouldn't allow them," Norton said laughing. "I'll bet he's queer."

"Know your opponent's weakness," Steve muttered to himself.

"What'd ya say?"

He didn't reply, just kept watching the hut.

Day after day, he sat watching for a pattern to the activity surrounding that small tool shed.

Guards would duck in after the end of each of their shifts, but only during daylight hours. He saw the faces through the curtains as guards entered and exited and those of the young girls inside.

He waited and he watched as he reasoned it out.

Two guards came one morning at sunrise and forced him and Norton to their feet and across the compound. Back in the officer's building, they were stripped down to boxers and tied up hanging from a rafter. Just the tips of their toes touched the floor.

"Today I have something new to share with you," said the commanding officer. "Perhaps now you'll finally share information with me and then sign these war-crime confessions for the criminals you are." He pulled back the blanket cover from the table and revealed a small generator.

"What's the matter," D. L. asked, "Congress didn't answer any of the letters you sent? Damn, I gotta get out and vote more."

"You both have been a most amusing challenge, but now we have more fun."

He ordered the guards to strap the wires to Norton, then they threw a bucket of water on him.

The generator was started and the switch turned on. The electricity jolted his body into convulsions as he screamed, then he stopped shaking as it was turned off within six to eight seconds.

Dan took deep breaths and moaned.

244

"You have something to say now?" the officer asked with a dirty smile.

"Damn," he answered in-between deep breaths, "that sure puts lead in your pencil. I gotta get me one of those for homecoming."

A second set of leads were put on Steve and when he felt the jolt he cried out, " I love you Angel!" then could only scream out in pain. When it finally stopped he just began murmuring softly, "Stay with me ... Stay, with me."

The switch was thrown again and again on them, but they both only repeated their name and rank for as long as they could.

Later, as they recovered from this new session of pain and questions, Norton moaned saying, "I don't think I can take much more of that again. Punches, knife cuts, a little beating... Hell, that's just a party in some rough parts of Jersey."

He moaned again adding, "But this crap...I think they've burned up something inside me. God it hurts."

"I've had it too," Steve answered. "Are you ready to try for home?"

Norton turned to him slowly.

"How?"

"Wake the others," he said quietly.

He led them over to a far corner of their prison and dug up some loose dirt he had reburied days before.

"See," Steve said, "the wood has rotted below from the water sitting here. If we pull together, we can break them free."

Each dug up the earth around the base of several poles and together they quietly pulled them apart.

"Come on," he whispered, "stay down low and in single file."

There were only two guards that stood in their way. Steve came up behind the first and put him into a choke hold, squeezing hard until he felt the life leave him. D. L. got the other.

The seven men made their way across the compound crawling from one dark shadowed spot to the next until they reached the shed hut. Then when all were inside, Steve pulled the curtains closed.

"You'd better be right about this," Norton said, "or we just bought us a long session on the new juice box."

They started moving tools, shovels, boxes of wire and nails about quietly. Finally, under one light crate Dan found it.

"H-e-l-l-o," he quietly sung out.

"Gentlemen," Steve said with a smile, "welcome to the Love Tunnel."

They looked over and saw the opening to a tunnel entrance.

"How'd ya know?" Preston asked.

"It had to be the only way the girls were getting in and out without being seen," he answered with a grin.

Steve peered back out the curtain at the officer's building. Hatred churned inside him as he picked up a shovel like a club. The officer's voice and face burned in his mind, mocking him, and he wanted justice.

As he raised the shovel a voice came from within his heart. "Just stay alive and come back to me," it whispered, "that's all you have to do."

He closed his eyes and cried a moment. Finally, he turned to help each man as they dropped down into the tunnel.

They made their way in the darkness by feel only. It seemed like miles before they reached an opening and crawled out into the jungle. It was still dark, but they figured out which way most likely led them back to the river.

Before daylight they had covered a lot of ground. They had moved in the moonlight faster and less cautiously than they knew they should in a jungle. That was because they wanted to put as much distance between them and the compound as they could before they were discovered missing.

By the fourth day, they began to feel safer and made their way more like soldiers than as fugitives. Steve led the point, carrying a bamboo spear he had sharpened on a rock, and Norton covered the rear carrying the same.

Preston had to be helped by two of the others as he was still weak from fever. Barnes limped as fast as he could on a leg which had been broken but had reset misaligned.

They came to a small rice patty and slowly moved through it. They were taking a chance out in the open, but they could make better time than going around the perimeter.

As they moved through the shallow water, suddenly one man cried out in pain. Steve turned and saw a snake, a constrictor, wrapped around his leg and he had been bitten.

He hurried back to him and jabbed his spear into it. It fell off and he helped the soldier up onto his shoulders.

"I know it hurts like hell," he said to him, "but it's not poisonous."

When they made it again to cover in the brush, he put him down and tore away the pants leg to use as a bandage.

Dan came up last and said, "Better keep moving," and he nodded.

Always they traveled with the sun to their left in the morning and on the right in afternoon. Insects buzzed and bit them constantly as they marched. They drank water when it rained from large leaves they could catch some in and often ate what crawled nearby.

As they sat one night under the moonlight, Dan noticed Steve patting his boot laces and muttering, "Stay with me," over and over.

He had seen him do this before during a patrol rest and at the prison compound whenever he was thinking.

"Why do you do that?" he finally asked pointing to his boot.

Steve smiled and undid his one boot lace. Underneath, he pulled out a Pontiac key fob tied to the laces from beneath and showed it to him.

"This," he said, "is Excalibur."

Dan stared puzzled asking, "And?"

"As long as he is with me, I am undefeatable."

D. L. grinned. "Have you got another one?"

"Sorry, he's one of a kind and serves only one king."

"You know why I like you," Dan said, "cause you're as crazy as I am."

They laughed and laid back to rest.

"It sure is peaceful tonight for a war," Steve heard him say, and then they laughed again.

By mid-day next, they spotted the river's edge and made their way along its banks. For the next two days they walked it, staying low and on 'Super Alert' at all times.

As they moved slowly through some high elephant grass he heard a cry from Darnel in front of him. D. L. hurried up, but found him lying down and gasping for air. The others came over, but he died within seconds. Dan looked up at Steve's face.

"What happened?" he asked in a cold tone.

Dan held up a green, spearheaded snake which he had killed. "It was a Three Stepper," he said as he tossed it.

"A what?" asked green weenie Barnes.

"If it bites you, you take three steps then you die," Dan answered as he eyed the ground around them.

Steve closed his eyes and said, "Come on, keep moving."

He worked carefully back to the river's edge and they followed, then he gave the signal to drop. They listened and then saw a chopper coming from down river, flying low as if searching. It was one of theirs and they jumped out from the brush screaming and waving as it approached.

Its crew spotted them and hovered for a pick up. The ropes were dropped and as Steve and Norton were pulled inside gunfire opened on them.

Two men were hit and fell back into the water from the ropes. The door gunner opened up on the tree smoke. Steve looked over the edge of the door and saw the last two still struggling to climb. He and Norton each grabbed the ropes and pulled them up a few inches at a time.

Preston's head appeared and Steve grabbed him, pulling him in. Norton reached for Barnes, but heard a shot and watched as his eyes went empty. He held his wrist tightly as Steve also grabbed at him and they pulled him inside. The copter lifted quickly and headed south.

They looked back in time to see the two bodies being carried away by the uncaring current. Steve ached inside as he pictured their faces and heard their voices echoing in his mind.

"God, I thought we were all home," he said solemnly with tears to Dan. "When do we stop paying?"

Dan turned to a crewman and asked for some coins, then he tossed them out the door and into the river below.

"Here's your fee you black-hearted Ferryman," he screamed out, "now carry their souls home! Everybody's going home today, I swear it!"

He continued to lean and stare far out the door as Steve grabbed and held on to him tightly. Finally, they both fell back inside exhausted on the floor.

"A chaplain once told me," Dan said mournfully as he stared at the blood on his hands, "that during the last 5600 years, the world's only known 292 years of peace."

He went silent for a moment thinking.

"That's like 20 to 1. My God Seaside, I could get better odds drunk and shooting craps in a Newark alley."

He closed his eyes and within minutes he was sound asleep.

Steve bowed his head and prayed quietly, then said, "Thank you Lord for Your mercy and for this chance to know a 293rd. Amen."

Chapter Sixteen

"There's not a joy the world can give like that it takes away."

-Lord Byron

Steve was booked on a commercial flight to Hawaii.

"I hope you make it home for Christmas," the stewardess said when hearing that he was headed for New Jersey.

The following day he had a layover, then connected with his flight for Sacramento to Fairfield Air Force Base. He waited there with another layover on Saturday.

On Sunday morning, he was to be channeled onto a flight to McGuire Air Force Base, near Fort Dix, in New Jersey. Upon arrival, he would then be taken to a hospital to be checked out further and then be released on Monday for a bus home.

The stewardess came over and asked if he needed anything.

He smiled and said, "Everything I need is waiting for me at home."

She smiled back saying, "Welcome home soldier," and then started serving snacks, tea and coffee.

As she passed by again, he asked, "You know, I think I would like some tea after all, would you mind?"

"Not at all," and she poured him a cup.

He drank it slowly, smiling at the thought of finally being with her again. He drank in the thought of her with each sip of tea.

"I am never leaving you again," he whispered softly, "I promise."

He fell asleep and she came to him in a dream. He could see her all dressed in white as she came down the aisle. Her smile beneath the thin veil outshined the chandeliers above as she came closer.

"Do you Susan LaRosa, take thee Stephen Clayton, for your lawful wedded husband? To love, honor and to cherish, in sickness and in health, for richer or poorer, till death do you part?"

He waited, then she faded from his sight as he was awakened by the announcement that they would be landing shortly.

"I do," he heard her voice echo from the past.

He had forgotten about the cup of tea in his hand. As he stirred up from his nap, the last drops split out and stained the cushion.

At the base he was examined for mental health issues and got the paperwork completed for his discharge. He was given the back pay due him and was informed he had been given a promotion to Sergeant while M.I.A. He tried to call home but there was no answer.

It was a cold Monday, with light on and off snow flurries, as he got a ride out to the bus terminal and boarded one for the ride to north Jersey. He watched others as they were riding to be with love ones for Christmas also.

"You going home soldier?" asked an older man sitting across the aisle.

"Yea, at last," he answered, "it's been a long road."

"Oh, how far?"

Steve looked out the window.

"To the dark side of the sun and back, " he said in a distant tone of voice, "but it's good to be back where two are always one."

"You all right?"

"I'll be fine, the moment I see her face and kiss her smile," he replied with a brightness in his eyes.

"Oh is that it," he said, "I should have known. Women have that effect on men sometimes."

"With some," Steve said with a sigh, "it can become a permanent condition."

As he rode his last bus for home up Route 46, he smiled at the landmarks passing quickly outside the windows. The Par-troy drive-in on the right, the batting cages and tee-off golf range, then the corner where the bus turned a hard right onto North Beverwyck Road.

He had watched as the other passengers had gotten off at each stop along the way and now there was just him, sitting in the back. The bus echoed in the emptiness with each bump until it finally stopped at the corner of North Beverwyck Road and Lake Shore Drive.

"Last stop!" the driver called out, then looked back to him and said, "This is as far as you can go soldier."

Steve walked up the aisle and smiled saying, "Yes, I know," and he got off.

It was late afternoon as he stood there in the snow. He looked across the street and saw the old Sunoco open, so he walked over. Inside was a young guy sitting on a chair watching him as he came inside.

"Can I help you?" he asked, eying over the uniform.

"I was just wondering if Chuck was around?"

The young man thought a moment, then said, "Oh yea old Chuck, naw, he don't own this no more."

"Oh wow, I used to work here a few years back and I didn't think he'd ever sell this place."

"He didn't, he died. A heart attack I think it was they said."

Steve was quiet as he looked around the office area. There were no more pictures of friends hanging up, or of Chuck with his old cars smiling next to them holding a rag and wrench. No more candy dish on the counter for visitors to take a piece free. His old desk was gone and a display was in its place showing auto accessories for sale.

"I'm sorry to hear that," he replied. "Well, you have a nice Christmas."

"I will, as soon as I can get the heck out of here," the young man snorted with his feet up against the window.

Steve smiled, then left and went back across the street. He paused and looked back.

"God be with you uncle, I'll miss you," he whispered, then he started walking down the hill for home.

When he reached his street he walked down it slowly, looking at the familiar houses. He knew every family and person in each one.

He smiled as he passed Elaine's house and remembered when she gave him his first kiss. On the right was Karen's, where he and Ken met two of her friends outside a bedroom window during a sleep over. They had a date with each before the evening was over.

He saw the tree in old Mr. C's yard where he had fallen out of and broke his arm at twelve, putting him in a body cast for the summer that year.

When he finally reached the dead end, he stopped to look at their little bungalow house. He closed his eyes as he could see each of them, working on dinner, homework and playing board games or watching television on the floor. The swing was still hanging on the front tree that he had swung Sue on so many evenings after they had dinner or after a barbecue in the backyard together with the family.

He remembered how he'd swing her, then grab and hold her a moment for a kiss, then let her go again. The lawn he had mowed and raked hundreds of times for fifty cents a week allowance and where they had laid and laughed together. The driveway where he had first seen the engine of a car as his dad tuned his up and where he sat with her in Excalibur, talking and kissing so many times. He was home.

He lowered his head and said a prayer of thanks.

His sister Anna was playing her record player and listening to her favorite 45, when she happened to look out and see him.

"Steve!" she screamed, "Steve's out there!" and she ran for the side door.

He saw the tears on her face as she finally came out the door and ran to him. She almost stopped, as if he weren't real, then smiled and jumped into his arms. He wanted to hug the breath out of her.

"Oh," he said, "I've missed you so much."

She said nothing, just cried and squeezed him tight as if he'd vanish.

"I knew he'd bring you home," she said smiling.

"He?"

"Yes, Santa!" she yelled. "I put you on my list when I wrote him every Christmas and asked him to find you and bring you back home. Sue would take me to mail it, except last year."

"She couldn't?"

"No, she couldn't come last Christmas, so I went myself up town and gave it to the mail lady. I didn't have an envelope, but she said she'd make sure he got it."

He smiled as he took off his coat and put it around her, then lifted her up in his arms.

"I had asked him to bring you home in his sleigh and he did, didn't he?"

Steve thought of the runners on the copter and smiled answering, "Yes, he found me and brought me all the way home." He reached into his duffle bag and said, "he gave me a present for you when he dropped me off at the corner."

She lit up as he searched through the bag and finally brought out a wrapped package and gave it to her.

"Can I open it?"

"Why not, it's yours," he replied smiling.

She carefully pulled back the paper. Inside was a real china doll with dark hair and eyes, wearing a geisha robe of red and white.

"Oh," she said with wide eyes, "she's beautiful!"

"She's a special dancer, " he told her, "and her name is…"

"Sue," she said. "She smiles like Sue."

He looked and was surprised that she was right, same little nose and perfect lips smiling.

"You're right," he commented, "she does look like Sue."

"Oh, I miss her," she said as she hugged the doll, "she doesn't come to see me anymore."

Before he could ask why not, suddenly other members of the family were coming out to find Anna and began crying and yelling as they saw them together.

He hugged each, then his mother appeared at the door and they stared at each other. She held her hand to her mouth, then over her heart and began crying. He went over and put his arms around her.

"They said you were dead," she cried.

"I know. I found it out when I reached Jersey while I was being checked out. I'm sorry, I thought you knew. I tried to call before coming home."

They all went inside and made him an early supper. He told them he really hadn't eaten, had just wanted to get home.

When he finished he went to the phone, then realized he couldn't remember her phone number anymore.

"I can't believe that I've forgotten everybody's number. What is Sue's again?"

Everyone suddenly got real quiet. "She not there anymore," his mom said and came over to him.

"She moved?" he asked surprised.

"Steve, she's married."

He put the phone down and stared at her.

"I'm so sorry. We were told, she was told that you had died in that battle Ken had gotten wounded in. They had your tags and you were declared dead."

He didn't move or say anything, just stared at her.

"Sue waited, hoping to hear something different, praying day and night for you but after so many years she had to accept it."

His mom came over to him.

"It almost killed her son. She died that day inside, I saw it in her eyes. I cried with her into the night."

She paused waiting, but he said nothing.

"She went on to college and finished, trying to make a new life for herself. She loved you so much but she had to move on. She met someone and got married last year. She has a little girl I heard from her mom."

She stopped, unable to tell if he was listening.

"Steve, did you hear what I said? "

He walked over and got his coat. "I'd like to go for a drive," he said giving her a kiss. "Is my car running?"

"Of course, your dad has been keeping it running well. The keys are on its visor."

"Thanks," he replied slowly, as if not really aware of the moment, and he went out to the garage.

He got into the car but then just pulled it out into the driveway and sat. His hands trembled and he waited until he was able to drive safely.

He drove uptown and finally pulled into the main lot of St. Peter's Church. He walked past the large shrine on the lawn where a full size nativity scene had been set up and he saw the infant in the manger with Mary. He went up the steps and inside the church.

It was empty as he paused in front of the basin, then slowly dipped his fingers into the Holy Water, touched his lips, then blessed himself. He walked slowly down the aisle, staring at the empty pew where he had first sat with her. He genuflected, blessed himself, and then knelt in the pew.

He stared up at the crucifix, then he prayed and he cried, then prayed and cried, long into the night.

He didn't come home that night. In the morning his mother called his friends, but no one had seen him. Finally, in the early evening, she got a call from Father Murphy.

"Your son is here," he told her. "I think since yesterday. I saw him around seven O'clock last night when I went for some papers, but he was praying and I didn't want to disturb him. When I came back an hour ago he was still there. I talked to him but he doesn't look well. He refused to leave when I tried to get him to go home. He just continues to pray. I think he has been crying also."

"Thank you Father, I'll get someone to go for him."

She called Joe back.

"Don't worry," he said, " I'll go over."

When he arrived with his brother Father Michael they went inside quietly. He was on his knees still with his head down. As they approached they could hear him praying.

"Please answer me. How much more? I can't bleed anymore. Oh please tell me this isn't real. Let me wake up in the cage again, at least there we were together. Dear God, let it be just a dream please."

They stopped in the aisle next to him.

"Steve, are you all right?" Joe asked softly.

He raised his head and looked at him. "He asks too much," he said, crying still.

They sat in the next front pew facing him. Mike touched his hand and said, "You have to trust in Him. All things are for the Good, if we trust that He knows best."

"Mike," he asked with a hoarse voice, "where can the good be in this?"

"He loves us, and He gives all of His saints trials to prepare them for His purposes. We must lean on Him and become perfect."

"Trials?" Steve asked. "I can tell you about trials," he said as he rose up. "I've walked through hell's gate itself. I've spit in the devil's face. I've seen and tasted a lifetime of pain and agony and death. I've stood burning in its flames, but always, always she was beside me, giving me strength, pulling me home. Well now I'm home, but home can't bring me to her."

"Let us take you home," Joe said.

"I have no home! No life!"

He walked up pointing to the altar. "Only He has the power to give me my world," he cried, "and He won't!"

He reached into his pocket and brought out the worn Pontiac key-fob and put it upon the altar.

"If you're gonna take my heart," he cried out, "then be merciful and take the rest of me too!"

He looked up at the crucifix, then fell to his knees.

"We've been faithful and true! You promised me!—-You promised us forever! Why! Oh God why!" He fell face to floor in tears, then collapsed and they called for an ambulance.

He was treated for exhaustion and then taken to the V. A. Hospital, but refused to talk or eat. A week passed but still there was no change.

"I know he hears and understands me," the doctor told Joe, "but he refuses to respond, to even try. I've seen the war take away a man's will to live before. He needs something to make him face whatever it is that he can't and deal with it."

"War isn't killing him, love is," Joe said choked up, " and they never taught him how to fight against that."

257

Joe stayed sitting next to him alone and praying. There was a knock at the door and his mother came in with the family.

"How is he?" she asked, knowing the answer as she looked at him.

"The same," Joe said. "Shouldn't we call her?"

"No, that would only cause them both more pain and they've had enough."

The doctor came in and asked, "Can I see all of you outside a moment?" They followed him but his mom asked Anna to stay with him.

"You wait here baby and talk with Steve. He doesn't feel well."

Anna went and sat on the edge of the bed, seeing his eyes half open, but looking at the ceiling. She opened her small backpack and took out the china doll he'd given her.

"Look," she said, "I put a prom dress on her. Sue made it for one of my other dolls, isn't it pretty?" He didn't look.

"I'm sorry you're not feeling well, but I have something else." She pulled out a small cassette player and said, "Sue and I made this tape of songs. We made a lot of them and I got most of them to keep, here listen."

She pushed the button and laid it on his bed. He could hear her and Sue's voices.

***

"Is it on?"

"Yes baby, you just talk in here. Go on talk."

"Are you gonna take him away when he comes home?"

"We will always be together," he heard Sue tell her, "no matter what, I promise. Once God puts someone in your heart, its forever."

"This is for you Steve," he heard Anna's voice say, "we're gonna sing some songs I learned. Ready?"

"Yes baby, I'm Ready."

"Okay, we're gonna sing the song, 'I can see clearly now'."

***

He heard their voices talking and singing then he started to cry.

Anna stopped the tape and said," I'm sorry, I thought you'd like it."

He touched her face gently. "Please play some more, you both sounded so good."

She smiled and turned it back on, then together they sang along. At the end of the song, he could hear Sue saying, "We love you forever Babe," and he cried for a moment until another song to him began.

Through the door window, his mom saw him singing with her as she sat on his lap. He was holding her 'Sue' doll against his chest.

She turned back to the doctor and said, "I don't think another evaluation will be necessary, he's just found his cure."

Everyone looked as she pointed to the room. He was smiling as they sang even louder.

"I love you," she heard him say to Anna. "I'll love you both forever," and he kissed the top of her head as he looked at the doll.

"Out of the mouths of babes," his mom whispered to Joe.

When he checked out the next day, he asked Joe to stop at the church. As he knelt inside, he lowered his head more than ever before.

"Forgive me Lord," he said, " I've been arrogant and selfish. I'm ashamed and I know she would be also for what I've done. I forgot she was a gift from You, a love I never deserved in the first place. I forgot that all I had ever wanted was for her to be happy and now I know that's why you made her move on. Thank you for saving her when I couldn't. I know now that she was always with me because You put her there in my heart, and gave us forever as You promised.

Now I promise to honor that perfect love you showed me through her. Please help me to be strong and make her proud. I ask this in Jesus' name, Amen."

He blessed himself, then went over and lit a candle.

He looked up and said softly, "I will light one every week, to cherish my love for her and my promise to You."

When he came out, Joe could see a radiant look on his face, as if he had just been blessed with peace.

"Steve, everything all right?"

"Joe, I was just given a new day," he said with a smile. "I'd like to do something good with it?"

259

"Sure, got something in mind?" Joe asked smiling back as he watched him looking out to the horizon.

"What we leave behind is as important as what we strive for remember, and Joe, I want to leave behind more than I've taken. I want to start a company and make a difference in people's lives. Care to join me?"

"Okay, what kind of company?"

"A Security Service like none before it. One that changes lives. Come on," he said walking quickly down the steps, "let's go buy Ken some lunch and talk."

As they sat in a booth at the Village Spa, they placed their orders with Mama and Ken turned to him.

"Look Steve it sounds like a good idea, but I still am a little confused on where we're gonna find the start up capital for this kind of thing."

"I've got that covered, if you're both in with me," he answered. "Joe talked it over with Cindy and they're willing to risk the nest egg they have for a house. I have my back pay from the army and you and I both have our V. A. benefits to tap. We can do it."

"That still can't be enough for employee wages, benefits, all the insurances and other stuff, " Ken replied.

"It can, if we're the guards for all three shifts to start out until we can afford others. Just uniforms for us and a small salary each. The remaining money goes back into the company. The rest is just basic business insurance, a bond, a small office with Cindy acting secretary and a license, simple!"

"All right, but what about a client to pay for it all?"

"I know how to get them," Steve said with a smile. "When I worked security before I was drafted, I learned from the management there. When I had down time I had to help out in the office sales. It's just a matter of submitting the right bid on the site."

They paused, watching his reaction.

"All for one?" Steve asked smiling. Ken looked back, then at Joe's grin.

"Okay one for all, but," Ken added, "if this bombs out, let it be on your heads."

Joe laughed. "I've been there before and we still won the tournament remember?"

Ken thought back to the match. "Yea, I remember."

Steve was quiet, thinking now about her also. He looked up at them and finally asked, "How is she, do you know?"

"They have been living out in an apartment in Fort Lee since they were married," Joe replied. "I talked with her mom and she said he had been offered a promotion, but they'd have to move to California. Sue said that she didn't want to move from New Jersey. I don't know what was decided."

"I know," Ken said, looking over at Steve's face and waiting for a nod to continue. "I heard he accepted it and went out this week. He also insisted she and the baby come right behind him as soon as he finds an apartment in Oakland."

Ken looked at him.

"Do you want to see her before she goes, I have her number and address?"

Steve just waved his hand as a no, excused himself, and went to the restroom.

"He's decided to let her live her new life, especially now with a baby, and forget about him," Joe said forcing himself to say the words. "He's agreed it would only bring her, and him I'm sure, more pain and hurt to see each other."

Ken sighed and glanced out the window into the parking lot with a distant look.

"I don't know how he can do it," he finally said out loud.

"It's because he loves her," Joe replied, "and only wants her happy. How happy would she be if she knew he was here?"

Ken smiled at him. "Of course you're both right, but God, I don't think I will ever know a love as pure and true as theirs was."

"As it still is," Joe corrected, "and forever."

Part II

Chapter Seventeen

"Can Oceans, Years and Tears Share One Heart?"

As Mass ended, Sue and Dawn genuflected from the pew. Father O'Malley greeted her as he stepped down from the altar and asked how she and the family were doing.

"Fine, thank you Father," she said with a half smile.

"She sure looks fine," he said looking at Dawn smiling at him, and how is your husband? I wish he would come to Mass with you."

"So do we Father, but he's been working long hours and doing weekends now," she sighed. "I wish he wouldn't but he insists he must."

"Maybe you both will be able to come to the benefit supper this Friday."

"We'll try and I'll tell him you asked about him. He'll be home early today, it's Dawn's birthday."

"Is it? And how old are you today?"

"I'm nine!" she answered with excitement. "Daddy promised to take me to the shore today. We're gonna go crabbing."

"Wow, you've grown so fast," he said. "Did he teach you how to do that?"

"No Mommy did, she loves the ocean too."

"Well Happy Birthday!"

"Thanks Father, I'm sure it'll be a good one."

He smiled at them, then went to the rear exit doors.

Sue went over to light a candle, as she always did every week in memory of Steve and another for this double special day.

"God watch over you," she prayed seeing his smile in her mind from that special time.

Later, Dawn helped her finish with the decorations and putting out the food for the guests soon arriving. One by one her friends and moms came to the door for the party. They served them snacks and drinks, then they started with some games as Sue waited for Wil to get home.

The doorbell rang and Dawn ran with her to open it.

"Maybe Daddy needs help with my present."

They opened the door and it was the clown Wil had hired for the party. Sue smiled and pointed him to the living room for his show.

Dawn took his big gloved hand and led him inside smiling as her mom looked up the street, then closed the door. She sat with Dawn and the others as Mr. Lotz-of-Pockets made them laugh with his magic tricks and antics.

As he usually did, he called the birthday child up for the grand finale. Dawn went and he dressed her up as a princess with a magic wand to wave over the empty box.

"Say the magic words with me!" he told everybody.

"HAPPY BIRTHDAY DAWN!" they all yelled as she waved the large wand. He opened the box and Mr. Bigfoot, the magic rabbit, popped his head out.

"Oh look," he said, "Mr. Big foot has a present for you."

He had her reach into the box and pull out a wrapped gift. They took a bow together as Sue snapped another picture.

After the show, cake and thank you gifts were given out to the guests, then the presents opened. Sue called the office, but still got no answer. An hour later, they waved goodbye to the guests.

"Did you have a nice day Baby?"

"Oh yes, but I wish Daddy could have been here."

"Me too," she sighed, then pointed to the magic present from the bunny yet unopened.

"I wanted to save that to open with Daddy."

"I'm sure he'll love that when he gets home soon, " she replied smiling. They put it aside and together started to clean up the house.

265

It was just after nine when Wil came through the door. She was sitting in the living room waiting.

"Where have you been?" she asked upset.

"Working at the office. I told you I wanted to get this work done for a Monday client."

He walked over to the bar case and poured himself a scotch.

"I called but got no answer there."

"I told you I was working and I just didn't want to be disturbed," he said in a firm tone.

"You missed her Birthday. We waited all afternoon for you. She fell asleep waiting to see you."

"The clown showed up didn't he?"

Sue looked coldly at him. "She wanted you. She turned nine today and you hardly spend any time with her."

He poured another drink. "I have to pay for all this, do you understand?"

"We don't need to be living in such an expensive apartment," she replied. "Driving such outrageous cars, belonging to golf and club memberships which we hardly ever use. We need you, working regular hours and eating dinner with us."

"I need those things, most for my business image. I don't hear you complaining about shopping and buying nice things," he stated with some resentment. "Well, they don't come cheap."

"You're the one who insists I buy the latest fashions to be seen in. It was you that put her in a private school and have us eat out in expensive places all the time," she stated bluntly. "You're never home for me to cook and to eat together, to share our day and talk about what matters, our lives together."

Sue pointed to Dawn sleeping on the couch. "There's what's important, family, not things."

She watched as he looked over at her, curled up, holding the present for him to open with her.

"I didn't ask for this life," she said, "I didn't want to leave Jersey, remember? This was your dream not mine, not hers, and I, I ..."

She went quiet a moment.

"We want to go home."

He glared at her saying, "You are home, if you make it one and stop complaining."

"Wil please, let's go back to Jersey. I miss it and my family and my friends. We don't belong here. I want a house of our own with a yard for her to play in and a garden of flowers. A place where we could have loved ones over on weekends for a barbecue. My mom and grandma ache to see us and watch Dawn growing up, please."

"I worked too hard to give this all up for some damn boring Norman Rockwell small town life."

"Please, don't curse," she begged quietly, looking over at Dawn sleeping.

"I like the action, the prestige I have here and the challenges," he said with a slight grin as he poured to top off his glass. "I'm not leaving."

"Wil, this life is burying us in debt. The phone rings off the hook looking for payments and I'm tired of not knowing what to tell them. Maybe if I went to work part-time we can get out of it, but only if you stop spending like you've been."

He turned to her with fiery eyes.

"I won't have you working and people thinking I need your money, and what I spend is my business since I earn it! You may be content to go back east and live like some common sheep in the herd," he mumbled. "Everyday getting sheered in the marketplace for a handful of pennies, but not me."

She watched as he took his drink upstairs while she went to the couch and held Dawn sleeping in her lap. She began crying, making a fist, then prayed softly. "Please Lord, send me the strength I need."

She slowly opened Dawn's gift. It was a hand puppet. A white bird with piercing blue eyes.

***

"Good afternoon On Guard Services. This is Pamela Emerson, how may I help you? ...Yes Mr. Windslow, Mr. Clayton took care of that personally. I faxed out a copy of his reported findings to your insurance company this morning and another to your legal department

…Yes sir, you're most welcome and thank you for using our services. If we can help you further, please feel free to call me. Thank you again Mr. Windslow, goodbye."

Ken came out from his office and called to Steve' s personal secretary. "Pam, has Mr. Clayton come in yet?"

"No, he hasn't," she replied, then they heard Joe call from his office.

"He won't be in at all today remember, it's May Fifteenth."

"Oh yea, I forgot," Ken answered.

Pam checked her date book, then questioned the importance of the date. "I don't have anything lined up for him here," she stated. "I sorry, but he didn't say anything to me."

"There's nothing wrong," Ken said, "he never works on this day. He has a date with a memory Pam."

She said nothing, just leaned her head a moment as if she missed something. Joe stepped out and said, "It was on this date that he had gotten engaged."

"I didn't know Mr. Clayton was ever married."

"He wasn't," Joe said to her adding, "and please, don't ever bring this up to him."

"No sir," she replied, lost in her thoughts. She saw Cindy come in and went over to her.

"Hi Pam, how's your day going?"

"Uh, fine. Cindy, could you tell me about something?"

"If I can, what?"

"Can you tell me about May Fifteenth?"

Cindy was quiet, then said, "Let's go in here." Pam followed her to Steve's office where she closed the door and pointed to a sketch hanging on his wall.

"She sketched that for him," Cindy said solemnly, "right after he proposed to her on that bridge on their prom night, May Fifteenth, 1969."

Pam walked over looking closer at it. "What happened?"

268

"Vietnam was what happened," she said. "Did you ever notice that no one ever sits in the front seat of his car, not even Ken or my Joe, when he drives?"

Pam nodded.

"That was for her only, and only Sue could drive Excalibur. They loved each other all through school. Their life was all planned out. Oh God, they loved each other beyond the words then she got the news that he had been killed. It literally almost killed her. He was her world. After years, she accepted it and had to move on. She married, had a child and moved away."

Cindy stopped, trying to compose herself.

"Then he came home. He had spent over three years as a P.O.W., the army had made a mistake, he was alive."

Again she paused, choking up.

"He loved her so much, more than life itself. When he found out, all he wanted was to die and would have but for the grace of God."

Cindy turned to her and said, "Pam, I would never have told this to you but I've known how you felt about him for a long time."

Pam looked away as Cindy came by her.

"He deserves to be happy too," she said to her, "maybe it will be you that can make that difference. Am I right about how you feel?"

"Since I first came here," she confessed. "The more I got to know him the more I fell in love with him, but he kept his distance." She lightly laughed. "I just thought he was shy at first. Later I figured he didn't feel the same and assumed he just wanted to keep things professional."

"I've seen the way he looks and talks to you. He feels the same but he just can't let it out."

Cindy thought a moment, then smiled to herself. "Tell ya what. The day's just about over so why don't you leave a little early. Oh, and I think that you might find it's a short cut for you to take River Road home today," she added with a wink.

Steve opened the trunk of Excalibur and took out a small bottle of champagne and two glasses. He walked up the steps and out to the center of the wishing bridge.

As he laid them down on the railing he paused to enjoy the end of the sunset as it reflected its last warm rays across the lake. He was hoping for a glimpse of the moon tonight, but was in no hurry to rush its coming.

Pam cruised along River Road slowly. As she came to the curve near the Hiawatha Pool parking lot she saw his car and smiled. Parking along side it she got out. He was nowhere in sight, but she saw steps leading to a bridge and slowly walked towards them.

He smiled as the first stars came into view and a near-full moon peeked from behind some clouds. He unwrapped the top of the bottle and set up the two glasses on the railing. Popping the cork, he made a private wish as it flew over his head into the river below.

He filled both glasses, then took one to toast the night sky."Happy Anniversary Love," he said as he sipped. "It will always be a great time," he whispered looking at the year 1969 on the label. He changed glasses and said, "To forever, as we promised," then drank from it also.

His 'Super Alert', which had never left him, suddenly made him aware that he wasn't alone. He turned to his right and saw a shadowed figure on the steps watching him. He felt his hand tremble and he put the glass down on the rail. The figure didn't move and his mind began to race, as did his heart.

"Sue?" he asked, almost afraid of the answer.

"It's me," came a voice, but not hers.

He strained to see and put a face to it. A moment later, Pam stepped out into the partial moonlight.

"I didn't mean to intrude," she said, then, "no that's not true, I did." She slowly moved towards him. He was dressed in all black, his tee-shirt, jeans and boots. She had never seen him without a suit or not dressed in his full field supervisor uniform before.

He watched as she came closer, still in her business clothes. Her white silk blouse, with granite-gray buttons, was now open at the collar. It shined in the light as her light-blue skirt swayed slightly with each step. He had never allowed himself to notice just how attractive she really was until this moment in the moonlight. She stopped within inches of him.

"What are you doing here?"

"I have something I need to tell you, but couldn't in the office."

He looked into her face puzzled, then saw concern in her hazel eyes as they caught a glimmer of the dim light. Her blond hair glistened like strands of fine gold over her shoulders and he could smell the arousing scent of her mild perfume.

She moved a step closer to him.

"I know why you're here tonight. How I know doesn't matter, what does matter is you. You can't stay alone like this," she said looking at his dark clothes. "You can't stay in mourning the rest of your life."

He turned away. "You don't understand the love I shared with her. It will never end for me."

Pam went around to see his face.

"A love like you had was special, I do understand that, but it takes two to make a relationship. Yours ended a long time ago while hers went on anew."

He didn't respond, only stared off towards the knoll out in the darkness that he knew was there.

"You have to move on too, it's over Steve," she whispered.

He spun around. "Don't say that, it will never be over for us. That girl was the love of my life."

She put her hands on his arms and said calmly, "I didn't come here to take away that love. I came here to offer you a chance for a second one, a new one."

He looked back towards her.

"I'm not here to replace her. I'm only here because I care and I've, I've fallen in love with you."

She waited for him to say something, but he could only shake his head at first.

"Oh Pam," he finally said lightly touching her cheek, "you deserve better. A man who can and will love only you. I have my love, here, in my heart."

"You have only a ghost!" she snapped out. "Can a ghost do this!"

She took his face into her hands and pressed her lips hard to his. He tried pushing her back but would have had to hurt her she was so determined; but more than that, he yielded because he enjoyed it. She felt so good in his arms and her taste was as sweet as the champagne.

When she finally let her lips slide slowly and softly from his, her eyes began to open. "I will love you, even if you won't let yourself be loved," she whispered. I'm not a dream. I'm real, I'm here now and I'm yours. If you'll let me, I know I can take this pain away."

She looked in his eyes but saw he was still held in his heart, not here with her. She turned and walked away towards the steps. When she reached them she cried back, "Wasn't it George Bernard Shaw who said, 'There are two tragedies in life. One is not to get your heart's desire, the other is to get it.'? Until now, I thought he was just being witty."

She descended down the steps and vanished into the darkness.

He turned and poured the remainder of the wine into a glass. As he held it he thought about both of them. Sue's joyous smiles on this bridge and now Pam's painful tears. He looked down into the river's dark water and poured out the glass.

"Enjoy it you black-hearted Ferryman," he said with a tone of disgust.

In the morning, he came out the elevator and noticed another girl sitting at Pam's desk. He smiled as she said good morning to him, then he went into Joe's office.

"Want some coffee?" Joe asked, holding up the pot.

"Uh, no thanks," he replied waving his hand back to her desk, "Where's Pam?"

"She called off!" he heard Cindy's voice say from behind, sounding upset, as she followed him in and closed the door. "Stephen Clayton, you should be ashamed hurting that sweet girl the way you did."

He turned to Joe who just sat quietly.

"I wouldn't be surprised if she quits and you never see her again," she continued, pointing her finger in his face, "and it'll all be on your head!"

"I didn't do anything," he said confused.

"You kissed her, didn't you?"

"Yea, I mean no. She kissed me."

"Well, what did you expect her to do!" she snapped back. "If she waited for you she'd of had a better chance of kissing a greased pig. And that's just what you are. A P-I-G, pig!"

Steve pointed back towards her in bewilderment as he looked over again at Joe.

"Don't look at me," he said waving his hands, "I didn't lead the girl on."

"Lead her on? What are you two talking about?"

"I'll tell you what we're talking about, you Don Juan," she jumped back in saying. "Flaunting your irresistible smiles at her daily and making suggestive innuendos over coffee. I mean, any girl could only take so much."

"Suggestive innuendos? Cindy, I asked her once if the coffee I gave her was sweet enough or did she need more sugar?"

"Would you just listen to that," she said looking at Joe. "Why, I won't be surprised if we get hit for sexual harassment."

"Okay, okay," he finally said with his hands held high, "I never realized I was being such a, a …"

"An ass?"

"Right," he said with a grin. "Well, I guess I'd better straighten it out before the lawyers start calling for blood. Do you have her number?"

Cindy handed him a paper she already had in her hand.

"This is an address," he stated with a raised eyebrow.

"Of course, you can't fix this kind of thing with a phone call, you have to do it in person. Now, the temp has rerouted your appointments so get going!" she yelped and then started towards him to make him move faster.

"All right Cindy I'm going, take it easy."

He got up and went towards the elevator.

"No need to hurry back," Joe added, watching as she stood grinning from the doorway, "we'll handle everything, won't you dear?"

Cindy turned to him. "What do you mean by that?"

Joe got up and went by her saying, "I am sure that I heard you yesterday insist Pam start using up her personal days immediately."

She rolled her eyes, then looked down a moment in silence. "Well, somebody had to do something about the situation."

Steve headed over to find the address and as he turned at the light in town, he spotted Pam walking down Lake Shore Drive with a grocery package.

"Can I offer you a lift?"

"What are you doing here?"

"I thought maybe we could talk. Would you mind?"

"That depends," she said, "on where I'd have to sit."

He got out of the car, taking and putting her package into the backseat, and then held the door so she could slip into the front.

"I was wondering," he said as they drove off, "if you were free to have lunch with me today."

"I might, if I could choose the wine," she replied, glancing over to see his reaction.

He smiled. "I've recently become very aware of your good taste. I'd be pleased to try another sample if you're still inclined."

She took his hand. "Very inclined," she said smiling.

***

There was a knock at the door and Sue ran from upstairs to answer it. It was a notarized letter from a lawyer in New Jersey.

"What is it?" Wil asked as he sat drinking at the mini-bar.

"I don't know. It's from a lawyer but I haven't opened it yet."

He put down his drink and came over saying, "Let me see that."

"It's addressed to me," she replied holding it back.

As she read it she began to cry. "It's my grandma, she's died and …" She stopped to take in the loss.

"Yea, and what?" he asked reaching for it again. She pulled it back to finish it. He waited as she read silently, then she suddenly turned with a look of joy on her face.

"She has left her house in Lake Hiawatha to me!" she sang out. Her heart overflowed with gratitude and the thought of going home and

274

living in that wonderful house. She closed her eyes and said a silent prayer for her grandma and a thank you to her.

"A house did you say?"

"Yes! I love that house. It has a large yard and a garden and flowers and fruit trees ... Oh its perfect!" she answered with joy. "Finally we'll have a home of our own."

Wil looked the letter over several times. "How long did she live there?"

"Almost all of her life, why?"

"Then it shouldn't have any mortgage on it. "

"Oh no, Grampa Dom made sure it was paid off long before he died. She only had to pay her taxes for years. She lived off of the insurance he left for her and some investments."

"It says here that she also left you some money with the inheritance of this house."

"Yes but I couldn't say how much that could come to, she was always very thrifty with her spending," she said, still dreaming of going home more than any money.

Wil paced the floor for several moments. "How much do you think a house like this is worth?"

She looked at him with a cold stare. "Don't even think about it. This is my house and I'm not selling it. We are going to move into it, that's why she left it to me."

"Well, I guess this is a good enough reason to go back to Jersey," he responded, watching as she relaxed again. "I didn't get that promotion anyway."

She looked at him sorrowfully. "Oh honey I'm sorry, and after all those extra hours you spent in the office. What kind of a company would do such a thing?"

He shook his head. "Well, maybe I can do better back in New York. I can easily commute from the house there each day."

She threw her arms around his neck crying, "Oh thank you Wil. You'll love this house too, you'll see."

"I'm sure I will," he said with a grin.

Over the next two weeks, while she flew back to Jersey to sign all the papers, he made the arrangements with a moving company. He also set himself up with a position in the New York branch. It wasn't as good a position as he was giving up, but worth it if he could get his hands on the inheritance money.

When he met them at the airport she and Dawn started to tell him about their trip and who they got to see while there.

"Yes, yes," he said, "but how much did she actually leave you?"

Sue turned and looked at him with that icy stare. "More than enough to pay off our debts and that's what it's going for."

"How much!" he repeated in a firm tone.

"Around sixty-eight thousand dollars after paying the legal fees. It was an insurance policy. Why do you need to know the amount now?"

"Well, I was trying to figure how best to invest it, that's all."

She went silent and just stared out the window. He became anxious for her to just say whatever it was she was thinking, so he'd know how to work around her.

At last she turned to him. "Wil, I put the money into several trusts in my name and one in Dawn's for her college. Ten percent goes to the church. Another percentage for taxes, then I plan on taking out what's needed to pay off our debts. The rest stays."

He pulled the car suddenly over to the shoulder.

"You listen to me," he said in a loud voice. "I am the one who makes the financial decisions for this family, you understand that!"

She said nothing and turned away. He grabbed her arm and pulled her around to him.

"You will give me that money, all of it, and I will decide how it is to be used, understand?"

"No," she said for the first time in a long while, "we can't risk losing it. You can't handle money well enough, let alone what has been given to us for our future. So no, you won't touch any of this inheritance."

He raised his hand as if ready to strike her.

"Don't you dare," she said through her clenched teeth and with a sudden fire in her eyes.

He paused, taken back by her firm tone and strong determined look, and he lowered it.

"Fine, you can handle it for now," he mumbled and pulled back out into the traffic, figuring he'd settle this once they reached Jersey.

***

"Got a minute?" Ken asked with his head in the doorway.

"Sure," Steve replied putting down some reports. "What's up?"

"We just lost the Baxter account. A mess up with the billing."

"Oh man. Tom Baxter has been with us for over six years. I'd sure hate to lose him over some accounting error. Let me talk with him."

Steve hit his intercom.

"Yes sir?"

"Pam would you please get Tom Baxter on the line for me?"

"Right away."

"How did this happen?" he asked looking at Ken's worried face.

"Oh, I'm afraid the outsourced accounting company I choose for the right price, just did the wrong thing again. I'm sorry, this isn't the first time something like this has happened."

"We will have to look into something more reliable," Steve stated with a shake of his head. "Would you ask Cindy if she could help us find some others to check out?"

"Sure, I'll go talk with her now."

"Mr. Clayton, I have Mr. Baxter on the line."

"Thank you Pam. Hello Tom? ... Fine thank you, but I understand there was a problem with your hours billed? ... Please, the fault was entirely ours. I'm correcting the problem as we speak, but I sure would hate to lose your business over this.

Could I take you out for lunch this afternoon and propose a deal I think may be of benefit to both of us? ... Fine ... Great ... Yes I know where it is, they serve excellent en trees there. I always said you had great taste. Look forward to seeing you again, bye Tom."

Steve took his suit-jacket from the back of his chair and hit his intercom button.

"Yes Mr. Clayton?"

"Pam, could you step in my office for a letter please?"

"Right away."

He reached into his top pocket and brought out a small box. Pam entered and closed the door. As she sat with her steno pad and pen, he motioned for her to please start and he began speaking.

"It has come to my attention that I have been showing an increasingly poor attitude in regards to the feelings of some employees. It was reported that I have made little effort lately to acknowledge their importance to this company, let alone to me personally.

One of the most recent unforgivable offenses has been to miss the birthday of Ms. Pamela Emerson because of putting business concerns first. I hereby am enclosing something which I hope shall redeem me in her eyes. Sincerely, and most affectionately, Me."

Pam put her pad down as he handed her the gift wrapped box.

"Happy Birthday Pam," he said, kissing her hand as she took it. "Please forgive me. I let less important things distract me, I'm sorry."

She smiled at him and opened it slowly. It was a diamond faced gold watch. She looked up at him stunned.

"Oh Steve it's just beautiful, but I can't accept this."

"I'm afraid you'll have to. I had it custom made so it's non-refundable."

He had her turn it over to the engraving which read 'A new time, a new wine'. She took off her watch and put it on. "I don't know what to say."

He reached out and took her hand. "Say you'll have dinner with me tonight. We can eat out at that street cafe you like so much."

"I'd love to," she answered smiling, then put her arms around him and kissed him tenderly. "Have I told you lately how much you mean to me?"

He took her hand and looked at the watch. "You just did, but you can say it again in an hour. The watch has an alarm setting." He touched her face and softly kissed her warm moist lips again.

There came a knock at the door, then it opened.

"Oh, I'm sorry," Cindy said seeing them, then left and closed it quickly behind her. She paused smiling as Joe came over.

"Is Steve in his office?"

"Yes," she answered as she moved to block the door, "but he's got his hands full right now. Don't worry he's handling it very well. They've just now reached the point of contact, I mean, a possible contract."

Introduction of 1983

Top Movies:

The Right Stuff
Local Hero
Never Say Never Again
Independence Day
Abuse
Lone Wolf
McQuade
Tell Me That You Love Me
 Breathless

Top songs of 1983:

Do you really want to hurt me? (Culture Club)
It must be Love (Madness)
One thing leads to another (Fix)
Hungry like a Wolf (Duran Duran)
Total Eclipse of the Heart (Bonnie Tyler)
Always Something There to Remind Me (Naked Eyes)
Every Breath You Take (The police)
Love is a Battlefield (Pat Benatar)
Don't Let It End (Styx)
I'm Still Standing (Elton John)
Beat It (Michael Jackson)

Chapter Eighteen
The Coming Fall of '83 - '84
"When Loves Collide, Worlds Divide."

It had been a hectic month moving from Oakland back to Lake Hiawatha and getting settled into the old house. The last of their furniture had arrived yesterday and Sue was glad it was over.

Feeling she deserved a break, she decided to treat herself with a trip to the beauty shop downtown.

She parked her BMW on North Beverwyck Road and thought it would be nice to walk a bit through town to really see how much it had changed over the last few years.

She walked casually along, checking out both the old and the new stores. When she passed the Village Spa Luncheonette, she paused outside its window, staring at the booths along the walls.

She smiled, remembering voices and laughter from the past and a cherry-vanilla coke with two straws. She gently touched the window, then walked on.

Tony Rudy's fine men's shop was gone and she remembered how all the guys use to work and save so they could go there to get the latest new 'High Roll' shirts and double knits.

"They always dressed so nice," she recalled, "even when they wore jeans. They were always cleaned and pressed with new colored Tee or dress shirts." She remembered also the 'Desert Boots' they'd wear or the highly polished, black 'Feather- Weight' dress shoes with onion-skin socks.

She smiled, knowing how she felt when they'd all get together to walk through town and the pride they had in their appearance. It made her feel appreciated and respected when out on a date in public with them.

"Oh guys," she sighed, "you were all so handsome and fun to be with."

She finally arrived at the beauty shop and went inside. She had a touch up trim on her hair and a manicure while she listened to the several ladies talking around her.

"I grew up in this little two blinker town and all I'm saying is it's just growing too fast for me. Too many changes and so many new faces moving in. There was a time when everybody knew everybody here."

"You're right Laura," replied another, "and everybody cared about their neighbors and their problems. Why just the other day, while I was out tending my garden, those new people across the street just opened their door and let the dog run loose alone. He came right over to my front lawn and did his business in my rose bed. Of course I went over to tell them, but they didn't seem the least bit concerned about it. The husband even said that if it bothers me so much, then all I had to do was to shoe the dog away and he'd go do it somewhere else!"

"These newcomers just have their own ways I guess," said another, "like that new family that just moved in next to me last month. They haven't done a thing to keep up the yard and old Mrs. LaRosa used to have such a lovely garden out front."

Sue's eyes widened as she continued to listen.

"She had such a way with those roses, but they're so over grown with weeds now I'm sure they'll not survive the season.

They've not even made an effort to introduce themselves, just stay inside or when next I look, the car is gone. I don't think I've seen their faces, but for a glance since they arrived."

"Didn't they inherit that house from that sweet old lady?" asked the hairdresser as she checked the drying time on one of the blowers.

"I heard they did," replied another, "and I heard rumor that they moved into it because they were having financial problems and couldn't afford to stay living where they were."

"Where was that?" asked the first.

"Out in California," she answered. "The husband applied to the club for golf membership, but I know from a reliable source that he was barely accepted after the background check on him."

She leaned over to the others and whispered, "They're very heavy in debt. In fact, last weekend at the club I heard that he likes to put on airs about how well he's doing. He works with a firm in New York City, but the truth is he was demoted with a huge cut in pay."

"Who told you that?" asked the other near her as she lowered her magazine.

"Oh, it's the buzz out on the course. I heard it from June Farraway and her husband is on the club's board."

"Oh my," remarked the other, "but they drive such nice new cars and their furniture was beautiful. I watched over my fence as it arrived."

"Just more airs," replied the first with a smirk, "and does he ever like to drink! He already has a high bar tab. I hear that if he misses paying it this month they plan on 86ing him or making him pay cash."

Sue kept her back to them as she lowered her head. She felt choked up and suddenly drew in a quick breath to hold it in.

"Are you all right?" asked the manicurist. "I didn't hurt you did I?"

"No," Sue answered softly, "you didn't."

As soon as her nails were done, she stepped to the counter to pay.

"Thank you Mrs. Walker," said the cashier, "and come back again soon."

Her neighbor heard and jerked her head up. Sue looked away as she went for the door.

"That was her," she heard the woman say to the others as she closed the door behind her.

She hurried to the corner to cross over to where she had parked. She shaded her eyes as the tears came, then quickly wiped them aside as she had done so many times before. She took a deep breath to compose herself, then she checked traffic before walking into the street.

As she was about to step, she froze. Sitting at the light, waiting to pull out from across the street, sat a maroon, 1966 Pontiac Le mans convertible. Its white top was up and the sun glared off its windshield so she couldn't see the driver's face.

She stayed standing on the corner, studying every facet of the car. It had rally wheels, white pin stripping and its dual pipes sang as it sped across, heading down Lake Shore Drive. She caught only a glimpse of its driver. He had brown hair and was wearing aviator style sunglasses.

"Excalibur?" she muttered. "Was that possibly his old car?"

She knew his family had moved to Florida; yet still, she ran to the other side of the street to watch its rear lights vanish from sight. She put her hand to her mouth, then ran to her car. If it was his, she just wanted to touch it again.

She got in her car and turned down the hill, hoping to catch it. She drove down past the old Lake Hiawatha pool lot, then around the bend into the lower sections but found no sign of it. She finally pulled over to the side of the Edward's Road.

"What's wrong with you?" she thought. "There must be hundreds of cars like that."

She covered her face and cried longer and harder than she had in a long time. "Oh God," she cried out, "don't do this to me, please don't!"

As the tears dried on her face she drove home, but she did not wipe them away.

***

Wil was about to leave his cubical for the day when he was buzzed by his supervisor, Mr. Jenkins, to see him first before leaving. He took the elevator up to the office and knocked on the door.

"Ah Walker, come in," he said waving. "I guess your family is all settled into your new home by now?"

"Pretty much."

"Good. Look we have a chance to land a new important client in Morristown, New Jersey, called On Guard Services. It is one of the fastest growing security companies in the northeast, with presently over two thousand employees and two branch offices. I need you go over tomorrow and see one of its partners to discuss their needs."

286

"Sure, who do I have to see?"

"Just check with the receptionist, you are expected at 10 am, and whichever partner is available will see you." Jenkins leaned over his desk to him adding, "If you make a good impression, they will sign up and switch all of their service needs to us. Their payroll, the billing, all of their accounting needs, understand?"

"Yes sir, I'll take care of it."

The next morning he arrived ten minutes early and reported to the receptionist.

"You can go right up to the third floor and ask for Ms. Pamela Emerson. She will take to see one of the partners."

"Thank you."

Wil went up the elevator and spoke with Pam.

"Please come this way," she said and took him into Steve's office. "Mr. Clayton will be here in a few moments, so please help yourself to coffee and a pastry if you wish."

"Thank you," he said, then walked to the breakfast bar and poured himself a cup.

Steve had arrived very early to look over some contracts in the conference room. As Pam came in to get him she found him asleep over the table.

He was moaning in his sleep, then woke up suddenly in a cold sweat yelling, "No!"

She ran to him. "Are you all right?"

"Yea," he answered as he fully awoke. "Just a bad dream."

"You want to talk about it?"

"No, it's nothing. I'm fine."

"Okay, you have an appointment waiting in your office," she said touching his shoulder.

"Thanks Pam."

As he waited, Wil noticed the pictures on the wall and a display case with several war metals and letters of decoration from Vietnam. A set of Army Sergeant stripes laid in the case also, with photos of soldiers posing together.

He smiled looking at them and the local commendations from the mayor and the sheriff's office to him and his company, each framed along the walls.

"A hero," he smirked to himself out loud.

"Not really," Steve said as he entered the office, "people are often too generous with praise. I was just doing my job. The real heroes are seldom known."

"Still," Wil said, "quite impressive Mr. Clayton."

"Please, have a seat Mr. Walker."

Will listened and then made recommendations which his firm could do to try and insure the company's needs would be met and in a timely manner.

"You make a good case for your firm," Steve said, "but I have a commitment to both my clients and the people who work with this company. I will need a personal guarantee."

"What kind?" Wil asked.

"I'd like you to work here daily and help to oversee these changes until they are running smooth on both ends, for say for six to eight weeks? Would you and your firm agree to this?"

"I would have no problem," he replied, "I'll call my company and I can let you know by this afternoon."

"That'll be fine, and if what you propose works well, then I'm sure my partners will agree to sign up for other needed services, after rate discussions of course."

"Thank you Mr. Clayton."

They shook hands, then Steve excused himself and left to meet with Joe. Pam returned to the office and informed him that the lunch she had ordered for him had arrived. A cart was rolled into the office and served out by the attendant onto the breakfast bar for him.

"Do you do this for all of your visiting consultants here?"

"Yes, the owners insist visitors are treated as guests," Pam answered, "I hope you enjoy it."

"I'm sure I will," he said, eying her shapely five-foot nine-inch form as she walked about the room.

"Say, are you free to share this?" he asked with a suggestive tone.

"No sir," she replied seeing a wedding ring on his finger. "Mr. Clayton would not approve but thank you for the offer."

Wil stepped in front of her and asked, "What about after you get off work?"

She smiled saying, "I don't think the man I'm seeing would care for that."

He grinned. "Oh, does he work here also?"

"Yes," she answered grinning back. "You're standing in his office," and, caught off guard by her remark, he quickly tripped to one side.

Steve returned to her desk. "Decide yet where you'd like to have lunch?" he asked reaching for her sweater.

"Yes, just a moment ago," she answered as she looked at Wil and he watched them get into the elevator. He went back and started eating his lunch as he jotted down some notes for starting the proposed services.

As he sat there, he looked up at the On Guard company Logo hanging on the wall. It was a photo of four hands, each holding up foil swords. A red one, a white, a blue and a fourth with stars all touching their tips, with its motto at the bottom, 'All for One, and One for All'.

A few moments later, a young secretary came in to lay some files on Steve's desk and she said hello to him. "Tell me," he asked as he pointed to all of the metals in the case and letters on the wall, "is Mr. Clayton some kind of a hero or something?"

"Oh yes," she said, "both during the war and here locally. The company has done a lot for the community. He was given commendations for several men he had saved, both before and after his being held as a P.O.W. That one was for arranging the escape that saved several others besides himself," she said pointing to a frame.

He turned to look at the army commendation, then noticed the sketch of the wooden bridge next to it.

"This says 'To My Love forever, Angel'. Does he know the artist?" he asked, wondering to himself if it had been done by his Ms. Emerson?

She paused thinking.

289

"I think he did. I heard they were engaged or something before he went to war, but then later she married someone else when she thought he had died."

"Really? Thank you," he said, and she smiled as she left.

Wil looked at it closer and saw at the bottom right corner the tiny signature of S. L.

His eyes widen. "Sue?" he said quietly to himself, then turned to be sure he was alone.

He felt a sudden chill and became uneasy.

"Clayton? Steve Clayton? So she was right," he thought, "he was alive."

His feeling became one of fear, then jealousy, as he thought of what she might do if she knew he was here.

Over the next several weeks he arrived at the branch each day and oversaw the changes to their accounting systems. He watched what he said around Steve and stayed clear of Pam whenever possible. He never told Sue about him being his client, but often she'd see him watching her. He'd ask where she had been or what she did that day. She wasn't sure what to make of how he was acting.

One Saturday afternoon, Sue took Dawn out to do some shopping at the Willowbrook Mall for clothes she'd need for the coming school year. On the way home, she decided to take the back roads instead.

As they drove past the Hiawatha Pool, she pulled in the lot and sat a moment looking at the entrance.

"What's this?" Dawn asked seeing the diving boards and part of the outdoor pool inside the large fenced in grounds, now deserted and closed for the season.

Sue smiled and sighed. "That's where I found true love."

"With Dad?"

"No I was only fifteen then, but he fought for me right there and I gave him my heart forever," she said in a distant voice.

"A guy really beat up somebody for you?"

"I said he fought for me, but yes, then there was a fight also."

She turned and pointed to the steps going up onto the wooden bridge. "Over there, many years later, he proposed to me on our senior prom night."

Dawn stretched to see the bridge. "Wow, and what did you say?"

"I said yes because I loved him with all my heart Baby."

Dawn sat quietly thinking, then asked, "Did you marry him before you did Dad?"

She watched as her mom's eyes teared up, shaking her head no.

"Mom?" she asked touching her hand. "Why are you crying?"

"I loved that boy so much. He was my whole world and I was his." She started to cry a little harder and covered her face.

"Mom don't cry, please. Did he hurt you?"

"Oh God no, he could never do that," she answered quickly. "He made me feel so beautiful, so loved. We were happy every day we had. We just wanted to spend the rest of our lives together, but he was taken away from me."

Dawn moved closer and held her arm. "How? Why Mom?"

Sue composed herself a bit. "He was killed during the war," she answered with her hand over her mouth.

She stared over at the lake a moment.

"They never even found his body to send home to, to me," she cried out through her fingers, while reaching out a bit towards the Island.

Dawn put her arms around her. "I'm so sorry Momma. You still love him, don't you?"

"Oh Dawn, we promised each other forever and as God is my witness, we meant it and I still do. He was my perfect matched set and we shared one heart in everything. I thought I'd die when he was gone."

"Matched set?" she asked.

Sue smiled and then laughed lightly.

"Yea, that's what we called our relationship some times because we both fenced in tournaments together. 'Matched sets' they were called."

291

Dawn pulled back with wide eyes. "You fought in matches with a sword?"

"I won Parsippany High School's first Championship," she declared, "and you should have seen the size of the guy I had to duel against. He was over a foot taller than me, at least!"

"Weren't you scared?"

"Terrified," she answered, "but it was a 'One for All' match and I was the chosen Musketeer. That means you have no choice but to stand."Dawn begged her to tell every detail and Sue was happy to remember that day, and how it changed her life.

"So, did you ever duel against him?"

Sue laughed. "Against Steve?" she chuckled out. "In more ways than I can remember. Most often in practice combat but sometimes verbally. Of course, that was always just to be playful."

She laughed to herself again.

She told Dawn about Renee at their prom and how she ribbed him; then about his first fight and the clip-on tie with her Uncle Joe. They both laughed together as she went on. Finally, she told her some of their tender moments and how it felt to share that special love.

Dawn turned to her smiling. "It sounds like you were made for each other."

"Oh we were. He made me feel so special, so wanted, so loved and so happy," she answered with another tear.

Dawn wiped it away for her as she went silent a moment, then asked, "So how could God be so cruel to tear you apart like that?"

Sue looked at her and said, "Dawn, don't ever say that. God is never cruel, He is in control always and knows what is best. As for me, He gave me a love from heaven. She paused reflecting, then smiled. "If I had only been given one day with him, one of our least important ones, I would still thank God every day for that gift. One day of perfect love is a lifetime Baby."

"Oh Momma you are special, he was right," she said crying. "I love you so much."

Sue hugged her tight and whispered, "If we had married and had a child, she would have been just like you. You are so much like him to me, in so many ways. I see him in you so often."

Dawn smiled on her shoulder. "That's because you always give me everything I need, and some of what you gave must have come with his love for you."

That night, after Dawn had gone to sleep, Sue sat up watching for Wil to come home from the club. It was nearly midnight when he came through the door, drunk.

"Hi honee," he said, slurring his words.

She held back her anger and said, "Hi. Why don't I help you upstairs so you can get some rest?"

He smiled as he leaned on her up to the bedroom where she laid him down and took off his coat, shirt and shoes.

As she went to cover him, he pulled her closer and held her tightly to him.

"Wil!" she cried out. "You're hurting me, stop it!" She tried to move away but he put his hand on her shoulder and pulled her down. He moved on top of her, pinning her onto the bed.

"Please Wil, let's just go to sleep for now."

"You mean till I'm sober," he stated, then he kissed her neck and she felt his hand squeezing her leg.

"Don't please," she said smelling the liquor on his breath, "not like this, please!"

Finally he stopped and looked at her. "What's the matter, we're married aren't we?"

She wormed out of his grip and slid to her side of the bed. "I just need you to be gentler with me. I want to be loved not mauled."

"I suppose he did it better?" he snorted.

She turned to him with a wildness in her eyes, then pushed him away. "Don't you ever say that again to me," she told him with warning in her voice.

"I'm as good as he is," he mumbled, "and you're my wife not his."

Sue went to the edge of the bed. "What do you mean, as good as he is?"

"Or was," he mumbled again. "In any case, you're my wife and your church says that you can't refuse me. Remember your vows?"

"I know my vows and yours!" she said in a loud and hurtful tone. "You promised to love, Honor and cherish me."

He lunged forward and grabbed her, pulling and holding her face down into his chest."Kiss me damn it!" he yelled.

She struggled for air, then scratched his chest to free herself. He cried out and struck her hard across the face, causing her to fall backward onto the floor.

She stayed sitting there a moment, looking up at him in shock as she held her cheek. Suddenly she growled out in anger, "Why you filthy! - - - Drunken! - - - " But then quickly covered her mouth and lowered her head in silence, trembling.

He snorted again saying, "You're gonna do for me what you'd do for him, you understand?"

She got up slowly and moved towards the door holding her face.

"What?" he asked as she stared back at him. "It's not like that was the first time a guy ever slapped you, is it?"

She opened the door and coldly said, "Don't you ever, ever touch me again," then she closed it and went to Dawn's room, locking the door. She sat quietly with her clenched fist hitting the chair's arm.

"Oh please forgive me, but I can't take anymore," she said softly in tears. "I need strength but I don't have any left. Oh, I feel so used and forgotten."

She dropped her head, still trembling and cried harder. Unconsciously, she raised her fist and slowly opened it. She suddenly felt its palm touch her lips and she remembered.

"Thank you Love," she moaned out, then fell asleep exhausted in the reading chair by Dawn's bed. The next day, she moved into the guest room with a locked door.

***

Cindy finished doing some personal errands. As she pulled into the company lot she spotted Sue entering through the main doors. She hurried to park and ran inside just as the receptionist was calling Joe's office number.

"Sue," she called out, "what are you doing here?"

Sue turned and smiled from behind her sunglasses.

"I just thought it would be easier if I met you and Joe here."

Cindy smiled back, as she glanced around saying, "Well, I'm sure Joe is still tied up so why don't we go have some coffee in the cafeteria and wait," then she asked the receptionist to call Joe as they walked off.

"So," Cindy asked, "we haven't seen much of you lately, how have you been?"

"All right. I finally got things finished at the house and Dawn's ready to start school."

"Wil's firm seems to be doing a fine job so far Joe tells me with their accounting needs, you must be pleased."

"He doesn't talk to me about his work anymore," she said with a disinterested tone.

Sue looked around, then noticed for the first time the company logo on the wall and she smiled at the motto.

"I'm glad to see the guys haven't forgotten their roots."

Cindy looked and realized what she was referring to. "Oh yea, they insisted on it."

"Ah, but why so many foils?" Sue asked, having not noticed the designs of each up close.

Just then Joe entered and Cindy took her arm. "There he is, let's get going before we're late for the opening matinée curtain."

Joe saw her eyes and replied, "Of course, we don't want to miss the start of the play."

They ushered her out and headed to the main lot for Cindy's car. As they pulled out the exit, Joe saw the Le Mans pulling in the main lot behind them. He quickly drove up towards the square and around it towards the playhouse.

Steve parked and came around to open the door for Pam.

"I'm glad you came with me," he said as they started towards the building, "I don't know why I couldn't focus on the presentation today."

"Didn't you sleep well?"

"Not really," he answered, "I tossed and turned, as if fighting with someone."

"Well, I think you've just been working too hard," she said taking his arm. "Next time let Mr. Tomineski do what he does best, the selling part, so you can concentrate on the field operations."

"It felt so real, like an attack, and I was fighting just for air."

"It was just a dream, try and forget it."

He nodded at her in agreement, then suddenly Pam stopped.

"What is it?" he asked.

"The play tickets," she said as she pulled them from her purse and looked at them.

"The ones we all got as gifts from the Baxter account?"

"I knew it," she said, "these are only good for today's matinée. Oh, and I really wanted to see it."

"So, let's go." he said with a smile. "We can finish up the paperwork in the morning, besides, I could use some restful entertainment today."

They got back in the car and drove towards the playhouse.

"We'll just make curtain," she said.

"What's this play about anyway?"

"Oh, it was written by a local playwright. It's a modern version of 'The Man of La Mancha'. You know, 'The Impossible Dream'."

"Oh yea the quest, a great play," he remarked. "I hope he does it justice."

Joe had been able to upgrade their seats to a box. As they made their way into the private balcony Sue felt thrilled to be able to see the entire audience and yet, be so close to the stage.

"I'll get us some drinks," Joe said and left.

"I heard this was a great story," Cindy said to her.

"Oh yes, it's a wonderful and moving play. Steve and I went to see the original version off-Broadway back in 1967, we loved it. I laughed and cried all through it and later again on our way home on the bus."

Steve and Pam were quickly ushered to their seats as the lights were already dimmed for the play to begin. They were seated in the middle, near enough to the front for a nice view. The play started and he watched to see how much the playwright had changed from the original, and if it was an improvement by going modern.

The setting had of course been changed to take place in an American small town. The characters were made teenagers, with Cervantes's Don Quixote now Don Quick, a boy who has a delusional quest to find the perfect girl. He finds her, his Dulcinea, in a sweet high school girl named Darla May; but who now has an undeserved soiled reputation and is hurtfully called Darla Will. He declares her to be the true queen of the prom and the most beautiful girl in the school.

"It has some merit," Steve thought as he watched it unfolding, "even some fun parts."

Later, as it moved on and he watched them lose their dream as the world shattered it, his heart began to ache remembering the sweetness of theirs.

When the play reached the moment of its version of Darla pleading for Don to remember how he made her feel, Sue began to cry. The scenes of Darla, who had been abused by ex-boyfriends and then hurt by her latest one to put her in her place, grew more painful for her to watch.

Then, when Darla had taken her pain out on Don for giving her the dream in the first place, Sue cried as his dream shattered also. She remembered the shame she had felt when she had screamed at Steve and God after she had thrown herself into the lake to die.

The closing scenes were well lit as the players were singing together and then Darla sang the new version of 'Dulcinea's reprise' to him.

***

"Won't you please bring back the dream of Darla May,
Won't you bring me back the warm and shining love
of Darla May, Darla May..."

***

The play had Don Quick asking her to help him remember the dream. So, she sang to him.

***

"To dream of an impossible love,

to fight against an unbeatable world,
to bear unbearable heartbreak,
to love and would die for this girl.
This was the dream, that was the quest,
to look in my heart and see only the best ..."

***

Sue was hearing both the new and the old lyrics in her mind and it tore into her heart. She lifted her sunglasses to wipe away the tears when suddenly, as the stage lights went brighter for a moment, she saw him sitting below her.

Her heart nearly leaped out of her chest as she stood up and leaned forward over the railing into the now darkness below. Again, she wiped her eyes, but it was too dark to see.

Steve's beeper went off and he told Pam there was an emergency on one of the sites.

"Please stay," he said, giving her cab fare.

"It's all right. Go take care of your people, I'll see you later."

He moved quickly up the aisle in the dark and went to a pay phone back by the restrooms to call the site first.

Sue could not shake the feeling that she had been right, that what she saw, who she saw was real. She got up and headed to the lower level. She came through the lobby and went into the lower seating areas.

Joe and Cindy had stayed, believing she had just gone to the ladies room, until Cindy saw a flash of her down below in the aisle searching.

Sue made her way in the half-lit aisle until she came to the empty seat. Pam looked up a moment at her, then back to the stage. Sue sighed and lowered her head as she went back to the lobby.

She went over to the glass entrance doors and stared out into the parking lot. A tear started but she held it back. It was near sundown as she aimlessly scanned the scene, then she froze as she spotted the rear of the Le Mans. She held her breath, fearing it wasn't what she hoped.

Steve resolved the problem over the phone and hung up. He started back to his seat and as he came into the lobby his reflection appeared in the glass before her like a ghost. He glanced at her as he passed, then saw her reflection also staring back at him, and he stopped at the sight of her face.

For a moment both said nothing, didn't move, only stared in the glass door. Each afraid the vision would vanish if they dared to look closer.

"Sue?" came a soft voice.

She didn't dare move.

"Sue!" the voice cried out.

She saw his reflection coming towards her and she turned to face it. He stopped, as if she wasn't really there after so many years of dreaming her to his side.

She was speechless as she inched towards him, then she ran and threw herself at him and she fainted. He scooped her up in his arms and carried her out to Excalibur as the cast sang the Impossible Love closing number from behind them.

He held her in the front seats, trying to bring her around. She finally moaned, then slowly opened her eyes. There they were again sitting in Excalibur, him smiling at her. She was sure it was a dream like so many times before.

"Wake up Angel," he said over and over, as he gently caressed her face, then saw her bruised eye and cheek as a car shined its lights at them.

She opened her eyes again and stared, then reached out and touched his arm, then his face and lips. Her eyes teared up, but she could say nothing. She felt his hand holding her face, his words to her saying, "It's all right, I'm here Love."

"You're dead," she repeated again and again, "dead, gone," but still looked at him sitting there, holding and touching her. Finally she sighed out loud, "If this is again a dream, then let there be no more mornings to take it from me." Suddenly she felt his lips on hers and she was lost back in her love. After several moments, she slowly pulled back to look again, he was still there watching her with those bright blue eyes. Her lips trembled, unable to speak.

"Forgive me Sue," she heard, "I just thought it was best to leave you with your new life and family. To just forget me, forget us."

She brought her hand up to caress his face, then she suddenly slapped him hard across it. "How could you!" she screamed, now punching his chest and swinging her fists at him wildly. "Could you forget about us!" She continued screaming and hitting him, then started to cry uncontrollably.

"Why would you think I'd be better off with you dead?" she cried out in anguish. "Why would you do this to me? Oh, I hate you!" she screamed, hitting and punching again. "I hate you! - - - Oh God, how I hate you! I, I …Oh God help me, I love you. I've died with you a thousand times."

She stopped hitting and fell into his chest crying up a pain from deep in her heart. A cry like that of a tormented condemned soul finally pardoned by an act of Grace.

He pulled her tight to him. "Oh Sue I'm sorry," he cried. "I was wrong and I knew it the moment I saw your face. I never meant to hurt you Love."

She slowly looked back up at him and saw his lip bleeding where she had punched him. She quickly took out a handkerchief from her purse and held it to his mouth. "Oh Steve I'm so sorry," she cried, "I didn't mean to do that. Are you okay?"

He gazed down into her face. "Like I died and went to heaven," he answered with a smile.

She laughed as he wiped away her tears, then saw him staring at her one cheek and she turned her face away.

"Please understand, I'm not the same innocent girl that you left behind," she cried.

He turned her face back to him and held it in his hands gently. "Angel," he said softly, "never deny that thou art My Lady Darla May."

"Oh, I love you so," she whimpered as she kissed away the last stain on his lips, hugging him tight, drawing breath, life from him again.

"Let's go somewhere we can talk and be together," he said as he started the car.

"Please just drive," she cried in-between her kisses and clutching back his arm to hide under again, "I am where I need to be."

The show ended and Joe came down to the lobby with Cindy. They looked around for Sue, but the usher said a gentleman had carried her out when she fainted. Joe questioned him more, then Pam came out and went up to Cindy.

"Pam, what are you doing here?" she asked somewhat shocked.

"Oh I came with Steve, but he was beeped and called away for an emergency at a site. I could use a ride back to my car at the office lot."

Joe overheard them and said to Cindy that they should go.

"But what about the person we came with?" she asked.

"She got a ride back home."

The two drove out onto old Route 24 and headed out into the country, up through Mendham, towards Chester and Long Valley. Sue sat up on the console, with her arms wrapped around him tightly. The late August evening air felt good coming through the vent windows, but she wanted more.

"Put the top down," she whispered and he slowed down, pulled the latches and hit the button.

As the top rose up and over her head she could see a canopy of stars above covering them. The harvest moon was full and its shining beams were as bright as the headlights before them.

She turned on the radio, changing stations, then she found a black leather tape case behind his seat and opened it.

"You still have our eight-tracks," she said with surprised joy and she took out a favorite and put it into the deck. It played 'Magic Carpet Ride' and she turned up the volume.

She kissed his cheek, then stood up. She opened her arms, leaning over the windshield, and embraced the raging wind against her as she sang along.

Steve started to reach up to steady her, but he could see she was fine, lost in the music and the excitement of being alive. He joined in, both singing as loud as they could as Excalibur tore through the darkness before them.

When they reached Chester she sat down beside him, rubbing his neck and shoulders as she smiled upwards to the heavens. He put his hand on hers and they continued through the small town.

Its little specialty shops were lit and people were walking slowly, peeking in each window at the crafts. They came out to Route 206 and turned right to continue cruising up towards Route 80 and then over towards Lake Hopatcong.

He took her to Bertrand Island Amusement Park and she grabbed him to go on some rides. They kissed through the Lost River ride and on the Ferris wheel. Then they walked along the beach front slowly, feeling the love in their Heart while others played games on the midway.

She splashed him by accident as she kicked into the waves barefooted. He smiled, then chased her until they tumbled into the sand together laughing, nose to nose.

They finally laid back on the beach, holding each other, as the fireworks started going off over the lake. She held her ears with each loud boom, but sighed out oohs and aahs with the growing crowd, as each exploded.

At last came the grand finale, which signaled the end of the night and everyone started to exit the park.

He helped her to her feet and brushed the sand off of her backside. He turned her gently and then kissed her against the moon's reflection across the calm lake behind them.

"I love you," they whispered to each other, and then left to head back.

Sue hung onto his arm tightly as he drove back into Morristown and around the square, then up to his apartment suite. He gave the keys to the valet and they went inside.

When she entered, she was impressed with the size and decor. It was very masculine in taste. Over the fireplace were four foils crossed. The furniture, though rugged, was very comfortable looking.

She walked around looking while he went to make them something to drink. She stopped as she passed his den and library. There were two wall cases of books, mostly literature and poetry. He had one section set aside for Lord Byron and she smiled.

His desk was massive, solid oak, with a swivel wing-backed black leather chair. Behind where he'd sit was a stained glass window picturing a wooden bridge and the grassy knoll in the distance, covered with wild flowers. It was a copy of the sketch she had made for him.

He came in, handing her a hot chocolate, then they stood together looking at the window.

"I knew you couldn't forget us either," she said.

"Not even for a moment," he answered. "Not in Nam, not here, not ever anywhere."

She leaned against him for a moment, then went into the living room and sat on the deep leather couch. He followed her in and sat across from her in a chair. She sipped her chocolate and felt the warm hint of rum as she swallowed.

"I hope you don't mind the rum, I add a little once in a while. It's a Kenny thing when he comes over."

"Oh no it's kinda nice, not overwhelming. I'll bet it helps in the colder weather."

"Sue," he started to say, then she interrupted.

"No, let me please."

He sat back and sipped his cup.

"I'm so glad that you're alive," she said. "I've prayed for you and to you it seems forever. I sit here and all I want is to be in your arms. I love you, maybe more now than ever before because I thought I had lost you."

He put his cup down and came beside her.

"I can't go on living without you," he said. "It almost killed me the first time."

"Me too, but I'm married. I have a little girl and a husband waiting."

Steve looked at her face, her bruised eye, and asked, "How did that happen?"

"It was just an accident," she said quickly. "I was careless and didn't see where I was headed is all."

He was silent looking at her, then he got up and took two foils off the wall. He tossed one, handle first to her, and she caught it with one hand easily.

"You were always a strong woman, fearless and stood up for yourself whenever you were wronged. I saw some of that old spirit in the car today, but I can't help wondering how long it's been between then and now that you've used it."

She lifted the sword and said, "He who lives by the sword … " She paused, then added, "Maybe you have too long."

He raised his and replied, "Touché," then lowered it.

"I have always tried to play by the rules and so have you," he said, "but there are some who have their own and ours don't apply."

He knelt in front of her.

"Sue, if I ever found out you were being hurt … "

She touched her fingers to his lips and took his foil, putting it together on the floor with hers.

"Did you want to fight or talk with me Love?"

His face softened and he kissed her hand.

"I want to know you're safe," he stated, "that you're loved. I need to know you're happy, that's all I've ever wanted for you."

She leaned in and kissed him tenderly. "I'm okay," she whispered, "but I'll never be happy without you so just hold me a moment."

They laid in each others arms without talking. He kissed her bruised face and she his cut lip.

"Oh, I don't want to go but I have to," she cried softly. "I have a little girl at home." She thought a moment, then added, "But even if I didn't, I took vows so I do it for love and honor."

Steve touched her bruised cheek asking, "Love for him?"

"No Babe, love for my God to whom I gave the promise."

She pulled him closer and tighter. "Please help me to be strong," she begged fighting back the tears, then stood up to kiss him gently one last time.

He reached down and took her right palm and kissed it, then folded her fingers closed.

"Just in case of …," he whispered.

"I know," she said with a smile, "and thank you so much for today. It will keep me happy for a long time." She touched her nose to his, then walked towards the door.

"But not forever?"

"No," she answered looking back, "not forever My Love. I can't be, because for me there is no divorce. Just know that I love you more than life and always will."

She closed the door and went out to walk uptown in the dark alone to her car. He watched from the window as she left, forcing herself not to look back, while he forced himself not to follow.

It was nearly two in the morning when she got home. Wil was waiting up, standing in the kitchen archway as she entered. She didn't look at him as she put her purse down and started to walk over to the staircase.

"Where were you?" he asked with anger in his tone.

"Out," she replied plainly.

"Don't lie to me," he said grabbing her arm to stop her from passing him by.

She could smell the liquor on his breath as she turned, then looked at him with hatred in her eyes.

"You talk about lying? You knew he was alive and said nothing, that was worst than any lie to me. He was my dream and you knew it. Couldn't you of at least let me know that he was alive and well?"

He grabbed her by both shoulders and yelled, "You saw him, didn't you! That's where you were, you were with him just now weren't you!"

"Yes I was with him, to say goodbye again," she answered choking on the words.

"Like hell you were!" he screamed and slapped her hard across her left cheek. She looked back up at him and then defiantly, offered him her right one. He raised his hand again but she didn't flinch. He paused, seeing the emptiness in her eyes towards him and then he let go of her arm.

She turned and slowly started up the stairs.

"Damn you Stephen Clayton!" he suddenly cried out.

She turned around as he grabbed her crystal bowl of the Island off the mantel and smashed it on the floor.

"There's your freak'n dream!" she heard him yell as it shattered into pieces across the darkened floor. "I am your reality woman and you are mine, forever!"

She stared at the fragments a moment and her right hand came up across her heart, then slowly became a fist. She drew in a quick breath as she looked down upon him.

"Forever can be a blessing or a curse," she said, "for it lives in the heart. You'd do well to look into yours before you dare make claim to it."

She turned as her tears fell, opened her fist and held it to her lips, then went up into the guest room. Seconds later, he heard the deadbolt bar the door.

He looked down and saw that the thick crystal base had remained unbroken. The Excalibur sword was pointing at him and he felt death's chill cross his heart.

Introduction of 1984:

Top Movies of 1984:

Ghost Busters
The Never ending Story
Against all odds
Conan the Destroyer
The Terminator

Top songs of 1984

If Ever You're In My Arms Again. (Peabo Bryson)
What's love got to do with it. (Tina Turner)
The Longest Time (Billy Joel)
On the Dark Side (John Cafferty and the Beaver Brown Band)
The Warrior (Scandal)
I Can Dream About You (Dan Hartman)
Somebody's Watching Me (Rockwell)
Almost Paradise (Ann Wilson/Mike Reno)
Against All Odds (Take a Look At Me Now), Phil Collins

TOP NEWS EVENTS

Haunted Castle of Six Flags Great Adventure in New Jersey burns down.
Several people die.

Chapter Nineteen

"It's the Fire of Passion which forges the blade's strength, but it's the Purity of the Heart that wields it with Honor."

"What is it?" Pam heard him ask in an irritated tone when she knocked on his door.

"I have the weekly reports for you to review," she said as she entered the room.

"Just put them on the desk," Steve said with disinterest and without looking up from what he was working on.

She came over and plopped them down in front of him. Startled, he looked up at her.

"Just checking," she said to his wild-eyed stare.

"For what!"

"To see if you still had a face. I haven't seen it in awhile," she answered calmly, then turned for the door.

"Pam please! I'm sorry."

She turned back around and waited in silence.

"You're right. I haven't been very ... You know, lately."

She came back over and put her hand on his shoulder. "Do you want to talk about it?"

He reached up and touched her hand, but shook his head no.

"All right, but I'm here if you change your mind," she said kissing his hand, then left as Joe entered.

"Problems?" he asked concerned as he closed the door.

"When hasn't there been one?"

Joe gave a short, quick nod, then handed him a fax. "Well here's another one."

He read it, then picked up the phone and dialed.

"Hello Roger, its Steve Clayton. I want a second squad to report for duty tomorrow in the morning at warehouse-three down in Newark ... Yea, at least twenty men with light riot gear. I'll meet you there at six, but have them at the gatehouse by seven ... Thanks, see you then."

"You want us to come with you?"

"No, you and Ken have enough to do because of so many out with the flu, besides, it's just another strike."

"It can become more than that if things don't cool off down there."

Steve grinned. "Well I could use some action, it's been too quiet for me lately."

"Some of these guys might not play by the rules, so watch yourself."

"Who does anymore Joe? I'm learning to expect the unexpected as the norm lately. Maybe I'm even looking forward to it."

"That's dangerous to think that way. You have men counting on you," he said with concern. "Don't get careless out there, you hear me?"

Steve picked up his customized nightstick. He flicked it open with a quick snap into a full metal baton in locked position and held it up.

"It's hard to be careless if you're prepared and willing to do what it takes," he said, then dropped it on the desk.

"I'm going out for a drive to relax before having to get sleep and deal with that site in the morning. Have a good night Joe."

He walked out for the elevator as Pam waved to him but he seemed lost in his thoughts. She went over by Joe who just stood at the doorway watching him.

"I'm worried," she said softly. "He's got something eating at him and won't let anyone in."

"Call Ken," he said looking at the elevator lights descending. "Tell him I need to be in Newark early, but I should be back here by noon."

Steve drove aimlessly until he found himself parked by the stop sign across from Sue's old house. The lights were out. After her dad died and little sister went to college her mom lived alone. He sat staring at the front steps for sometime, then he drove off and found himself parked across from her new home.

He watched the shadows passing the downstairs windows. In a short while they vanished and the top three room lights came on. He could make out her shadow now as she turned out her light last around ten O'clock.

At about ten thirty, the middle room light came on and he could hear a man's voice.

"Let me in!" it yelled.

Sue's room light then came on, but the yelling continued. He could see her shadow backing up to the window. There was more pounding on a door, then vulgar language and the cursing out of her name.

He got out of the car and went to the porch. He rang the doorbell and pulled down his black ball cap low over his eyes.

When Wil opened the door, a fury of fists tore into him and he went down head first, like the Titanic, deep into the dark shag carpet. He slammed the door and then walked slowly back to Excalibur murmuring, "Thunder may frighten, but Lightning strikes," then drove off in a storm of dust.

Sue came cautiously down the stairs when she heard the commotion, carrying an umbrella point first. She found Wil unconscious on the floor but breathing. She opened the door slowly but saw no one, then looked down and noticed a large silver coat button shining up at her. Etched in its center was a pine cone.

The next morning, Wil called off from work after having his nose set at the hospital. Sue waved her car keys at him as she headed out to go shopping. The button was hanging from its ring.

She went over to the Headquarters and told the receptionist that she was there to see Ken.

"Just tell him it's Susan Walker and it's a Code Red. He will understand."

The receptionist called and was told to immediately escort her and Dawn to the elevator.

When the doors opened, she came face to face with both Ken and Joe.

"Are you all right?" they asked.

"Can we talk privately?"

They went into Ken's office while Pam took Dawn to watch television.

"What's the problem?" Ken asked.

"Last night, someone came to my house and punched Wil in the face, breaking his nose and bruising several ribs, among other things."

"Do you want an officer posted there while we look into it for you?"

"No. I didn't see anyone but I know who it was, he dropped this." She held up her key ring and they saw the distinctive style button. "I saw it on his overcoat when I was at his suite."

"You went with him to his apartment?" Ken asked amazed.

"Yes!"she snapped back. "Just to talk with him Ski!"

"Of course, why else?" he said, suddenly feeling ashamed for having even asked. " I'm sorry Sue. I shouldn't have even thought different."

"It's all right," she said softly with a smile, touching his hand.

Joe stepped out into the hall and went to the coat rack. He checked Steve's black overcoat, then came back in and nodded to Ken.

"Guys, we were together the night of the play and agreed not to see each other again, but I need you to talk with him."

She looked away a moment.

"I'm afraid that he will do it again, even worst if he thinks, well that…"

"That you're being abused?" Ken asked reaching for her sunglasses as she stopped him.

"Oh Sue," Joe said, "why didn't you tell us? I'd of taken care of it for you."

"That exactly why I didn't Joe," she said with fear in her eyes, "and why I couldn't say anything to him either. I knew he'd do something like this. It's not what I want. Please help me stop him."

"If he knows, you're asking a lot," Ken said.

"He knows," Joe stated. "That's what's been eating at him these past weeks."

Joe paced, thinking.

"I'm afraid she's right. If it happens again and he finds out, he will do worst. I've seen it in his eyes," Joe said nervously.

"Well, we'll go and have a talk with him now," Ken said pointing Joe to the door. "You just wait here Little Sister."

They went over and knocked, then entered and closed the door behind them. Steve was sitting back in his chair, staring off into space, thinking.

"What's up?" he asked as he finally noticed them just standing quietly.

"Doing little search and destroy missions are we?" Ken asked.

He looked questioning at him then Joe said, "If you're going to do this kind of thing, don't leave behind your calling card," and he tossed his button onto the desk.

"It's got nothing to do with you," Steve said picking it up. "Just leave it alone."

Ken looked over at Joe saying, "Ya know, if you'd just hold him I could beat the hell out of him."

Steve looked at Joe and yelled, "What if it was Cindy? Would you want me to stop you!"

"Cindy is my wife," he said.

Steve raised his hand, pointing at him. "Don't go there Joe, she's my life too."

"So what are you gonna do to stop him?" Ken asked. "You know it's gonna happen again, that's the pattern, or is that what you're counting on?"

Steve came over to Ken as if he was about to hit him, but then caught himself and turned his back.

"He doesn't even know it was you who hit him, so why should he stop?" Joe commented.

"I don't care if he knows who does it so long as it gets done," he answered with a tone of fatality.

"Okay, go!" Ken said. "Go now into my office and you tell her to her face that you're gonna kill her husband. Go on, tell her!"

"She's here?" Steve asked, suddenly looking pale.

"And I'm sure she just heard everything we've said," Ken answered.

Steve closed his eyes a moment, then slowly went and opened the door. Pam was standing near her desk looking at him with fright. He walked into Ken's office and Sue stood up as he closed the door.

"Why?" she asked with a look of despair.

"You know why," he answered in a gruff tone.

She came over to him and gently held his face. "I'm asking, for me, please don't do this. If you love me as I love you then you'll stop now."

He closed his eyes and lowered his head to his chest with a deep sigh as he saw the pain in her face. "Please leave him," he begged.

She caressed his face with both hands. "I have left it all up to God in prayer. He knows how to best deal with it. Trust me, trust Him My Love."

"You ask too much Sue," he replied with a painful tone.

She kissed him saying, "But still, I'm asking. Pride, Honor and Respect, remember?"

"All right," he said, forcing out the words. "I'll try, I promise."

"Thank you Babe," she whispered, then smiled up into his face with watering eyes. "I know how hard this is for you. I need you to stand with me, help me to be strong, not to fight for me. I need you to pray with me Love. Pray that we'll do His Will, His way, and not ours. Can't you see that?"

He raised his eyes to hers and saw himself in them. "I am always with you Sue," he cried softly. "As you stand, so I stand. So if His Will is yours, then it must be mine too. I'll pray it be so."

She pressed her cheek to his and their tears touched. "I love you so much," she cried into his ear. "It'll all work out, I know it will." She took his hand. "I have someone I want you to meet." They went to the conference room where Pam was having a soda with Dawn while watching the television together.

"Dawn, this is your Uncle Steve," Sue said waving her over.

"Hello," Dawn said smiling as she shook his hand. "Are all of you brothers?"

314

He smiled down at her. "You mean with Ken and Joe? Oh we're better than just brothers, we're the best of friends," he answered, knowing they were both at the door behind him. He leaned closer to her, looking at her light brown hair, her deep brown eyes and perfect little nose. "So much like your mother, and that smile … Perfect."

He turned to Pam. "This is Mrs. Susan Walker," he said, "Wil Walker's wife and her daughter Dawn. Everyone, this is Pam my personal secretary and my special girl."

Sue looked up at her and smiled with a polite hello. It was then that Pam recognized her from the theater aisle.

"I believe we've already met," Pam said. "Weren't you at the opening of the Impossible Love play when Steve was called away on business?"

"Yes, I was," she answered.

"I don't remember seeing you in the lobby afterwards though with everyone else."

"No, I had already left with someone before it ended."

"For business reasons also?" Pam asked, glancing towards Steve as he continued talking with Dawn.

"Yes, personal business," she replied, "very personal."

During the next couple of months, Steve seemed to be himself again. He was performing his daily tasks with a passionate purpose and true focus on the company's needs and future.

Pam noticed it also, the way he became affectionate towards her again. Still, she was bothered by wondering about his relationship with Sue. Finally, over coffee downstairs in the cafeteria she sat with Cindy and asked her about it.

"You already know about what happened between them," she said to her.

"Yes I understand the past, it's the present I don't understand. I mean, she's married now and she has no intention of getting a divorce, so why are they still an item?"

"They're not an item," Cindy answered with certainty, "they haven't seen anything of each other since that day in the office."

"But she still comes here and goes out with your husband and Mr. Tomineski for lunches and such."

Cindy turned to face her directly. "They're friends, have been since school. You don't just end something like that, especially for that group, they are all Musketeers!"

Pam paused. "So, that fourth foil is for her isn't it?"

"Yes, she is like a little sister to Joe and Ken. They would never have thought of leaving her out of something as important as the company logo."

"And for Steve, is she a little sister to him also?" she asked sarcastically.

Cindy stared at her, then stated, "The color green doesn't suit you."

"Jealousy? I'm not jealous she's married. I'm the one he's dating," Pam stated back as if to convince herself.

"Then everything is fine isn't it?"

"But I know he'd run at her beckoned call," she said flustered.

"So would Ken, so would my Joe and so would I," she declared. "Sue is part of this family, she always will be, so if you want to be with him you better get use to it. Some things are forever."

Pam stirred her coffee for several moments, trying to think it through.

"He still loves her, I mean passionately loves her, doesn't he?"

"Without a doubt," Cindy answered calmly. "Theirs was a True Love from the beginning, a gift from God, and everybody that knew them could see it."

Cindy looked in her eyes. "Even now you can see it. It's eternal, and yes, he would die for her in a moment. Can you handle being in a relationship like that?"

Pam turned away a moment, caressing her watch, then said, "I love him and I believe my love is strong enough to win over his love from her."

"His love is not a prize to be won Pam," she said. "It has to be a gift or it's nothing."

She started to cry. "I don't want to lose him Cindy. I love him so much."

"Then that's what you do, just love him and don't worry who else does. It's the love you two share that's important. Sue can't help loving him for the rest of her life, but she would never do anything to hurt him. Even if that meant seeing him loving you. The other's happiness is the center of their love for one another."

Pam wiped away her tears, then looked up at the fourth foil on the wall. "I don't know if I'm that strong," she confessed.

"If you truly love someone, "Cindy said touching her hand, "you'll always put their happiness first."

***

Ken went down to the gym to work out a bit. He thought he'd be alone after office hours on a Friday night, but was surprised to find Steve there. He watched quietly from the top stairs as Steve worked out, attacking barehanded and with bare feet on a full bag. Seeing him kicking it, punching, jabbing and then ending with a round-house kick up high to the chest or head areas. It was like watching a dance.

"Don't you ever get tired of trying to sneak up on me?" Steve asked with a grin without looking up.

"No," he answered now heading down the stairs, "cause one of these days, your built in alert will blow a fuse and I'll be there to save your sorry butt."

Steve laughed. "It already happened remember, you took a knife meant for me."

"That doesn't count. I distracted you back then, otherwise you'd of heard him coming before he was even recruited."

Ken watched as he was being particularly hard on the bag tonight."You got a personal grudge with this bag?" he asked.

Steve stopped and turned to him. "Can I tell you something, tip to tip, straight out?"

"Musketeers is plural for a reason," he answered, "and if for no other reason than to just be there for the other."

"Ken you were right, I did want to kill him."

"I know," he replied softly, "and I understand why. One because of what he was doing to her, and then, because he was the only thing standing in the way of getting her back." Ken came closer. "I also

317

know that if the time came and you were about to tear his heart out, you wouldn't be able to do it because of her. "

"And what about Pam's? What am I doing to her heart with all this?"

"Only you can answer that. When you do, be honest with yourself and with her because she deserves it."

"Oh God," he moaned, "sometimes this world asks too much."

"Like Sue has of you?"

"Oh Ken, what am I going to do without her?" he cried, then he beat the bag several times before dropping to his knees.

Ken knelt beside him. "You're gonna live and make her proud of you. You're gonna honor the greatest love I've ever known. Keeping it pure as God's own Grace, as pure and true as the day He first gave it. Sue has, and you will too. You can't ever lose each other, you both live in One heart."

"I try to ignore it," he said softly, "pretending everything is fine when I'm with Pam, but that One heart is bleeding and I'm drowning in it. Oh God help me I ache so bad," he moaned out, clenching both fists tightly.

"He will," Ken said in a calming tone. "He gave you the faith, the trust comes from you."

Ken helped him to his feet and they walked out to the lockers.

"In three days it will be a new year, 1984," he told him. "Ask Him to make it one of resolution for you."

***

The next several winter months were long and harsh, so the coming of spring was welcomed by all. Steve paid for his purchases and then stepped into the store's revolving door at the same time Sue did coming in. They stopped midway looking at each other, then he let her continue on inside and he came round to meet her.

"How have you been?" he asked trying to take in as much of her at once as he could.

"I've been fine," she answered with a smile, "and you look well."

"Oh, I'm okay I guess," he replied still fighting the urge to reach out and touch her.

318

They stood silent for a moment then she said, "I guess I'd better get on with my shopping."

"What have you come for?"

"Just some things I saw were on sale."

He didn't want her to leave, so he said the first thing he could think to say. "Would you mind if I kept you company, I'm not in any hurry?"

She smiled saying, "I'd love that Babe," and took his arm gently.

They browsed at first and then she made her way into the women's section. He just watched her every movement; the way her hair fell to one side as she'd look down or the sparkle in her eyes whenever she found an item of interest. He could smell her scent as he stood closer and wanted so bad to just hold her again.

Sue did her best to act natural but inside she just wanted to put her arms around him, kiss his lips and draw life from him again.

When they got to the undergarments, she saw a short, thin, lacy nightgown and absentmindedly held it up to see. He suddenly turned his head and she laughed.

"This still embarrasses you?"

"Oh no, I just thought I saw someone I knew."

"Oh yea, me too," she said with a joyful smile. "You, back in Caldwell about seventeen years ago," and she laughed again.

"Oh Sweety," she said sighing into his eyes, "you're still so precious."

He smiled back, trying to avoid getting too red-faced; but it was so good to hear her laugh and see her smile again.

As they stepped out into the sunshine, still smiling and laughing, a BMW pulled up with its lights on. It blew the horn causing them both to stop and look. Wil was at the wheel, his business completed, and waving her to come.

"I have to go," she told him as the warm glow left her face, "but I loved seeing you."

"Goodbye Sue," he said solemnly and watched her leave as Wil stared coldly at them.

He stood there, heart wrenched, as she put herself into the car. It was all black like a hearse. Her eyes stared back at him but never blinked and her hand didn't wave, just remained propped up against the window towards him. Her face grew pale and lifeless as his image faded. He felt their heart bleeding, then it ached and burned, as the car proceeded up the hill slowly, then dropped from sight.

Every instinct screamed for him to storm hell's gates. To rescue her from this nightmarish Purgatory she was doing penance in for both of them.

He walked the crosswalk slowly to the other side and then back to his empty apartment. As he opened the door, he tossed his bag into a darkened corner and then went to the window. He put his hand to the glass and stared down upon the path she had taken into the darkness that night she left him, so many months before.

"Just know that I love you more than life," he heard echoing in his heart, mind and soul. He turned and looked at the door. "No, I can't be happy," he heard again, "not forever My Love." Not forever, not forever repeated over and over in his head until he pressed his hands to his ears, wanting to scream to try and stop the words.

"Leave it in God's hands?" he asked moaning out loud. "What I need is hold her in mine." He fell to his knees and cried out, "God has our love become an offense to You now? You know there is no greater pain for us than knowing the other is hurting. One Love, One Heart, that's what You gave us, that's what You made us. So why now won't You save us?"

He turned his eyes up to heaven and declared, "Whatever price you want me to pay for us to be together, I will pay it I swear."

Suddenly the doorbell rang. He wiped away the tear that had started in his eye and opened it. It was Pam.

"Hi. I thought you might like to come shopping with me this afternoon and keep me company. It's such a beautiful day, isn't it?"

He reached out and took her hand. "Yes, I would like to get out. Staying here alone is just making me feel down."

"Then come with me and I promise to make you happy," she said quickly with a smile. "Forever," she added, "if you'll give me a chance."

The next day in the conference room, as Joe sat with Steve to discuss schedule changes for a new site, a call came for him.

"Yes," Joe answered his secretary Alice.

"You have a call from Janice on line two."

"Thank you I've got it. Hello Janice …What? - - - When! - - - No, don't move her! Call an ambulance and we'll meet you at the hospital."

He slowly put down the phone and turned to see Steve looking at him.

"That was Janice, there's been an incident. We have to go to the hospital now, it's …"

"It's Sue," he said, "isn't it?"

Joe nodded. "Sue and Dawn. It's bad Steve let's go."

Joe saw the rage grow in his eyes as he got up, jabbing his pen into the arm of the chair.

"What are you going to do?"

"Find him," he answered in a tone that chilled Joe like an ice-dagger down his spine. He threw back his chair and headed for the door.

"Steve no! - - - She's hurt bad and! - - - Wait, she needs you now!"

Steve continued towards the elevator as Pam stood up, hearing Joe calling for him.

"What's wrong?" she asked him, but Steve didn't stop walking. She turned to Joe as he tried to catch the elevator door before it closed, but missed it.

"What's happened?" she asked upset.

"It's Sue, she's been hurt. Call Ken and have him located Wil Walker before he does."

It was a Saturday afternoon and he knew exactly where to find him. The Le Mans screeched into the parking lot of the golf course country club and parked up near the door in a fire zone. With the top down, he just jumped over the car door and made his way up the steps. He walked swiftly around the wrap-around porch to the large patio doors that led to the bar lounge.

He slammed the doors open and stood with the day's bright sun flowing into the darkened room from behind him. All talking stopped and faces turned to look at him. His eyes scanned the room, then he spotted him back by the billiard table.

"William Walker!" he called out with judgment in his voice as he stared with fury at Wil standing there with a glass full of scotch.

The faces turned to the back as William stepped forward from behind the billiard table, now holding a cue stick he had found lying there.

"You beat them, then come here and celebrate!" Steve cried out.

"This is no business of yours," Wil replied nervously, "she's my wife and you stay away from her. She's Susan Walker, that's whose she is now!" he added as he pointed the cue stick at him.

"What value is a pearl to a pig?" he muttered back in disgust.

Wil watched as he walked defiantly towards him. People got up from chairs to make room as he approached, flipping a table out of his way. When he reached the table he pulled a stick from the wall holder and held it out.

"You wanna test your steel against mine, fine. I'm gonna skin you alive, one strip of cowardice at a time," he told him with his eyes ablaze. Steve whacked the end of his cue on the table's edge, splintering it into a sharp point. "You ever say her name again with those foul lips and I'll cut them off!"

Wil lunged forward at him with the heavy end of the cue swinging downward towards his face. Steve stepped aside and parried the attack with a single stroke, then jabbed him hard with the point into his stomach. Wil fell back, heaving up a vomit of scotch.

"Crawl you snake," he said. "Bleed like you made them," and he cross-swung the tip into Wil's face. He then brought up the heavy end into his chin, knocking him backwards flat onto the floor.

"Somebody call security!" Wil cried out in fear from his bleeding mouth. As he got to his feet and prepared to defend himself Steve lunged at him again. He attacked gracefully, yet with malice, jabbing

322

Wil hard in the ribs with the cue. The blow might have punctured his left lung but for a wallet being in his breast pocket to stop the tip.

Steve came back striking more cuts to his face, neck and arms. Finally he cracked his cue across Wil's knuckles causing him to drop his stick. He then laid his aside and it came down now to bare hands.

Wil felt a hard blow to his eye, then another across his cheek and fell backwards onto the bar. There was a frosted mug of beer sitting there and he grabbed it. He threw it and it struck and shattered on Steve's head, yet still, he kept on coming at him with a fury of fists.

The blows seemed endless, to his face, chest, stomach and eyes. Wil swayed and staggered as he tried to see from where the next one was coming. He held up his hands trying to protect himself but couldn't. He tried to kick him in the groin, but Steve caught his leg and pulled him off balance and down again to the floor.

Wil made his way under a table and then got to his feet again. He turned and was met with a round-house kick to under the chin, flipping him backwards into a chair, exhausted and crying. Steve lifted him up to his feet and held him there by his shirt as he grabbed the sharp cue back into his right fist again.

Suddenly he heard a voice inside say, "Please don't, for my sake!" He stared at the dazed, bleeding face as he then heard Wil's words echo also saying, "She's my wife, stay away from her!"

He remained with fist cocked aiming the stake at his chest, while still holding him up.

"Please don't, it was a promise!" cried the inner voice again.

He thought of her. "How bright her light that shines my night," he murmured to himself, "yet here, I hold the sword while she holds the right."

He dropped the cue and lowered Wil down into the chair behind him, letting him go. He turned and gazed at the bright light coming in from the open doors, then quietly walked past the room of faces and out into it. He got to his car and drove off.

Moments later, Joe pulled up and was met inside with a team of On Guard security officers. As he entered the team leader recognized him and approached.

"It was over before we arrived," he told him, "but Mr. Walker said that it was Mr. Clayton who attacked him."

"Stay here," Joe said to him and he walked over as Wil looked up from the chair with tears.

"I don't know why you're still breathing," Joe said as he lifted him up by the neck. "You must have had an angel on your shoulder. I don't know why he didn't kill you but if you ever lay a hand on those girls again, I promise you, I will!" Joe grabbed his hair and jerked his head up. "Do you understand me?" Wil nodded, then passed out and Joe dropped him into the chair.

Joe returned to the team leader. "Captain!"

The officer came over. "No sir, I'm a lieutenant," he answered correcting him.

"This is your chance for a field promotion, Captain," he said with bold authority, "as long as I don't see Mr. Clayton's name anywhere in your report. Do we understand each other?"

"Yes sir!"

Joe went out and then drove off in his metallic red Corvette. A short time later, he found the Le Mans parked near the entrance to the Island. He walked out to the grassy knoll where Steve stood looking out over the lake. "Are you all right?" he asked as he came up from behind.

"She once told me here how safe she felt in my arms, but she's in that hospital now because I put those arms around her. I caused all this Joe, all this pain."

"It was a drunken jealous husband that did this."

"And who made him that way!" he screamed out, then lowered his head. "I might as well of beat her myself with these two hands," he cried. "Oh God forgive me."

"You listen to me," Joe said as he roughly jerked him around. "The love you two have for each other is as real and solid as the ground we're standing on. Love doesn't cause pain, it's a refuge from it. It heals, it doesn't hurt. Now, that girl is lying in that hospital and she needs healing so I'm asking you, are you crying for her or for yourself?"

"You lousy, self-righteous! - - -" Steve screamed as he swung round at him. Joe caught his fist in mid-air and squeezed it tight in his bear-like paw.

"That's what I thought," he finally said as he released him. "Stay here and whine, I'm going to the hospital." He turned and walked towards the parking lot.

"Joe!"

He stopped, but still with his back to him, as Steve walked over and stood next to him.

"Have I ever thanked you for being my friend?"

"We ain't gonna hug or nothing, are we?" Joe asked with a raised eyebrow.

Steve let out a short laugh, then Joe looked down asking, "How's your hand?"

"Lucky catch," he replied as he massaged it.

"It's the Irish in me," he stated with a grin and they left together.

When they entered the main entrance they were met by Janice. "How is she?" Steve asked.

"I'm not sure, they took her into the E. R. and haven't told me anything."

"Go sit in the waiting room," Joe said, "I'll see what I can find out."

As they sat Janice looked over at him. "It'll be fine," she told him. "What happened?"

"Wil accused her of sleeping with you. She denied it and he hit her. She grabbed Dawn and ran out the door towards my house, but he caught her on the lawn and knocked her down. Dawn grabbed his arm as I came out and I saw him punch her. Then he kicked Sue again and again."

Steve put his head in his hands as she continued.

"He kept asking her if she still loved you and each time she said yes, he'd kick her over and over again." She stopped as she saw tears oozing out between his fingers. "I'll get us some coffee," she said softly as she touched his knee.

He wiped his eyes then went to the window. Outside cars drove by; people were walking, talking and smiling. The treetops swayed in the gentle breeze. Flowers lined the walkways. It was a beautiful day. Above, the blue sky carried a milky white cloud lazily across its ocean-like vastness.

***

"That one looks like a cruise liner," he heard her say.

"And where is it going?"

"On a Mediterranean cruise, stopping in Spain and then Greece and ending in Italy for a Roman holiday," Sue answered with wide eyes.

"You want to go to Rome?" he asked.

"Maybe someday. My grandma told me about it, she was born near there." She smiled adding, "I'd like to throw coins into the fountain square and make a wish."

He pulled her closer. "And what would you wish for?"

"I can't tell you they may not come true then, but mostly, I'd wish that you were there with me."

"I'm with you now," he whispered.

"Then I already have the best of my wishes," she said as she leaned up for a kiss.

***

"Steve?" came a voice calling. He turned, it was Joe. "They're rushing her to surgery now," he said, "she has internal bleeding."

"Can't I see her?"

"Not now, I'm sorry," he replied touching his shoulder.

"Here," Janice said offering him some coffee.

"No thanks. Joe, where's the Chapel?"

"I'll take you."

As they entered through the stained glassed door he saw Dawn up front, kneeling with her head down. Joe stayed by the door as he watched him go over and kneel next to her.

"Oh Uncle Steve," she cried and he held her. Joe closed the door as he went out.

He looked at her bruised face, kissed her on the forehead, then looked to the altar. "Lord," he said softly, "I know I have no right to ask, but still, I'm asking. Please don't take her, for this little girl's sake, please don't."

"Oh Momma," she cried out as she buried her face under his chin. "She kept saying that she loved you, again and again, and he kept on kicking …"

"Shh, I know," he whispered in a choked up tone, "I know." He lifted her chin up. "He's a just and merciful God, isn't He?"

"Yes," she said through the tears.

"Then pray with me little one. I'm sure He'll listen to you."

Hours later, as they sat in the Chapel with her head on his shoulder, Dawn asked, "When did you first know that you loved her?"

"I wasn't much older than you when I fell in love with your mom. I'm not sure if there was any one particular moment," he answered thinking. "If I had to pick one I guess it was when she smiled at me in a math class. It was days after I had given her a small bottle of perfume called 'Heaven Scent' for Christmas."

Dawn smiled. "She still has that bottle. It's empty, but she keeps wild flowers in it."

"Small round flowers with red and blue centers and white edges," he thought out loud.

"Yes," she replied, surprised he knew.

He smiled. "She called them American Dreams. They only seem to grow wild out on the Island."

The door opened and a nurse came in. "Miss Walker?" Dawn sat up. "Your Mother's out of surgery and in her room now."

"Can I see her?"

"Yes of course, follow me."

They were led to the second floor and the nurse pointed to the I.C.U. sign. The two went down the hall and up to the nurse's station.

"I'm here to see my mom, Mrs. Walker."

"She's in room three, but it's family only."

Dawn took Steve's hand. "It's all right," she replied, "this is my dad," and she led him through the door.

The sun was just beginning to set outside her window as they entered the room. They paused a moment as they saw her there lying still, with her eyes closed. Slowly she opened them and turned to look at the two quiet figures.

"Hello Baby," she said softly.

"Hi Mom," she replied, as she held Steve's hand and walked over to sit near her. "Are you all right Mom?"

"I'm fine, but look at you two," she said seeing the cuts and bruises on both of their faces.

She raised her hand to Dawn's bruised cheek. "I'm so sorry Baby."

"I'm okay," she said as she looked at Sue's I.V. Tubes, the bandaged face and her left wrist in a cast resting on her stomach.

"Shh," Dawn added, "just rest Mom, please."

Steve held back the tears as Sue smiled up at him. "Hello My Love," she whispered.

He knelt down by Dawn and kissed Sue's hand. "I prayed just to hear your voice, to see your smile and God's been gracious enough to hear me."

"And I asked the same," she said smiling.

He smiled back as a tear broke and fell from his eye onto her hand. "You are so beautiful, like an American Dream."

"And your touch," she said with a sigh, "is like a summer's day on a grassy knoll."

A tear began in her eye as she gazed up into his. "Come and take some love from heart," she begged, "I can't hold it all."

He got up and leaned over her, then ever so gently touched his lips to hers. Dawn squeezed Sue's hand while reaching over to put Steve's on top of theirs.

"I'm so sorry Steve. I should have kept believing in you, in us. I should have waited for you longer, after all, you did promise," she said with trembling lips.

"You were dying Sue and so was I. I felt it so many times and I knew I had to get back to you somehow. I tried Love, oh how I tried."

"And you did," she said smiling.

"Yea, but too late. A lifetime too late," he moaned out. He looked at her lying there beaten and his heart bled. "Oh Babe!" he finally cried out loud. "Why didn't you just tell him what he wanted to hear?"

"I couldn't!" she cried back with closed tearing eyes. "When he asked if I still loved you, all I could see was your face." She turned quickly and looked up to him. "Into Beauty's eye, one dare not lie. I could only say what my heart would allow."

He reached out to wipe away her tears but she stopped him saying, "No don't. These tears are ours and I want them!"

"So do I," he whispered as he slowly dipped his fingers into them, put them to his lips, then he blessed himself.

"Oh how I love you," she cried taking and kissing his hand.

The door opened behind them. It was Wil. He said nothing as they turned to look at him, then he walked over but stopped a few feet from the bed. He looked at Sue and tried to speak but could not. She saw his bandaged face and hands.

"Hello Wil," she said.

Dawn started to get up but stopped when she felt Sue squeeze her hand.

"Oh Susan I'm sorry. I didn't mean to do this."

"I know and I forgive you, if you can forgive me."

"For what?"

"For letting you believe I loved you, while I knew I would only love him all my life. I'm so sorry Wil, I never should have married you. You deserved a wife who was yours completely. A real love not a pretense."

"But I love you Susan," he said in a begging tone.

"I know you think so, but I can't live a lie anymore. For both our sakes, please go get your things and move out. We both deserve better than we've had. I love you for caring, but I can't come back to you again."

"I'll stop drinking," he pleaded.

"I'll pray you do and I'll ask God to forgive me for all the other hurt I've caused you," she said with pain in her voice. "What you needed was never mine to give."

"So it's over?" he asked as the sun's last rays vanished outside the window.

"Yes Wil, finally."

He lowered his head, then slowly turned and left.

"God forgive me," she cried softly as she closed her eyes.

"He's a merciful God, isn't He?" Dawn said to her as she looked up at Steve.

He smiled down on the girl's teary face and nodded. "Yes He is."

Chapter Twenty

"Whatever price you want me to pay, I will pay it."
-Steve Clayton

Sue was able to leave the hospital after three weeks, but her doctor said he wanted her back for more tests. She was glad to be home again as Steve and Dawn helped her from the car. Inside she immediately wanted to do some cooking.

"You'll stay and have dinner with us?" she asked touching his arm.

"Sure. What can I do?"

"Well, I thought I'd make us some homemade baked mac and cheese with beef sirloin tips…Oh, and I have some homemade bread ready to bake also."

"Sounds terrific," he said.

"If you'd grate the cheese, that would be great," she said grinning and he laughed.

"I can help with the bread," Dawn said, "I know how."

"Thanks Baby."

It was so good having them with her. She felt like it should have been this way from the beginning.

When they had finished eating he helped Dawn clear the table. Sue picked up the pile of mail that had been set aside for her and went to rest in the living room. She opened a few, then suddenly paused in silence.

"Sue? Where do you want me to put these pans, they're all washed?" he called from the kitchen. There came no answer.

"I'll go ask," Dawn said and went out to her. She found her upset and she knelt by her.

"Mom, what is it?"

She held out the official papers and said, "They're divorce papers from your father's lawyer. It says he wants half of all the money I inherited and half the house too."

Dawn became angry. "He doesn't deserve any of it Mom!"

"That's not the way the state looks at it," she replied, then she turned to her. "Please, I don't want Steve to know about this."

"But maybe he can help," she urged.

"Please Baby, I'll handle it."

Reluctantly, Dawn agreed.

Sue wiped her eyes quickly as he came in from the kitchen holding up the pans. "Oh in the lower cabinet please, thanks Babe," she said smiling.

"I'll get them," Dawn said to him and took the pans back into the kitchen.

He came over to her. "What's wrong?"

"Nothing," she answered with another quick smile. He looked at her for a moment, still sensing something.

"Angel, what is it?"

"Nothing I told you. I guess I'm just a little tired, but everything's fine."

He knelt by her. "I'm always here, even to just talk, you know that."

"I know Love and thank you. Now, how about some of that great cake Cindy gave us for our dessert?"

The next afternoon she called his lawyer. He said Wil might be willing to let her keep the house if she'd give him all of the trust funds.

"That'll be everything we have, even Dawn's college funds," she said. "Please, ask him to understand this."

"He does," he said, "but he feels that he was the one wronged here and that's why he's filed for mental cruelty."

"For what?"

"He said if you don't agree to the terms then he'll have to file instead for adultery and go after child custody also."

Sue was silent a moment.

"Hello Mrs. Walker, are you there?"

"Oh yes, I'm right here," she answered in a firm tone.

"What shall I tell him?"

She stood up from her chair with a fist. "You tell him, On Guard!"

"What? Wait, hold on … He's sitting right here and wants to talk with you."

"Susan, what's the problem? I'm entitled to this money."

"Is this what you meant when you told me in the hospital that you loved me?"

"What's love got to do with it? This is a property settlement."

"Wil, you'd do this after what you've already done?"

He was silent a moment.

"Look," he said, "I've checked and you should have several thousand dollars, plus there's the house. Let's just cut to the chase and do it okay? I want what's due me, so just put your mark on the papers and send them back here. I'll fill in the blanks."

Dawn heard the conversation from the stairs and watched as Sue clenched her teeth, holding her right fist up to her chest. She went and lifted the extension in the hall and listened to them.

"Wil I'll be right over with your papers, just you wait there."

"Good, now you're being reasonable. All I want is what's fairly due both of us." He paused, then added, "After all, you're getting the best deal here. You get the house you always wanted. You finally get back your precious lover boy and you can both have the kid as a bonus."

"Wil I want this over too. Just don't leave until I get there."

She hung up and headed to the back sewing room, now being used for storage. She got down on her knees and prayed for guidance.

"What would you have me do and when do I stop paying?"

She laid her head against a stake of boxes, then suddenly a long round leather case fell from above and landed in front of her. She stared at it a moment, then smiled upwards. "Thank you," she said and flung its strap over her shoulder.

Dawn stood at the bottom of the stairs as Sue gathered up the divorce papers from the table. "Mom I heard. You can't give him what he wants, it's not fair!"

Sue turned to her. "It will be more than fair to have this over, you safe with me and this house still ours." She packed up the papers and stuffed them into a grocery bag. "You wait here," she said to the young troubled face.

"No Mom, don't!"

Just then, Excalibur pulled into the driveway. "I called him," Dawn told her, then she ran out to meet him.

"You have to stop her Uncle Steve," she cried out to him from the porch. He hurried up the walkway and Sue came out the door behind her so he stopped.

"Good," Sue said, "I need a ride please," then put her stuff and herself into the front seat.

Steve and Dawn talked on the porch a moment, then they went over to the car.

"What do you want to do Angel?"

She smiled at him and said, "To give him what's fair, if that's what he wants."

He looked over at Dawn's frightened face.

"Would you two kindly get in the car and drive me over to his lawyer's office, please?"

"Whatever you want Babe," he answered.

"You can't!" Dawn yelled to him.

"Do you see her face?"

Dawn looked at her mom.

"There's no changing her mind when it looks like that," he stated. "She used to look that way before a match and it meant she's already visualized the outcome of the set. Now, all we can do is let her play it out, understand?"

Dawn agreed with a nod, but was still unsure about the whole idea as she got into the back seat. They drove out to the Parsippany plaza and all went inside.

Wil and his lawyer were sitting in the back conference room waiting and were surprised when the three of them arrived.

"Felt you needed moral support to make a mark on some papers?" Wil snickered.

"Oh, I'm not all together here just to support her," Steve said, "I'm here to keep things fair is all, for everyone."

"Would all of you excuse us," she asked, "so I can have a few minutes with Wil first?"

"Let's give them some privacy," Steve said as he ushered the lawyer and Dawn out, and then winked at Sue as he closed the door behind him. He stood against the other side as he heard the lock click from inside.

Sue then walked from the door and laid the paper bag on her end of the table, looking at Wil sitting at the far end in his chair.

"So," he asked, "where are the papers?"

She poured them out of the bag in a pile.

"Have you signed them?" he asked impatiently.

"I will now," she said as she opened up the tube case, removed a long black foil and placed it on the table.

"What's that for?" he laughed.

"That's for you. This one, this is mine," she answered as she pulled out another with stars on its handle and unscrewed the safety tip. She held the papers from moving and cut a large 'S' into the one marked for a signature.

"What are you doing?"

"Making my mark," she replied. She unscrewed the tip off the black foil and tossed it to him handle first, but he fumbled and dropped it. "You said you wanted to cut to the chase, well let's, now that we're on equal ground." She walked around the table, pointing her tip straight out, and told him to pick up the sword.

"No," he said, then she jabbed him in his stomach. "Are you crazy!" he cried out.

"Pick it up, now!"

Steve smiled as he listened, blocking the door. Dawn and his lawyer ran over to the small inside window of the room and saw her with the sword held up to his face.

"I'm calling the police," his lawyer said going for the phone but Steve stopped him.

"I wouldn't do that, that'll just make her mad," he said with a grin. "Don't worry, it's just a few minor points they have to work out first."

"I said pick it up!" she repeated, then stuck his hand.

"All right!" he screamed and bent down taking the foil with both hands.

She took a step back and then held out her tip to cross against his."On Guard!" she said, then started striking his foil as he backed up to the wall. He waved it out at her with both hands wildly as she played with him. Finally, she lunged forward and jabbed his arm.

"Damn! Stop it!" he cried out. "Have you lost your mind!"

"Actually," she said calmly, " I just recently came to my senses. We've taken as much as we're going to from each other, understand me?"

He stared blankly.

"I'm not going to take one more moment of abuse from you and you're not going to take one more thing from us. Do you understand me!" she yelled as she stabbed and cut his hand, causing him to drop the blade.

"Yes! Yes damn it!"

She moved her blade's tip quickly up under his chin and pressed lightly, slightly cutting into the skin. "I've asked you never to curse around me. Have I finally made my point?"

"Yes, all right," he answered shaking with tears flowing, "just don't hurt me anymore, please!"

She pulled the tip back, then moved away two steps, still prepared for any attack. "Now listen," she said, "and see if any of these names ring a bell for ya. Darcy Lang, Jenny Calter, Nancy Gilbert, Sally Windton ... just to name a few."

He looked blankly at her again.

"Did you really think I didn't know?" she asked with anger burning in her eyes. "I talked with all of them. They each confessed how they had an affair with you and how poorly you treated them after."She lowered the tip and aimed it at his groin. "They've all agreed to happily testify on my behalf in court if I wish," she said coldly. "If they do, that will mean you'll not only end up with nothing from this marriage but pay alimony and child support for many years to come."

He sat down in his chair, watching her as he grew pale. "So what now?" he asked trembling.

Sue threw the papers off of the table at him as he covered his face. "Now, you're going to get that fancy lawyer back in here and have him draw up a new divorce for you. One that states it is for incompatibility, not mental cruelty, and that you want to walk away without taking anything from us. We both just walk away clean and free of each other."

"Fine," he snorted, fighting the tears of fear.

She went over and unlocked the door, then opened it. "Mr. Hennings, thank you for your patience. We've come to a mutual understanding and are ready to do what is fair for all."

His lawyer went in and spoke with him as she grinned at Steve's smile.

"Mom!" Dawn cried out running from the window and throwing her arms around her neck. "You were awesome!"

Steve came over and picked her up at the waist declaring, "And still the reigning Champion!" She kissed him as she hugged his neck. "I love you," she heard him whisper, "and I never had a doubt."

Later, Dawn sat on her front porch as Steve enjoyed his coffee and wanted to ask him a question but remained quiet. He could sense it so he said, "Ask."

"How'd you know I had something to ask?"

"You give me the same vibes as your mom. I could almost always know when she felt something."

Dawn moved closer on the bench. "I never saw Mom stand up to him like that before, what made her be able to do it after all these years?"

Steve leaned into her. "Pride, Honor and Respect," he said, "but it was being home again that gave her the strength to stand up for them. You can always draw strength from your roots and of course, your father made at least three major mistakes with your mom."

"What were they?" she asked as she laid her hand on his.

"First, he thought she was weak because she left his abusive ways in God's hands. Second, he then threatened to take away her home and you. That was a really big mistake."

"And the third?" she asked anxiously.

"The third? Oh, you already know that one," he said kissing her forehead.

Sue went to see her doctor as scheduled on the following Saturday and had the tests run. He said he was concerned over the fact that she seems to be having nerve problems with her right arm since the beating. He also felt there might be some possibility of brain damage, but wanted to run a scan on her first. She sat calmly listening and agreed to continue the testing.

After she got home she felt the need for a short nap. As she rested peacefully, suddenly her sleep was shattered and she awoke crying out Steve's name. She took a cab to the headquarters, but when she got there she found everyone tense and just went straight up to the offices.

There had been trouble brewing down in the Newark warehouse district. Steve had spoken with the clients, recommending extra men be put on each site. Only seven out of the thirteen agreed to pay for the extra cost.

He had put four extra squads on standby and had two more on-call. He knew that meant paying partial stand-down pay out of his own pocket for the next few days. It would be worth it, he figured, if all hell broke loose as he suspected possible and his men would have backup ready.

There had been several incidents between residents and the police over the last week and the neighborhood was extremely restless. A riot was very possible, so he made continued patrol visits to each site to check on any unusual activity.

When he came into the Lambert site entrance he noticed several trailers with seals, loaded for shipping. There was only one tractor in the yard backing up its trailer into a slot near the side fence line. As he got out of his company van a voice yelled out to him.

"Hey Seaside! Looks like you just can't stay out of trouble's way." He turned and saw Norton smiling from the tractor's cab.

"What are you doing here?" he asked him as he walked over to the truck.

"Well, this is what I use to do for a livin'," Dan answered, "so when I got home I used my back pay and bought one of my own."

"And Audrey Ann?"

"Would you believe she came with the truck?" he replied with a grin as a smiling red-head popped her head out of the sleeper saying hi.

"I couldn't believe that she was still waiting when I got back," he said shaking his head, "I guess I was worth it after all."

"Yes, you were," Steve stated with a smile as he watched her hugging his arm, "and by God it's great to see you again."

They shook hands, then Steve told him he'd have to stay in the yard with his truck until a team arrived to back him up.

"I've got to secure this place and lock those gates while I still can."

"Need some help?" Dan asked.

"Thanks, but you're a civilian now and I have the rank here. Just stay put and, as always, keep your head down or I'll shoot your sorry butt."

Dan laughed, lifting off his hat and fanning his brown hair. "Don't worry about us we'll be cool, but nobody's gonna mess with this truck I promise ya." The two locked themselves in the rig as he watched Steve return to his van.

***

As Sue entered their floor, she heard voices from all directions, some on the phones and others yelling from the offices. She ran to Joe's office as she heard him call out, "Cindy, call down to the last squad and have them meet us at the van for the Lambert Site. Steve is there with only twelve men in light gear and I'll need them!"

"Joe?" he heard Sue's voice ask and turned to see her frightened face at the door.

"It'll be fine," he told her, "back up men are on their way now to support him." He called out to Ken, "Are you ready?"

Ken came out of his office in full riot gear. "Yea, let's go!"

She shook with fear, just seeing the expressions on their faces and the urgency in their actions. The shields, helmets and guns being gathered up by men in the office to carry down to the van waiting outside made her heart race.

"I'm coming with you," she said.

"Not a chance," Ken replied, "it's a full riot zone down there. Stay here, we'll call when we've contain the situation."

"Ski!" she screamed.

"No I said!"

Cindy came over and hugged her. "It's alright, let them do their job. I know how you feel," she said watching Joe loading his sidearm and grabbing his riot helmet, "but there's nothing we can do but wait. They're the best task force in the east."

Sue watched as they all went down in the elevator and others down the stairs rather than wait for it to come back up. In moments, the floor was completely empty and quiet except for a phone ringing which Pam answered, confirming the call in. She walked slowly, in a daze, past Pam's desk as she was calmly talking to the officer on the phone.

"Yes, please report immediately to zone four. Code red, officers need back up."

Pam hung up the phone and looked over at her trembling. "Come on," she said softly. "I just made some fresh coffee in the conference room," and she took her by the arm.

"No," Sue said firmly, "I'm going there. I know he's in danger. I saw his face, his eyes! He's going to get hurt!" she stated with certainty. "I saw it. There were gun shots and then I saw him fall to his knees. He was crying out as I woke up screaming to him! This isn't the first time I felt his pain. There was blood on his hands and his uniform," she told her as if watching it happening that very moment.

She looked straight into Pam's eyes. "He's gonna die if I don't get to him, I know it!"

"All right," Pam said shaking, "I'll take you."

***

"All the other sites are now fully covered," Joe told Steve from the van's phone. "We should be with you in about forty minutes or less."

"That's fine," Steve replied calmly. "So far they've stayed on the other side of the fences, looting stores across the street. I just wish I could see some cops but I guess that they have their hands full downtown. Don't worry, we'll hold this 'till you can get here. See ya man."

"Yea," Joe said, "see ya."

Steve hung up the van phone and looked at the twelve other faces outside. "They're all just green weenies," he thought to himself, "not one has ever seen hand-to-hand yet." He got out and called them all over.

"All right, I just got off the horn and a full squad is on its way right now, they'll be here in minutes. For now we need to set up a fire line, just in case, to protect this property, the personnel inside and each other until the reserves arrive, understand?"

All nodded and Steve smiled.

"Anybody here ever heard of Thermopylae?" One hand rose up. "What's your name officer?"

"Pavlos," he answered.

"Tell me what you heard."

The young man stepped forward. "It was where 300 Spartans fought and held off nearly a million Persians from overrunning Greece."

"He's right, and all we have to deal with is maybe a hundred or so untrained rioters. A piece of cake for this team, am I right?"

"Yo, yes sir," cried out the twelve.

At that moment, some fighting had broken out near the main gate and there was screaming and banging of bats on the metal fencing.

Several office workers came out the front doors to see what was happening. Steve yelled for two officers to get them back inside and secure the door. Several other workers watched from the windows on

341

the second floor as he shouted orders to the team to set up a defensive line.

They were in just regular uniforms. They had no guns, body armor, helmets or shields; just asps or batons and some pepper spray. He concentrated his line twenty feet inside the main gate, being where there was the most action. It was also shorter than the high barbed fences around the yard and buildings. He spread his men arms-length apart with the line of gray uniforms standing like a stone wall.

"Now," he said, "no retreat, no surrender. This far and no farther, right!"

"Sir, yes sir!" they responded.

He watched as the mob screamed through the fence at them as they held up chains, metal pipes and bats. He went over to the company van and turned on the radio full volume. It was a rock station and it was playing 'The Warrior' by Scandal. He got back in the line, with his asp fully extended and stood next to Pavlos who leaned to him and asked, "You do know that the Spartans all died, right?"

"Naw," Steve whispered grinning, "they all became immortal. You remembered them, didn't you?"

The officer laughed.

Voices from the mob called out saying, "Just give us the supply trailers and we'll leave you and the buildings alone."

"Molon Lave!" Steve yelled out loud.

"What did he say?" asked one of the other officers.

Pavlos the Greek, surprised Steve knew the language, answered grinning, "He said, 'Come and take them!'"

***

Joe got off the van phone and turned to Ken. "The north sites are all covered," he said, "but the rioting is moving down to the fourth zone, his site."

"How much longer?" Ken asked.

"Maybe twenty minutes."

"Move it Mason," Ken said to the driver, "I'll pay the ticket!"

Pam drove the company car like a demon down Route 280, passing and zigzagging between the tractor trailers and other cars. As they came to the exit they spotted the squad's van and followed it.

Sue was fixed on just getting there in time as both vehicles flew through the streets like apocalyptic angels. She prayed that he'd be all right and that the guys would reach his team in time.

When they reached the warehouse district they were forced to stop. The street was full of overturned cars burning and hundreds of rioters looting everything in sight, as well as fights on all sides.

The van doors swung open and the squad formed a V-formation with full body shields up to wedge its way through the massive chaos.

The girls sat in the car watching, then suddenly several men began pounding on the doors. They screamed obscenities and made vulgar gestures towards the frightened women.

Pam started the car and drove in a panic through some of them until she reached the van with Officer Mason inside guarding it. He saw the car being attacked and tossed out a tear gas canister. It disbursed the mob long enough for him to get the two into his secured vehicle. Once safe inside, they were able to compose themselves enough to thank him.

"Just stay put," he said as he reached to answer a radio call from Joe.

"What happened back there? Over."

"A pair of our secretaries had their car attacked sir. Over."

"What? Who are they and what are they doing here? Over."

He turned to ask and Pam took the mic. "Joe it's me, Pam, and Sue is with me. Over."

"You two stay with Mason, you hear me! Over."

"Yes sir."

They sat watching through the bullet proof windows as the mob returned and overturned their car.

Back at the site, a car suddenly came crashing through the main gate. It was followed by dozens of people waving clubs and fists.

"Stand and hold," Steve yelled out, "and protect the man next to you!"

343

When the first set reached their line, the men used their batons to defend themselves. As the waves of attacks became more savage the team in turn let loose on the mob without mercy. Noses were broken; heads and arms were heard to be cracked. It was now a matter of survival for the force of thirteen.

Two came upon Steve wielding bats and he took out the first with a kick to the kneecap, the second with his asp to the head. Pavlos was hit in the face with a flying bottle. His broken nose started bleeding and spread across his face in streaks like war paint; still, he stood and continued swinging at the oncoming flood of screaming rioters.

As they fought, Steve grew proud of these green officers, for as soon as one fell he got up again. He ordered them to form a circle, back to back, to now protect each other.

As the mob increased and stormed them, Joe suddenly appeared at the gate with the full riot squad moving into the grounds. Tear gas was tossed and the rioters panicked when it saw the reinforcements with guns and shields approaching. It began to disperse somewhat, yet still there was continued hand-to-hand within the circle of officers.

Mason pulled the van up to the gate and blocked the entrance at an angle. The girls spotted Steve being brutally beaten as he swung back at his attackers. Sue opened the side door and ran out as Pam followed, trying to catch her.

Gas and smoke were everywhere around them as they got almost to the center of the fighting. Just as she caught Sue by the collar, she heard her cry out, "Gun!" Pam looked and saw a middle-aged man aiming a revolver into the circle and then he fired it. Both women froze as one of the officers fell. He cocked it again and Sue screamed to Steve, then grabbed her right arm and side as she suddenly was wrenched in pain.

Pam pointed to the gunman as she ran towards Steve screaming his name.He looked up in time to see the gun aiming at him. It fired just as she dove to push him out of the way. He watched as her eyes widen and heard her gasp, "Oh Steve," then she fell into his arms. Sue screamed and watched helplessly from her knees, holding her side as she saw Pam drop to the ground. She forced herself up and limped slowly towards them.

The shooter cocked again, aiming into the circle of uniforms, then a louder shot was heard and Sue saw the man fall and drop his weapon. She turned to see a driver, with brown hair and beard wearing a Stetson, holding a smoking gun from the door of his tractor. She watched him climb down and walk over to the gunman. He continued to aim his revolver until at last he stood over him.

Dan took two coins out of his pocket and tossed them down to the wounded man, who was holding his bleeding arm and crying out in pain. "You'll need those for the ferryman," he said with hatred in his eyes, then cocked back the hammer and pointed it down into the screaming man's face.

"Sarge don't, please!" he heard Steve cry out to him. "There's been enough pain here today, please Dan, no more."

D. L. turned, seeing him kneeling in the dirt with Pam, and he shoulder-holstered his gun. He walked back to his truck as Audrey ran and threw her arms around him crying.

The gunman got up and fled into the chaos of smoke and rioters as Joe ran over, retrieving his handgun to later help identify him.

Ken checked the fallen officer and he was still breathing. He radioed for an ambulance as he saw the mob vanishing from the lot and street because of the gunfire. He finally turned to see Steve on his knees holding Pam's head in his lap. Sue had reached them and was kneeling also.

Pam bled into his hand as he propped her up and she cried out, "Please Steve! In God's name please don't move me!"

Steve began to break down as she laid gasping for air. "Somebody!" he screamed, "Oh God, somebody call an ambulance!"

"It's coming," Ken said touching his shoulder, while trying to hold back his own emotions as he looked down into her face.

"Oh Honey just lie still," he cried holding her, "it'll be okay."

Pam looked up at him, then over at Sue. "Yes," she said, "I think it will be."

He leaned down and kissed her face over and over.

"Stay with me darling," he whispered, "please, hold on." His tears broke loose and fell onto her cheek as he tried to keep her head up out the dirt.

As the squad secured the lot, each held back their own tears as they watched on. Sue took her hand and felt her squeezing it as the pain increased. "Love him," she said up to Sue.

"I'm so sorry," Sue cried softly while kissing her hand. "Forgive me."

"No, please forgive me," Pam replied as she turned her eyes back to him. "I love you Stephen Clayton. You have your second chance now." She tried to take a deep breath but cried out a moment because of the pain. "Please Steve," she whispered, "say it just once to me."

He held her face, as he felt her breath on his, and said softly through the tears, "I love you Pamela Emerson."

She smiled and touched his face, then closed her eyes as the alarm on her watch went off.

Days later after the funeral, he stood alone in his suite as he opened a bottle of wine she had given him and poured two glasses. He sipped from one, then smashed it in the fireplace. The other he carried over to the window, together with a book of Wordsworth.

The doorbell rang.

"Come in," he called out and Sue slowly entered. She said nothing as she came beside him. She put her arm around his waist as he continued turning the pages of Pam's favorite poet.

He stopped as he found, 'She Dwelt Among the Untrodden Ways' and he looked up into the night stars. Finally, he read aloud.

***

"She lived unknown, and few could know
When Lucy ceased to be;
But she is in her grave, and, oh,
The difference to me!"

***

Sue turned her face into his side and cried. "I'm so sorry Steve. I know what she meant to you Love."

He put his arm around her and kissed her cheek.

"She was so special Sue. She offered me all she had … Gave all she could, even …" A tear fell from his eye and she touched his face, turning it to her.

"She knew like I did," she said softly. "She knew you were a man to die for."

"I love you Babe," he said now crying harder, "and I loved her too!"

"I know, I do too," she whispered, "and I will for the rest of my life."

Chapter Twenty-One

"Let One Dream Come True."

"Mrs. Walker, the tests show that you received damage to your brain during your attack," Dr. Watts said.

"It's Miss LaRosa now since my divorce," she corrected.

"Miss LaRosa, your brain is not sending the proper nerve impulses to your muscles, causing them to shut down. For now it's your arm and side, but later your chest and lungs could be affected. If that happens, it will become hard to breathe and it may not pass, until finally with no signal coming, your heart could stop."

"Isn't there anything I can do?"

"These attacks may get more frequent and severe, I don't know for sure. There is a specialist down in Toms River that may be able to offer you more hope. I spoke with him, he's the best in this field. Here is his number, please see him. He has a new procedure. Together with proper follow-up therapy, he has had high success causing that part of the brain to begin to compensate for its injuries."

"Thank you doctor."

"Please don't wait long," he urged from the doorway as she left his office to pay the bill out front.

"Mom, what did he say?" Dawn asked nervously.

"He said it was in God's hands."

"That's all? Isn't there anyone else we can see?"

"Yes, he gave me the name of a specialist down near the shore who might know more, with more tests."

"So we'll call him and get you there as soon as possible."

"No Baby, I can't afford any more medical bills right now and that would be extremely expensive. No, I'll just leave it in God's good hands for the moment."

When they got home, she had some calls on the answering machine and she played them back.

"Hello Ms. LaRosa, this is Tom Price from Yetterson Advertising. We have reviewed your recent resume' and thank you for applying, but I'm afraid the position has already been filled. We will keep you on file though. Goodbye."

She sat, unmoved as she listened to another rejection recorded, then there was a call from Cindy.

"Hi Honey, thought maybe you'd like to go out for lunch. Call me, bye."

Sue called her back and they met at the Headquarters.

Steve returned from making site rounds and went straight up to the offices. As he passed Pam's empty desk he paused, then stepped into Joe's office.

"I guess I need a secretary," he said solemnly as he poured himself a cup of coffee. "Would you ask Cindy to find one for me please?"

"Already done," Joe replied with a grin and a pointing finger. "She started this afternoon."

He turned to see Sue walking out of his office with some papers. She was wearing a dark blue business-like skirt, with a matching vest and a white blouse. He found it most becoming.

"Oh, there you are," she said coming over. "Mr. Clayton, you need to sign these for payroll to be able to process the new hires."

Steve stared at her a moment, then said, "Would you come with me please?" and they went into his office.

"What in the world?" he asked.

"Cindy told me at lunch that you still needed a new secretary and I told her I wanted the job." He was silent, so she came over to him.

"Steve I'm not trying to take her place," she said softly, "I really do need this job. I'd be proud to support and share in the work you do here, all right?"

He smiled back. "All right Miss LaRosa. You have a thirty day trial period before benefits kick in and thank you for choosing On Guard Services."

"You can thank me on payday Mr. Clayton," she said smiling out the door, "and that top new hire sheet to sign, that's mine." He laughed to himself and then signed the papers.

Sue worked as hard as she could, learning everything Cindy and the secretaries showed her. She was always professional dealing with the three owners, especially with Steve, yet was still able to maintain the closeness they needed towards each other. She loved her position and being so close to him and what he did. They had built a great company.

Sue was so glad to have benefits again, but as the weeks went on she found that the costs of the specialist and tests had quickly maxed out her medical coverage. She knew she had to call and cancel any further visits for some time. As she was finishing up for the evening, Cindy heard her on the phone with the doctor and explaining the situation.

On the following payday, she found that her paycheck included a supplement package expanding her medical coverage. She was taken back as she read it and felt guilty, so she went and knocked on Steve's door.

"Do you have a minute?"

"Yes Sue, what is it?" Steve replied looking up from the reports he and Ken were working on.

"I think a mistake has been made with my benefit package."

"Oh?" responded Ken as he glanced over at Steve.

She came over and showed it to them.

"No, it's right," Steve said.

She looked at them both sternly. "This is far greater than I was explained when I was hired. You guys can't do this," she said firmly, "it's not right."

Joe stepped in carrying another report and Ken told him what she had said.

"No," Joe answered smiling, "it's the right package for you Sue."

"I want what everyone else here receives," she insisted.

"Well okay, now you have it," Steve said and she looked at him bewildered a moment. "We gave it to all of our employees. How can we take it back now?"

She looked to the ceiling, then smiled back.

"You guys are too much, really. Thank you."

"Our pleasure," Joe said, "and besides, all of you deserve the best we can offer."

She brought her hand up to her eye as she turned to leave. "Thank you again and God bless you," she said.

"You're very welcome," they answered.

Steve asked to drive her down to Tom's River for her last visit with the specialist and she was glad. She was getting scared as most of the past tests had been negative for her condition. She was running out of hope and there had been an increase in the attacks, though they often went unnoticed by others. Steve had seen several of them, but said nothing as he knew that was how she wanted it.

When she came out, he stood and she went over and put her face into his chest. He wrapped his arms around her as he looked at the doctor shaking his head from the door.

"Come on Angel," he said softly, "I'll take us out for a drive along the shore. It'll be a beautiful evening and we can drop the top." He held her against him as they walked out the door.

He headed towards Seaside as she stayed with her head against his arm, saying nothing until, "I can smell the sea," she said.

He looked as she closed her eyes, breathing in the air. "It's just ahead Babe, be there in a few minutes."

She smiled, rubbing her face on his arm and then kissing it. "I love you so much," she said feeling the tears coming. "I don't want to die yet. I want ... I need more time with you. We've lost so much already," she cried out softly.

He pulled up into the parking lot near the beach and boardwalk and stopped. He reached over and hugged her tight.

"I know," he whispered with a kiss to her cheek, "but each day with you is a lifetime to me."

351

"Oh I love you Steve Clayton," she cried out. "My whole life I've loved you and now it's going to end before it can really begin."

"Doctors don't know everything. Only God knows the number of our days, you know that Little One." He held her face and kissed it, then came around and opened her door.

"It's not over until He says so. With His help we can fight this together, every day, and make each count as a blessing for us. I know this in my heart, in our heart Angel."

She threw her arms around his neck and he lifted her out of the car. He carried her to look with him out over the beach and the waves as evening was closing with the sun nearly set.

When the last rays went under the horizon, they went back to the car and she sat on the edge of the hood as he looked for a tape to play.

"It is beautiful tonight, isn't it?" she asked while gazing up at the stars.

"Yes," he answered looking over at her, "very beautiful."

He put a tape into Excalibur's new cassette player of the soundtrack from the movie 'Eddie and the Cruisers'. It started playing the song 'Boardwalk Angel'.

She smiled as she turned to him. He came over, lifted her off the hood, and put his arms around her. They began to dance as he sang to her.

"You have been the greatest part of my life," she said looking up at him as they swayed together. "You and those blue eyes that can always see the song in our heart. Promise me we'll sing it forever."

"That I can promise Love," he said, spinning her around gently as Excalibur played on.

While they danced another car pulled up, then a second. After awhile, the other couples got out and started dancing by their own cars also as the music played on.

When the song ended, Sue said with burst of light in her eyes, "Play something fast now," and he chose to play 'Wild Summer Nights'. Her face lit up and the two started to rock and sing along out loud, shaking their faces into one another and dancing around the car. The others quickly joined in and soon all were singing, often screaming, along as it played.

They moved with each other, dancing like it was their first time there. Sue began smiling and laughing like she hadn't in years. She threw her worries up to the heavenly stars, feeling free and happy, as her heart sang with his.

They spun around and met nose to nose singing, then he lifted her up in the air by the waist as she cried out with her eyes shining, "Wild summer nights!" When he lowered her, their lips met and kissed tenderly but with a passion stronger than ever before.

As they drove back up the parkway later for home, she purred next to him.

"Oh Steve, this morning I thought the worst was coming today, but now, I feel like the world hasn't got a chance against us."

"It doesn't," he said back smiling. "No matter what it throw at us we'll always get up again and it knows that can't be beat."

"Oh Steve," she sighed, "I've needed a night like this for so long and with you." She looked at him without saying anything more, but he could see what was in her eyes.

"We will soon Love, I promise."

She turned away, knowing he had read her thoughts of love, of being with him as they had dreamed.

"Steve, you know that his divorcing me wasn't enough," she said softly, "there's still the church."

"I know, but I have faith that He loves us, at least as much as I love you. God didn't make us One heart to keep us apart. I know He plans to bring us together forever."

She heard the conviction in his voice and said, "I believe it too." She closed her eyes, feeling the warm night air on her face and the soft touch of his hand on hers. At last, all doubts about their dream flew from her soul and were cast out into the darkness behind them. She smiled as Excalibur carried them forward into the bright path of its lights, onward to a new life.

It was a week later, as she was pulling into the driveway, that Dawn came running out waving a Fed Ex envelope.

"Mom," she screamed with joy, "look what I got for my birthday!"

Sue got out of the company car just as she handed her the opened envelope. She looked inside and found a letter with two tickets for a Mediterranean cruise. It was to leave from Florida on June 22nd and airline tickets were included.

She read their names on the prepaid tickets over again. It was true. She opened the letter and read it.

> May, 15, 1985
> "HAPPY BIRTHDAY DAWN!"
> "Please ladies, I wanted to give you these in person but was afraid you might not accept them. As you can see, it is for one double cabin together. I have a separate one for myself to accompany you for what I pray will be an unforgettable cruise to Spain, Greece and Rome.
> Sue please let me give this to you and Dawn. It was a dream you had a long time ago and I want so bad to share it with you both. I want to make all of your dreams come true, if you'll let me. I love you both more than words. I'll be over tonight after work at seven to see you.
> —- Love Now and Always, Steve."

Sue held the letter up to her mouth reflecting, then looked at Dawn's anxious face as she was holding her breath for her response.

"Well Momma?" she finally asked in a pleading tone.

"I have to think about this Baby," she said, then went into the house to prepare dinner.

At seven that evening he pulled slowly into the driveway. He parked and turned off the engine, then sat still looking at the door. He could see the living room lights on but no one came out. Finally, he took a deep breath and walked up to ring the bell.

He hadn't been this nervous since that snowy night so many years ago when he had come to give her that Christmas gift. It was even more like prom night had been when he had that ring in his pocket ready to ask her that night for her hand.

Dawn came to the door and smiled.

"Hi Uncle Steve, come on in."

He entered and she took his overcoat to hang up.

"Where's your mom?"

"Oh, she's been upstairs ever since she made dinner for me, but she didn't eat. She's still thinking about your letter, I'm sure," she said with a tone of uncertainty.

She kissed him on the cheek saying, "I don't know what Mom is going to say, but that was a thank you from me for such a wonderful birthday gift. I love you too."

He smiled. "Well thank you. I hope she'll say yes but I'll understand if she doesn't."

He sat on the couch as Dawn made him some coffee. He felt like a teen again as he waited for her to appear at the stairs.

"'It had been easier facing her dad last time, then her now," he thought.

After about twenty minutes, and two cups of coffee, he heard the bedroom door open upstairs. He felt his mouth going dry and his heart racing. A moment later she appeared at the top of the staircase, then slowly began to come down.

She was wearing a strapped, flowing white dress that swayed with each step as she descended and a matching sweater lay on her shoulders. Her golden brown hair was up like a crown, held by a small, engraved silver clip etched with a wave. There were tiny silver-pearled earrings swinging gently from below her ears about an inch, like stars from heaven.

When she finally reached the landing, she turned to him and he stood up straightening his shirt and tie a bit. She looked at him silently.

"Wow," he said, "I didn't know that you had planned on going out tonight. I'm sorry, I should have called first."

"I hadn't, until your letter came."

He studied her face a moment, then she said, "Yes I'd love to go, if ... "

He came closer and took her hand. "If what?"

"If you let me take you out to dinner and we go dancing tonight."

He smiled and answered, "Okay, but don't expect to take any Liberties later, after all, I'm not a pushover for a pretty face."

She smiled back, then leaned into him and blew a warm kiss onto his face. He felt his knees weaken a bit as she held his hand firmly.

"I don't deserve you," she whispered.

"No you deserve so much more, but all I have, all I am, is yours."

"A gift from God," she said with a sigh while leading him to the door.

"Yes! Yes!" cried Dawn from the kitchen and they laughed as he put on his overcoat and held the door for her.

Chapter Twenty-Two
"I hear Our Song whenever You Smile."

After several days of Atlantic Ocean breezes, endless horizons and gorgeous sunsets with her love at her side, it seemed more than her heart could hold.

In the morning, breakfast always came to her adorned with a new arrangement of fresh flowers and card telling of his love for her. When she returned to her cabin each night, there were a different colored rose and a handmade Swiss chocolate lying on her pillow.

During the day, they enjoyed sampling fine foods, attended great shows and of course, there was the dancing. They'd take countless strolls around the ship, pausing to kiss and hold each other while gazing over the waves. It was more than she ever imagined it would be and she thanked God for every moment and for him.

Dawn had made friends with some teens and started doing more with them. She was glad to be able to let them spend some time alone. She had grown to love him as much as Sue.

Early one afternoon, Steve came to get her and led her topside to the bow. He held her as he pointed ahead of them.

"Mons Calpe," he said to her.

"What does that mean?" she asked in a tone of wonderment.

"The Pillars of Hercules," he answered in a whisper to her ear.

Sue stared at the huge rock in the sea. "The Rock of Gibraltar," she sighed out. "Oh Steve, it's magnificent."

"It's British territory," he told her. "Made of limestone, standing 1396 feet high and it contains tunneled roads, mostly used by the military."

He paused as they looked at it.

"But the most amazing thing to me is that there is a flowering plant there called a Gibraltar Candytuff. It's only on this rock, in all of Europe, that it grows wild."

She smiled. "Like our American Dreams only grow wild on our Island."

"Exactly Love," he said hugging her. "That's our first stop and then up to the top!"

Her eyes widened at the thought of actually being able to stand on it.

When they made port, they first went sightseeing in the local markets. Later, they took a taxi over to the cable car which carried them to the very top. The girls loved it.

"It's like being on top of the world!" Dawn said to him.

"The gate to the Mediterranean," he replied with a smile. I heard that John Lennon and Yoko Ono were married here and Jules Verne wrote about it in one of his novels."

After their brief stopover in Spain, the cruise continued into the Mediterranean Sea and towards Greece. That first evening in they prepared for a special dinner, the Captain's dinner, the ship was giving later on. Sue was making every effort to look her best so this formal evening would be perfect.

As she looked through their outfits, there came a knock at the door. She opened it and a steward stood there holding six different gowns, three on each arm.

"These are for both of you to choose from for the evening if you wish," she said, "and you both have open appointments at the salon."

"Oh Mom, would you look at these!"

Sue thanked her as she laid them out.

"How can we choose just one?" Dawn asked with excitement.

"You don't have to," came a voice from around the door in the hall. "They are all yours to keep," Steve said, "if you like them."

Sue came and hugged him. "You are just too much. Now you have to stop doing this," she said looking at him sternly.

"Ask me to stop breathing, it's easier," he said looking into her eyes.

She shook her head then smiled. "You're impossible. Just being with you is all we want."

"But thank you!" Dawn said over her shoulder.

"You see what you've done?" Sue asked, then leaned to him and said, "Still, I love you for it."

"Maybe you're right," he admitted, "I should back off on some of these small indulgences. What's important is we have a good time together."

"You're what's important to me," she said caressing his face.

He smiled, then left them to get dressed.

It was a little early, but the girls decided to go down to the dining area anyway and left word for him. When they arrived, they were taken to a front table that they were told had been reserved just for them.

"This is just a dream," she kept saying to Dawn.

"I know," she replied, "but I never want to wake up if it is." She looked over at her mom and asked, "How are you feeling?"

"Oh, I'm fine Baby," she answered, but Dawn sensed she was feeling some discomfort.

"I have your pain pills, if you need one."

"Thanks but I'm fine at the moment. Besides, they make me drowsy."

Moments later Steve arrived. He was dressed in a fine white tux with black tie, and he slowed his approach to enjoy the sight of them sitting there in their gowns.

Sue had on a pale blue with a flared bottom and a row of white stars running down each of her long sleeves. Dawn's was white with pink trim and a splash of soft flowered prints throughout it.

"You both look wonderful," he said gazing back and forth at each. "They compliment each of you so nicely, but beauty needs so little to be perfect," he added with a smile.

Dawn blushed a bit, but Sue smiled back with a glow from the heart that he loved to see on her.

"So," he asked, " are you ready for a fabulous evening? " He looked over at Dawn who winked at him.

"It's hard to believe all of this," Sue said with a look as if it would all vanish when the clock stuck midnight.

He reached over and touched her hand. "It's as real as my love for you."

They were served a wonderful dinner and enjoyed some dancing, then there was an announcement that a surprise had been arranged for them. Sue looked at him but he shrugged his shoulders.

"I don't know anything about it Babe."

The curtains opened on stage and it was the Beach Boys live. Sue let out a scream and grabbed Steve's hand.

"This first song is dedicated to the both of you," the MC said as he pointed to their table. He encouraged them to get up onto the dance floor as he led the applause, then the band started playing 'Little Surfer'.

"Oh Steve, it's the first song we ever danced to when we went steady. How could they know?"

"There's how," he answered pointing to the wings where Joe, Ken and Cindy stood smiling.

"Oh my God," she said looking, then waving back at them as she lowered her head against him. She started to cry as the band played on while Steve sang in her ear.

When the song ended, everyone applauded as they returned to their table and greeted the whole gang.

"I read they'd be on this cruise, so when Steve asked our help with your bookings we made sure this was it!" Cindy said thrilled.

"Oh I love it. Thank you all so much," Sue said with a joyous smile. "The Beach Boys live and all of you here … it couldn't be better!"

"Where did you come from?" Steve asked.

"We all flew out and boarded in Spain," Joe replied, "but not just to hear the Beach Boys."

Ken smiled with a 'thumbs up' as Dawn handed Sue a large envelope. She opened it, then covered her heart and started crying again.

"It's all right," Dawn said to Steve, "just wait for it."

He took Sue's hand and squeezed it lightly. "Babe?" he asked quietly.

"Oh my goodness … I can't … I can't believe it," she answered in-between breaths. "Dawn when you had me do this I never really believed it would happen."

"Show them Mom."

Sue held open the letter. "It's from the Church. They've granted my Annulment," she cried out. "I'm not married in the eyes of the God anymore!"

Cindy got up and hugged her.

"Oh, I'd nearly given up hope for this," Sue said nearly crying again.

"It wasn't easy," Dawn told her, "but here's why it happened." She turned pointing to a man with his back to them at the next table. He stood up and faced them.

"Michael?" Sue asked.

"Mike Reily?" Steve then asked amazed.

"Father Michael, if you please," he answered as he pointed to his collar.

"I don't understand," Sue said choked up.

"I know what you've gone through," he said, "and then Joe told me more, so I looked into your situation. Later, I then went to see the board in Paterson and pleaded your case. They all agreed, you never had a marriage."

Mike smiled. " But it was really the honesty they sensed in your answers to the questions that persuaded them. I'm happy for you," he added and kissed Sue on the cheek as she hugged him.

"Oh Father," she said, then turned to her daughter. "I love you Baby."

"I love you too Mom," Dawn said back, then looked at her uncles.

Joe smiled as Ken said, "We mainly came because we really wanted to be here for this."

Steve turned around as Joe leaned down and whispered, "Dawn got this for us and we had it enhanced a bit."

He felt a small box put into his hand under the table, looked down and opened it. It was the original engagement ring he had given her, but now around it was a ring of other diamonds to showcase it.

"It came out of your share of the profits," Ken said shrugging his shoulder. "Now go on and ask the girl."

Steve looked at Sue's puzzled face. "Uh Sue," he stammered out, "I've always known what kind of girl you were, uh ... I mean are and that's why I waited again for the right time ..." He paused feeling unprepared and uneasy.

Ken leaned to his ear and said, "Ask her now or start thinking tags to your mom in Florida when I get back."

"God's timing is not mine but it seems He has decided," he continued as he took her hand and then fell to his knees. "Sue, so many dream of a chance to love while others just dream of being loved. For me, we have always been the dream together and one I could never wake up from. When I slept I held your face and loved you, and when I awoke you were there loving me. I never deserved that love, anymore than I deserve heaven, but God has loved me enough to give me hope for both. If you share this dream, as I pray you do, then I'm asking for your hand so I can put my heart in it and yours in mine. To have and to hold forever. Angel, will you marry me?"

He opened the box and took out the ring. She looked down at it but said nothing. Seconds passed, then they heard her moan out, "Oh dear God," and started crying.

"Was that a yes?" Ken asked Joe.

She began to cry harder.

"Oh my heavens!" Father Michael exclaimed, "This has all just been too much, we're sorry."

Sue shook her head, but kept crying.

Steve put his arms around her. "Shh, it's all right. You don't have to give an answer now," he whispered kissing her cheek.

"Yes I do," she said still crying.

"No you don't," he said firmly, then took her by the arm and led her out of the room to the hallway.

He held her in his arms alone quietly for several moments, letting her just cry. When she seemed less upset he took her face into his hands.

"Angel I'm sorry. This was not the way I had hoped to ask you."

"I know that," she said with a smile. "If it was, then it wouldn't be you. It's just that ... "

She stopped and then leaned against his shoulder as he gently stroked her hair waiting. She finally kissed his cheek tenderly, then looked back into his eyes.

"It's just that, when I saw the ring and heard your words, I was suddenly back on a bridge in moonlight. My heart was pounding and love was flowing through it like the river below. Then a gentle voice said, 'It's all right. The bad dream is over and you're home again. Now wake up and tell him 'yes.'"

A tear rolled down her cheek and he kissed it.

"We are home Babe," he whispered, "forever."

"Yes we are," she softly cried looking up at him, "and yes My Love, I do want to marry you." She held out her hand and he gently slipped the ring over her finger.

They turned back to look as they heard the band start to play 'Wouldn't it Be Nice' and they smiled.

"Would you like to dance?"

"I love to dance," she answered glowing, then took his hand as they began to sway alone in the doorway. Her gown flowed like a dream around her as he heard her say, "The magic is forever."

Dawn saw them and pointed for the others to look as the two seem to be lost in a world of their own.

"You've always made me feel like a princess while treating me like a queen," she sighed out.

Smiling warmly into her sparkling eyes he spun her around and whispered, "You're a blessing from heaven and I love you. How could I do otherwise?"

"And I love you," she whimpered back with a kiss to his hand, "but I still love to hear us say it."

Later at the table, everyone wanted to know when they would set the date.

"You could get married in Rome!" Cindy suddenly yelled out. Steve looked at her for an answer.

"That would be very romantic," she replied turning to him, "but I have always dreamed of us being married back home at St. Peter's. Do you mind?"

"Of course not, it sounds perfect. Michael, would you marry us?"

He smiled back at them and said, "I would be both honored and blessed."

"Okay," Ken said, "how about a honeymoon in Hawaii on us?"

Steve smiled. "What do you think Babe?" he asked looking at her.

She leaned in towards him. "I want to go to the Jersey shore for a honeymoon. Please?"

He was taken back. "You want to go to Seaside?"

"I was thinking more of Cape May," she answered with a smile, "we've never been there. You've taken me to the other side of the world today, but my heart will always belong to New Jersey. The rest of the world just revolves around its shores for me."

When they arrived in Greece, they saw everyone off as they boarded to fly back home, while the three continued their trip. They visited Athens and the Parthenon, then found a guide and were showed the real Greece. It was the tour of a lifetime. Sue had a few minor attacks but said nothing as she smiled through every minute of it, although he noticed.

"What a beautiful country," she declared.

"The best for you is yet to be seen," he told her.

Her face lit up as she said aloud, "Italy, and my Rome."

The night before they were to land in Italy, they stood out on deck holding each other quietly. The sea breeze filled their senses and reminded them of home and weekends at the beach.

"What date do you want to set?" he asked.

She caressed the arms around her a moment, then asked, "How about the first Saturday in May?"

"Why that day?" he asked somewhat shocked.

"Hum," she cooed softly in his arms as she enjoyed playing with him. "I'm surprised you have forgotten."

He thought hard for several moments. "Don't tell me," he said and then thought some more.

"That was the day … " she began but stopped as he said, "Wasn't that when Momma G. named a sandwich special after us?"

She lightly slapped his hand and turned away pouting with disappointment.

Seconds later, she felt his arms come around from behind her as he whispered, "Or was that when I promised you'd wear a wedding ring before you gave yourself to me?"

She turned slowly in his arms with wide eyes. "I can't believe you remembered."

He kissed her tenderly on the tip of her nose. "I have never made a promise lightly, especially the ones to you."

"Oh Babe, I love you so," she said leaning back up to his lips and their kiss flowed through their heart like a spring breeze.

As the limo carried them to their hotel in the Eternal City both girls took in every site they passed. Dawn snapped pictures of people just walking on the street, as well as any special sight their driver Tony pointed out to them.

They were given directions to some of the best places to eat around the area and went by limo to try little samples of the many cuisines of her heritage. In the evening, they finally ended the day with an excellent dinner in a hideaway recommended by Tony, whom they insisted join them, and then they returned to their hotel rooms.

The next morning, after a light breakfast, Sue made inquires about a small town she wanted to visit and found it was only a forty minute drive away. She went to his room to ask if he'd mind taking them.

When she knocked on the door, he thought it was the porter bringing him his cleaned shirts.

"Come in," he answered, and she entered to see him bare-chested standing in his pants. She suddenly froze in horror as she glanced into the mirror behind him.

"Oh dear God," she cried out as she saw his backside slashed and scarred. She felt a sharp pain in her side and started to drop slowly as he ran to catch her.

"Oh Sweety," she cried as she ran her hands across his bare back while he held her, "what in God's name did they do to you?"

He lifted her up in his arms and carried her to the bedside where he sat, still cradling her.

"Sue I'm sorry," he said kissing her face as she trembled. "I wanted to break this to you gently, later on."

She composed herself a little, then asked, "Please, let me see?"

He turned around and her tears fell as she touched his back with her fingertips, then kissed it murmuring, "Oh why?"

"It doesn't matter," he answered, "that pain has passed."

"I've never really understood what you must have gone through until now," she said with anguish in her voice.

He looked at her lovingly.

"It was you that got me through it," he confessed. "The thoughts of knowing I'd hold you again like this one day."

He held his hand over her heart and said, "It's the scars they can't see that have cut the deepest, like the ones you carry in here for the both of us."

She stared into his eyes, as he wiped back her tears, and she caressed his arms and face.

"The world has taken so much from us," she said. "It just never understood that I'd of given all to be held like this by you for even a moment."

"I love you Sue LaRosa," he cried holding her tightly to him. "More than life and beyond its reach."

They laid in each other's arms until Dawn finally came for them.

Later as they were leaving the hotel, Dawn asked, "Now, where is it we are going?"

"To where my grandmother grew up," Sue answered. "Her sister still lives there and I had written we were coming. It's just for the day."

"What's been left behind is as important as what you strive towards," he told her, while winking at Sue.

He went and got a rental car for all of them to drive out there.

As they came up to the farmhouse, they slowed down as Dawn took pictures, including the animals on the farm. The countryside was full of olive gardens along the road and Sue suddenly felt so close to her Grandma again.

When they pulled up to the house he helped them out and said he'd come back for them after supper.

"You can't leave," Sue said taking his hand.

He felt awkward and replied, "Maybe it would be best. Your family here is strict Catholic. I don't want to embarrass you with questions about my not being your husband."

"You have to come," Dawn said to him holding his other arm.

Sue touched his face. "I love you so much for caring," she said, "but I have written them already and now I have the Annulment from the Church to show them if they ask. Everything will be fine. Come please and let us share our family with you."

He stared over at the house as an older woman came out and waved them to come.

"Please, you're family too," Dawn said.

Sue took his hand. "And even more to us."

They walked together and were greeted with open arms, including him, as each came out and hugged them all.

The visit was all she had hoped for. Pictures were shown and a tour of the farmhouse and grounds were given with pride. Dawn captured every moment she could with her Kodak, especially the ones where they had Steve and Sue feeding the goats and chickens as they were being butted around the barnyard in the feeding frenzy.

The real foods served at dinner were surprisingly different from what they had expected, especially the desserts. They looked wonderful, but were not overly sweet as they had imagined. It was a memorable visit for everyone.

On the drive back to the hotel, Dawn had fallen asleep in the backseat and Sue laid up against his arm as she always loved to do.

"Thank you so much for this dream," she said stroking his arm.

"I thank God for giving me the means to do it," he said softly, "and for the help of good friends."

"We're so blessed," she commented about their lives. "The good things truly are forever with us."

After a couple more days of tours, they finally were ready to board for their flight home.

"Wait!" Sue called out to the limo driver and she held out three coins. "The Fountain, please!"

Tony smiled back to her and turned onto the main road. When they parked she grabbed both of them and handed each a coin.

"Now close your eyes, make a wish and toss it over your shoulder into the water," Sue said excited.

Dawn laughed as she counted, "One, two, three!" and each threw backwards.

"Don't say what you wished for or it may not come true," Sue warned them.

"We have to get going or we'll miss our flight," he said leading them towards the limo.

Before they reached it, a car came around a curve towards them and its tire blew out. The car instantly tipped on its side, then rolled over at them. Steve pushed them and they all dove behind the limo a second before it would have hit them.

As they got up, the car started on fire and they saw the woman driver trying to climb out of the window. Tony and Steve ran to help pull her out and they carried her over to the limo as Sue tried to calm her. She started to scream and point to the burning car. Dawn looked and saw a child belted in the back seat and ran to it.

"Dawn stop!" Steve yelled.

She reached the crushed door and pulled on it until it gave way with a creak of metal on metal and partly opened. She could just slip inside and started undoing the belt as the child was screaming in her ears. Steve came to the door, but couldn't fit through it.

"Hurry!" he cried, reaching in for her as the flames appeared in the front seat. She grabbed and lifted the little girl then slid back through the opening.

He threw his arms about them screaming, "Run Baby, run!"

When they were barely fifteen feet from the now engulfing flames, the car exploded. The opened door flung and struck them as he covered the girls. All were thrown forward and down onto the street.

Sue and Tony ran to help them up, shouldering them over to the limo. Steve had been hit hard to his head and was dazed, then passed out as they reached safety.

When he came to he could hear the whining of the sirens, voices calling out and people running about him as someone wiped his face and eyes. His head throbbed and he could feel the heat from the fire as the flames lapped and crackled the twisting metal.

"Sue! Dawn!" he suddenly called out.

"Shh, we're fine," Sue answered as she continued to wash the blood from his eyes. "The little girl is too."

"Oh, my head feels like an engine block fell on it," he moaned.

"It was a door," she replied as she tried to gently clean the cuts. "Please hold still Hon so I can see how badly you're hurt."

The heat covered his face like a suffocating mask and he held up his hand to block it.

"Sue?" he called out.

"What Babe?" she answered, trying to check the bleeding at the back of his head.

"Angel," he said more softly.

She knelt to his face as his eyes reflected the burning light from behind her.

He reached up for her hand.

"Sue, I can't see," he said in a whispered gasp as she watched his blue eyes being consumed in the fire's red and orange flashes.

Chapter Twenty-Three

"You must be fit to give before you can be fit to receive."
-James Stephens

As they sat quietly in the E. R. waiting room, the hours passed like days.

Dawn looked over her mom. Sue was praying, but with a glassy stare as if disconnected from the moment.

"He'll be okay, won't he mom?"

"I pray he will," she answered softly, then Dawn saw a tear roll down her cheek.

"They have very good doctors here," Tony said touching her hand. "They will take good care of him you can be sure."

"Stefano Claa-ton?" the doctor called out as he came into the room.

"I'm with Steve Clayton," Sue snapped out as she quickly rose up. Tony translated what was said by them and for them as they watched the doctor's gestures.

"He has several cuts about his face. I have bandaged him and he can remove them in a few days."

"And his eyes?" she asked fearing the answer.

"He has no eye injuries that I can find. The blow to his head may have caused his blindness, but it's too early to tell."

"May we see him?"

"Yes of course, right through here."

Sue held Dawn's hand as they entered the emergency area and then she saw him getting dressed near a bed. As she came quietly over, his bandaged head rose up.

"Sue?" he asked sensing her near.

"I'm here Babe," she said as he held out his arm. She moved quickly to get under it, pulling his hand to her chest and kissing it. She gazed up at his bandaged eyes and asked, "Are you ready to go?"

"Yes, I've laid around here long enough. Ask Tony if he knows a good place for pizza," he said with a smile.

"What would you like on it?" she asked quickly to keep from crying.

"Oh, how about we leave that to the maker this time. He should know what's best."

They led him out and into the limo. Dawn held his other hand as Tony drove them to another hideaway spot he knew.

When they left the restaurant, he asked if there was a local church where they could attend Mass that evening.

"Yes, there is one just around the corner from your hotel," Tony replied. "Mass starts at seven pm."

"Then would you please come back for us at six-thirty?"

Later, when they entered the small church and found a quiet pew, they knelt and prayed. Sue held him constantly by hand or on his side. Inside all she wanted to do was cry; but instead, she focused on his needs and found joy in any simple thing she could do for him.

As the weeknight Mass was about to begin, some late arrivals appeared at the rear doors and made their way up to the altar. When they passed, Sue's eyes widened and she blessed herself.

"Steve, it's the Holy Father."

"What?"

"It's the Pope," she cried softly, "John Paul, himself!"

His Eminence turned to the local priest and to the handful of faces in the pews.

"I was compelled to come here tonight," he said humbly, "because God himself pulled at my heart. I do not know why, but I never question the call of the Holy Ghost."

Tony leaned to them and interpreted as all sat amazed.

"With your permission Father," he said to the old priest in a pleading voice, "I would be grateful if you'd allow me to assist you with the Mass tonight."

The priest bowed and kissed his ring, as his Bishops sat to the one side and the Mass began.

When it had ended, all of the parishioners were invited to come up for a personal greeting and to speak with him. Sue and Dawn each took one of Steve's arms and, together with Tony, they made their way in the procession up to the altar. They could hear as each spoke with him when they kissed his ring, and some seemed to be asking for a special blessing as he touched each head.

When at last they came before him, Tony spoke a moment in Italian telling his Holiness about them. The Pope smiled and Sue put Steve's hand onto his ring. Steve dropped to his knees, kissing John Paul's shoes as he found them by touch.

"Have mercy," he cried.

"My son," he heard him say as the Pope leaned down to him, "come and face me."

He rose up as he felt the hands on his shoulders. Moved with compassion, John Paul put his hand over the bandaged face. Steve quickly reached up, moving the Pope's hand over onto Sue. "Not my eyes Holy Father," he said in a pleading voice, "for I've seen the face of God's Love. But pray and heal my Heart."

The tears Sue had been holding back fell as she knelt beside him. The Pope touched both their heads as he closed his eyes to pray.

"Most Heavenly Father, I ask for their healing according to Your Will, in our Lord Jesus' name. I pray also, that I might love as great as these. Go with God my children. Bless you and thank you."

When they landed back in Newark Airport, Ken and Joe met them in a company limo. They waited at the front as Sue and Dawn led him out.

He paused at the curb in front of Ken and said, "You changed your aftershave Ski."

Ken was taken back a moment, then smiled remembering his uncanny 'Super Alertness' and sensing it had now been heightened with his loss of sight.

Joe held the door as Sue helped him into the back seat. "We have set up the best to look at him," he whispered to her.

"Thank you Joe," she replied and kissed him.

"It was that blow to your head that caused your blindness," Dr. Murphy from St. Clair's Hospital said to both of them. "It may just return on its own, all we can do is wait for now for some signs."

"So there's a chance?" Sue asked with hope in her voice.

"Oh yes, there's always the chance, but it's out of my hands for the moment and in God's."

They thanked him and left for home with Dawn waiting out in Excalibur. "What did he say?" she asked her mom.

"As with all things Baby, it's in God's Hands."

Steve sensed that they weren't headed towards Morristown. "I thought you were taking me home?" he asked her.

"I am, you're staying with us at the house."

"I can't do that Babe, it wouldn't appear proper. I'll be fine back at the suite."

"Let people think what they want. I need to be sure you're all right," Sue said with a finality in her tone.

He smiled. "Sue, the Bible says, 'Do not give the appearance of evil', so I won't soil your reputations with gossip or false accusations. Please Babe, take me home."

When they got to the apartment she told him to rest on the couch while she made him some coffee. Dawn came into the kitchen and put her arm around her.

"We have to have faith Mom," she said looking at her solemn face.

"I do Baby, but I can't help hurting for him."

Sue came back and found him asleep, sitting upright on the couch. She put the cup on the table, then curled up next to him with her head on his chest. Dawn came in and saw them together.

"Mom?"

Sue turned to her.

"You haven't had any attacks since Rome, have you?"

She didn't answer.

"Then that was a miracle."

Sue looked over at him and lightly put her fingers on his closed eyes. "No, I had my miracle already." She lowered her hand onto his chest near her head. "I never could have imagined that I'd love or be loved this much. I can't help but love this man Dawn."

"You really are a matched set Mom. I can't help but love him either."

Sue closed her eyes as she gently stroked his arm crying, but now with tears of joy.

"Don't ever settle for a love less than this Baby," she finally said, "because that's what the world will try and sell you. Wait for God to send you the real thing."

Dawn knelt near her and asked, "How will I know the difference?"

"Oh," Sue sighed smiling and said, "he will never take, only give, because he himself will be a gift and one you never deserved. He'll put a song in your heart and sing it with you forever."

Dawn went out to make some tea. When she returned she found Sue asleep, still smiling, curled up under his arm and his chin resting against her head. She went and got a cover and put it around them.

"I love you," she whispered to them as she turned off the light. She heard a sigh, then left them to dream beneath the blanketed grace of moonlight as it flowed over them from the Den's stained window.

Chapter Twenty-Four
"Riddles are just Questions within the Answers."

There was a knock on his suite door. "Come in," he called as he remained looking out the window.

Sue entered with packages and put them on the table.

"I bought you some things I know you need. Here's something special I got on sale at Shop-Rite with a coupon, it's that sauce you like so much. I thought I'd make us veal-parm tonight."

"Thanks Babe," he said as he remained staring out the window.

"Is something wrong?"

"Maybe we should be sure of what we're doing," he said turning and then his arm bumped over a lamp, smashing it to the floor. "Oh God!—-See!" he suddenly yelled out, backing up against the window.

"It's all right," she said to him calmly as she ran to pick up the pieces.

"No it isn't!" he replied upset. "I'm a helpless invalid Sue! I can't work anymore. I can't do what I do anymore. I can't even provide for myself."

"You're a partner in a great company," she stated.

"I'm a liability, that's all." "It isn't fair to the guys, to you - - - I can't help anyone!"

"You listen to me Stephen Clayton," she said getting mad and upset, "you are no invalid! You asked me to marry you when you knew I was dying. Was that out of pity?"

"No! I love you."

"Well I don't pity you either!" she cried back in a firm tone. "I love you and I want to be with you."

He turned towards her voice and cried out, "I'm blind Sue!" then reached out his hand. "I can't even see your face, your smile, your eyes," he added with pain in his tone. "I can't even find you in my own living room!"

Choked up, she reached out for his hands saying, "Then let me find you." She took hold of one and put it on her eyes, then the other on her mouth. "See now," she said smiling, "they're right here Babe. You will never lose them."

"Oh Angel, I feel like half a man. I feel helpless and useless!"

She put her arms around him saying, "You are more of a man than any woman could hope to find. You give me life, is that useless?"

He felt her smile widen as she said, "I didn't fall in love with your eyes or the speed of your legs. I fell in love with your heart. How can you think I wouldn't want you because you can't see this world? Can you still see the song in my heart?"

"Always," he answered from his heart to his lips.

"That's why I want to marry you," she said firmly. "No one else can see it or hear it, only us."

He smiled as he touched his nose to the tip of her perfect one. "Forgive me Sue. I was just feeling sorry for myself I guess," he said lowering his head.

"You have a right to feel hurt," she told him as she hugged him tighter. "I know I did when I was dying, but you gave me hope." She reached up and gently stroked his face. "And you have it too, that you may one day see again. In the meantime, don't let your blindness make you lose sight of your goodness."

"I'm sorry, I never wanted to hurt you," he said holding her face.

"Then just don't ever stop loving me or push me away," he heard her say in an angel's whisper. "Don't ever stop being you, being us."

They went to the couch and he laid his head in her lap. Within minutes he fell asleep as she gently stroked his face and hair. A short time later she watched as he began moaning and struggling. He suddenly woke up with wild eyes as he cried out, "No!"

"God Babe! What is it!" she gasped as he sat up in a sweat.

He kept breathing heavy until he realized where he was. "It's nothing," he said, "just a bad dream is all. I'm fine."

"Fine? No I don't think so. You've had them before, haven't you?"

"Now and then. It's just some memories from the war."

"Tell me," she said holding his arm. "You promised never to hold anything back from me, remember?"

He paused, closing his eyes a moment, then looked off with a faraway stare.

"It was just a short while after I had been captured. Another group of American soldiers had been found and were brought into our lockup.

I didn't see him at first, then I heard a voice say, 'Got room for a good old boy over there?' and when I turned around it was Tucker. He had come back several times looking for us and the last time they were shot down."

Steve paused smiling.

"He just stood there with that stupid grin. Just looking at me and shaking my hand, as if we were bumping into each other at some church social.

I reached out and hugged him, then noticed the guards watching so I led him over in a corner to sit by Dan. We joked and laughed, then all of us went to sleep."

His eyes squinted as he remembered being woke up with a bright light in his eyes.

"They came in the night and took Tucker out. For the next hour or more, all I heard was him screaming."

Steve's eyes started to water as he stared out towards the window in his darkness, as he had back then through the bamboo bars of the cage.

She squeezed his arm and kissed it as he began shaking.

"Finally it stopped," he said, "then two guards came and got me. They brought me into the hut and tied me to a chair. I looked up and saw Tucker hanging by his feet with his arms tied behind his back. He was slashed and bloody, barely conscious.

The officer said that he was sure Tucker would appreciate it if I'd tell him the truth this time.

'I've told you the truth,' I said, 'we were taking men out, not bringing any in. There's nothing more to tell! So let him who has ears hear!'"

Steve turned his head towards her, his eyes were wide, filled with pain.

"Then Tucker said, 'Don't give him spit,' and that filthy!—-Black-hearted devil! He grabbed a knife and very slowly started cutting Tucker's throat out!

'You're doing this!' he yelled to me as he kept cutting. 'You and your lies!—-Your stubbornness! You are killing your friend.' Then he wiped the blood from the knife onto my face."

Sue's felt a tear in her heart as she watched the pain flash from his eyes and bleed out from his words.

"And he laughed!" Steve cried out. "He just kept laughing as he left the room while Tucker hung choking…Gurgling in his own blood for a breath! His eyes pleading to me for help! I screamed out, fighting the ropes, but all I could do was watch him die. I was helpless! Useless!"

Steve reached out and touched her face.

"He died because we were friends and because he came back to help me, but I couldn't help him! I couldn't save him! I cost him everything, his very life, because he cared about me."

She pulled him into her chest and cried with him.

"Oh God Babe, it wasn't your fault, he knew that. He's at peace now Love," she cried, "the pain is over for him. Let it be over for you too now, please."

He raised his head a bit and said, "It was days before I could tell my sergeant what had happened to him."

"And what did he say?"

"He said make his sacrifice count."

She took his hand and kissed it. "And you did. You got your sergeant and all the others out of there and saved them."

"Not all of them," he mumbled remembering their faces.

"If you had saved only yourself then you would have honored him. That's why he came back."

"Oh Sue, I just don't want anybody else to pay for my shortcomings. I don't want you to have to pay."

"I love you Steve Clayton and what you call shortcomings are blessings to me. I have a man who sees me for who I am and loves me for it," she said through smiling tears. "And he can do this with his eyes closed."

They held each other without saying another word, until finally she felt him relax and laid him back. As she kissed him, he surrendered to her caring caresses and felt the love that she was breathing into him.

"I know you would have done the same for him," she cried in a whisper while holding him tight as he now slept, "but I thank God you didn't have to."

On Monday she picked him up and they drove to the office. Sue worked at her desk managing his appointments while he finished up in a conference with the partners, their accounting head and their sales manager.

"So, that's where we stand this quarter," said Tab Whistner. "You are working in the black, the revenues have remained level and steady, though not much growth."

"I have salesmen out everyday working to maintain good rapport with our existing clients, as well as following any leads for new ones," Jeff Roberts remarked, "so I'm open to anything more we can do."

"We need to concentrate hard on those new leads but keep building the quality of our existing services," Joe stated. "The contract for Coswell Industries is coming up for renewal and I got the feeling that they may consider a lower bid this time out. We'll need to show them why we are really the best choice."

Jeff shook his head and added, "I'd hate us to lose that account. It could really hurt us and cost some jobs."

"Maybe we could include roving mobile patrols in the new bid at the same price," Ken proposed, "and increase our incentive plan with the guards for outstanding service with a new bonus system."

Tad Whistner agreed. "If we lost Coswell, you might have to lay off a lot of people."

Ken looked at Steve who had little to say and nothing to ask, which was not like him at all.

"Thank you gentlemen," Ken said. "Please leave your reports on my desk and we'll let you know how we want to handle this by Friday."

When they had left, he turned to Joe.

"So, I guess the best way to handle this is to go public and sell off most of our company shares before we go belly up, hey Joe?"

He winked and Joe grinned, looking also at Steve's non-response.

"What do you think Steve, sell it all?" Joe asked loudly.

Steve jerked his head up suddenly. "I'm sorry, uh ...What? Go Public? Sell? Are you both crazy!"

Ken laughed. "I guess it's true what I've read about on how the very thought of getting married can affect some people."

"Oh," Joe asked covering his laugh, "and how's that?"

Ken moved behind Steve's chair and whispered, "That it can become a progressive disease. In his case for example, it started out in the knees, then moved into the chest to his heart, and now it has affected his mind."

"What did it say was the cure?" Joe asked still grinning.

"Well to start with, something warm, soothing and relaxing, but it has to be administered by someone with a very delicate touch."

Ken pushed the com button.

"Yes sir?" answered Sue's voice.

"Could you come to the conference room please? Oh, and bring your coat."

"Uh, yes sir."

"What are you up to?" Steve asked but got no reply as Ken looked to the door.

Sue entered looking puzzled and closed the door.

"Ski?" she questioned.

"Your future husband isn't feeling himself today," he said. "We think what he needs is a break for some soup and sandwich with a side order smile this afternoon. Any suggestions?"

She smiled back.

"Oh, I think on Mondays the Cafe' has a really nice special between eleven and three. If I call now, I'm sure we could get a quiet seat near the garden."

"Just what the doctor ordered in the article," he replied, then turned to Steve and said, "now, go get cured."

"Thanks guys. I guess I'm not much use around here today anyway."

He helped Sue on with her coat and grabbed his off the rack.

"I'll call you later," he said as he took her arm.

As they finished eating, she noticed that he was being quieter than usual. "What is it?" she finally asked.

"Oh, I've been thinking that maybe I should sell out to the guys. I can't do my share like I use to, it isn't fair that they carry me. I suppose I could find something different to do now, besides, I feel a change coming on me."

She remained silent, waiting for him to continue as to what he might like to do instead, but he just sat there sipping his coffee.

"Maybe you could go back to school, to college?" she eagerly proposed. "Take some classes in writing like you once wanted. Maybe even get your degree to teach."

"I have always regretted not going, but I guess I never wanted to without you there."

"I can be. I'd love to take more courses in art and I'm still available to help you with the math," she chuckled softly.

"Yea, that was another stumbling block in my decision," he replied laughing with her. "Okay, maybe after we're married. Right now, I can't help but feel there's something more I need to do with the company."

She knew that look when he'd drop off into a deep thought. His head would turn upwards slightly to the right and he'd stop listening. She reached over and put her hand on his.

"Promise me you'll think about school also?"

"I will," he said, breaking his concentration a moment to feel her hand in his, "I promise Love."

She took him shopping with her so she could price some things for the wedding and reception. While they walked through the stores, he stopped to hold his head often.

"Are you sure you're all right?" she asked several times.

"Yea fine, it's just a headache but it passes."

She watched him as they shopped, but he insisted it was nothing.

Back at the suite, as they were discussing the wedding plans, she noticed that whenever she got up, he seemed to follow her as she moved. It wasn't like he usually did with just his head tilt listening, but now with his face. She watched him closely some more, then decided it was just her.

When she had to go and pick up Dawn from school to bring her back for dinner, she just kissed him and left.

He made coffee and poured some into two travel mugs. With cane and overcoat on his arm, he carried them down the elevator and went out the door. Thomas the doorman was standing undercover of the light rain as he came out.

"Hello Mr. Clayton," he said as he grabbed the door for him, "it's a bit damp out here for a walk."

"Oh I just wanted some air with my coffee and thought you might like one also," he replied holding the second cup out to him.

"Well, that was kind of you sir."

"Please call me Steve," he said raising his cup in a casual toast.

"All right Steve, but only in private."

"Thanks, it makes me feel more at home after a day at the office."

As they both stood under the overhang of the awning by the doorway, they casually talked about the weather, then work and finally each other's health.

"I've been having problems with my legs, poor circulation I guess," Thomas confessed as he kept moving to stay comfortable while standing. "It helps to soak a bit after a day's work."

"I always enjoy a hot shower after work too, but mostly for the stress," Steve stated. "I have been getting headaches lately. I guess it's just from work also."

"Maybe from nerves about the wedding?" Thomas asked with a laugh.

Steve nodded with a smile.

"Your Miss Susan is such a lovely person. I know you will both be very happy."

"Thanks Tom. We already are."

There was a commotion near the corner as a group of teen boys ran in the rain towards them and then went into the alleyway. Thomas went over and yelled in to them.

"I've told you boys that you can't go in here. The owner doesn't want anyone hanging out."

One of the teens laughed at him. "Get lost old man," he said with a wave and then turned back to his friends.

Thomas walked over to them and said firmly, "He wants me to call the police if you won't leave." They just stood there ignoring him until he added, "All right, if that's what you want," and he turned to go inside.

Two of the boys lunged forward and grabbed him. "Just give us your wallet old man," one said as the other began searching his pockets.

"Let me go!" Thomas yelled, then cried out for help.

Steve heard him and walked quickly to the alley entrance.

"That'll be enough!" he yelled holding out the point of his cane. He heard someone approaching from in front of him quickly and he thrust forward with the cane, hitting his mark.

"What the ...?" came a voice in pain, then it cried out, "Go! Get him!"

More steps came from his right and he swung out, striking someone hard in the chest area. He could hear him fall to his knees gasping for a breath and he immediately came down with the cane on him, catching him on the shoulder.

"Mr. Clayton, behind you!" and Steve felt a sudden blow to his head.He fell forward onto his knee, then swung his cane around to his left and hit a pair of legs. The sound of his opponent falling next to him caused him to reach out and grab at his jacket. He pulled him closer and punched at his face until his attacker went limp.

"Let's get out of here!" cried out a voice from behind him and he heard footsteps running off to the street.

"Mr. Clayton, are you all right sir?"

"I think so. Could you give me a hand?"

Thomas took his arm and helped him towards the front door just as Sue pulled up the drive.

"No!" he heard her cry out, then Thomas, "Get away from them!" as he left him leaning on his cane and ran ahead. Steve made his way towards the sounds of the struggle as he heard her and Dawn fighting off the teens.

One yanked Sue out of the car and got behind the wheel, as the other pulled Dawn into the backseat.

"Let go of me! Oh God, please Don't!" Dawn screamed as she was pushed down on the seat and the guy got on top of her. Sue grabbed for the car door as they prepared to drive off, pleading with them to stop. Suddenly, she saw Steve standing in front of the car with his cane held high.

"You hurt them and you die!" he yelled out, then threw his cane towards the sound of the voice at the wheel.

It struck the driver in the face and he floored the gas, driving blindly forward into Steve's opposing figure. Sue screamed as he was thrown up onto the hood, hitting his head on the right fender. The teenage boys panicked and jumped from the car, vanishing into the street's thick fog.

Sue called to him as he slid slowly down from the hood and into the path of the car. It was still in gear and creeping forward. Dawn reached from the backseat, trying desperately for the key to stop it.

As the front wheel was about to roll over him, Excalibur suddenly stalled out. Dawn grabbed the key on the dash and turned it off, then slipped it into park.

Sue hurried over and fell to her knees beside him, taking and putting his head into her lap.

"I'll call an ambulance!" Thomas cried out and ran inside.

She cradled his face as Dawn stooped down near her calling his name. Still dazed, he opened his eyes and said, "So much like your mother, especially that perfect nose, but your hair is a mess."

Sue gasped as he turned to look at her.

"My brown eyes, how they shine for me."

"Oh dear Jesus thank you," she cried out in a half prayer. "It's the love that shines for you," she said now kissing him over and over.

The rain finally stopped and the sun was breaking through as the E.M.T. drivers finally finished checking him over. They were amazed that he had survived miraculously unharmed, let alone could now see as well.

"God has been patient with me," he told them, "and merciful." He invited them up for coffee but they thanked him and quickly left.

Sue continuously held onto his arm, as if it were all a dream she might wake from to find him really gone. He sensed it and smiled constantly at her, squeezing and kissing her hand gently often.

"I just thank God," she repeated as she walked with him.

"So do I Love," he whispered back, "for really opening my eyes."

"What do you mean?"

He took her back into the alley.

"I saw this just a few minutes ago," he told her, then pointed to the back wall of the apartment building. She looked and there, some four feet high and six feet wide, was a painted mural of black and white teens dancing and hanging out on a corner. It had such great detail, you could even sense the mood of each character.

"Oh Steve it's beautiful," she said looking closer. "Whoever it was has a lot of potential. Checkout the shading and the way they used it. Do you think you know who could have done this?"

"I have no idea. What I do know is that somewhere out there are kids with some real talent." He paused to look out at the town, then shook his head adding, "But for lack of an opportunity, they'll just end up jailed or dead instead of realizing their gift. It's shameful to see it go to waste like that."

"No Steve, we can't let someone like this just slip through the cracks. To let them throw their life away for something as empty as theft or assault? They deserve a chance to be more."

"That's what I began thinking when I saw it. Maybe free art supplies given out at the Green Square or a cash contest for top drawings or …"

"Or maybe …" she said interrupting, then went silently pacing. "Maybe an Art center where they could come for free and learn. Learn from real teachers who want to reach their artistic souls. To feed and fuel that raw talent and make it soar. Maybe even a place for writers and hopeful actors, for music and dance. Maybe we could even …"

She stopped when she saw him holding his head.

"Steve?"

"It's just a lot to think about right now I guess," he said still rubbing his forehead.

"Are you sure you're all right? How do you feel?" she asked taking his arm.

He looked over into her eyes, then smiled and touched her chin.

"I feel like dancing. How about you?"

Her eyes lit up in joyous relief. "What? Where?"

"Why here of course!" he laughed out, then took her to the car where he turned on the radio. He swept her to him and they began to dance around Excalibur in the driveway as Dawn and Thomas watched in disbelief from the front doorway.

Her heart swelled with joy as they lost themselves for a few moments in the music and again she was dancing in his arms.

"You're crazy, do you know that?" she cried out laughing as they swayed about.

"Just crazy about you," he replied touching nose to nose. "We can talk about the art center idea later, but for now, how about we have dinner at the Governor Morris tonight? The Rizin Starz is doing a benefit show there until tomorrow. What do you say?"

"The Starz, really? Tonight?" she answered with bright eyes. "What should I wear?"

"Anything you want, but your smile most of all."

That evening they arrived just in time to pull up behind Joe and Cindy, whom they had called and invited to join them. Ken was already there with a date and waved from the main doors.

"Please be sure to park Him next to a sleek, classy, dark top," Steve told the valet as he handed him the keys and a twenty.

Sue laughed as Dawn stared up at him puzzled.

"It's a triangle thing," Cindy said to her. "Don't even try and figure it out."

Ken stood waiting at the door and hugged him as he entered. "I can't believe it man," he said almost crying, "but I thank God for it."

"So do I Bro," Steve said smiling back.

"I got us a great table up front like the last time we all were here, remember?" Ken said with his hand on his shoulder.

"At least this time you're not dressed like a flaming arrow," Joe commented from behind and looking at his conservative jacket.

"You never did get it, did ya?" Ken said frustrated. "I was creating a mood!"

They sat around the table enjoying drinks and reminiscing about the prom for Dawn, but mostly for themselves. Sue felt like she did on that night so long ago. She felt alive, excited and in love. She could not stop smiling or laughing, nor slow down the racing of her heart as the music began.

He led her up onto the floor to dance slowly as the band played the song, 'With These Hands'.

She held him tight while they sang it to each other, pausing only for him to kiss her once on the side of her neck. "I love you," their eyes said to one another as they exchanged glances.

Dawn began to cry with joy as she watched the way they touched and looked at each other. Cindy reached for her hand saying with a near tear also, "They have always been like that. So much a part of the other."

Joe heard her and said, "Steve once quoted Mark Twain saying, 'the difference between the right word and almost the right word is the difference between lightning and a lightning bug.' I believe the right word for their love is 'Perfect'."

Dawn smiled as she remembered, "Don't ever settle for a love less than this."

"You're right Mom," she thought, "there is only one kind of love, a true one."

Steve held her face in his hands as the song finished, then she leaned in to rest against his chest as he kissed the top of her head tenderly.

"The song of our love," he said softly, "is a prayer the angels can sing but only we can hear."

"When I say I love you," she whispered, "I sing it with them."

The next number started and they both were filled with its energy. The two instantly burst alive on the floor as the words sang in their hearts and their feet carried them away.

They sang out loud as they moved swiftly across the floor together. He held her as she flung herself backwards with her face shining up at the revolving ball of lights above, as it threw off thousands of sparks in all directions like an exploding sun. She jerked her head forward again as they rubbed noses singing, almost screaming, the lyrics.

Their hearts almost burst with joy as they clung to one another in a dancing frenzy. It was that place they loved. The moments where they could come together and bond the love in their heart that no one else could see or hear or touch but them. They became One.

Finally, nearly breathless, they returned to the table for a break.

"Oh this is great!" she exclaimed to the others, then noticed them lying back. "Why are you just sitting there? Aren't you guys gonna dance!"

"Sue," Cindy replied, "when Joe and I were teens we could never keep up with you two."

Joe smiled adding, "But the next slower one we will, I promise."

The Tom Jones song, 'What's New Pussycat?' started playing and Steve grabbed Dawn to get up.

"Come on try it," he said to her. "I know you've got some of your mom in you, let's prove it!"

She followed him out to the center floor and, following his lead, she began to dance. Within minutes, she was moving in-sink with him and laughing in her mother's voice.

"I love you Uncle Steve," she said as he twirled her around. "Promise you'll never leave us."

"Where could I go Little One?" he answered smiling. "I live in your heart."

It was the best concert they could ever remember, as each song made their hearts sing stronger to the celebration of their lives together. Joe and Cindy even began to lose themselves on the floor. They slowly came to realize that it was what they felt inside, and not the perfection of their steps, that made the heart sing.

As he drove them back to their house, Sue laid once again against his arm. Excalibur purred along the road as if having had a great night also.

"Thank you so much Uncle Steve," Dawn said as she hugged him.

"You're welcome," he replied, "and thank you for the dance."

Sue held him close as she kissed his hand. "I have no words left to thank you with," she said holding up her engagement ring, "except, I love you darling."

"And you know I love to hear you say it," he replied back with a kiss. "To be able to see you smiling, dancing and full of life," he whispered, "that was love in motion for me Angel."

The deadline of preparation she had made for herself for the wedding never seemed to be enough. She worked with him on the details several days a week, as well as with her mom, Dawn and Cindy.

"I pray it will be perfect," she'd say over and over.

Dawn repeatedly replied, "It already is, it's you and him. How could it be otherwise?"

Sue would smile, but then turn looking upwards as if for a sign of reassurance.

One warm August morning, Steve called and told her that he wanted to pick them up for a ride into the past. When he pulled into her driveway he saw them already waiting on the porch.

"Where are we going?" Dawn asked as she climbed into the backseat, while Sue quietly sat in the front bucket and gave him a kiss. He turned back and gave her a half upturned smile.

"We're going back eighteen years, give or take a forever."

Sue looked over at him questioningly with a grin, but didn't ask anything.

They drove out to Route 46 and then headed east. Within minutes he was pulling up to park on the main street of Caldwell. Sue smiled as she commented on how little it had changed over the many years.

"Oh some things have changed," he said pointing to the little boutique shop storefront where she had once stood checking out a wedding dress. It was now a video store. Her heart warmed as she remembered the moment.

"Oh, it's a shame that it's gone," she said turning to him. "They had such beautiful dresses there."

"Yea well," he sighed, "some things do change as we said."

He pulled back out and drove them over to Route 24, going up into the quaint streets of Madison. There were many lovely, little shops along the main street as they cruised slowly. It was always a nice town to drive through, with its homes and businesses so tastefully displayed with great care and pride.

"Why are we here again?" came a voice from the backseat.

"I just thought your mom might find it interesting to drive around some of the places we use to go when we were younger, " he said as he pulled into a parking space. "Oh, and to see this."

Sue looked around casually then suddenly cried out, "Oh Steve, it's Anna Amora's Fashions!" She turned back to him with a shock of awe on her face.

"And some things just change location," he added smiling.

Sue looked back again seeing that now, instead of just a little assorted boutique', it was a full-size specialty bridal shop. A sign read, 'Dream gowns custom-made to your desires'.

"I thought that maybe you might like to explore your gown possibilities here first," he said, "and with a little help."

She looked as he pointed to the cafe' tables on the sidewalk up two doors from the shop. There, sipping coffees, were Cindy and her mom. They spotted the Le Mans and started waving to them.

"You are a man to reckon with when it comes to my emotions," she said touching his face. "Oh thank you Babe so much," she added with a heart-warmed glow.

"Look at all the gowns!" Dawn yelped out and hurried her mom to let her out to look closer.

"Go on," he whispered. "Cindy will call me when you're ready to leave." She moved up onto the console so Dawn could get out as she went to kiss him. "Something with pearls always seems to suit you," he told her softly and she smiled into his eyes.

Later that evening, as Sue was putting away the last of her dinner dishes, Dawn came into the living room and sat quietly next to Steve on the couch.

"What is it?" he asked and she smiled.

"When you marry Mom you will adopt me, won't you?"

He smiled back and said, "Of course," then paused a moment. "And what else?"

She let out a short laugh, amused yet amazed, because he seemed able to read her thoughts like that. She looked up again but now with a more serious gaze.

"When Mom becomes Mrs. Clayton can I have your name also instead of Walker?"

Sue could overhear them and stopped to listen from the kitchen archway.

He looked into her eyes and said, "If that's what you want but listen to me Dawn. You are a LaRosa and no finer heritage exists. They are the best family I have ever known. The women in your family are the strongest, most loving, most giving anyone could find."

He paused a second, then told her, "I once saw three LaRosa women create a gown here in under two weeks that should have taken months. It was a vision, a gown worthy of our Blessed Mother. I will never forget how your mom looked that night in it."

Dawn's eyes widened and shined. She could see the love in his face as he remembered their night together.

"You be proud of who you are Little One," he said holding her chin, "and you make them proud. That's what's important."

Dawn gave him a hug then went up to her room as Sue watched, wiping back a tear, then she came out to him.

"You have given her more love this past year than she has ever known before from her own father. You are such a gift to me," she said now crying.

He got up and held her. "No Sue, both of you are the gifts I once thought I'd never have. I'm the one most blessed by the love shared here. I was empty and now I overflow inside. Thank you Babe."

She leaned up and kissed him.

"Oh Steve what you are to me I have yet to fully understand, but what you mean to me is so easy to love."

A week later, when she arrived for her first fitting of the gown, she felt a dull pain in her chest, as well as a nagging headache. She took some pain medicine but it got steadily worst by the hour. As the seamstress was taking her measurements, Sue grabbed her chest and then suddenly collapsed.

Dawn called for an ambulance, then had the office reach Steve who was away setting up a site near the shore. He arrived at the hospital just as she was taken to a private room for observations.

Joe, Ken and Cindy waited in the hall as he entered slowly. Seeing Dawn sitting at her side, he stopped by the door. Dawn looked up and went over to him, hugging him tight and crying.

"She never said anything," she told him.

He looked at her sleeping with the oxygen tubes beneath her nose then, taking Dawn by the hand, he went to her. He lightly touched her hair and she opened her eyes.

"Hi Babe," she said softly. "I'm sorry, but I just don't have the strength to last as long as I'd hoped. "

He knelt beside her and put his arms around her.

"We could have waited until you were well enough," he whispered.

"I've felt for some time that this was coming, but I wanted so bad to have our dream. I couldn't chance waiting anymore. He held back his tears and she touched his hand saying, "No, don't hold them in. This time let me wipe yours away." His head fell to her as he let out a deep moaning cry and she kissed his tears. "I need to see Father Michael," she told Dawn and she ran for the door to get Joe.

Steve raised his head and begged her to fight back against this, but she smiled saying, "I've outlived the time already the doctors gave me because of your strength and love. This is one of those moments that most can't accept or understand, but I pray you will. Oh please, just hold me."

He put his arms around her and looked in her eyes.

"Oh Steve," she cried, "I wanted so much to make love with you."

He smiled, now brushing her hair, and replied lovingly, "We have Sue. Every time we looked at each other. Whenever we talked, touched, smiled or laughed. But when we heard the music and danced Babe, always, we made love."

She sighed. "I wanted so much to have your child. When Dawn was conceived I could only think of you."

"You did Angel," he whispered back. "I felt you ... I heard you call my name through the darkness of that hellish cage. I was there with you Love, believe me," he cried out softly through the tears.

"Oh Sweety," she said with joy in her voice, "then promise me you'll take care of our daughter."

"You don't need to ask me that, I love her as I love you," he said with a kiss. "She's a gift of that love."

He held her gently and she cried again asking, "Oh Stephen, why does it have to be like this?"

He closed his eyes a moment and sighed, then looked down into the hurt he saw in hers.

"No, it doesn't have to be this way," he said with anger in his tone. He touched his nose to hers and whispered, "I'll be right back." He kissed her as Father Michael came in and left her to say her confession. He ran down to Excalibur and took a small box from its glove compartment. When he returned, she was struggling even harder to breathe than before. He called for all of them to come in.

"Michael, please marry us now," he pleaded.

"You don't have a license," he said, "it wouldn't be legal."

"Please Mike just say the words," he begged. "We only need to hear the words from you Father."

He turned to Sue and she smiled with a glow as he helped her up on her pillow to face everyone. He opened the box and took out the two gold rings. He showed her the inscriptions inside each of 'I Promise' and she sighed with her eyes shining.

"Dearly Beloved, we are gathered here today to witness the joining of this man and this woman in the bonds of Holy Matrimony."

Sue suddenly held her side and gasped for a breath as Steve put his arm around her and held her hand tightly. Father Michael took a deep breath and continued quickly.

"Do you, Stephen James Clayton, take thee Susan Maria LaRosa for your lawful wedded wife? To have and to hold, in sickness and in health, for richer and for poorer, to love, honor and cherish for as long as you both shall live?"

He looked into her eyes as he put the ring on her finger and said, "I do, forever."

"And do you, Susan Maria LaRosa, take thee Stephen James Clayton, for your lawful wedded husband? To have and to hold, in sickness and in health, for richer and for poorer, to love, honor and cherish for as long as you both shall live?"

She slid his ring onto his outstretched hand and raised her hand to his face. "I do. Forever and a day."

Father Michael paused, then said, "I now pronounce you Husband and Wife. What God has joined together, let no man put asunder. You may kiss the Bride."

He leaned down to her, stoking her hair, as she said, "Every breath I take is for you My Love."

"Then give me life Angel," he said and they kissed as if for the first time.

"It's time for us to go back home and live the dream," he whispered sweetly to her and her eyes brighten.

"Oh please Steve, yes," she cried softly.

He turned to Dawn. "Please Baby help her to get dressed, then go stay with your Grandma."

Dawn smiled and hugged him. "Love her as she deserves," she said in a whimper.

"I always have," he whispered in her ear with a kiss, "now hurry."

Joe grabbed his arm asking, "What are you doing?"

"There's nothing they can do for her here Joe. I'm taking her home to heal and where the world can't touch her. Forever will be ours as we were promised."

"Steve no! You take her off of that oxygen and you'll kill her for sure!"

Steve turned for the door but Joe continued to hold onto his arm tightly.

"Joe, don't you understand?" he said with desperation in his eyes. "It's her dream, our dream, and it was a promise. It was 'The Promise', and I have never broken a one to her! This is one wish that was meant to come true."

Joe stared at him a moment, then smiled saying, "You'd just get back up if I knocked you down, wouldn't you?"

"Joe," he answered putting his hand on top of that huge fist of his, "today you're just not that strong."

Steve wheeled her out to the front entrance where he had parked Excalibur and helped her into the front seat. She kissed Dawn and her mom, then hugged everyone else with tears of joy in her eyes.

"Wait!" came a voice from the doorway as Cindy ran towards the car with an economy size box of rice. "I got it from the kitchen!" she explained as she held it out for all to take a handful.

"God bless you!" Cindy cried out as they all threw a shower of the white rain over them. She turned into Joe's arms and then cried as the car drove off with the sun hanging low in the sky.

Sue continued to take short breaths as they made their way to the rear entrance of the Island. It was when they finally reached the other side of the metal bridge that she suddenly was only aware of the Island's fragrances. They filled her with each new breath and lifted her spirits above the pain. Her heart sang as she gazed over at him.

He pulled up as close to the knoll as he dared. He went to the trunk and got a blanket which he spread out over the sweet scented bed of flowers.

As he unrolled it a single bottle of wine, long hidden in the darkness, tumbled out along with a plastic wine glass. Startled, he paused staring at it then picked it up slowly. Its label read '1969' and he smiled as he placed it on the blanket with the greatest of care.

When he came over to the car he pushed in an old eight track of 'Anne Murray's Greatest Hits'. He smiled, then lifted her out of the seat and sat her on the hood. Taking several steps back, he held out his arms to her as Excalibur began playing, 'Could I have this dance'.

Sue's eyes widened with her smile and slowly she lowered herself to the ground. She watched as he grabbed at the air with his fingers towards her.

"Come to me Babe," he said softly.

She inched her way to him, focusing on her balance with each step, until at last she was in his arms.

They began to dance slowly in a circle, her arms tight about his neck, as he held her securely around the waist. Her head rested on his chest and she listened to his heartbeat while her tears soaked through his shirt. He felt their warmth bleed into his heart.

"I love you so," she whispered as he lifted her up and carried her to the knoll.

"Oh Sue, come home with me now," he said as he gently laid her down amidst the bed of their dreams. He took a flower and put it in her hair. As their eyes melted into one gaze, the love of her stirred in his heart and it quickly began to write words as fast as his lips could form them.

***

"Come Voyager, sail with me
to an Isle of green that holds a Dream;
we'll stand together on the wooden deck

and wish it True,
a Promised Love, for me, for you
and cheat the ferryman his due;
for our sea to cross is but a stream
and from the beginning, we were the Dream."

***

She took a deep breath as her love poured from her eyes and down her face.

"Oh Steve what you do to me," she cried. "You kiss me now or I'll clip you good."

His lips smiled then surrendered to hers as the last rays of the sun were setting beyond the far end of the lake.

They opened the bottle and he took a sip of the wine, then turned the glass a full turn and she drank. He then kissed the tear from her eye and she, one from his.

"So many tears," she said, "yet still our love shines. Forever comes in many ways My Love, tonight will be only one of them."

She then slowly undid the buttons of her white blouse and laid back on the blanket. Smiling up at him, she pulled its corner over his shoulders.

He put the glass aside, then kissed her hand.

"A gold ring on your finger. No regrets in your eyes, only love shining back," he said with a smile.

"I need all of your love my husband," she whimpered as she took his hand and put it to her chest. He could feel her heartbeat in the palm of his hand. He closed his eyes as he felt his own beat now in rhythm with hers.

"I live in your heart Angel," he whispered, "now and always."

Her breathing suddenly became painful and shallow so he cradled her tenderly. "Listen," he said softly, "do you hear the crickets?" She listened with him as they sang to her from the far side of the lake.

"Now listen how others sing back from the north shore, and now those here around us, then again from across the lake. Do you hear Babe?" She listened quietly with him as they grew louder with the setting sun.

"Breathe in their song Sue and when they stop, let it out to them lovingly."

She began to breathe in sync with their music. Slowly and deeply in, then slowly out. Within moments, her breathing became steady and normal again.

"Make love to me," she pleaded with a tender caress.

As he held her, the love in her heart melted and flowed through her like life itself and she pulled him even closer.

"Only God could make such a man for me," she cried out. "I've waited my whole life to be made love to," she told him in-between kisses. "I've waited for you. Oh Sweety, love me."

As their lips met again, they gently rolled in the fragrant garden while gazing at the moonlight now beginning to shine in their eyes. Above them, amidst a thousand dancing lights, a shooting star fell like a tear from heaven and blessed their loving embraces.

Later, as the harvest moon dropped low in the sky, he stroked her hair while gazing at heaven's face resting on his chest. He sensed her breathing and with concern asked, "How do you feel?"

She looked up slowly, with a glow that could warm any winter, and answered, "Loved." Then she began crying.

"Sue, what's wrong?"

"Nothing," she said smiling and hugging him tight. "It's just a girl-thing, and because I love you."

"Sleep now Angel," he whispered smiling.

"I'm afraid to," she said. "I'm afraid that I'll wake up and this will all just be a dream."

"It is Sue, it's ours. Just know I'll always be here dreaming it with you." They closed their eyes and together they fell into a deep sleep.

When the sun's new rays warmed his face he awoke. He turned to find her nestled under his arm, but could hear her shallow breathing. He could feel her struggling in pain as she held her chest.

"Sue please," he begged, "just wake up and it'll be all right!"

Her eyes stayed shut as she continued gasping for air. He shook her, called to her again, then slowly stroked her gently and held her close to his heart.

"Oh Lord! You tell us that a day with You is as a thousand years," he cried out. "So what I'm asking for, by Your own measure, are just minutes to You while years to us. If You love her half as much as I do, and I know You do, then I know You'll hear my prayer. We can do so much together in this life, so what are a few more years for things to be right? She has so much more to give."

She gasped harder, now moaning in her sleep.

"Oh God, what more do you want from us? What's the price of love! - - - And when is it paid in full!

All I have is Yours, even her I know that, but let us have our love for a time then she can come to You. You know my heart, You gave it to me. Let me share it with her for just a few of Your minutes. It was a promise, please!"

She cried out in pain and he held her tight as he lowered his head onto hers crying.

"You took her from my life once to save her life, but why would you take now when she is my life? Oh, whatever this trial is give it to me. She's had enough."

"He has given it to you," she said softly up to him. "This is, your trial My Love."

She took his hand saying, "Steve, one day of a perfect love is a lifetime remember? Now, forever awaits as promised."

He felt his heart burn and bleed as he pressed his cheek to hers.

"I love you Sue!" he cried out. "Don't leave me. I'll be like a cloud without a sky."

She smiled as her tears touched his face and whispered, "I love you too. So come and take that love from my heart, I can't hold it anymore. Let it live on in you."

"Please Sue," he begged, "don't please."

"And both were young," she said smiling, "and their One Heart was beautiful."

He turned quickly and their lips met, and their hearts touched, as their love flowed from one to the other. Seconds later, he could feel her last breath blow upon his lips.

He felt a sudden sharp pain and grabbed at his chest, as if part of his heart had been torn away. He fell forward crying uncontrollably.

Worried, Joe and Ken had come looking for them. As they reached the wooden bridge they heard him scream out, "Why!" and the sounds of the Island went silent.

"I won't be long," he cried out, "I promise!" and then he collapsed over her.

Chapter Twenty-Five
"The Love Shared."

"Steve please, you've got to take it easy," Joe said. "You had a heart attack man, please sit down."

Dawn came into the church and Joe went to her. "Talk to him please. Get him to calm down."

"Please don't overexert yourself today," she said coming over and taking his hand. "I'm asking for me."

He looked at her as if he heard Sue speaking. "Oh Dawn, just let me walk with her down the aisle."

The pearl casket was lifted. Ken and Joe at the front and four Captains of the guard service, all in full uniform, behind them. Steve walked slowly at its side with his hand on top. He stared at the flame of a white candle up on the altar. It was flickering but continued to burn strong and bright, despite a strong gust of wind coming from the open church doors behind them

Once in place, the lid was opened by Father Michael and Sue was shown dressed in all white. Dawn placed the small bottle of Heaven's Scent with American Dreams at the foot of the casket, then knelt down next to the Musketeers to pray.

Joe took one of the Dream flowers and placed it onto her hands. Ken took one also which he placed in beside her. "I love you Little Sister," he moaned softly, then turned away to hide his tears.

Dawn handed Steve a ring on a chain. It was his initial ring, the same one she had taken to go steady. He smiled at her, kissed it, and then wrapped it around Sue's fingers. Her face glowed from the chandeliers above, as did Dawn's kneeling next to him, and it warmed his heart.

Joe stood up in the near-empty church and said, "Pride," as he put his hand on one of the gold handles.

"Honor," Steve added still kneeling as he put his hand on Joe's.

Ken stood and put his hand on theirs. "Respect," he said softly. Dawn got up, adding hers onto theirs. "And love," she whispered with tearing eyes.

The two guys went and took their seats in the front row next to Cindy and her children, as others began to enter for the service. Steve stayed, reaching in and gently stroking her hair.

"Your grandfather once told us we were too young to know what love was," he said to Dawn as he smiled at Sue. "But to us, love was as natural as breathing and as simple as just whispering each other's name." A tear broke and rolled down his face. "The voice of an angel," he sighed, "and the heart of heaven itself."

"She got her wish," Dawn moaned out softly.

"Her wish?"

"The one she made at the Roman fountain," she answered. "I knew then what she had wished for."

She looked up at him and smiled.

"She wished that she could finally live, love and die in your arms, and she did. You couldn't have made her happier, I know it, and I love you for doing that."

He cried and she held him, wiping away his tears, as he reached in and stroked Sue's cheek.

"Go with God My Love," he said.

He lowered his head a moment and then started to get up. Dawn took his arm to steady him.

"Oh God," he mouthed softly as he got to his feet and stared up at the statue of the Sacred Heart near the altar. "Thank you for sharing her love with me my Lord."

At the cemetery in Hanover he tore off a silver button from his coat. He then placed it onto the pearl lid as it was lowered into the family plot he had purchased.

As he knelt before her, he grabbed a handful of earth and begged softly, "Please be patient with me. I shouldn't be very long then I'll go straight to you. The shortest distance between two hearts is a song and I sing to you. I know you'll be there. Where else would God keep an Angel?"

Ken helped him up while Joe stood by Dawn. Steve turned to her and asked, "I was hoping to get your permission to be buried here beside your mom."

Dawn hugged him tight and replied with a tear, "Where else would I want my Father to be?"

He gazed at her and said tearfully, "You have so much of her in you, you truly are you mother's daughter. I'm so glad part of her lives on. You promise me you'll always make her proud."

"Oh I promise Daddy," she said crying on his shoulder.

Later that evening, as they were walking back from dinner at a local restaurant, Dawn told him how much she missed her already. He stopped and held her young face in his hands.

"She will always be with us," he said. "I see her in you every moment. Every time you smile, in the sound of your voice and the way you kneel in church." He paused for her to look up at him, then said, "In the way you carry yourself with confidence, yet with gentleness."

He turned with her and again started walking.

"Still," he added, "if times come when she feels far away, I want you to just look up."

He pointed to the night sky and she raised her head.

"Do you see those bright stars, the real bright ones? I believe those are the loved ones God has taken from us, but He lets their Crowns shine brightly so we can know they are watching over us."

"I wish I knew how to find the one that was Mom's," she sighed.

"Oh that's easy," he whispered, "just look for the brightest one."

Chapter Twenty-Six

"God gives you love to live and He expects you to make it grow."

-Grandma LaRosa

"Dawn, how have you been?" Joe asked as he came into the company garage and found her sitting on the trunk of the Lemans.

"Grandma and I cry a lot Uncle Joe," she answered quietly.

He hugged her softly. "Yea I know, so do we."

"I've been waiting for Dad to come down so we could talk. I haven't seen him since dinner after the funeral."

"He isn't here. He hasn't been out of his suite in over a week since he left his car here and walked home. We've tried to see him but he won't answer."

"I know he's hurting too," she said, "I can feel it." She looked into his eyes as she asked, "Take me to him. I need to see him, please?"

Joe kissed her forehead. "Come with me Baby," he said touching her cheek, "you'll see him if I have to take the door down."

They got into his car and drove over to the apartment.

"I'll be fine Uncle," she told him as he opened the Corvette door for her.

"Are you sure you don't want me to go up with you, or to wait to see if you'll be needing a ride home? He may not even see you."

"I have Mom's key, it'll be fine thanks."

Dawn went up and rang his bell. She waited then rang again, but still got no answer so she used her key.

"Daddy, it's me," she called out. "Where are you?"

She glanced around, then saw his arm on a wing-backed chair near the window which looked down to the walkway that led to town. She came over slowly, then saw his face. His beard was grown-in from not shaving and his clothes were wrinkled and out-of-sorts. He didn't move as she came by his side, only continued to look out the window with a glassy, trance-like stare. She reached down and touched his hand.

"Daddy, are you all right?" she asked softly. "I've been worried, everyone has. You don't answer the door or the phone … You haven't even been to work. Have you eaten anything?"

He didn't respond, only stared ahead.

Finally, she squatted right down in front of his view and looked him in the eyes. "Talk to me!" she yelled and she shook him.

At last, he moved his head towards her.

"Sue?" he muttered.

"No, it's me Daddy."

He looked into her brown eyes and smiled. "Hello Little One, I've missed you."

She smiled. "I've missed you too," she said with a hug. "Look I'm starved, have you eaten?"

"Uh, no, I haven't been very hungry," he answered somewhat in a daze.

"Let me go to the kitchen and see what I can find." She got up and began to hunt through the fridge.

She made tuna melts with some soup and set it out on the table, then called for him to join her. She waited but he didn't come.

"It's ready, did you hear me?"

She went into the living room but he wasn't there. His bedroom door was shut so she went over and knocked.

"Please go home to your grandmother Dawn. I need to be alone."She tried the door but it was locked.

"You've been alone enough, so have I, so please come out and talk with me." She waited with her head against his door but he didn't answer.

"I'm hurting too you know!" she cried out. "She was my whole life and until I met you, the only person who loved me! Or was I wrong about you! You said you'd never leave us. You told me that what we leave behind is important. Well I've been left behind, aren't I important! Aren't we what she loved?"

She slowly slid down the door onto her knees crying.

"You told me it was important to make her proud. Would she be proud now? We're all that's left of her, of who she was and what she cared about." She cried harder, then got upset and started pounding on the door. "Did we bury her legacy with her that day too!"

She paused, then said, "No, no. I'm a LaRosa and I want to make her proud." She choked up a moment then, "Oh please Daddy. I need you, please!" she cried. "I don't know how to stop the hurt. I don't know what to do, please."

As she cried against the door she suddenly could hear him crying and moaning also from inside. She gently put her hand on the door and said softly, "I'm sorry Daddy. It'll be all right, I love you."

The door opened and she saw him looking down at her through his tears. He dropped to his knees, held open his arms, and she ran into them.

"Forgive me Little One," he cried hugging her. "I thought only of myself and not the promises I've made."

She looked up at him as he caressed her face, then he wiped away her tears.

"I love you," he said, "and I am here for you always, I promise. You're a gift from God and her and I've been blind again. I just couldn't understand why He would give me back my eyes to see a world without her. I just don't understand it or why He had to take her from us."

"I don't either."

She looked to the side and saw the Bible on a shelf behind him. She went over and took it down, then hugged it.

"He promises that one day we will understand," she said. "Meanwhile, lets try and find some comfort in here as Mom always did."

Steve sat on the couch with her and he laid the Bible on the table in front of them. He opened it at random as he thought of Sue. When he looked down he saw that it had opened to Matthew 13:46 and he read it aloud.

***

"Who, when he had found one pearl of great price, went and sold all that he had, and bought it."

***

On the following Monday he returned to the headquarters. As he passed the conference room the guys spotted him and followed him into his office.

"Steve, you ready to work?" Ken asked with concern.

He looked up and smiled. "In a way, got a few minutes?"

They both nodded and sat with him as he removed some papers from his briefcase.

"I had our lawyer draw this up for us, please read it." Joe took the papers and as he finished each, he passed it to Ken to read.

"This says that you're selling out nearly all of your company shares to us and for below their value," Joe stated in disbelief.

"Why?" Ken asked.

"I need the money for something else."

"What?" Joe asked puzzled. "If you need money just ask us, you know that."

"I do and thanks, but this is for a promise I need to make come true. Besides, I can't live by the sword anymore," he said touching his hand over his heart, "I just don't have it in me."

"It's for Sue, isn't it?" Ken said knowing the answer.

"For both of us really," he replied, "and for many others I hope." He handed them another set of papers showing the layout of the project.

"An Art Center?" Ken questioned as he looked at the plans.

"A 'Free' Art Center," he replied with shining eyes. "Where any kid can come and learn for free how to use the gifts God gave them. They'll do it through drawing or painting, writing, music or even in the dramatic arts. See here, it will have a small stage with seating."

"If you're counting on just donations and part of your income to run it, this looks like it might cost more than you can afford," Joe stated looking at the bottom line figures.

"Well it can start out smaller, then hopefully grow as its student body does."

"Wait a minute," Joe said and he called the Accounting Department Head to come up to the conference room and then he called Cindy to join them.

"What you propose is feasible," Ted their accountant said as he looked over the plans and costs. "You could use a lot of it as a company write-off each year as its major sponsor, but the rest would come out of your own pockets for say, maybe the next six years. Maybe even longer if you have to continue to add more funding to it along the way until it hopefully becomes self-supporting."

"I'm in," said Ken.

"So are we," Cindy said looking up at Joe nodding.

"Okay, if that's what you all want. I'll start on it immediately."

"One more thing," Steve added. "It needs to be called 'The American Dreams Art Center'."

The others smiled and it was agreed.

"I love you all," Steve said choked up and hugged each, save Joe who took his hand.

The first building chosen was found to be too small. Ted hunted and finally found them a larger one not far from the center square of Morristown, although it would need restoration as it grew. He got them a very good price on it and with great terms.

Steve backed off from the firm. He became an instructor only for the Task Force and remained a partner at the insistence of the others. They would only buy half of his shares and paid him their fair market price. He entered college as a part-time student on Saturdays and after work. Dawn helped him with his math classes and helped out at the art center after school.

Teachers from all around Morris County began to come and ask if they could donate some of their time to teach. It became the hub of interest within the area after only three years, but funding was tight.

Dawn stayed with her grandma as her legal guardian. Mrs. LaRosa sold her house and they moved into Sue's which had been willed to Steve and Dawn.

Grandma took the master bedroom. Dawn took her old one, which she shared with Sarah for awhile when she came home from college. After two months, Sarah accepted an administrative position to run an outreach center for seniors near Trenton and moved down into her own apartment. She stayed in touch by phone and came back to visit often. Steve then moved in and took Sue's guest bedroom, on the family's insistence, and at last they all were a family.

One night, as Dawn went through many of the boxes which were in storage in the old sewing room, one kept sliding back whenever she pushed it aside. She finally looked inside and then brought it to Steve.

As he looked through it, he started to become very emotional. It was all of the letters he had sent to her while he was in Nam. She had bound each for protection and with each letter she had made several sketches of whatever he had told her about in that letter.

There were sketches of the men he had served with. She had caught the very personalities of each because of the vivid details he had given her when he wrote about them.

Other drawings were of the two of them, showing happy times as well as the pain during their separation.

He could see the joy and the agony in each as they portrayed the good and the bad moments. The smiles, then the sorrow or pain on their faces, even the look of death of the ones he had lost. He also noticed the stains from her tears on his letters, which she must have read often, and he kissed each darkened spot as he cried to her. There were over two dozen sketches covering the time he had been free to write her.

As he stayed up all night reading them again and touching his fingers to the drawings, he began to feel a growing need to share them.

Each night soon after, he started retiring early to his room. Sue's mom and Dawn would watch television while they'd listen to him working at his typewriter upstairs for hours on end and they'd smile at each other.

By the end of the year, he had written a novel based on those letters and included her sketches in each chapter. He made inquires with his college professors who recommended some publishers to whom he could send it out to for consideration.

After many rejections, mostly from major publishers, he got a call. One up and coming publishing company down in Trenton asked to see him about his work. He drove on down and met with its head writer and one of the editors.

"We like your book," the editor Bob Jenkins said. "It's not really anti-war like many others, but touches more on the personal side of the conflict." He paused then added, "We might want to put it to print, but we felt that it should first be touched up by our head writer here to make it more entertaining for our readers. Would you mind changes like those?"

Steve sat silent for several seconds and then answered, "I didn't write it to entertain. I wrote it to share. To share in the hope that maybe no one else would ever have to go through what these men did, or what she and I had to. I was also hoping to give these men the respect they deserved, but never got. If you didn't see their souls in her sketches then you've missed the whole point of the book completely." He got up as they remained silent, thanked them, and then headed for the door.

"Please Mr. Clayton, just a minute," the head writer Travis said.

Steve turned back, still standing at the door. Travis glanced a moment at his editor, then back to him and said, "Steve, I am a Nam vet also and trust me, I saw their souls in your writing and in the way she must have bled for them as she drew. What we're asking here, what I'm asking, is just a chance to help you make that book the best it can be. What it has to say has to be said, and there are very few changes I would ever want to make in it. I assure you, each change will have to meet with your approval before it is sent back to Mr. Jenkins and his partner for possible acceptance."

Steve walked over to him and took his hand. "If you've been there, then I know I can trust you."

"You can Bro. Let me keep the book and then I'll call you to look at my suggestions."

Steve smiled and nodded, then all shook hands and he returned home.

After several weeks of working with Travis on some changes in person, by phone and in writing, Steve finally got a formal letter from the editor of acceptance. A personal note was also included from Travis thanking him for the chance to help and Steve thanked him back in the book's dedication.

In March of 1992 it went to print and was released in the late spring. The title he and Travis had agreed on was used.

In May Steve went on a book tour promoting 'To My Heart Afar', written by Stephen J. Clayton and Illustrated by Susan M. LaRosa. It made the best sellers list almost immediately.

As the royalties started coming in Steve began to use them to expand and improve the Art Center. It was over the next several months, when word got out that it was the book's sales co-funding the center, that the donations steadily began to pour in for the school.

The center started producing some of the finest prodigies from New Jersey. As each student showed promise through hard work, they were given a chance to have their names posted nationwide for colleges to see their talents firsthand and a chance to offer them scholarships.

Dawn and Cindy started up an in-house service to handle these inquiries and the portfolios each needed to send out. They solicited referrals for each student from community leaders throughout the areas as well.

Private and business donations continued coming in, and trust funds were willed to it. Its fame began to spread from the ads paid for by On Guard Services as one of its major sponsors, but always, it remained a private enterprise, never seeking or accepting government funding.

It was insisted upon by its founders that the world could never influence its operations or its criteria decision making. It was forever to remain a Free Christian Based Organization with the Bible always having the final say in its decisions and policies. It was open to all to attend classes without any pressure to convert to the Catholic faith. All families wanting their children to attend signed an agreement of their understanding to these terms. Its underlining mission, beyond just helping to meet the earthly needs of its students, was always based upon the Christian adage of, "Preach the Gospel, and if necessary, use words."

Many times over the years would its founders find themselves in court fighting against the influence for changes from a faithless outside world, but never did they yield. Always they stood side by side in the fight for what was right, what was true and what was good. The Christian flag continued to fly high over its classrooms and at the entrance for all to see.

Steve spent many hours working the stage for its students and helping them on their lines or with their stage fright. He also mentored the ones writing, as he himself grew through his college studies. He could always feel Sue by his side as he worked effortlessly with all kinds of teens.

"You just keep giving me reasons," he'd hear her whisper.

The students prided themselves in their efforts of doing assorted fund raisers to support the center. It continued to remain a private, growing and living entity within the community, and was loved by all.

In mid-summer of 1992, as Dawn was preparing to enter Princeton College in the fall to pursue a degree in Law, she came into the exercise room of the center. Steve was there practicing his fencing as he always did on that day. She stood silent and watched him.

"For You my Lord and for my Queen, this school I'll defend with you both by my side," she heard him say as he finished his set.

She slowly went over and he turned. He smiled, then noticed that she was carrying Sue's foil case.

"Teach me please," she asked as she took out the star-handled foil.

"Why do you want to learn to fence?" he asked in a firm tone.

"To find out what I'm made of, of course."

He laughed, seeing her smile, then asked, "How long have you been waiting to say that to me?"

"It seems like forever, but mom did show me a little."

412

"Really?" he replied surprised. "Let's see what you remember first."

He tossed her a mask and glove, then they took starter stances and went through the basic moves and steps.

"Very nice," he commented.

"I know how to parry also," she said and had him attack her. She focused on his advance, but then lost her footing and fell back off the mat.

"I know," she said, "it's focus and balance."

"You master those two things and they'll carry over into every facet of your life."

He reached for her hand and lifted her back up on the mat. "Okay, let's try it again with you advancing on me."

She took stance, then cried out, "Heel, Toe, Heel, Toe," and moved him back towards his mat's edge. He suddenly advanced forward two steps and held her sword close to her chest with his. She smiled at him, then blew him a kiss and pushed off, striking his padded blade arm to the floor on the retreat.

She pulled off her mask and her shining brown hair shook over her shoulders as she stood looking at him proud and smiling.

He paused a moment, looking at all of her five foot, four inch pose, then laughed.

"I once warned your mom that only one weapon was suppose to be used in this sport."

"Know your opponent's weakness, she'd often say," she answered back with a wink and then a laugh.

"Yes she did," he replied laughing with her, "and she was a master at it."

He walked over to her and gently held her chin. "I love you Little One, she taught you well."

She smiled up to him and replied, "She was one of a perfect matched set, so I learned from the best."

By her second semester away at college Dawn had dated two young men, but never allowed herself to be distracted from her studies. Becoming a lawyer was her passion and nothing had been more important to her.

Then one afternoon, while she was hurrying to make it to class for a mid-term exam, she pushed open a hallway door and knocked down another student who was about to enter through it.

The six foot, blond haired young man just sat there stunned as he realized this little girl had just taken him down.

"Oh, I'm so sorry," she said as she started picking up his books and papers now scattered all about the floor. "Are you all right?"

He shook his head yes as he stared up into her warm brown eyes.

"Oh good," she said, then ran down the hall for her class.

"Hey, what's your name?"

"Dawn Walker," she yelled back and then vanished into a classroom.

When the bell rang, she made her way out into the hall and ran into the same young smiling face again.

"Oh sorry," she said as she bumped into him, then moved around him to continue on.

"Wait a minute," he called out and put his hand onto her arm. She immediately grabbed hold of him and flipped him. A second later, there he was sitting on the floor again.

"Do you do this to every guy who tries to talk to you?"

"No, just the ones who think it's okay to put their hands on me," she replied firmly.

"I just wanted to talk with you, but slowing you down is like standing in front of a bus."

She let out a laugh, then reached down for his hand. "You're right, I'm sorry," she said. "It's just a reflex action to so many loose paws around here."

"Where'd you learn to do that?"

"My dad and uncle taught me, they're ex-military," she answered, "and now own and operate a security task force."

He dusted himself off and asked if he could just walk with her, at a safe distance, to her next class. She smiled and agreed.

"My name is Sam Dupree. I'm studying to become an architect."

"I'm studying law. "Have you been here long?"

"No, this is my first semester," he said. "I just hope the next four years aren't as rough as today has been."

She laughed.

"You'll be fine, most of the ladies here are a bit more subtle than I am."

He smiled back, then said, "Well if you don't mind the company, I think I'll rather just keep on taking my chances to get to know you better."

She began to blush a bit, then smiled warmly as she looked back up into his gazing blue eyes.

"Besides," he added, "you never know when my honor might need defending and I'd feel a lot safer knowing you were nearby." She laughed, then walked a little faster trying to keep up with his wider strides.

They started dating steady within the month and she really enjoyed his company. He took his studies as seriously as she did. He told her how hard he and his parents had worked for him to be able to come there, and that nothing was going to stop him from his goal.

It was only when she learned that part of his tuition was coming through a football scholarship that she began to get nervous. He sensed something had come between them and questioned her about it.

"It's football," she finally said, "that's a bit of a problem."

"I don't plan on going pro, it's just a means to my end."

"I know that," she said. "It's not me, it's my family."

"Why, did they go to a rival college?"

"No they just don't like that kind of sport. I mean, they really don't like it!"

"Why not, too rough and tough for them?"

"No, not really," she replied. She thought a moment then said, "Look, everything should be fine when you come home to meet them this Easter Vacation. Just don't mention it, okay?"

"Sure if that will make you feel better, but I am a bit proud of being such a good player. I guess I was hoping that maybe you were too."

"Oh I am proud of you, it's just my folks. I just have to find a subtle way of breaking it to them is all. Once they've gotten to know you better I'm sure it won't matter. In fact, I'm sure they'll be as proud of you as I am."

He smiled and gave her a slight hug. "Whatever makes you happy," he said softly.

When they arrived at her house she took him in to meet Steve and her grandmother. As they entered the kitchen, Sam came in smiling ready to shake hands but stopped cold as he saw Steve sitting at the table cleaning his revolver.

"Dad, this is the boy I told you about. Sam, this is my dad Mr. Clayton."

"Nice to meet you sir," he said nervously.

Steve spun the barrel as he checked how well oiled it was, then he snapped it into the pistol.

"Well, it's nice to finally meet you too Sam. Have a seat and let's talk."

Sam looked over at Dawn as he slowly lowered himself into the chair. Steve placed the gun on the table and sat back.

"Ever do any shooting?" he asked the boy.

"No sir. Guns weren't allowed in the house as I grew up, not even for hunting."

"Oh, it's just a tool like any other," Steve said with smile, "when you need to get a job done."

"Okay Daddy, maybe if you're finished cleaning it now you could put it away?"

"Sure Baby," he said still smiling and slowly holstered it as he looked at Sam. Dawn covered her smile a bit as she looked over at Sam's nervousness.

"He's not dangerous," she finally said seeing his face. "Right Daddy?"

"Me? No, I just like to talk and understand the relationship anyone may be having with my daughter."

"We have never had any relations, ever sir," Sam suddenly spit out. "I give you my word!" he then stuttered more. "We're just real good friends. I do care for her, but I would never do anything inappropriate in regards to her person. I can assure you, I wouldn't even think of it!"

"Why not, what's the matter with me?" Dawn asked. "Don't you find me attractive?"

"You're beautiful," he told her, then turned back to Steve and said, "in an architectural kind of way."

"I see," Steve said, "you mean she's kind of like a big building or giant statue?"

"Exactly," he answered.

"You think I'm huge?"

"No, you're perfect," he said to her, "in an architectural kind of design."

Dawn laughed, then hugged him.

"Sorry, but all my boyfriends went through this when I was in high school. It's just a Daddy-thing I have to bear."

He turned to Steve and saw that he too was smiling.

"Hope this indulgence of mine hasn't put you off, but my little girl is very precious to me and I like to be sure of those she dates, understand?"

"Of course," he said with a sigh. "Did I pass?"

"Yes you have. Now, you just have to get by her uncles."

Sam watched as Dawn shrugged her shoulders.

"So," Steve asked, "do you like any kind of sports like track?"

"Oh yea, I'm a football player," he replied proudly, then quickly covered his mouth as he watched Dawn cover her face.

"Really?" Steve remarked resting his hand on top of his pistol. "Ya know," he said leaning into him, "you might not want to mention that over dinner at her Uncle Joe's today."

In 1993, a huge crowd attended graduation ceremonies at Ramapo College to see Steve receive his degree in teaching. The attendance was so great that the college had to present him with his degree twice, once inside, then again outside for the ones who could not be seated. He was moved by the community's support as he stepped up to the outside podium and addressed them.

"I'm touched by all of you coming today, but the person you need to honor most today is yourself." He motioned for Joe, Ken, Cindy and Dawn to come up with him.

He put his arm around Dawn and said, "The American Dreams Art Center exists because of your faith, hard work and the inspiration from a local girl. A woman whose love for her home state, for others and for her Lord, has made room in your hearts to love your neighbors and to give these kids a chance to see their greatness.

She inspired us all when she once said, 'What you leave behind is as important as what you strive for,' and you, all of you, are her legacy. You are all now and forever, Musketeers!"

The five raised their arms up high with fingers touching and the entire audience raised theirs in salute to them, and in loving memory of their beloved Musketeer past.

The audience cried out, "All for One, and One for All!"

"They are One Heart because of you My Love," he whispered up to the heavens, "and I never had a doubt."

Between teaching full time now at the school and overseeing the classes of the task force, Steve's schedule was extremely tight. Still, he always made sure that he had time set aside for family.

He would have backyard barbecues at least twice a month at either their home with grandma and friends or at Joe and Cindy's with their children. He made sure to talk with Dawn at least three times a week by phone and be available if she needed him. Of course, every Sunday after church he'd always visit Sue and bring her fresh flowers and talk.

One of his proudest days came when Dawn graduated with honors and then passed the bar exam. She went to work for awhile as a public defender in Morris County, then later, wanted to go into private practice. When she was ready to tell her family, fearing that they might think she was foolish for leaving a steady job with income and benefits, she turned to Sam for support.

"They'll understand," he told her as they sat in his convertible watching the waves coming in on the shore as the sun set. "They did the same thing starting from scratch with their company."

"I know," she replied nervously, "but I want to do this on my own and I'm afraid they won't understand when I tell them that I don't want their money or help doing this." She paused, then added, "I love them all and I don't want to hurt them by turning them down."

Sam smiled and gave her a hug. "They're a strong bunch and they'll understand. Besides, I have a good job with the firm up in Essex County and when we get married next year we'll make out just fine Babe."

"When we do what!" she asked jerking her head up suddenly.

Sam reached into his pocket and brought out a diamond ring.

"I love you Dawn. I'm not very good with words, but when I look at you I see life, a life I want to share. You bring spring into mine year-round and any dreams I see for happiness always have you in them."

He paused, holding out the ring. "Every time I look in your eyes I know why God gave me mine, to see us together. I'd hoped that maybe you felt the same?"

She smiled with melting eyes and said, "I do, and for a long time now. I love you too Sam."

She held out her hand and he gently slipped it on as she whispered, "Yes," then they kissed as the sun's last rays yielded to the new moon's bright soft glow.

She smiled up at him a moment, then suddenly panicked and went pale.

"Oh God," she said, "getting married? I've never even mentioned ever having such idea to any of them. They won't be ready for it."

"Well, now we can tell them about it at the same time we do about your career decision."

"Oh great," she said holding her left hand up. "I'd rather be caught wearing the Hope Diamond and face the three of them in full riot gear. At least then I'd get a trial first and then hung!"

"What? Why?" he asked puzzled. "You're a college grad and a young woman so why should they have a problem with it?"

"You don't understand. To all of them I'm still just a little girl."

"Yea, so?"

"So little girls don't talk seriously about love and marriage to their guardians. After all, what do children know about love? To them, love is just ... "

She stopped a second, then suddenly smiled and turned to him saying, "It's just as simple as breathing, or my saying your name."

He smiled. "Hey, I like that."

She took his hand and held it against her face. "You're right they will understand," she said, "but you do realize that you'll have to ask my father for my hand, and do it alone."

"I'd face him and your uncles for you," he said smiling, "and I won't leave until they've all said yes. They'll have no choice."

She smiled softly as she caressed his face. "Oh you are so brave and so naive, but I love you anyway."

"What do you mean?"

She put his arm around her shoulders and sighed.

"Does the word 'subtle' mean anything to you my, 'Oh yea, I play football,' hero?"

The family welcomed him warmly and helped to give them the finest wedding ever to be seen at St. Peter's church. Father Michael stood up at the altar with Sam and his best man ready to begin the ceremony. Dawn and Steve waited outside in the vestibule and talked as he held her.

"I'm so nervous Daddy, I can't stop shaking. If you weren't here, I think I'd just drop to my knees when those doors open and I see him."

Steve smiled and said, "Believe me, I understand."

He felt his eyes starting to water and looked away for a moment. She took his hand and kissed him saying, "Don't hold it in, I can't either."

He looked back into her eyes. "You look like an American Dream Little One," he whispered as he pulled down her veil.

She smiled warmly and whispered back, "I love you so much."

When the doors opened, she dipped her hand into the Holy water and blessed herself. He did also, pausing only to first touch his lips. As he walked down the aisle with her, he watched as her white gown swayed gently across the floor while its long train seemed to just float behind her.

The light from the chandeliers paled in comparison to the glow on her face. He smiled as he glanced at her bouquet, seeing his Dreams mixed throughout the roses. As he held her small hand in his, he sensed Sue smiling from beyond the glow of the white candles on the altar. Not since he last held her on the Island, had he ever felt this blessed.

"Who gives this woman?" Father asked.

"I do, he answered and lifted her veil to kiss her forehead and touch his nose to hers. He put her hand into Sam's and then took a step back.

During the reception at the Black Bull Inn in Mountain Lakes, she danced with him for the traditional 'Father-daughter' number. When it ended, she squeezed his hand to keep him on the floor. She smiled, then nodded for the band to begin playing, "What's New Pussycat'.

He looked at her and laughed, then spun her around. She tilted her head backwards and gazed at the lights above laughing in her mother's voice as she followed his lead. "I love you," he said as she jerked her head forward again smiling. Her brown eyes flashed love and life in all directions as he watched her blossoming into womanhood before his eyes.

"May God keep you in the palm of His hand," he said to her as they returned to the tables for dinner.

When they returned from their honeymoon at the shore, Dawn was anxious to start her practice. She found a small office on a side street in Morristown and was able to rent it out by the month cheaply, in exchange for doing some repairs and renovations.

She and Sam worked on it nightly and on weekends while she started advertising for clients. She even went down into some shady parts of town alone to meet with low income women. Many of them desperately needed help with child support or spousal abuse.

Her heart ached as she listened to their stories and she vowed to help, regardless of their ability to pay. Word of her services began to spread and within two years she had to add on several paralegals to her staff to keep up.

She also kept in touch with the public defenders office and would take on some of the overloaded case loads they often got of deserving clients. She slowly became known throughout the community as a starch advocate for women and children's rights. This sometimes though became a mixed blessing for her.

She got a call from Steve one day for an invite to go out to lunch. They met at the street cafe' and talked about their work. He could see how overworked she was becoming and was concerned.

"I'm fine Daddy, really," she said sipping her coffee as she glanced over some legal papers and made notes.

"I was wondering how much time you and Sam have been able to spend together these past few months. I mean, what with your work and him working projects in South Jersey so often."

"We talk on the phone all the time," she said, "and we just had dinner together the other night since he came home for some down time."

Steve reached over and put his hand on hers.

"Baby, you have to remember the important things and that's the two of you. If you don't find the time, then time will find you out. Out in the cold and alone, and you'll never see it coming until it's too late."

He leaned towards her and tilted his head into her eyes.

"You know that you and your mom always came first and my work second. Please remember, his love is a gift not a right, and one you never deserved in the first place. He's a good man and he will always need to know that you need him and that being together is what you live for."

Dawn dropped the papers onto the table, then started to cry on his arm.

"I love him so much Daddy, I tell him so, but I do miss the time we use to have together. Our work is just so demanding. It's hard you know?"

"I know Little One, but if you lose the joy of each other, then all the work in the world will come to nothing. The real work is always between the two of you. Even a gift has to be cared for or you lose it."

She looked up at him, then kissed his cheek. "I love you Daddy," she said as he handed her his handkerchief to wipe her eyes.

"You keep it," he said, "to remember how you felt just now for the days to come." He looked over at the papers and asked, "Can those wait?" She nodded with a smile, kissed him, and then left for home to be with her husband for the rest of the day.

Sam eventually also went out on his own as a consultant and joined her in sharing the small office space together. It didn't take long before they outgrew the tiny facilities and were in need of a much larger place.

One day while they were having lunch with Cindy, near the Green center square, they mentioned it. They wondered if maybe she could help them locate something better.

"I think I know a place," she said. "It has lots of parking, is secured, and the rent includes heat and air conditioning. It's got two office areas with a lot of room and a quiet view too."

"Sounds expensive," Sam said with a shake of his head.

"It's been empty for some time, so I don't think so. It just needs some added office walls, a little carpeting, and a couple more overhead lighting units put in from what I saw. Oh, and your willingness to put up with some noisy tenants downstairs on occasion," she said.

"I guess it can't hurt to look at it," Dawn said looking to Sam.

"Good," Cindy replied excited. "I'll make a call so you can see it tonight if you'd like?"

"All right, how about sevenish?" Sam asked looking at their faces. "We can meet you at the headquarters."

When they came into her office Cindy was with Joe and they were just finishing up some work.

"We're all ready to go," she told them and took Joe's arm as they headed towards the elevator.

"I think you both are just going to love this place," she said almost giggling, and then they suddenly noticed that the elevator was going up, not down to the lobby.

When the doors opened they were met with Steve and Ken. It was the top floor of the building, which had been left mostly unfinished and was being used mainly for some storage of office supplies.

"Okay, " Dawn asked, "what's going on?"

"Well, we heard you both were looking for a bigger office," Steve answered, "and we could always use the rent money instead of a giant closet. So, how about it?"

He took them by the arms and walked over to the windows, then out the sliding door onto a nice balcony. "Quite a view wouldn't you agree?" The two stood breathless as they stared across the evening lights of the town.

"I know the cost of space in this town Daddy," she said with a look and tone of warning, "and the cost per foot of something like this would be prohibited for us to even consider. I thought I made it very clear that we will always pay our own way, so what are you up to?"

"What? Are you telling me that you're not willing to give your father the same deal you gave a stranger?"

"Meaning what exactly?" she asked moving closer into his personal space.

"Well I … " he replied, trying not to stare into those wide brown eyes too long. "I mean you both fixed up the last place for a break on the rent. Can't we work out the same deal here? After all, you'd be doing me, uh, us a favor by making this a real source of new income. We just can't ever seem to find the time to do it ourselves."

Steve turned to the guys for a little help, so Ken spoke up.

"It's simple," he said, "we want to keep this building a family operation if possible and we could always use a little 'free' legal advice. So are you game or is this just too much for you to handle?"

"Too much for me to handle!" she said walking over to him pointing her finger. "Uncle Ski, are you aware that the woman in these shoes just forced Wagener Industries to its knees in court last week and had it pay its unskilled workers two years of unpaid overtime, plus penalties!"

"Sure, but you didn't have to swing a hammer like you'd have to with this project."

"Oh yes she did," Sam interjected. "She carries a gavel in her briefcase and she threw it at their attorney when he called her his sweet, but young, learn-ad opponent."

"I'll bet that went over well with the Judge," Joe remarked in a low tone.

"She threatened me with a hundred dollar fine if I ever threw it in her court again," Dawn said. Then she smiled adding, "And then she gave him a fine of fifty dollars for his showing continued lack of respect."

"Okay, point made," Ken said. "So, yes or no. Come on, we have a lot of boxes that would kill for this space."

Dawn smiled, then laughed. She looked to Sam and he nodded.

"All right," she said, "talk to us about the deal and the terms."

Introduction of
2001

Major News Events:

*The world's first self contained artificial heart is implanted.
*The United We Stand: What More Can We Give benefit concert is held in Washington, D. C.
*Sept. 11th—The twin towers of the World Trade Center have fallen. One first, then the second followed.

Top films of 2001:

*The Musketeer
*A Beautiful Mind
*The Princess and the Warrior

Top Songs In 2001

There You'll Be (Faith Hill)
Hero (Enrique Iglesias)

Chapter Twenty-Seven
2001

"A Girl To Die For."

It was the beginning of a joyful Christmas season when, on December fourth of 2000, Dawn announced that she was expecting her first child. Steve's heart swelled with the love of her as she and Sam told him first.

"I think it's going to be a girl," she told him with a glow, "it's just a feeling, but I can't shake it."

"I just pray it's healthy," Sam said.

"So do I," Steve replied as he touched her smiling face. "I can't believe you're going to be a mom," he sighed, looking deep into her eyes, "just be a good one."

She smiled. "Oh I will. I had the best to learn from, and you Daddy."

Over the next several months both Steve and her uncles made sure she got to every one of her checkups whenever Sam was away.

One afternoon in April, as she entered the elevator to meet Joe in the lobby for an appointment, there was a man inside when the doors opened. He was in his thirties, dressed in jeans with a dark hooded jacket. She got in and smiled as she pushed the button.

"You don't remember me, do you?" asked a voice from behind. She turned looking at him. "You wreaked my life and stole my family from me. How can you not remember?"

Dawn began to tremble, glancing at the floor lights above as they descended way too slowly.

"Who are you," she finally was able to get out, "and what do you want?"

"I want my life back," he said in an empty tone and grabbed her from behind with his arm under her neck, almost choking her.

"I want my wife Arlene back and my son but I can't have them, you saw to that. You said I was a no-good husband. A lousy father you said, well I'm not! I loved them. I needed them! Who are you to stick your nose into our lives? You filled her head full of lies and she left me."

Dawn thought hard.

"Arlene? ... Arlene Stapleton? Yes, I remember you now," she said. "You'd beat her and the boy in drunken rages. You would have killed them one day if they stayed."

"You killed my life by getting them to leave. Well I found them Ms. Lawyer and they won't be leaving me ever again."

He pulled out a hunting knife, stained red from the blood now dried on its blade.

"Now you're gonna learn what it's like to lose a family, a child," he said holding over her stomach, pressing its tip against her.

"No! Please don't!" she screamed out as they reached the lobby level. Joe heard her and ran to the doors just as they were opening.

"Get back!" Stapleton yelled at him as they stepped out.

"Fine," Joe replied backing up slowly and waving the reception guard at the desk to stay put. "Just let the girl go," he said calmly, but firmly.

"Oh no, she's the whole point of this," he replied. "She's never gonna hurt anybody again. She's gonna pay up her dues!"

The elevator doors opened again and Ken appeared with a pretty blond whom he had made a date with for that evening. He saw the knife and dove for it as the doors closed behind him on the young lady.

As they struggled, Joe grabbed Dawn as she butted her head back into Stapleton's nose and pulled her from harms way. Ken squeezed a pressure point on Stapleton's wrist and he dropped the knife. Then he jerked his arm around and flipped him to the floor. Stapleton moaned in a daze for a few seconds, then opened his eyes.

"Get up Buddy," Ken said to him as he reached down to lift him up. Stapleton slipped his hand into his jacket and then there was a gun shot. Smoke rose slowly from a small hole in the jacket's pocket as Ken fell to his knees, holding tightly to his chest.

"You piece of dirt!" Joe screamed as he pounced on him, tearing his jacket off his back, then throwing him up against the wall. He grabbed him by the throat, lifting him off the floor with feet kicking wildly, and began chocking the life out of him. Stapleton's eyes began to roll back, yet still Joe squeezed tighter.

"Uncle Joe!" Dawn screamed, "Don't, please!"

She ran over and put her hands on his as she stared into the blind fury of his burning green eyes. "Stop please, for me," she cried softer and he looked down at her. "Don't do this," she begged, "for Cindy and the kids, please stop."

He let go and Stapleton fell limp, but gasping, as the desk guard cuffed him then radioed dispatch a Code Red for police and an ambulance. Dawn went over and knelt by Ken as Joe just stood there staring at his life's blood spreading across his dress shirt.

"Little One," she heard him mutter, "are you all right?"

"I'm fine Uncle Ski. Please don't move, the ambulance is coming."

"I don't think I can wait for the ride," he said squeezing her hand a moment until the pain subsided, and then he looked up into her face. "Wow, I never saw that coming. I haven't led the best of lives. I always figured I still had time to set things right before the end, you know?" He took several deep breaths, then added, "I guess I really messed up."

"There's still time," she replied sobbing. "Uncle Ski, you just saved my life and my baby's. You've risked your life many times for all of us. For my Dad in Nam and for my Mom here."

"She told you?"

"Yes, she always loved you so."

He closed his eyes thinking about her and smiled. "She's the one that got away you know."

"No she didn't, you were always very special to her. She'd always smile whenever your name was mentioned. You've been a blessing to so many and touched so many lives for the better. You touched mine."

His breathing started to become shallow and the pain increased each passing second. She put her hand on his chest to help slow the bleeding.

"Listen to me," she said softly. "Greater love has no one than this, than to lay down one's life for his friends! Our Lord knows your heart, talk with Him, ask His forgiveness and believe on Him to save you."

"Help me Dawn, please."

Ken prayed with her and they ended with the Lord's Prayer.

"Uncle Ski, God is love and John tells us that he who abides in love abides in God, and God in him. I will see you again, that's a promise."

"You'll tell your little one about me, won't you?"

Dawn smiled. "She'll know and love you as I do."

"I never told anyone this, I guess cause it didn't suit my image," he said, "but my middle name is Leslie. I just wanted someone to know and remember it."

A moment later, his smile widened and a tear fell from his eye as he gazed upwards. She heard him whisper, "Oh Little Sister, I've missed you. Show me the way home," and then he was gone.

Tears rolled down Joe's face as Dawn leaned to kiss him goodbye.

"We won't forget," she cried, "not ever, I promise."

When her baby daughter was born later in August, she was proudly baptized, 'Lisa Leslie-Maria Dupree'.

Ken's death was hard on everyone, but Steve seemed to carry it around like a red-inked entry on his life's balance sheet. It was one he knew he could never repay.

Whenever he visited Sue, he'd then go and sit long over Ken in silence. Joe saw how he couldn't get past it, so one Sunday afternoon he met him at the grave site.

"I loved him too you know," he said as he stood quietly behind him.

"I know Joe, but he didn't save the most important pieces of your life, time after time, like he did mine."

"No, he didn't," Joe replied as he came to stand beside him. "He just made mine a better one for being my friend and I couldn't repay him for that either, except to try to be the best friend I could to him."

"You are and were, to both of us," Steve remarked softly.

Joe stooped down and pulled out a couple of dying flowers from the vase on the headstone.

"The day he died a part of me almost did too," he said up to him. "If it weren't for Dawn, the life I had might have ended that day with his. For the first time in my life Steve I wanted to kill someone, until your daughter made me realize it would cost me everything. My freedom, my wife, my kids, even my very soul. I owe her like you feel you owe him."

He rose up and Steve looked into his eyes as he continued.

"No we can't repay them, but God does it in other ways. The daughter you and Sue raised so well, she helped him in his last few moments to be save and go to heaven. Is that repayment enough? What greater reward could he have gotten?"

Steve lowered his head, fighting back the tears, then looked upwards smiling.

"You're right Joe. He knows best how to handle these things. It's better to just pray and believe, and then leave it in His hands."

Joe smiled, then whispered, "Well with Kenny, He sure has his hands full now."

Steve laughed out suddenly, then they headed back home.

***

The air was cool and crisp like the early fall leaves that morning of September tenth. He had woke up very early and felt a desire to be near her and to talk. He wasn't feeling himself so Joe was glad to drive out to the cemetery with him.

As he knelt on the dew-damp grass talking with her he put some fresh Dreams in the vase, then sprinkled a few over her.

"I picked these today from the knoll before coming over. They are the last of them for the season I'm afraid. I remembered how you use to love to pick them before they were all gone.

I saw Dawn yesterday. She's started a new branch in her law firm offering sliding scale services to low-income people in all of the surrounding counties now. You can be so proud of her Babe and Sam is doing well also."

He sat back on his heels to rest a moment, and then continued.

"I had dinner with them last night and he told me about a project he was helping to design down near the shore for seniors. He loves her very much and they are so happy together. They have 'The Gift' Angel.

Oh I saw the baby again, she has your eyes and I love to look in them. I think she likes me, she drooled on my sleeve.

As for me, you know I've backed off teaching the task force, but I attend most of the training sessions to watch how they're being taught. Somebody has to be sure those green weenies are prepared out there. I've also been an adviser for S.C.O.R.E., it helps people trying to start up a business. I do it after teaching at the center. That's about everything for now Sue, except that …"

He lowered his head, staring at her name before him and he reached out to touch it.

"I know that I've been longer then I promised, but I got busy. You know I've never been one to leave things unfinished," he said in a chocked up tone. "I guess for you it must only seem like it's been a couple of minutes, but to me, it's been a lifetime Babe."

He fought back the tears, then said, "Please keep praying over the family. The world is so fast-paced today and we want them to remember the important things. I'll be back next week, so until then, I'll see you in my dreams Love."

He slowly got up and turned, then saw the morning star above. It sparkled and then flashed back at him for an instant. He took two steps, then felt a sharp pain in his chest and fell to his knees.

"Oh Sue, I miss you so much!" he cried out.

Joe saw him fall as he was waiting near the car and hurried over to him. "Easy there," he said as he helped him to his feet. "What is it?"

"My heart," he replied taking a deep breath.

"Come on, let's get you to the hospital."

"I got it under control," he said getting some of his breath back.

"Then do it for me, okay?"

"You're a good friend Joe."

"Forever remember?"

***

"It was a bad attack this time," the doctor told Joe and Dawn, "but he refuses to go to surgery." He hesitated, then said, "Of course, it would only be a slim chance anyway even if he did. I don't think he will make it through the night, I'm sorry."

Father Michael came out, wiping his eyes, as he had finished hearing his confession. Joe turned to Dawn and said, "Let me see him first for a moment," and he went into his room.

Steve opened his eyes and smiled.

"Heavens Reily, you look like you lost your best friend."

"Why did you refuse the surgery?"

"Oh heck," Steve chuckled, "they're talking about taking my heart out and giving me a bunch of plastic and tubes. I told them no, someone took my heart a long time ago. Besides, I got a girl waiting for me and Kenny's already there, ready to pick me up when I see her again."

"My God Sweety," he said hurting.

"Joe her love sings to me. I gotta go."

Joe smiled. "I love you man and I'm gonna miss you, but you go to her."

"One for all?" he asked smiling.

"Yea," Joe answered tearfully, "and all for One Heart," then he hugged Steve for the first time ever.

"Is all the paperwork in order?"

"Everything is set," Joe replied. "Your company holdings, the book royalties and complete control of the center go to Dawn and her family. You have my word."

"I know I do," he said with a smile, then grabbed at his chest from a jabbing pain for a moment until it passed. His breathing got heavier, harder each time.

"She's calling me Joe. I can hear her lips saying my name."

Joe went and got the family. "Hurry," he told them. Dawn entered, followed by Cindy and Sam holding the baby.

"Daddy?" she called softly with tears.

He opened his eyes and smiled. "So beautiful like your mother," he whispered, "but so much a woman unto yourself. I am so proud of you."

He frowned at her hurtful look. "Why the tears? You promised me when the time came you wouldn't."

She smiled back and said, "I know, but it's just a girl-thing Mom use to say. We can't help it."

He looked at Sam and said, "You never stop loving these little girls you hear me, cause I'll know."

"Yes sir," Sam replied holding a tear. "I never could stop, you know that Dad, but I promise."

"Oh Daddy," she cried as she took his hand, "I love you so."

"Then I have all a man could want. The love of family and friends, my Lord and soon my Angel again." He stopped to silently hold in another stabbing chest pain.

"Don't hold them in, remember Daddy?" she said while letting him squeeze her hand as her tears fell. "It's okay to cry, we all do, " she whispered softly with a smile. "I cry my tear into a river clear, and its ripple thunders in My God's ear."

His eyes widened in surprise. "How do you know that verse?" he asked startled.

"Mom told me she found it carved in the wooden bridge. She knew it was you and she etched over it with paper and pencil. It became the marker she used in her bible."

"Oh Sue," he moaned out, then suddenly gasped hard for a breath. His face took on a sudden glow as his eyes opened again. A smile grew brightly as he stared upwards.

"Oh my brown eyes shine like stars," he whispered with a cry as if into her ear. "And they tear no more, cause He's wiped away the ones that I never could. Sue please," he cried softly, "come take the promise from this broken heart and let it live in Ours again."

A bursting tear rushed to his smile and then he was gone.

Dawn kissed it away from his cheek. "Go home, oh good and faithful servant," she whispered crying. "Please hug him Mom and don't ever let go ever."

"Run to her Sweety," Joe cried softly. "You run as fast as you can."

Dawn reached into her pocket, pulling out a small delicate gold crucifix and put it into his hand. She gently folded his fingers saying, "Give her our love Daddy."

After his funeral, the family gathered with Dawn and Sam at their apartment. Joe gave them the legal papers Steve had him prepare of his holdings and Steve's key to her mom's house.

"Now that both your grandma and your dad are gone he had hoped that maybe the two of you might want to raise your family there."

Dawn took the key and squeezed it tight.

"I use to be afraid in that house when I was little," she stated coldly and paused for a breath, "then he came and made it a home with his love for us. He made me feel safe and wanted and special. He took away the bad memories and made room for joy and laughter. It's a beautiful home, isn't it?" she asked looking up at Sam and he smiled nodding.

"It has a wonderful yard for family gatherings and for little Lisa Leslie to play in," she said. "He kept the garden so nice like mom loved to see it. I think we can really make it the home they both had hoped it could be."

Joe reached back into his briefcase.

"I have something else I think he'd want you both to have." He brought out Sue's original sketch of the bridge which had hung in his office, together with a poem.

"He had written this for their wedding day. I was going to read it as best man at the reception. I could never bear to part with it, but now, I think it belongs with her sketch in this home of yours."

He held the frame against his chest a moment.

"Steve once told me that he had thought writing was bearing one's soul on paper.

Later he said that he learned, that true writing strips one's soul naked to the bone and bleaches it out in the sun for all to see."

He stopped a moment, trying not to cry. "Whenever I read this, I can see what a difference they made in my life having known them."

Dawn took the framed poem and read it aloud with Sam.

***

"THE WISHING BRIDGE"

A moonlit glance and sweet romance
echoing laughter, sighs and goodbyes
as One Heart cries through stormy eyes,
from the hopes of promises made, but never to fade
once spoken on a bridge made of dreams;

It sings, of forever rings
made to encircle star-crossed fingers,
and of a heavenly love that still lingers
born on a bridge built of dreams;

stars light the course of its water's force
as it carries life's joys and pains and death,
while the night wind waits and holds its breath!
- - - remembering,
when two became One, outshining the sun,
once born for a bridge of dreams;

Now wildflowers sing a song, of a love so strong
that its fragrance they grew to envy,
while the moon bows down, to a fullness never found
until was born on a bridge of dreams;

so time will hold, this heart of gold
as a treasure today and forever,
yet the world will understand never, it seems,
the love dreamt by two, by me and by you,
on this bridge to our American Dreams.

Chapter Twenty-Eight

2006

"Score: Heaven 2, the World 0."

Dawn got a call from the On Guard garage mechanic telling her that the Le Mans would have to be towed out of her parking spot.

"I'll be down to pick it up," she told him.

"Ms., it won't start," the mechanic told her. "I've checked but I can't find anything wrong with it. It just won't run."

"I'll be right down," she repeated.

She came down the elevator from her top floor office and went over to where he was still turning the key. All Excalibur would do was crank, but not even try and start.

"It beats me," he said as she took the keys.

Dawn walked around the car. "I know you miss them, so do I Baby, but let's be strong for them okay? I promised the family Seaside this Saturday with you."

She slowly sat in the seat and put the key in the ignition. "I love you," she said softly and then turned the key. It caught instantly and the pipes began to purr.

"Thanks Love, now let's go. Some lunch for me and High-test gas for you," she whispered, then drove it out of the lot as the mechanic stood watching amazed.

***

Joe carried the flowers in a small basket he always kept in his car. It was just in case he found himself wanting to go walk the Island to remember their love when he missed them too much.

440

Later at the cemetery, he stood at the two headstones side by side and read them again.

***

Susan Maria LaRosa	Stephen James Clayton
His Beloved Wife,	Her Beloved Husband,
Our Heaven sent Mother.	Our Heaven sent Father.
1951-Forever	1951-Forever

"ONE HEART"

***

Dawn was working late that night when her secretary buzzed her.

"I'm sorry Mrs. Dupree. I know you didn't want to be disturbed, but Mr. Reily is here and I ..."

"It's all right Joyce, thank you. Please ask him to come in right away." She got up from her desk and walked towards the door as it started to open.

"Uncle Joe, are you all right?"

"Yea. I was out walking and suddenly I just found myself here. I'm sorry, I didn't mean to disturb you."

"Never Uncle Joe. Family first, remember?"

"I just needed to talk with someone."

She took his arm and walked him in as the secretary closed the door. They went, over to the large couch and sat down.

"I went to visit them today. I'd been to the Island and got them some more of those flowers they loved."

"I know," she said smiling, "I've seen them in the vases whenever I visit them."

"I do it now and then, but today ..."

"What is it?" she asked moving closer.

"Oh Dawn I miss them so. It wasn't fair. They should have had the life they had planned from the beginning."

His eyes began to tear and he turned his head. She put her hand on his shoulder and held tight to his arm.

"I miss them too," she sighed out, "but God had other plans for them, only one of which was having me."

Joe looked into her eyes and smiled. "I can't argue with Him there Little One. It's just that sometimes it's hard to see it all clearly," he added choked up. "I mean the rhyme and the reason of it all. The 'Why' of it all! They deserved so much better."

"Yes they did. Come with me," she told him as she helped him out of the couch.

She led him over to the sliding glass doors of her office and brought him onto the balcony outside.

"Did Daddy ever tell you about the Crowns of Heaven?"

"Yea, when Kenny died," he said softly while gazing up slowly into the clear night of stars and a full moon.

Dawn stared up with him, then quickly pointed. "There!" she said with excitement. "You see those two bright ones off in the northeast over Lake Hiawatha? Do you see! - - - The ones side by side, twinkling like they're moving!"

"Yea, I see them," he answered with a smile suddenly appearing on his lips.

"There they are Uncle Joe, singing and dancing together in God's Heavens forever as He promised. Happy and in love, and watching over all of us."

He glanced down a moment to see the glow of awe in her eyes, then back up at the two beacons bursting through the darkness.

"Their love is a world without end," she sighed with contentment, "and their light shows us the way."

Tears finally broke and ran across his freckled upturned cheeks as their lights shined down on his face. He lifted his arms up, as if to hold each one in his bear- like paws.

"Touchdown!" he cried out as she smiled upwards hugging his arm.

"When you can hear the music," she whispered joyfully, "you just gotta dance."

THE BEGINNING.

Epilogue

A True Love will never break your Heart,
It keeps the One you shared forever.

Without knowing that Love, that One Heart,
you'll wander like the 'Tin Man'
in search of a cheap substitute.

Pray God sends you THE GIFT.

—Dawn Dupree

Would you like to see your manuscript become a book?

If you are interested in becoming a PublishAmerica author, please submit your manuscript for possible publication to us at:

acquisitions@publishamerica.com

You may also mail in your manuscript to:

**PublishAmerica
PO Box 151
Frederick, MD 21705**

www.publishamerica.com